Two Spoons of Crazy

A novel by

Jennifer Ward

Two Spoons of Crazy
Jennifer Ward

PUBLISHED BY WINDFALL PUBLISHING LTD , UK

ISBN: 978-1-0686273-3-0

First Published 2024 by Jenny Ward Ltd t/a Windfall Publishing UK.

AUTHOR WEBSITE: https://jenniferward.uk

Join me on my journey...

Facebook: https://www.facebook.com/profilephp?id=61558384782238
Instagram: https://www.instagram.com/jenren_author/?hl=en
TikTok:

"For you, Lon

With so much love.

Thank you for proof-reading this book 282 times, and then politely losing count! Thanks for the all the cups of tea and encouraging words while I re-worked it 282 times.Of all my crazies, you were -and are - the best one.

Special thanks to my daughter Sheldene, who bullied and believed, my biggest critic and my biggest fan. Thanks too, to Shaun, whose guiding hand in this family allowed me this space, where I could fulfil this dream.

And friends, there are many. Wendy Carter who stepped up when I couldn't any more, the words were dancing before my eyes. Paul Dixon, who helped me in those dark days, with endless, endless support. Lesley Atholl, right up there. And last but never least, Ken Cram, who believes in me, no matter what.

What would I do without you all.

I am blessed."

Jen

Author Notes & Trigger Warnings

ON THE MATTER OF SPELLING:

Please note the spelling could confound, as the intention was to write using American spelling, (which spelling makes more sense, I will concede) but I was *taught* to spell by Catholic nuns, and it was either the Queen's English, or a sharp rap on the knuckles.
So, if you spot a lapse, dear reader, forgive me and know that the very thought of my book going into the world with American spelling has me in therapy ;)

SCENES THAT MAY BE DISTURBING, OR TRIGGERING TO SOME READERS.

A few passages infer, but do not describe in any great detail, pedophilia or sexual assault. There are passages that portray mental health struggles and mental decline, and the resultant shooting scene readers may find distressing. Indeed, it was distressing to write it, but such things do happen in real life, and perhaps the recollection of such a chapter in this book could serve to make us more mindful to the plight of others, and that, dear readers, is a good thing.

Overall the book describes various assaults on a committed relationship, and examines in a purely fictional scenario how diverse the response to such assaults can be.

It has scenes of seduction and sexually explicit content, and reader discretion is advised. If you feel uncomfortable at any point, please prioritize your well-being.

Blessings

Jennifer Ward.

TABLE OF CONTENTS

PART SCENE

PROLOGUE

The words were intriguing but made no sense.

"Mommy, the cat's poop is talking!"

Josie Rollings opened sleepy eyes. Her four-year old was standing at the side of her bed, her little face anxious.

Six kittens later, her careful schedule blown to hell, she was late and rushing for her appointment, her cheeks rosy with exertion, cursing the fact that there was no parking close to her accountant's office. She had parked miles away –actually, a matter of some five hundred yards, but she was in heels, so...

Josie drilled her way down Figueroa Street, past the Wilshire Grand, left into 7th Street. She hated downtown Los Angeles. It was always manic, noisy, and oh, the endless, endless road repair and construction!

On the sidewalk, off the sidewalk, on the sidewalk. For a chubby woman, she was surprisingly nimble, and with her purse clutched tightly to her bosom, she focused on her destination: her accountant's office—and the IRS guy waiting there.

The wooden trestles' warnings of 'CONSTRUCTION AHEAD' were her particular challenge. She was in her professional finery, but she was already feeling hot and clammy but this morning her rather heavy thighs were trundling her along at a fair lick.

Josie was intent on avoiding the building debris, hoping to preserve the heels on her far too expensive shoes. Cursing the ubiquitous road-works, she squeezed between the narrow opening in front of the news vendor, lifting her purse high, taking care not to let the grubby barrier soil or snag her outfit.

The photos caught her attention first, not the headlines.

The little girls' faces, actually. Then, she looked at the

man's face, then the woman's. Smiling faces, staring out of the front page. Her first glance had been perfunctory, but the faces looked familiar.

Josie moved on. Then from some far recess in her mind, she felt herself slowing down, turning around. She was being ridiculous, she chided herself, yet her heart was suddenly thumping. She slowed her walk, determined to be mistaken.

Her steps faltered. She reached for a copy of the newspaper.

How strange, her hand was trembling.

The news vendor held out his hand for the change, but she didn't notice. The traffic noise had a new, unfamiliar echo, a strange whooshing, as if the ocean was bringing its flotsam to downtown LA.

Something about the Brea, where she lived!

Nothing ever happened in the Brea. Josie stared hard at the photos. Four victims of a shooting. Four smiling faces.

The damn headlines wouldn't stand still. Briefly, Josie wondered if she was having a stroke, but dismissed it–surely she was too young?

Case had once told her it could happen to anyone, anywhere.

Her gut was churning ominously, as if her bowels were going to betray her, here on this busy street. And this peculiar sensation, the blood draining from her head, as if someone had pulled a secret plug she never even knew was there.

Josie tried again to read, but the words were jumping around on the page, confusing her. If she read aloud, perhaps...

FAMILY SLAYING AT EQUINE HAMLET

> The equine hamlet of the Brea is reeling after residents awoke this morning to find no less than four of their own shot, in what appears to be a family murder-suicide.
> Grim-faced medics described...

The always competent, hands-on Josie Rollings suddenly found herself plopped on the sidewalk, her legs betraying her, splayed and undignified in front of her, and quite, quite useless. Her grasp on the tabloid loosened and it slid gently off her lap onto the sidewalk. Curious passers-by moved around her, some skipping over her, rushing past. For them, life had not stopped.

The newspaper vendor was saying something, but he was speaking from inside a tunnel, so she couldn't understand him, not at all.

Josie understood she was sitting on the sidewalk. She knew she should never be sitting there, but it was quite impossible to stand. Kind people were attempting to help her to her feet, but her damn legs weren't working, so they set her down again, looking at each other helplessly. A black woman, her face pinched in concern, began to make sense through the cacophony inside her head.

"Where're you headed, hon?" The stranger looked troubled, turned aside, half-addressing a gathering crowd.

"I think she knows these people!" She turned back to Josie, her face anxious, her head bobbing up and down. "I think she does! Look at how she's staring at those pictures. C'mon, let's get her up..."

The woman on the pavement was in distress, of that the stranger was sure.

Josie tried to focus. She was vaguely aware of an anxious face in front of her, far too close. She was feeling queasy, perhaps it was the woman's perfume?

"Hon, you know where you should be going?" The woman was bending over her. "Let's get you there. You gotta an address, hon?" she was asking, her manner gentle.

Josie tried to speak, but she found she couldn't speak, couldn't think.

The woman straightened up, looking over her shoulder for some help.She snapped her fingers impatiently, beckoning a gaping cabbie to lend a hand. The sound jerked the man out of his macabre fascination with the fancy pants sitting on the sidewalk.

He turned his attention to the woman. She seemed to know something.

He stepped up to assist, addressing himself to Josie. "Here, let me help you, ma'am."

Between the two of them, they managed to lift Josie and settle her unceremoniously inside the rear seat of his cab. They stepped back, puffing and out of breath, looking at each other, unsure what to do next.

Josie sat dumb, inert, trying to grasp what was happening. She was feeling very nauseous, and she wondered if she might throw up. They would insist on talking to her, these people, but why on earth from so far away? Why did everything sound hollow?

And why was she in a cab, for God's sake, when she had her own car? Of course, she would never be able to drive it, not now. Ivor would simply have to fetch it. That kindly lady was talking to her again; she wanted to know where Josie was going.

Where was she going? It was simply too hard to think. If only Laine was here, she would know what to do.

Laine!

The puke finally came, spilling onto her new outfit, her shoes, and the back seat of the cab. The Brea. She had to get home.

"The Brea," she gasped, when she could speak, "take me to The Brea."

14 weeks earlier...

WHEN IT'S GOLDEN

CASE

Dr Case McAllister was waiting.

He had been waiting for some fifteen minutes.

Which meant his usually calm face was starting to pucker into a frown. He stood to the side of the steady tide of visitors streaming in and out of the hospital's glass doors. Some of the hospital staff called out greetings, but most elected to scurry past.

They knew that face.

Case responded, distracted. He was late.

He ran his fingers impatiently through thick, tow-colored hair, hair he kept short and close-cropped because otherwise, Laine would tease him and call him 'my Julius Caesar'.

Six feet two in his socks, built like the quarterback he once was, his eyes narrowed as he scanned the visitors, seeking a certain face, and the deepening frown suggested he was coming up empty.

Dark shadows of fatigue under his eyes accentuated their striking gray-blue hue. He was, the nurses gossiped, appealing, if macho was your thing. And if, perchance, those steely eyes fastened on you, accompanied by that quick grin, well then, that whole alpha male thing, that kinda popped right on into your head!

The surgeon stood to one side of the throng, arms crossed, frowning, his feet slightly apart, in that bracing stance that bigger men often assume. His demeanor implied authority, and a casual observer might have correctly speculated that perhaps he was a rather important cog in Granger Clinic's hierarchy.

Case McAllister sighed.

It was nearly seven-thirty, and unquestionably, they were late. It was visiting hour and the parking lot outside was full, yet no sign of Kevin. Today, Case had an appointment. An important one, in the McAllister family calendar, and yet, here he was, waiting for Kevin!

A few yards away, to the right of the huge glass doors, almost hidden between two parked ambulances, a couple of nurses stood puffing on their politically incorrect cigarettes, grateful for the all-sacred smoke break. They nattered to each other quietly, in a good position to observe the hospital's eye-candy, if the damn ambulances didn't move.

They saw him take a call and watched his scowl morph into a grin. They glanced at each other and rolled their eyes, smirking. The wife.

Unaware of their scrutiny, Case hesitated, debating what to say. There was no escape. He was toast. He took a deep breath.

Upbeat, that was the way forward, and he leapt in before she could ask.

"Hi hon, I'm still here, waiting, Kevin should be here soon. Any minute now," he said, rolling his eyes heavenward.

With Kevin, there was a better-than-average chance they would be a lot late. He knew she had made reservations for Gaucho's and tonight's celebration would be a Big Deal.

To his surprise, his wife sounded surprisingly sweet, un-fussed.

"No problem. Just checking where you are!"

"Sorry hon, you know I would never be late for my own birthday!"

Laine McAllister could hear the smile in his voice.

Yeah, right, she thought, but she said nothing.

"But perhaps, call the others and let them know?" he suggested.

"Sure, sure, don't fret," she soothed.

Case was surprised at her relaxed response, and relieved. He was working too long and hard these days. But today, today was his birthday, and as all married men know, the day belonged to his wife.

"You know I would never be late, clockwork, that's me." he teased.

At her end, Laine gave a wry smile. If only...

Through the glass, Case had noticed the nurses and was vaguely aware they might be chuckling about him. He turned away, in case they could lip-read.

"All going according to plan?" he asked, secretly hoping that it wasn't, and maybe he could buy time. She had commandeered his car mid-rounds this morning, and now, here he was, stranded, having to rely on Kevin, of all people. He could hear Shana bawling in the background, and the ire in her wail widened his grin. Laine clearly had her hands full.

"Sort of," came the distracted reply. Case knew the bellow would have claimed her attention. "Have to go. Don't rush. See you soon, hon." She hung up.

He pocketed his phone, feeling better. That had been painless! Well, he was temporarily off the hook—as long as Kevin pitched up within minutes.

He checked his watch again. It was seven-goddamn-twenty-two. Where was the asshole? His phone was off, even worse.

It would be over to that shrew secretary of Kevin's, Mrs. Sheppard, to save their collective bacon.

LAINE

For Laine McAllister, this was a perfect moment, a challenging viewpoint, given that her five-year-old could be heard bawling in the background. The operator had her on hold, and almost certainly, the caterers were running late. Still, she knew now, at this very moment, her life was perfect.

The party was more than a party, it was a celebration.

The scare turned out to be just that, a scare.

The McAllisters were to remain a family of four.

Thank you, God, thank you. Her eyes rolled to the heavens in gratitude. Definitely, a snip-snip for Case. Two kids were more than enough, adorable as kids were. A son would be nice, but statistics pointed to yet a third daughter, so, regretfully, shop shut!

She gave a soft, happy sigh of contentment. Case's tenure had been tabled before the Board, and—, drum roll here, she had a real shot at the State Championships.

For Laine McAllister, little inclined to spiritual covenants, there came a rare sense of the Universe's grace, that day as she stood patiently in her kitchen, holding the phone to her ear.

She smiled happily, for no reason in particular.

She had no inkling.

There was no warning at all.

KEVIN

Less than three miles away, on the fifteenth floor of a stately old office building in Lower Los Angeles, east of Barker Street, Case McAllister's annoyance at his absent friend was effortlessly surpassed by the ire of one Mrs Felicia Sheppard, Personal Assistant to Kevin Daniels, Attorney at Law and recently appointed partner in the prestigious firm of Nicholson and Jacobie.

The lights burned brightly in Kevin Daniels' office suite, a lone beacon of toil in a floor of dimmed offices. After devoting some nineteen years of her life to the firm, the good Mrs Sheppard relished the prestige of her seniority. Everyone knew it was an unspoken rule that such seniority precluded one from lowly duties such as overtime, giving generously as one did the required pound of flesh from nine to five.

She pursed her lips in disapproval as she pounded at the keyboard, her fingers swift and practiced as they flew almost unguided, her mind oscillating between comforting thoughts of Kevin Daniels' ultimate downfall and the words in the draft before her. Her young snot of a boss was on the phone, his babble hindering her concentration, delaying the start of her long weekend. Exasperated, she pushed her chair back, intending to close her door firmly against the distraction of his voice. She paused mid stride, her interest piqued by...

Well, it was the tone, really. He sounded as if he were... Pleading?

Mrs Sheppard eased herself back into her chair, pretending to resume her typing, giving the keyboard fake taps, taking care not to alert him to her eavesdropping.

Kevin Daniels, groveling?

Snatches of conversation floated through the partially open door that led to her boss's office.

"You're holding a gun to my head—" Silence.

"I don't ever want—"

She craned her neck, straining to hear.

"Can't afford..."

Long silence now. Then she heard him sigh.

"No, way, way too dangerous. Things are hectic here at the moment." There was another long silence. She heard him rocking his chair gently, the way he did when pondering a problem.

"God, I wish I was thinking straight. It's telling on my work, dammit."

At the last, Mrs Sheppard sniffed in disgusted agreement, nodding her head. And just who was paying? Her, that's who.

Intrigue slowed her fingers, dissipating some of her indignation. More than the content of his words, from which she could make neither head nor tail, it was the tone of Daniels' voice that titillated her.

He sounded positively cowed. The cavalier Kevin Daniels, undone?

She sniffed in disdain. He duped everyone with those glossy good looks and charm, but not her. Well, not for very long, anyway.

She paused at her pretend-tapping as she heard his tone change.

"Corey, do not pressure me, dammit."

She started guiltily when he banged his hand on his desk in anger.

"Corey? Corey?"

She could hear Kevin Daniels was mad.

'Corey' was obviously gone.

A second later his chair squeaked as he spun around, and she knew he would be gazing moodily out of the window with his back to the door. She glanced at her wristwatch. Seven-thirty.

He's probably forgotten he has to fetch Dr McAllister. For a moment, she was tempted not to remind him, and her eyes gleamed malevolently. No. Rather get rid of him, then she would have the place to herself.

He swung around at her soft tap on the door, startled to see her in the doorway.

He's forgotten I'm even here, she thought.

"Mrs Sheppard. Are you still here?" He closed his eyes momentarily, his face puckered in guilty recollection. "God, I'd forgotten. You're finishing the Ferguson brief, aren't you? Sorry I left it so late, but—" he gestured, deeming any further explanation as pointless, annoying her still more.

Kevin Daniels paused, noting his PA's hands clasped before her like a schoolmarm.

"Anything wrong?" he ventured mildly, masking his irritation.

Mrs Sheppard closed her eyes for the briefest moment. Nineteen years, and still she had to bow and scrape. But at Nicholson and Jacobie, the only difference between a Partner and God was God didn't have a corner office.

"Dr McAllister?" she prompted, one painted eyebrow raised in mild reproach.

He looked at her, his face blank. Why did the damn woman insist on speaking in capital letters? Then he gasped.

"Jesus! I'd completely forgotten. I should have collected him fifteen minutes ago. Oh Christ, what a day! Whew, thanks." His smile was warm, embracing. "Lucky that you're still here!" He made a futile attempt at organizing the papers on his desk, then gave up, shrugging in dismissal. He stood up, clearly pained at leaving such disarray.

"God, I am so dead, absolutely screwed!" he muttered. He snatched his jacket from the coat stand, then stopped short, a thought occurring to him. "I have to fly, but I imagine you're nearly through?" He looked at her, anxious to be gone.

"Oh, a while longer," she replied unctuously. "No matter, give Dr McAllister my best wishes for his birthday." She managed a thin smile.

"You just run along..."

He favored her with yet another of those smiles that had so charmed her in the beginning.

Before he became so secretive.

"Mrs Sheppard, you're a gem. Okay then! See you Monday. If you get stuck, call me." But they both knew she wouldn't.

He paused in his headlong rush before the Michael Sowa print of the Diving Pig, adjusting his tie in the glass reflection. She stepped primly aside to allow him through the door. She cocked her coiffed head, listening to his departing steps. A moment or two later, she heard the elevator doors close.

Elvis has left the building.

Satisfied she was alone, her eyes darted around the plush office, coming to rest on the cabinet that housed his selection of whiskeys. She opened the cabinet, tapping a shellacked nail over the bottles, trying to decide. Which little nightcap tonight? Talisker was her favorite.

A few moments later, she sat back at her desk, sniffing her generous tot appreciatively. She flexed her fingers and began to type.

* * *

In the elevator, 'Elvis' ignored the No Smoking sign and lit a cigarette. At this time of night, it was unlikely there would be anyone in the building, and frankly, he didn't care. Christ, Case would be furious!

His thoughts turned to Corey, and his unspoken threat.

Kevin was dismayed to see his hands had a slight tremor.

He inhaled deeply on the rogue cigarette. He had given up smoking.

Mostly. But this was an emergency.

How had he ever got himself into this mess? He sighed. The truth was, this 'mess' was a train wreck long, long headed his way.

The elevator doors opened and he stepped out blinking into the gloom of the parking basement. He ground the cigarette out underfoot, uncaring of the surveillance camera recording his transgressions. He glanced up into the CCTV lens, casually flipping a bird at the camera. His childishness amused him, but when he opened his car door, he was relieved to see his hands were steady. The prince would be waiting, doubtless in a snit.

Snit? Case would be wild.

The thought made him smile.

ROXIE

Most of the other superstars described Roxie Tanner as hugely talented, fanatical about detail. And, a total bitch.

Her friends said she was driven, a self-starter, gifted.

Perhaps just a teeny difficult?

Her therapist said she was bright, had a 'typically obsessive personality,' and some 'challenges' regarding her ability to determine the 'relevant' from the 'irrelevant.' Perhaps, he cautiously ventured, her EQ 'might need some work?'

Translation: Control freak with a temper.

Roxie's husband, one Jeremy Carter, an accomplished war-time correspondent with reputed wizardry when it came to the written word, he had dug deep.

He came up with whack-job.

Of course, when he said that, he was standing right in front of her with a grin on his face, prepared to fend off the blow that would surely follow.

Roxie didn't take offense. She understood his humor and she knew Jeremy had enormous respect for her talent.

As for the rest, well, the truth was very few people in her world had the balls to point out any of the star's shortcomings.

She reflected pensively that it was, in fact, Jeremy's understanding of her 'fanaticism' with her craft that she would miss. The thought made her good mood wind down a notch, and she brushed it aside. Today, she chided herself, today she was centered, the universe was showing the way forward, once again.

Still—. Jeremy. She sighed.

Roxie had resolved two matters in her head, issues that had been murky. She had no patience with murky. She was a do-or-die sorta gal.

One, she had won a starring role as a feisty girl-mechanic, a waif who inherits a derelict gas station and sets about challenging Big Business. It was a romcom, where the unlikely scene-stealer was a '59 Cadillac DeVille.

Two, she wanted a divorce.

Which was a bummer, because she was fond of Jeremy.

But the time had come...

She had shared the latter decision with her agent Patricia Halliwell, or Trish, as everyone called her, expecting ructions. Would this blip derail the movie deal?

To her surprise, the thick-skinned Trish managed to be both kind and cavalier, no easy feat. "Leave it all to me, hon," she reassured Roxie, secretly pleased. Husbands could be bothersome, especially if they had a brain...

"I'll handle them." 'Them' being the movie people.

Roxie was only too happy to let her handle that little problem. But there was the little matter of privacy.

"Okay, but I still need to have 'the talk' with Jeremy first, so please, stall everything till then, okay?" she cautioned, her voice stern. Not everything was for the tabloids.

Roxie frowned, remembering the conversation. Her request notwithstanding, her record company already knew of the looming divorce. The PR machine had already held a strategy meeting, and basically, she just had to push the go-button—

She grimaced. So, the key people in her career all knew about the impending divorce.

All that remained was for her to inform her husband.

Would Jeremy be heartbroken? She doubted it. Distressed, perhaps, but he once told her a good war correspondent needed to close out 'all the emotional crap', and Roxie had never been quite convinced she fell outside of that category.

She shrugged, dismissing the thought. It was no biggie. Besotted guys were tedious. The marriage had served her. He looked good in a tux. Now, however, their marriage was boring, and Roxie didn't do boring.

Initially, when it became apparent that Trish had already mentioned her imminent divorce, she was peeved. But the label execs hastened to assure her they would sit on everything until she said 'go'. In the end, she decided Trish was paid to be the big mouth. Wasn't that what agents did? Still, her marriage was private, and her damn 'failures' were ever more private.

She sighed. Roxie understood all too well that most tabloids were destined for the bottom of the birdcage, and she also knew the studio would indeed put a lid on it all until the 'timing' was perfect. Translation: release the story when they could exploit it to the max.

Promises were given, but they whispered in her ear perhaps 'the word' should come in time to promote the movie. "Just a thought, Rox? Angst, and all that sort of thing, the fans will love it, hon. But no pressure!"

Jeremy was away on an assignment in Ukraine, there was still time to think. Still, it was sad, three years of marriage coming to an end.

Again, Roxie felt her joie de vivre stutter–enough of that!

No dwelling on divorce. Too, too dreary.

But the thought niggled.

It seemed wrong, somehow, that Jeremy would be the last to know.

RUNNING IN PACKS

Outside the hospital's main door, an Aston Martin swept up and parked carefully underneath the NO PARKING sign.

Kevin. Case thought, with his shiny new toy.

Indeed it was. Kevin was extracting his lanky frame from the driver's seat and stretching, as if he had driven some three hundred miles, rather than just three.

Case rolled his eyes, hefted up his bag and strode from the lobby, feeling slightly self-conscious about heading towards Kevin's latest indulgence. He was aware of the damn nurses gawking, lurking between the ambulances and tittering.

A security marshal peeled off from the doorway to warn the owner of the Aston he was illegally parked.

Kevin's face broke into a grin at the sight of Case bearing down upon him. He turned and held up his hands in an affected apology to the security officer.

The marshal instructed Kevin to move his car, but without much sincerity. His eyes were drinking in the car, his admiration undisguised.

The two nurses watched Doc McAllister apologize to the security officer, then the doc turned, chastising the driver of the car.

"Dammit, Kev, we're late as hell!"

"Kev" seemed in no hurry. He had his phone out and was making a call. He began to speak to the person at the other end, ignoring both Doc McAllister and the security officer, his impudent grin seeming to underscore that his lot was not to park out there, with peasants.

"Superman..." the younger nurse breathed in awe, gaping. This guy was gorgeous. She wondered idly if hunks ran around in packs.

The older nurse snorted. She wrinkled her married nose and sniffed in dismissal.

"Personally, I'm not big on pretty men. Invariably, they're gay."

Her younger colleague had no such reservations; she gaped at Doc McAllister's pal, awe-struck. He was as tall as the doc, but kinda lanky, his hair dark and thick, just long enough to make you want to muss it, but gently, take your time, sort of thing. The eyes were soft and dark, and eyelashes like that on a man were just plain wrong! The smile he gave his friend was complacent, as befits a man who has absolutely everything. She watched the newcomer flick non-existent fluff from a perfectly tailored suit, unaware or oblivious to the stares of curious passersby.

The nurse sighed, audibly and long, to the amusement of her companion.

"Hey, Case!" Superman was calling out to Doc McAllister, who was opening the passenger door. "How's the birthday boy?" he said loudly, intending that those close should hear. He chuckled, amused at the doc's answering scowl.

The nurses looked at each other. Birthday! They watched the doc toss his hold-all behind the seat.

"Show some respect for the leather-work, dammit!" The man the doc called "Kev" was protesting loudly, addressing the doc across the roof of his car. "When you pick the leather for these seats," he said, "you get to fly to England, and you choose your own goddamn bull," he ended with a grin.

"Kev, we're so late, damn! Let's get going!" The doc gestured Kev should get back in the car, impatient, but they could see he was grinning.

Kev seemed in no hurry. "I guess I got a bit... Involved. Sorry," they heard him say, patently insincere. "Anyhow, I made the call. Our wives know we're on the way."

Then Kev folded himself back inside the car.

They watched the doc manipulate his own solid frame into the low-slung car, cursing, demonstrating none of the other man's grace, and like a lid slamming shut on a box of chocolates, both car doors closed simultaneously.

The two nurses glanced at each other, the younger one smirked.

She couldn't resist it; "Wives. So, not gay!" she crowed.

The older nurse snorted. It was time to get back to work.

BEST OF FRIENDS

Case glanced around him, respectful of Kevin's choice of car, but a three hundred-thousand-dollar car was not for him. His passion was vintage American. The McAllisters' indulgences ran to a sixteen-hand gelding named Donatés, the only serious male competition Case had for his wife's affections.

His wife's passion looked poised to escalate into a full-blown career, a career in showjumping too long kept on hold by motherhood, and that career might stretch their resources. Case was thoughtful. There was a fair-to-good chance that if she and Donatés were as good as people in the know thought they were, then Laine would get a sponsorship. and that would help a bunch.

But that could be a while coming.

Case did not doubt at all that his wife would be a champion. The real challenge would be financing her chase to the Olympics. According to Jason Ballard, his wife's trainer and owner of the stables where Donatés was homed, Laine's chances of sponsorship were 'good, to very good.' Jason should know, having been an Olympic contender himself, back in the day.

Case sat silent while Kevin guided the vehicle through traffic, grateful they were at last on their way. On the highway, with the powerful motor eating up the miles, he began to relax.

He complimented Kevin on his new car and then his thoughts turned to Laine's mishap with her car. "Strange, Laine's car packing up today. I had it serviced just the other day." He shrugged, "Anyhow, she caught a lift into the clinic with Josie and commandeered my car." Case closed his eyes and leaned his head back on the headrest.

"Now I'm stuck with you, an asshole who can't tell time." The insult was delivered with the easy familiarity of old friends. "But thanks, pal, for the lift."

Kevin smiled. "No biggie. How's it feel, thirty-eight?"

Case thought about that. How did it feel?

"Actually, if you really want to know, I feel good. Life has been good to me. I feel content, and..." he searched for the right word, "kinda worldly? All this, and I'm not even forty," he finished smugly.

Kevin snorted in derision. "Worldly? You? Balls. You've never been tempted, so content, sure, but worldly? Never. You, my friend, are a cliché. Two kids, Chevy, mortgage, dog, ugly damn dog, yudda yudda yudda." He sniffed, warming to his theme, "Texan beauty for a wife. You're the all-American prince!"

Case grinned, Kevin's jibes bouncing off him. Yep, he was Mr Lucky. He might be offered tenure soon. That would help. He was still —only just— the father of two, thank God. And of course, he, Case McAllister, was the lucky SOB who had snaffled the one and only Laine Hamilton, now Mrs Laine McAllister.

Life was good!

They traveled in easy silence. After a few moments, Case asked, piqued by Kevin's curious turn of phrase, never been tempted.

"What do you mean, never been tempted? Tempted by what?"

Kevin shrugged, ostensibly concentrating on the road. There was a moment's silence before he replied.

"Life, sonny, just... life. You always take the high road. You are unaware of the—" Kevin stopped himself, suddenly feeling he was wandering out, past shallow waters. Caution, he warned himself. "—the challenges life can present," he continued. Good save, Kevin.

He snuck a sidelong glance. His pal was always such a black-and-white kinda guy. "You remain ever an innocent!" Kevin said, his tone light. Yet a fleeting shadow passed over his face, unnoticed by his passenger.

Case snorted his disdain. What rubbish! He was a surgeon, for Chrissakes, he knew about life, its frailty, the treachery. And the reward.

He wondered idly why Kevin's cars were always so damn low. If Kevin would insist on spending so much money on a car, why not buy something comfortable? His ass was too close to the asphalt, it was like being in a damn wheelbarrow!

The ludicrous thought made him chuckle.

Kevin heard Case's chuckle and an unfamiliar stab of resentment seared through him. Life was always so fucking simple for his best friend. He pushed the churlish thought from his mind. The turn-off was up ahead.

What if Case found out—!

They were finally on the dirt road leading to the McAllister homestead, in the mink-and-manure suburb known as the Brea, where city-dwellers could indulge their yen for all things equine and country. Perfect for aspiring show jumpers like Laine. The lots were all around 5 acres, but few homesteaders practiced any degree of husbandry. Mostly, they were the so-called "horsey" people.

The Brea had a village high street which offered the essential services, but for bigger needs, there was Calabasas, or Los Angeles was a thirty-six-minute sprint.

Case saw the gables of his home, top left of the valley, adding its silhouette to the surrounding maple grove. It was one of the original farmhouses in the area. Laine had fallen in love with the trees, the view, and especially loved the rather sorry-looking old house. "It's all perfect," she whispered to him when they first saw the house, anxious that they should appear as savvy buyers to the hovering realtor. "It has a good vibe, Case! Okay, so it needs a little remodeling..."

Little? Hell. It was a damn money pit.

The Reichmanns were their only neighbors. The two neighbors could see each other's house by gazing out across the north paddock.

The Reichmanns also had two little girls, about the same age as Shana and Liesel. The girls had begun to wear a pathway between the two homes.

Kevin turned a sharp left into the McAllister driveway, too fast for Case's liking, always aware of kids, the pet geese, the dog.

"Jesus. Slow down, Kevin!"

"Fuck you," Kevin said mildly. "I'm a maestro behind the wheel, as well you know. And here we are!" He swung the car skillfully into the lean-to, grinning at Case's sharp intake of breath as the tail of the car fish-tailed alarmingly in the loose gravel. They cleared a pergola pole with seemingly inches to spare, coming to a halt with a noisy scrunch.

Case was surprised to see Laine's car parked alongside his Chevy. This morning, it was at the garage being checked out. Good, that probably meant it was something small. His eyes fell on his own special baby, a
Harley that he had rebuilt from scratch. It stood proud and gleaming under the lean-to.

Case McAllister—born to be mild, was Kevin's familiar chirp.

Tomorrow, Case resolved. Tomorrow would be the perfect opportunity to take it for a run to the clinic. What the heck, he was only going in for a couple of hours. It was Columbus Day; the roads would be quiet.

Case understood the plan was Kevin would drop him off, and then promptly leave to collect Ashley, but Kevin appeared in no hurry. He shrugged. Ashley and Kevin never bickered. Next to Laine and himself, they had to be the happiest couple he knew. And Ashley was well used to her mercurial husband by now.

Laine, he thought, now that's another kettle of fish!

He wondered where Ollie was. Usually, the sound of a car, any car, brought the dog, sometimes even the girls, rushing out. Perhaps they hadn't heard Kevin's car arriving, but it was unlikely. The sound of tires on the gravel was distinctive and quite noisy.

The house, usually well-lit, was now in unusual gloom. Perhaps the family was in the kitchen, at the rear of the house. He noticed with growing disquiet that although the house was in darkness, the front door was ajar. He frowned. Sometimes, this property was too damn isolated.

Case tried to quell an irrational sense of disquiet. He glanced behind him. Kevin was burrowing for something or other in the car's trunk. Case approached the door, straining to hear the children's voices, Laine's voice? Nothing.

Where was the dog? Alarm bells were starting up inside his head, and abandoning any pretense of calm, he quickened his pace up the porch stairs and shoved at the door, stopping short in an unfamiliar gloom. Every single light in the house seemed to be off.

He paused, listening. Towards the middle of the sitting room, he heard a faint shuffle. Yes, definitely breathing. Someone was trying hard to quiet their breathing.

He froze.

There was more than one.

PICKET FENCES

FRIENDS AND NEIGHBORS

"SURPRISE, SURPRISE!" A chorus of voices sounded in his ears with the high-pitched squealing of his girls eddying above them all. Relief flooded through him, ousted almost immediately by acute embarrassment. He knew he had a dumb grin on his face, but he couldn't shake it off. No wonder Kevin had seemed so nonchalant about running late.

They were all there!

Their friends, some of the locals and some of the people in his department at the hospital, fellow doctors, with wives and nurses already in two distinct camps.

A frantic tugging at his legs finally claimed his attention, making him look down. Laughing, Case scooped his two daughters into his arms. They were getting bigger by the day. He grunted as he lifted six-year-old Liesel, the elder child, into one arm and four-year-old Shana into the other. Shana was fast catching up to her sister in weight; big boned, like her Daddy,' was how Laine described her.

Their eyes shone with excitement, and he could imagine what a fun game this must have been for them. High off the ground and exposed, Shana buried her little face in his neck, coy amid this noisy crowd, while Liesel bounced up and down on his hip, delighted to be at the center of attention.

"Happy Birthday, Daddy," they chorused, demanding attention, giggling and wriggling, making it hard for Case to respond adequately to the good wishes being showered upon him.

"Yes, Happy Birthday Daddy," murmured a soft voice behind him.

Case sensed his wife's presence before he saw her. She approached him from behind and gently drew his cheek to her lips, her eyes aglow with pleasure at having pulled off the surprise.

Laine McAllister looked stunning in a woven sleeveless dress that clung to all the right curves. Her breasts were just a little too voluptuous to give her 'the perfect figure,' and tonight they seemed deceivingly unfettered beneath a neckline designed to challenge any vows of fidelity. Her dark eyes sparkled and danced as she watched her husband accepting all the backslapping, the good wishes.

She invoked an incongruous mix of imagery; fragile blooms, babies, – and Playboy. Luxuriant blonde tresses and a warm smile seemed to epitomize the good life. She had that best of all smiles, an infectious one. She stood a little back from her husband, serene, her face alight.

Case too, was beaming at it all, unusually boyish. The girls began to squirm and wriggle in his arms, impatient to be set down. He put them down carefully on the floor, turning to his wife.

Case teased Laine that she was his 'seventh' sense. A sense no one else could see, only him. His true North. He felt her squeeze his arm, and then she left him to attend to her duties as hostess, whispering to him he should excuse himself and change.

"Come see, Daddy, come see Grandma." The girls tugged at his hand, and he looked around in surprise.

Mom? She had called him from San Diego this morning to wish him well for his birthday. She was here!? Then he spotted her standing quietly at the rear of the crowded room, her face sporting a rare smile.

Judith McAllister made her way politely through the swell of guests towards her only son. Seeing him here, surrounded by these good people, she felt stark adoration in her heart for her only son and younger child. In a moment she was at his side. Always reserved, she held up her cheek for a kiss, embracing him with a quick, awkward hug. Displays of emotion were for other people.

Disregarding her inherent reserve, Case hoisted her off her feet with a whoop, delighted to see her. He swung her around, then put her down. Embarrassed but inwardly pleased nonetheless, she stepped back, breathless, a woman unused to 'horseplay.'

"Happy Birthday, son. Many, many more."

Judith was a tall, upright woman in her sixties, her hair swept up in a classic chignon, her attire suggesting she was rather a businesswoman than a party-goer.

She had her own imposing aura. Never a beauty, but almost all would have described her as a 'handsome' woman. Tonight, her usual reserve was gone, and her normally stern features were softened by a broad smile, a smile that had became so elusive after the tragic death of her husband twenty-five years ago.

The idea of a 'surprise' party was anathema to her, but this evening was not about her, it was about her son. Looking into his eyes, the conversation around them faded into a dull buzz, suddenly it was her late husband who stood smiling at her, with those same faded blue eyes.

Jim. All these years later, and the bile could still rise in her throat and choke her. Judith struggled to rally herself, today was a happy day, not to be tainted by memories of Jim, for God's sake!

"Grandma, Grandma. You're not listening to me. C'mon, let's go watch Sing, let's go-ooo!" Dancing from one foot to the other, her granddaughters tugged impatiently at her hand.

Case was replying to someone over her shoulder.

With an effort, she turned her attention to the little girls. They were the present. Jim was the past. A little unnerved at her unexpected lapse, she took their little hands affectionately into each of her own.

She gave a sweep of her head, indicating the rest of the room.

"No party for me, I'm afraid," Judith said with a smile, feigning regret.

But they both knew she was only too pleased to leave.

Case smiled. Mom was not a party gal, not ever.

He kissed her forehead lightly in understanding, and gratefully she led her excited granddaughters from the room, heading for the annex, where they would sleep over with Granny.

Case was suddenly aware that everyone sported party glad rags, and here he stood, quite disheveled. Hastily he made his excuses, needing to shower and change, and headed for their bedroom.

His clothes lay neatly on the bed, ready for him. In the bathroom, he was pleasantly surprised to find the old ball-and-claw cowboy tub had been filled in anticipation of his arrival. The water wasn't piping hot, but it was warm enough.

He stripped swiftly and stepped into the water and lay back with a happy sigh, languid, enjoying the steam and the quiet, determined to steal ten minutes for himself, party or no party.

He loved this old bathroom, with its carefully chosen clutter. Laine had refused to get rid of the old tub, insisting they redecorate the bathroom with the old ball and claw bath as the focal point. Case offered token resistance, finding little to entice him in the dilapidated old tub with its chipped and stained sides, but after re-enameling, Laine was proven right.

It was tranquil here, a favorite spot for a 'cowboy' to think. He closed his eyes in contentment.

Suddenly the bathroom door burst open, and Kevin strode in, a glass in each hand.

"One for you, —and one for me! For the birthday boy," he declared, handing Case a whiskey sour. He leaned against the door jamb, ankles crossed, and took a sip from his glass, his lanky form filling the doorway. He eyed Case lazily, but in truth he was wondering if the opportunity would present itself.

Certainly not tonight! Shitty idea.

Case was glad of the drink.

He sipped it, wondering if Kevin had something on his mind. Was it just him, or was Kevin more wired than ever these days?

"Thanks, now leave me in peace," Case instructed, enjoying his drink, his eyes closed in a vain attempt to recapture the tranquility Kevin had so rudely chased away.

"No. You're not the boss of me!" They both grinned at the old chant. Kevin swirled the clear liquid in his glass, trying to imagine what Case would say.. if—

Keep it light, Kevin. "One; too many women out there to pester me. Two; Ashley hasn't arrived yet. Three; I feel like annoying you. It bugs me to see you so smug."

Case grinned. Despite what Laine described as Kevin's 'vulgar' good looks, Kevin remained impervious to the many 'invitations' proffered by his grateful—and needy— women clients.

Those brooding eyes simply howled at them for mothering, or at the very least, breastfeeding.

Yet none of their wiles ever moved Kev. Frankly, their theatre bored him. He had dated the ever-composed Ashley since college, their marriage an inevitable sequel to a long, rather predictable courtship. He loved his wife! Like Case, he was happy.

Their lives had gone neatly to plan. Wives they loved, successful careers. Life was good.

Kevin's thoughts were quite different. He eyed Case, sipping his whiskey, reflecting. He and Case had been best friends for, what was it, twenty-seven years? Best friends at school, Best Man at each other's wedding, the bond between them was unshakable, all-enduring.

But when Case finds out—

Case was leaning back in the bath, his eyes shut, and Kevin felt an alien melancholy threatening to swamp him. Melancholy had no place here, dammit.

Tonight, they were celebrating, for fuck's sake!

But again, that churlish envy; Case suffered no indecision, ever. His life always followed a plan. Case's path was to follow in his late father's footsteps, and study medicine. He had been steadfast, despite vigorous and unexpected opposition from his mother.

Kevin, ever frivolous and indecisive, had opted at the last minute for law. Today, he was tagged as a shrewd gun-for-hire whose reputation in the divorce courts of California was growing quickly.

Kevin lurched and slopped his drink as he was shunted unceremoniously aside.

Laine swept into the bathroom.

"Go Kevin, go do your duty," she admonished, shoving an obedient Kevin out the door. "You're our party-trick! The women are already looking for you!"

Kevin rolled his eyes and sighed, but he departed obediently.

Laine caught up her hair in one hand as she leaned over the bath to bestow a kiss on her husband's head, swishing her free hand in the water, checking to see if the water was still warm. Case put his glass carefully down on the floor, and freed of his handicap, he circled her waist and pulled her protesting to a kneeling position next to the tub.

"You're making me wet," she complained but offered only token resistance. "Case McAllister, this is your party, and you can't spend the night in the bathroom." She paused, charmed as always by the familiar glint in his eye.

"Hmm... Alright, give me a birthday kiss, a special one," she said, smiling at him.

Laine had a full, generous mouth that somehow always teased him, beckoning him. It was like a half-open door that only he could walk through. He could feel the fine strands of her hair sticking to his damp arm. He kissed her, taking his time, marveling anew she was all his! Her free hand trailed through the water slowly up his leg, the manicured nails scratching lightly at his inner thigh, making his groin quiver. She felt the involuntary twitch. Game on.

Abruptly, she stood up, pleased at this reassertion of her feminine power. She flicked droplets of water casually from her hand, showering his face in fine drops of dismissal, ignoring his exaggerated groan.

"Enough. No time," she cooed with a wicked grin. "I have guests to attend to, but maybe—" She turned at the door to face him again, sashaying her hips in a slow, sensuous circle, eying him through half-closed lids, her tongue playing with the underside of her top lip, feigning lecherous desire.

"Maybe—? Later? We can play cowboys and 'ho's'!"

His 'ho' suddenly exploded into giggles. "I love you," she declared, abruptly solemn.

"I love you far too much. And—" the teasing light in her eyes was back, "—I can't wait for tomorrow. It's been a long time since we took time off, without the girls. You have such long hours lately. I should have remembered all the warnings about being a doctor's wife."

Case knew her comment was not reproach. He shrugged. "Cheer up. Remember you have a weekend with absolutely, and pos-it-ively, the best lover in town."

"Oh?" She looked surprised. "Who else is coming, then?"

They both laughed. He watched her take the perfume bottle off the vanity, and dab a little top-up drop behind each ear, affecting that little side-to-side flick of her head, a gesture so familiar to him.

"Corny. You are so cheesy," he intoned. His drink was almost finished. Time to get out.

She peered at her reflection in the mirror critically for a second, gave a satisfied nod, and turned to leave. "Hurry," she chided as she departed.

He heard the bedroom door close, and he leaned back in the tub, stealing one last minute. He gazed wryly at his rapidly deflating erection. Idly, he traced circles in the condensation on his whiskey glass, watching the little droplets merge and swell, then slide to the bottom. After a few moments, he raised his glass in a solitary salute to his wife.

It would be good to get away tomorrow, just the two of them. He would treat himself to a ride on the old Harley, just a quick nip-in to check on his patients in the morning.

He heaved himself out of the bath, relishing the prospect of a weekend alone, just the two of them.

That's how it was, for the McAllisters, that night of the party.

No menace in the air, no premonition, nothing at all.

MIA

"Laine?" The voice was soft, nervous. Laine turned in the direction of the soft call.

"Mia! Glad you could come. Where's Rudolf?" Dumb question, she thought as the words left her lips. Rudolf Reichmann's braying laughter had been ringing out across the patio for the last hour. He had arrived without his wife, explaining she was 'seeing to the children'.

The two couples never socialized, but tonight, Laine had deemed it polite to extend an invitation to their only neighbors. They would hear the noise from the party anyway.

Better to have them here.

The Reichmanns hailed from Serbia and although Mia's accent was still thick, her English was more than passable. A petite, elfin woman with pale skin and dark eyes that somehow always seemed feverish, those same eyes were now darting anxiously about her, as if she were plotting an early escape.

Laine felt an innate empathy for the skittish Mia. Both women had two young daughters, all of a very similar age. The four girls attended the same junior school, and the mothers alternated weeks in carpooling their children to and from school.

Laine harbored a dark suspicion that Rudolf beat Mia, if her regular bruises were anything to go by. But Mia never ventured any confidences, and Laine, uncharacteristically for her, refrained from asking outright, sensing the woman's humiliation.

But sometimes, when Mia dropped off her children, sporting new purple welts on her arm, or wearing far too much make-up, make-up which failed to hide the bruising, it was all Laine could do to hold her tongue.

She tried once to open a conversation, and the woman had been so vehement in her assurances that all was well, and was so patently embarrassed, that Laine felt loath to go down that road again.

It was a sensitive issue, and unless Mia wanted to speak freely—?

"Laine?" Mia interrupted Laine's unwelcome musings.

Laine noticed the woman was still clutching her purse, her face wary. She smiled at Mia, feeling mean-spirited and shabby with her meddling thoughts.

"I'm glad you managed to come. Rudolf's over by the fire with Ivor Rollings, you know, from the drugstore. You can hear his laugh anywhere," she joked, wincing inwardly at her fake cheeriness.

"Here, let me take your purse to the guest room. You go ahead and join Rudolf, " Laine reached for Mia's purse and dropped her hand in surprise when Mia stepped back in a panic, clutching her purse to her chest.

Laine would feel her purse was heavy, because of the gun inside. Rudolf insisted she keep her gun on her at all times. This was America, full of crazies, he said.

"No. It's okay." Mia faltered, flushing. Laine was looking at her askance. "—I will go join him later, perhaps now I just do my makeup, fresh?" Mia was in fact loathe to join her husband.

Doubtless he had drunk some by now, and would humiliate her in front of Laine's guests.

Surprised at her neighbor's intensity, Laine shrugged agreeably. "Here, let me show you where you can leave your things." She linked arms and led Mia through the house, where she left her in the guest room to 'adjust her make-up.'

"Take your time," Laine reassured her. Mia always seemed too tense, too uptight. She made a mental note to try the "difficult" conversation again, sooner rather than later.

The party was in full swing. Everything had been set up to give an ambiance akin to a country jamboree, complete with bales of hay and lanterns everywhere. It was all very rustic and charming. Over at the bar, Kevin stood with one arm around his wife Ashley, and the other around Lindy Mallors, Case's nurse and receptionist at his rooms in the clinic. Lindy Mallors had a keen sense of humor and tonight, her eyes sparkled as she enjoyed this unusual glimpse into her boss's domestic life.

Over at the fire pit, Case stood smiling at the tableau at the bar. Kevin, as ever, surrounded by women. Next to him, his wife, Ashley, looking on in amusement.

As a couple, everyone agreed they were an excellent match.

The McAllisters' horsey pals were there, as well as some of the 'villagers', all eager at this opportunity to shuck off the humdrum, air their party gladrags and enjoy an evening with their delightful hostess.

Laine had that most agreeable of all qualities—she was an attentive listener. And as with most good listeners, the talkers vied for her attention. She was also indisputably Ballard's star rider, and her fellow riders amongst them held her–and her magnificent bay, Donatés in awe. A group of fellow riders from Jason Ballard's prestigious Redwood Stables sat chatting on pool loungers, the light from the pool washing their faces in an eerie blue hue. Their faces lit up as they debated whether Laine–with her Donatés–had a serious shot at the Olympics.

They were all of one mind: maybe.

A couple sat perched high atop a few stacked bales of hay. They were talking spiritedly, discussing the pitfalls of crossing from amateur to professional showjumping, the younger man toying idly with the handle of a lethal-looking pitchfork embedded in the bale.

The music was loud, the laughter ringing out amidst the noisy chatter and clinkity-clink of glasses.

A radiant Laine flitted between the guests. It may have been Case's party, but it was her night. For the last twelve years, he was nearing his goal, as Granger Clinic's nominated specialist in reconstructive surgery. The flip side to that was time together and alone seemed increasingly rare. Watching her husband loosen up, she resolved that this year she would see to it that they relaxed more, found more time for each other. He was spending longer hours at the clinic, as his list of patients grew.

She understood. Tonight, when all the guests had left, it would be like the old days, when it was just the two of them. The children were sleeping with Judith in the annex, so there would be no walk-ins or wails in the night to disturb —or distract—them.

Roll on tonight.

RUDOLF

Laine was relieved to find the decks cleared in the kitchen, all the food appeared to be outside, save for a couple of platters of canapés waiting their turn. The kitchen door shut out most of the noise from the party outside, and she stood for a second, debating whether she should take the canapés outside now, or leave them for late-night nibbles.

She opened the refrigerator, looking for Avian water. She was reaching for a bottle when a shadow fell over her and burly arms closed around her waist, drawing her close. Large hands moved up to cup her breasts, and she could smell sour, booze-tinged breath over her shoulder.

"What the hell!" she gasped, struggling to twist around and see who this was, somehow not surprised to see Rudolf Reichmann's round face, ruddy and gleaming, a thin film of perspiration glistening on his fleshy cheeks. She blanched at the acridity of his breath and twisted her head away from the stench in disgust.

"God, let me go!" It was difficult to muster dignity while she was struggling to free herself, to hiss at him quietly, aware of guests nearby, perhaps coming in at any second. She held her breath momentarily to claim a brief respite from the stench of him. It was no good. She had to breathe.

"Your wife has arrived. I think you've had too much to drink." She pushed at him in vain, as much irritated as shocked, but he held her fast against the open door. Vaguely, she wondered if the damn mustard would stain her top.

As neighbors, they were no more than polite to each other, but Rudolf Reichmann had never been the slightest bit forward, or 'improper'.Usually, he was indifferent with her, to the point of rudeness.

He was pulling her up against the bulge in his crotch, grinding himself into her. Revolted, she increased her efforts to get loose, painfully aware of her fast-waning dignity. He was breathing in short and ragged pants his tongue caught in a speculative leer between yellowing teeth. He stooped to kiss her and Laine felt her stomach heave with nausea at the slobber on her cheek.

Spittled, squishy lips were pressing against her cheeks. She wrenched her head away, struggling to keep down the bile in her throat.

Oh God, she was going to throw up on her new dress, because of this oaf.

"Rudolf. Don't be stupid! Let me go," she hissed. Furious and disbelieving at the man's boorishness, she hesitated to yell for help, preferring to handle this idiot herself, rather than create a scene. The kitchen's swing doors swung open with their familiar squeak, and Mia walked in, looking vacant and lost.

Her face paled in shock at the tableau before her eyes, Laine, contorted and grappling with Rudolf, who seemed unaware of any interruption. After a stunned split second she flew at her husband, her face horrified.

"Are you crazy?" she cried, stricken, tugging ineffectually at her husband's arm, trying in vain to pull him off their hostess. Reichmann appeared set to ignore both women, then suddenly he let Laine go and stepped back, smiling affably at his enraged prey.

"Only a little joke. Why such a fuss?" He grunted and looked around. There was only Mia in the kitchen, that mosquito he had been foolish enough to marry. He scowled and turned towards his wife, his heavy frame looming threateningly over the shrinking woman. He paused, vacillating between circumspect restraint, and the pleasure it would give him to swat this bitch down, once and for all.

Laine was trying to collect herself, and for a horrified second, she thought Reichmann would strike his wife, right there, in her kitchen.

"That's enough! Get the hell out of my kitchen!" she exclaimed; her voice choked with fury.

The bloodshot eyes swung away from his wife, and he turned to stare at Laine, his expression oddly vacant.

He said nothing. Instead, he gave a hearty belch. The menace from moments before evaporated in an instant. He turned to leave with a sardonic sneer. Stupid bitches.

Women! They were all the same.

Time for a drink anyway.

"Sure, sure. No hard feelings." He held both his hands up in mock deference, placating, docile. "You're a knock-up! What do you expect? She," he spat the word out, looking contemptuously at his wife, "she doesn't know the meaning of the word woman." He snorted in disgust and sauntered out.

He was hungry.

Hopefully, the food was out on the table.

"Knock-up?" Laine was lost for words. What the hell did he mean, 'knock-up'?

"He means knockout," Mia ventured timidly, reading her expression. "—Attractive."

Perhaps it was hysteria, but Laine began to laugh.

Mia gaped. Her hostess was laughing! Her eyes were unblinking as she stared at Laine, her eyes unusually large, huge and rounded, her mouth slack with shame.

Laine tried valiantly to calm herself. She was hysterical and this poor woman looked distraught, ready to faint.

"Mia? Mia, are you alright?" She gave Mia a little shake. "He's had a few too many, don't worry," she said, groping for calm. Laine was unable to hide the tremor in her voice.

Slowly, Mia's eyes took on some life, a deep flush of shame mottling her face and neck.

"Laine, I'm so sorry. I, I—" Her voice trailed off. Her eyes darted about her, as though seeking the escape she had contemplated earlier.

"I leave immediately. And I take Rudolf." She turned to leave.

"No!" The word burst from Laine's lips.

Mia stopped mid-flight, turning to stare at her in confusion.

"I mean, no," Laine finished lamely, biting her bottom lip in agitation. That sonovabitch had looked at Mia as if he would kill her. There was nothing Laine would have liked better than to see Reichmann leave, but she suspected he would probably cause a scene, or worse, batter this mouse of a woman when they got home.

Jesus, she needed a drink!

"I tell you what, have a drink to calm your nerves—forget about him. Here, have a beer? Vodka? Wine?"

Mia nodded dumbly. She did not drink but perhaps this was not the time to tell Laine such things! With trembling hands, Mia poured a beer into the glass, ignoring the foam that spilled onto her hand. She obediently sipped the foaming head as if sipping medicine, her eyes averted.

Laine leaned back against the kitchen counter, trying to show composure, but feeling more than a little unnerved by her scuffle with Reichmann.

Both women started as the kitchen door swung open again.

A jovial Kevin and Ashley sauntered in, rescuing Laine from further thought.

"C'mon, c'mon! Where's the hostess, we're ready for the toasts." He stopped short, staring at Laine in surprise. She looked pale and... odd. He noticed the other woman for the first time. He shot a glance at Ashley. Yes, she too sensed something. Something was amiss.

He rallied himself. "Hello, I'm Kevin Daniels. Friend and servant of this good family. And you are...?" His smile was open and friendly, his curiosity veiled. God, this little woman looked petrified. What a mouse!

"Meet Mia. She's my neighbor. Kira's mom. You've seen Kira and Bernadette here before, Kevin. The little girls from next door." Laine's introduction was brisk and Kevin failed to notice the slight tremor in her voice.

"Yeah. Sure." He extended his hand in greeting, a smile on his face.

Mia shook it shyly, painfully aware that her palm was clammy and damp.

Laine took Kevin by the arm and gazed up at him, her back to the others, her eyes transmitting a silent S O S.

"Kevin, be a friend and take Mia to the bar, and guard her with your life. As you can see, she's rather shy. Her husband Rudolf—" Laine swallowed, " —the big chap with the reddish hair, he seems to be busy?" She ended her entreaty with a smile like honey.

"Sure thing," he said easily. "You and Ashley bring the rest of the champagne; I'll take the lady. Seems a good deal to me." Obligingly, he led Mia out of the kitchen, but not before he shot Laine a swift, quizzical glance. She responded with the merest shake of her head, deflecting questions. He shrugged inwardly. Later.

Ashley took up one of the canapés platters and followed him out, smiling at Laine, promising to be back in a jiffy.

Ashley felt a tad mystified. There was something strange with Laine, something she couldn't put her finger on. She looked quite... rattled.

Alone in the kitchen, Laine made a beeline for the freezer and reached inside for an unopened bottle of Vodka, twisted the cap off, and poured herself a generous tot. She gulped it down, shuddering at the raw taste.

Her nerves were jangling. Who would have thought—? She rubbed her right breast gently; it was still tingling from Reichmanns fumbling grasp.

Laine felt uncharacteristically jumpy. She headed for the door, towards the music and people. She needed the comfort of her husband.

ASHLEY

Ashley Daniels was the ideal mate for the gorgeous Kevin.

Perhaps not as attractive as her husband. some would say, but impressive in her own right. Svelte and elegant, her auburn hair in a shiny bob, the rather small brown eyes made up to perfection, she looked every inch the fashion-buyer she was.

As with all women shiny and tinkly, there was an invisible 'Don't touch' aura that hovered around her, keeping people at bay.

—Which was a shame, because only a few words with Ash, and one's preconceptions dissolved.

Her husky laughter caught you by surprise because it was unexpected and infectious.

She sat now in the shadows, almost hidden on a felled tree trunk, away from the festivities, idly watching her husband with that skittish little neighbor from next door.

Ashley never doubted her husband's love, just as he would have found the idea preposterous to doubt hers. That boyish exuberance, when properly muted in sober attorney's garb had lulled many a client into easy confidences they originally had no intention of disclosing. Their sessions with Kevin Daniels served to arm many a jaded or rejected spouse with their own mental machete, which machete's sole purpose was to cleave what assets they could from said bastard of the moment.

Invariably, his clients were happy to yield control, allowing the lanky lawyer to take up the torn tapestry of an abandoned life. Rarely was their faith misplaced. Testimony to his remarkable strike rate was his recent appointment as a partner to Nicholson and Jacobie.

And she, Ashley, everyone agreed, was his perfect mate!

One of four senior fashion buyers for Macy's, Ashley made frequent trips overseas in pursuit of inexpensive excellence for the masses. But these days, Ashley found these jaunts, once so exciting, were less and less appealing, more and more wearying.

Increasingly it seemed to her that their marriage lacked fire.

And children.

The thought snuck in, unwanted, and lately, ever-present. There it was, the heart of the matter. Their marriage lacked children.

After thirteen years of marriage, Ashley felt her childless marriage had made her, too, a victim of Kevin's own shitty childhood.

She tipped the ash from her cigarette with a soft sigh. Earlier in their marriage, she had hoped he would change his mind. There seemed so much time, then.

Not for them, children. That was the deal they struck years ago, and a smitten Ashley had blindly agreed. Children were not important.

But the truth was, she had changed her mind!

It was clear to her now; she had no doubt at all.

The sophisticated Mrs Daniels would chuck her career in a heartbeat, for one Kevin Daniels, junior. Or perhaps, even a little Ashley Daniels? Ashley allowed herself a smile at the idea. A little girl.

What a delicious thought!

She sighed. Their sex life was infrequent, damn near non-existent lately. But then again, Kevin had never been a particularly physical person, and neither was she, she supposed.

She drew on her cigarette, observing the party shenanigans from her hideaway.

She watched Laine, always smiling and gracious.

Laine was always so damn—Ashley struggled for the right word. So damn wholesome, she decided. And sexy, too, which was should have one or the other, that was only fair!

Ashley adored Laine. Hell, everyone did! Laine had parked her dreams of being a showjumping champion without a minute's hesitation when her girls were born, relishing motherhood, ecstatic with her small family.

Ashley did a mental tally.

Her own sex-drought was nearing four, no, nearly five months, the last being a rather mechanical birthday fuck.

Actually, not even fucking. Copulation. That's what it was, as boring as the very word. What would Laine advise her to do, she wondered?

It was Laine, after all, who was the psyche major at college!

She would be dismayed, and unhappy for me, Ashley decided. She and Case were so very close. Kevin always teased Case he was like a prince, reigning with his princess.

Ashley felt a twinge of despair. She gave herself a mental rap on the knuckles. Didn't she have the kindest and best-looking husband?? And wasn't her home beautiful?? Kevin was also her best friend, not just her husband. There weren't many wives who could say that!

And so on and so on and so on, argued her head.

Yet her heart, her heart felt a bit empty, as if there were room for more...

More what?

Children, replied her ungrateful heart. A sudden movement behind her made her start in fright, but it was just Kevin.

"Hi, hon. I've been looking for you?" He sat down beside her on the old tree trunk, his arm encircling her in an affectionate squeeze.

"Why the big sigh?" He took the cigarette from her, waggled his finger in admonishment and took a drag. "Temptress!"

That Kevin smile blazed out at her.

"Did I tell you, you look fabulous! Stunning." He kissed her forehead lightly. "I'm starving. Are you ready to eat? The food is all out?"

Ashley smiled up at him. He was such a boy. Always showing her off.

Yes, she could have done a lot worse than Kevin.

Things would work themselves out.

LETTING IT SLIDE

"She's finally joining us!" Josie's voice was teasing as Laine approached."That outfit positively demands bad behavior!" She tilted her glass in homage.

"Laine, hon, you look gorgeous. It makes me green-eyed to look at you! Ugh." She quaffed the last of her wine in a swift gesture of mock disgust.

Laine managed a laugh, but Josie's words unnerved her. Out of the corner of her eye, she saw Rudolf on the patio, in conversation with Lindy. He was doing the talking, but Lindy was barely listening, her eyes frantically signaling another man in the corner, mutely begging him to rescue her.

Laine made a concentrated effort to join in the light-hearted banter.

Case saw his wife and left Ivor's side and came and stood behind Laine, locking both arms around her in an enveloping hug.

Laine felt her frayed nerves starting to settle. That man was a thug, and she would be very wary of him in the future. She turned to smile at him.

He was surprised. He sensed a somber mood behind her smile. Where the hell had that come from?

"C'mon, let's dance." He led her to the makeshift dance-floor and he held out his arms and she stepped gratefully into them. In a few moments, they were being jostled by other couples around them.

"What's up, hon?" He looked at her, concerned. "Something up with the girls?"

She pondered dismissing the nasty episode for a moment, but she knew Case could sense something was amiss.

"Nothing, —serious, that is."

Case was rubbing her back in a soothing motion as they danced. He felt perplexed. Just a short while earlier, she had been on top of the world.

"C'mon, spill." he coaxed, pulling her close.

With her mouth close to his ear, she told him quickly of the incident in the kitchen, caressing his ear with her lips every now and then to diffuse the content of her words. She refrained from a blow-by-blow version, saying only enough to let her husband know Rudolf had been "out of line.'

"I think he's just plastered," she ended, feeling irrational. "But never, ever leave me alone with him," she added vehemently.

Case said nothing for a second or two, but Laine could sense his anger in the rigidity of his embrace.

Case was angry, but after a moment, he decided it would be best to leave it. Laine was faking calm, but she was clearly agitated. She had never before complained to him of anyone making a pass, and he knew she had fielded many, many passes.

However, she seemed to be calm enough now.

As if reading his mind, his wife snuggled in closer and whispered in his ear, "Relax, darling. He's a fool. Mia sure has her hands full. Just let it go."

"Sickening, that's what the two of you are. Just look at the pair of you!" Ashley's honeyed tones interrupted their apparent tet-a-tete.

A few couples around them laughed at the good-natured teasing, but Laine ignored them and snuggled in closer, burying her face in Case's neck, relishing the clean, familiar smell of him, glad to be safe within his arms.

He held her close, his anger fading.

Afterwards, he would wonder; was that the moment he took his eye off the ball?

THE LATE SHOW

The celebrations went on into the night.

The music got louder, and the liquor flowed. Tongues and morals loosened.

In one clandestine instance, the prickly, uncomfortable hay had to be carefully brushed off a bare backside. One itch gone, replaced with another.

The laughter was loud and constant, the chit-chat was idle, increasingly slurred.

In the wee hours of the morning, the music slowed, softened, and gradually guests bade farewells until only a few die-hards were left. The Reichmanns, the Rollings, the randy Jason Ballard with his latest conquest, a few persistent Granger party animals, including Lindy.

Most stragglers were preparing to depart.

Ashley had come in her car, and after being assured by Laine that the cleaners would come tomorrow to manage the celebration debris, she left her husband to make his own way home.

To Laine's chagrin, the wretched Rudolf Reichmann looked set for the night.

He sat on a low patio wall eying the stragglers balefully through a whiskey-sodden haze. The party had soured for him. The women that were left were married, and Mia was far too friendly with that pretty boy, shaming him. He watched how Laine McAllister played up to that pompous Ballard bastard from the stables. They looked too cozy.

Women, they were all whores.

He grunted in disgust to nobody in particular, muttering to himself, as drunks tend to do.

He had ignored his wife the entire evening and spent the last half hour in a heated discussion with some moron about wind turbines, that being one of the many subjects upon which Reichmann considered himself an authority. When the other party to this conversation bade a slurred farewell, Reichmann felt disgruntled.

He wasn't ready to go home yet.

Mia desperately wanted to go home. It would be a quick walk through the paddock to get home, but she was hesitant to leave the McAllisters to suffer her husband alone. If she left him in this state, assuredly he would do something embarrassing! No, better to stay at his side, try to keep him in check. She didn't really have any friends, other than Laine, who was more of a good neighbor than a friend. He might cause a scene, and then the McAllisters would shun her.

And worse, maybe their children would no longer be welcome here. That would be dreadful.

She resolved to stay, try to get Rudolf to leave. urge him when the opportunity permitted.

She sat quietly, contriving a smile when curious eyes found hers. She was fretting about the children. It was too late, and Mrs Costaz had agreed to babysit, as long as it wasn't too late. She disliked driving at night.

Mia thought about her younger daughter, three-year-old Bernadette. Bernadette was having bad dreams. She really should be getting home. In Serbia, there were always people around you. People you knew, who smiled at you and chatted about the weather, the economy, anything. Here, people were too busy, and always in a rush.

She wished Rudolf would move to the suburbs. There were some nice suburbs in LA. Here in the Brea, it was more like a village, and everyone appeared to know everyone. The mothers at the school frequently went for coffee. She herself had never been invited, which was hurtful, but then again, she was very shy, and perhaps it was better.

On odd occasions when the children were at school, she would sit in the coffee shops and observe the bustle. The truth was, she was lonely. Thank God for the children.

The thought of them spurred Mia into action. She glanced around.

No one was paying them any attention.

"Rudolf, it's late. I think we should leave." She tugged at his sleeve timidly, her heart beating a little too fast, praying he would behave.

Irritable, he flung her arm off.

Wives. They were more trouble than pleasure. Laine McAllister had returned to the patio after seeing Ballard off. He saw her glance in his direction. Unconsciously he licked his lips. Now there was a woman who would make a man feel like a man! Just the thought made his mouth dry and suddenly, he felt thirsty. He saw Case approaching out of the corner of his eye.

Mia was tugging at his arm again. "I'm staying," he snapped at her. His tone changed as Case came within earshot. "I am going to have a drink with my neighbor here," he said, feigning bonhomie. He grabbed at Case's arm as the man walked past.

Case paused in his stride, looking first with surprise, then with distaste at the huge paw on his arm.

"Join me for a drink?" Reichmanns rasping tone jarred the quiet night air and caused others to turn and stare, but Reichmann appeared oblivious to the abrupt lull. However, his host's repugnance was not lost on him, and his temper flared. He sneered. "Too good for me?"

Mia's grip tightened on her husband's arm. Case glanced at her. Mia's eyes were frightened, her face pale. She looked defeated. He hesitated, unsure how to handle this oaf who was clearly drunk.

Mia tugged at her husband's arm again, and roughly, he shoved his wife away. Unprepared for the force behind his crude shove, she stumbled and would have fallen had Case not caught her. Case steadied her, then turned to Reichmann, thoroughly riled.

Reichmann was peering over Case's shoulder, wondering if the drinks were still out.

"You've had enough." Case took a deep breath, contriving to contain his rising temper. "I think Mia wants to leave anyway," he said.

Reichmann shrugged, indifferent. "Then let her fuck off," he said mildly. He wanted that drink. But this fool stood in his way, blocking him.

The few stragglers glanced at each other. Was this going to end badly?

Mia gave a soft moan, and she covered her face with her hands, her shoulders bowed in humiliation.

Reichmann's eyes narrowed with malevolence, and he turned away, teetering slightly. The two men were the same height, but Reichmann was overweight and heavyset and built like a wrestler. A man not used to people opposing his will.

He thrust a belligerent jaw inches in front of Case's face.

"She's whoring with your friend, you know?" His voice was jarring, the words slurred. He looked at his wife, then jabbed his thumb in the direction of Kevin. He rocked onto a back foot, his expression smug.

Kevin looked at Reichmann, absolute incredulity on his face. Then he shrugged and glanced at Laine. This was her night. and this sonovabitch was going to fuck it all up.

Sensing his train of thought, Laine reached out and grasped Kevin's hand in a tacit gesture of support.

Mia paled and whispered something to her husband. "Rudy?" Her voice was barely a whisper. She pulled at her husband's arm frantically, dignity abandoned, imploring him all the while to come away with her.

He ignored her, his eyes hooded, sizing up Case.

Mia kept at him, tugging at his arm.

Irritated, he lashed out, his backhand connecting with a dull smack against her face. The horrified stragglers saw her almost lift off her feet, and then she was a crumpled heap on the floor.

Reichmann turned towards her, his arm raised to strike her again.

Case heard his wife's horrified shriek of warning. He moved swiftly and grabbed Reichmann's wrist and held it fast. Kevin was instantly to be at Reichmann's other side and he wrapped both his arms tightly around Reichmanns left arm.

Together, the two men pinned Reichmann fast.

Kevin's breathing was short, his adrenaline pumping. "Try it again buddy," he challenged.

Case closed his eyes briefly. Déjà vu. Always, Kevin and jealous boyfriends. They had played this very game a few times, in those years, himself and Kevin. But this crap belonged in the past.

A glance at the whimpering woman on the floor told him that this was the present, and here was a justifiable reason to be 'that' Case of old, one last time.

He thought about it, then dismissed the thought immediately. No need to spoil the night because of this drunken asshole.

"Take your hands away. Quickly." The menace in Reichmanns voice was unmistakable, and he glared at Kevin, then at Case. They were all three tall men, but the burly, thick-set Reichmann loomed huge next to the lanky Kevin.

"Case..." Laine's voice was strained. A groan from Mia galvanized her into action, breaking the tense frieze. She helped the stricken woman up off the floor. Mia had blood trickling from a split lip.

Case prized Kevin's arms off the bristling Reichmann. He felt his temple doing that throbbing thing again, heralding a fight. God knows, he wanted to tear the sonovabitch apart, but he told himself to remain calm.

"Kevin, let me handle this, buddy," he said firmly.

Kevin hesitated, he looked at Case curiously, then he shrugged. He stepped away. "It hardly seems fair, but it is your party."

Case eyed his neighbor. Fuck good manners. They should have never invited this prick. Just the look of him, those broken veins mapping the fat cheeks, it repulsed him.

And then, there was the matter of Laine... "Reichmann, this really wasn't necessary," Case said softly.

He stood before Reichmann, rubbing his jaw thoughtfully, a man disappointed in the vagaries of his fellow man. He looked down at the floor, his hands on his hips, then glanced across at Mia and Laine.

Laine was leading a dazed, stumbling Mia inside. Case nodded, pleased. Good. They were safely inside.

Time to deal with this.

Kevin was watching the two men warily. He knew Case of old. This would explode.

A contemptuous smirk spread across Reichmanns face. He lunged past Case, trying to grab Kevin. In a lightning movement, Case's right hand balled into a fist and connected with Reichmanns jaw with jarring force.

There was a sickening click as the man's teeth snapped together, and he bellowed in pain as his lip mashed into his teeth. His nose felt as if it had been ripped from his face. He lurched back with the blow but didn't fall. He stood swaying, disbelief in his eyes, and then he bellowed in rage and swung at Case.

Almost immediately, another fist crashed into his ribs, expelling the air from his lungs in a fine spray of spittle and blood. Reichmanns eyes clouded in confusion, and he wheezed, gasping for air as he slowly buckled to his knees. Case stooped to help him to his feet. Reichmann stood tottering and ready to crumple to the floor again, but not before Case dealt another savage blow, mashing already pulpy lips to a bloody mess.

For a moment, it appeared Reichmann would stay standing, take another blow. He stood for a moment, dazed and weaving on unsteady legs, then, to the watchers' relief, he seemed to implode and folded almost gently to the floor, gurgling, an unsightly bloody froth coming from his mouth.

Reichmanns glassy eyes stayed fixed on Case, but he had no breath to sound any retort.

"Case!" Case heard his wife's cry, and reluctantly, he stepped away, his wife's distress giving him pause. He was itching to hit the bastard again.

On the floor, Reichmann closed his eyes and curled up in pain, his knees pulled to his chest, desperately trying to breathe. The transfixed onlookers shuddered at his breathing, a strange, gurgling, whistling sound. He was struggling to get to his feet and grabbed at a pitchfork that was stuck in a decorative straw bale as an aid to help hoist himself up.

Case felt Kevin's hand on his arm, tugging him away. He flexed his hands and looked with a measure of surprise at his bloodied knuckles.

He nodded. It was over. Case walked towards the pool, and he dropped to his haunches, intending to rinse his bloodied hand in the water.

"Case!"

Josie's shrill scream pierced the silence. He sensed, rather than saw something go whizzing overhead. He glanced up in time to see the pitchfork go flying inches above his head, tines pointed forward in lethal flight.

Had he still been standing, it would have embedded itself in his back. The warning scream had come from Josie, who watched Reichmann tugging the pitchfork from the ground, apparently to support himself, then saw him suddenly lunge forward, hurling it with force at Case's back.

Kevin too, had seen Reichmann's intention, but his clumsy, frantic kick at Reichmanns body connected a fraction too late.

Case was still squatting at the water's edge. He stared at first in disbelief at where Rudolf was kneeling, grunting in pain from Kevin's wild kick, then he looked at the pitchfork settling on the bottom of the pool, its stark outline wavering crazily in the water. He stood up slowly.

Kevin noticed that Reichmanns nose looked ominously skewed, but hey, he was a lawyer, not a doctor! He looked inquiringly at Case.

Short little Ivor was the first to react. He walked over to the man and with surprising strength, pulled the hapless Reichmann quickly to his feet.

Reichmann looked as if he was about to pass out, and he allowed himself to be led away, staggering and stumbling after Ivor, still making those ghastly gurgling noises as he struggled to breathe.

"Come on," Ivor snapped, "I'll leave you at the ER!"

Josie shook herself, as if coming out of a trance. She would need a car to get home. Laine's seemed to be in a daze and her hand was clenched around the weeping Mia's wrist. Gently, Josie pried the woman from Laine's grasp. Making soothing sounds, she led the distraught woman away, towards Laine's car.

She would take Laine's car and return it in the morning. But priority number one was to get this woman home.

Scarcely aware of anything, Laine stood rooted, her face ashen. Her dark brown eyes were huge, fixed on her husband, shock robbing her of speech.

Case gave her a wry grimace and shrugged in a gesture of apology.

He sighed.

What a fuck-up. He had seen Reichmann's nose was broken, but Case was unrepentant.

The last party-goers were disappearing at speed, each with their juicy story to tell on the morrow.

Kevin tried to lighten the mood. "Helluva entertainment, Case. Next time, why don't we slow it down, have the women mud-wrestle?"

Case gave a wan smile. He saw his wife grimace, roll her eyes skyward.

"Case? Are you okay?" Laine was asking him. Her eyes were fixed on her husband. She had never, ever seen him in a fight before. Yes, Kevin had sometimes regaled them with funny anecdotes of long-forgotten brawls...

Funny? How the hell could that ever be funny? Case's clinical pounding of that bastard had stunned her. Her husband was rarely riled, and she had never imagined he could ever resort to violence.

Yet that sonovabitch could have killed Case! She felt intense anger stirring deep within her, bringing with its intensity a surge of revitalizing energy. She had to concentrate to speak coherently, mentally thanking God the children were safe in the annex.

"I need to give Josie my keys." Dazed at how the evening had ended, she went inside to fetch her car keys.

Kevin rubbed his foot tenderly, wondering if he had fractured his foot against that buffoon. The pumping adrenaline was subsiding and as a consequence, the pain in his foot was growing. Nonetheless, he smirked. Case had not lost his touch, that was for sure.

Case eased his wedding ring off his swollen finger and placed it carefully in his pocket. He sat down next to Kevin, seeing Laine's horrified face in his head, and seeking some twinge of remorse within himself.

There was none.

Kevin looked up at him expectantly.

"Well?" Case said. But his tone did not invite discussion or reproach.

Kevin shrugged, more concerned for his aching foot than anything else. He paused in his ministrations to his throbbing foot, a smile playing at his lips. "Case, my man, you missed your vocation in life. You really should have been a boxer." He looked at Case with such frank admiration that they both burst into spontaneous laughter. The heavy mood broken, Kevin shook his head disbelievingly. "What a punch. You've improved since college." He stood up, grinning. "Oh well, time to be off."

"Foot okay?"

"Yeah, bruised, that's all." Kevin was nonchalant.

"Lawsuit here?" Case asked, only mildly bothered.

Kevin grinned. "Fuck him if he can't take a joke!"

Case accompanied Kevin to his car, but he was distracted. Laine would be waiting for him... Trouble.

Inside the house, he turned off the lights and went upstairs to their bedroom.

She was already in bed, wide awake, and he could see immediately from the glint in her eye her mood had changed–she was ready for battle. She drew the covers up to her chin in a gesture of angry exclusion, saying nothing to him at all. He stood in the doorway leading to the bathroom, studying her for a second, hesitant, trying to find the right words.

Here was real trouble. Forget Reichmann and his crap.

Case sighed and walked around to her side of the old four-poster bed and sat down. As usual, it creaked ominously, as it had been doing for a hundred years. He tried again to think of something to say, something that would redeem him, but all thoughts or apologies seemed trite and inane.

Laine eyed him, waiting.

"Want to talk...?" he asked at last, giving up. It was the best he could find. He noticed she was trembling under the covers and concerned, he gathered her close to him. He saw she was trying hard not to cry.

"Laine, honey, it was a great evening," he said. "Try and forget the last bit." His words were met with stony silence. He frowned, concentrating. Think, McAllister. What to say, what to say?

Attack is the best form of defense, maybe.

"He threw the first punch, sort of." Case offered eventually, knowing he sounded beyond lame, childish even. But it was the best he could muster.

She glared at him.

Nope, that wasn't working. Pleading maybe?

"Can't we forget it, Lainie? Please?" He stroked her hair and held her close. He was pleased to feel the trembling had stopped.

"And you still haven't given me my present? Where is it?" he teased, looking under the covers, trying to distract her. Fat tears began rolling down her cheeks, but she gave a small, watery smile at his teasing.

"You could have been killed. You were so damn... damn primitive. And that poor woman! I've wondered for a while if he beats her. Imagine if little Kira and Bernadette see that sort of thing regularly?" Her words were barely audible and she began to weep.

Case felt his heart contract in a painful squeeze.

God, he loved her! He held her close and when the tears stopped, he lifted up her chin and kissed her gently on the lips, wanting to convey his love, wanting to fix this the one way he knew how. She responded distractedly at first, distraught, then slowly her mouth became fierce and hungry, wanting.

She broke away from his embrace.

"Get in," she instructed solemnly, patting the bed beside her. "I want you close, up against me. -No, don't wash," she said, as he started towards the bathroom, "Just get in. Please," she said softly, her voice husky. Case stopped short, surprised at the urgency in her voice, the desire in eyes that just a moment ago were weeping. Her unexpected reaction quickened his pulse, making his groin respond involuntarily. Quickly he stripped off and climbed into the bed beside her, leaning over her. Laine clamped herself hungrily onto him. Instead of the long and tender foreplay she had envisaged at the start of the evening, now she felt consumed by an urgent, overwhelming need to make herself one with him, to draw him into her warmness.

Here, deep inside her, she could keep him safe.

JUST ONE SPOON...

GOD BLESS HOLLYWOOD

Roxie Tanner swung her legs off the bed and stretched. She padded across the room to the glass wall and pulled back the drapes to take in the view, the day. The sun was well and truly up, and a tranquil Pacific shimmered in the distance. Another glorious California day, and somehow, it felt full of promise.

She clasped her hands above her head and did her wake-up Yoga, a few half-moons, warm-up bends, mountains, the discipline ingrained. She was excited. This afternoon, she was meeting the movie's director, Matt Priestly A smile played on her lips as she thought about her role, a female mechanic. Well, he was a good director, and the role would open other doors. She shrugged.

God bless Hollywood!

Her life would soon mimic art–or at least–her movie. Soon, she would be alone, hand to forehead here, out of love and alone, not unlike her movie role.

The producers rather liked the idea of a 'woe is me' publicity reservoir that could be used on tap.–Although they took care to feign the correct amount of distress at the 'sad news', but it was BS, and both they and Roxie knew it.

Still, it was good form and the execs good form.

She was alone in the house today; Juanita, her housekeeper, was off. The gardener was off too, enjoying his long weekend, but Roxie's diary was full. Today it was all work and the endless, endless schmooze.

Some, of course, might not call it work, but work it was, the smiling, the gushing, being charming.

Oh, so endlessly charming! She had no less than four functions to attend this weekend, one fundraiser and one photo-op, two gotta-be-there socials.

She gazed out onto the beach. In the distance, she could see a lone angler trying his luck with an enormous rod. It was a bummer to wake up alone on a day like today. Jeremy? Should she call him? She dismissed the thought immediately. No, no, not a plan. What if she was tempted, and broached the divorce thing? That was a conversation one should have face-to-face. Perhaps Phillipa?

Roxie dismissed that immediately. Phillipa would be horrified to be woken up before noon.

From left field, a sudden gust of that old melancholy blew back those curtains in her head, curtains pulled tight, to close out those memories.

Enough of that. She shrugged it off quickly before it could settle.

Not today.

Today she had things to do, places to go, people to see–no time for maudlin crap. She picked up a pair of binoculars to see what the angler was reeling in–something small. Probably rock cod.

Her reverie was interrupted by the intrusive ringing of her phone. Trish, her agent.

"Hey..." She moved up to the foot of the bed to bask in the sunshine pushing past the drapes, enjoying the warmth on her bare skin.

"Roxie? Roxie, are you awake?" Trish's tone implied Roxie ought to be awake. Roxie rolled her eyes. Play nice, she warned herself.

"Yes." She sighed. Far away, she could see the fisherman departing. She hoped he had been successful. It was the kind of day where everyone should be successful.

"God, you sound awful. Are you sick?" Trish asked, immediately concerned. The worst thing that could happen to a singer was to sound sick.

"No, I'm not sick," Roxie replied irritably. "I'm recording–it was a long session last night."

"Oh. Okay. Good." No threat there, then, to her prize cash cow. To business; "The meet at Matt's house today- just a few pointers, hon."

'Matt' was Matt Priestly and the director of Roxie's debut movie.

Roxie groaned. "What now?"

"We-ell," Trish drawled, "It's kinda, today it's sorta like a bonding session, hon, you know, seeing the 'fit', as it were."

"Uh-huh." Charm. That she could do.

"Oh, he asked if you could kinda look the part, hon?" Trish said sweetly.

"Look the part??" Roxie wrinkled her nose, perplexed. "What does that mean?" She thought about it.

"Female singing mechanic? Dungarees? Vaguely butch?? Jeans, boots? Missing tooth? Baseball cap?" She rattled her suggestions until they were both laughing.

"Hon, the role is a Cinderella part, so kinda... waif it up, you know what I mean?? They want you," Trish assured her, "but the producer, he thinks you're kinda of a glamour puss! He was unsure about you for the role. But Matt insisted, and he, with my help—" she said, justifiably smug, "-won out!"

Roxie was smiling. Glamour puss?

Yep, money could do that.

"I think I can figure something out!" she said casually, "Might be fun!"

"And you keep that Manning in check!" Trish warned. Trish had a love-hate relationship with Roxie's manager, Charles Manning. Managers. They got in her way.

Roxie could feel her good mood ebbing away.

"Trish, that's a side of the business I don't worry about. You do your bit. Let Charles handle the rest. Now I'm late, I must go."

"Fine, fine, hon," Trish soothed. "Oh, they're delivering the car this morning. I told them around 9 am?"

Roxie frowned. What was she on about?

"Did I not mention it? The DeVille. The Cadillac. You're going in the Cadillac, in character, as it were. Just humor them, hon," she said soothingly.

"Here? The car's coming to my house??"

"Sure. He wanted to see you in it, 'wrap you into the role' as he put it. So, he's sending it to you, to let you 'immerse' yourself! 'Good thinking,' I said to him. He'll see for himself-you're a natural!"

"Oh my God!" Roxie was horrified. Some old banger was coming here, and they expected her to drive it??

Trish rushed on. "Having you arrive there in that bucket, that will make him them for you, you know, for this role. Maybe some sorta Thelma and Louise thing he's got going on, who knows," Trish said,

"Point is, it would be great to show him you're a chameleon, hon, a fucking chameleon!"

A Cadillac DeVille? What was that exactly? Roxie shrugged. Some kind of a coupe, she knew that much. Her stomach was growling. She was hungry, and wondered if she should have fruit or eggs.

Trish was all business. "You have to be there around two-ish. The car's a bit beat up, but hey, that's the part." Trish began to rattle off some facts she had researched about Cadillac DeVilles, 'that might be conversational gambits, hon, let him see you've got brains too.'

Roxie zoned out. Something about Matt saying the 'drive-train' was costing four thousand dollars alone. Blah blah.

"I must go. I've got dance downtown at ten. Catch you later, bye!" Roxie hung up, not waiting for an answer.

The phone rang again almost immediately.

It was Jeremy.

Roxie frowned, debating. She decided to let it ring. When it stopped ringing, there came the inevitable buzz of a message. He was delayed and would see her in two weeks or so, probably. Probably?

She frowned and looked at the phone, pensive.

Two weeks? Probably?

It should have mattered, but it didn't.

Roxie gazed out of the window. There were a couple of joggers on the beach, running with a dog.

One day, she mused, perhaps she would get a dog...

—But, to the matter of Jeremy?

Well, she had two more weeks before she had to cross that bridge.

Freshly showered, Roxie stood before the wall-length mirror debating her 'waif' look for her luncheon-meet with Matt. The face in the mirror that stared back at her was relaxed; most said it was a beautiful face.

Roxie herself was skeptical. Her nose was too Roman, her lips too pouty. A sensual mouth, they said, but personally, she didn't see it. But the big thing —the great thing— she photographed well.

Her eyes were her secret weapon. Below perfectly sculpted brows were eyes a deep, brilliant jade. They were particularly green this morning! No shadows to hint at the late nights in the studio. Good. The mane of auburn curls would prove a challenge. Good genes and a fantastic hairdresser made her look expensive, even when stark naked.

Plus, success makes one fucking awesome, she thought with satisfaction.

How to change that awesomeness. Dress down? She chewed her lip, thinking. The role called for "early twenties," and she knew with her hair in a ponytail, she looked like a kid, younger than her thirty-two years.

In the end, she decided on no makeup, save for oodles of mascara.

As she applied the mascara, she reflected that these same eyes would soon pin the producers up against the damn wall! Too glamorous indeed! What did they know.

Finally, with those old jeans she could never find the heart to throw away, an old Fleetwood Mac T, a Dodgers baseball cap, her ensemble was complete. And, of course, her old faithful, big, really big, Chanel sunglasses.

She dressed quickly, grabbing a hoodie she had purchased years ago on tour in Europe, a tatty but precious reminder of the hungry years.

She twirled in front of the mirror. Transformation complete. She looked positively loathsome.

Satisfied Matt would see his waif cum mechanic cum pop star, Roxie went down to the kitchen and fixed herself a light breakfast of muesli and fresh fruit, followed by toast and Nutella. She smiled to herself, knowing that Juanita would be secretly horrified that a "seemple breakfuss could makka this mess."

Her breakfast was interrupted by the bell. The kitchen monitor showed an enormous car in the driveway. A giant, monster of a car.

Her chariot had arrived. Roxie strolled outside, crunching on her toast, remote in hand, to get a better look. The young guy driving the car waved at her in greeting.

"Special delivery for you Miss Tanner!" he called out, taking in her tatty gear. She sure looked ordinary.

The gates swung open and Roxie gazed at the car in dismay, her hand over her mouth. "So this... monstrosity is a '59 Cadillac DeVille?" She was aghast at the sheer size of it.

It was also scrap, or very close to it. The blue paintwork was patchy, and every panel had a dent of some sort.

This was her passport into Hollywood. Roxie flung a half-eaten piece of toast into a large porcelain planter pot brimming with geraniums, her appetite fled.

"There's no way that I can drive this, this heap!" she wailed to the grinning young man. She stared at the car in dismay and chivvied herself. It's a part in a movie, not a lifetime sentence. Consider it a challenge, Rox!

The young driver of the car was smiling. "Nah, it's easy," he reassured her, trying to hide his awe at being this close to Roxie Tanner. He was also more than a little amused at her panic. "Just a bit big, kinda," he conceded. "But you'll get used to it." Like hell she would, he thought, but hey, he was just here to deliver! A car had pulled up behind him, and he gave a thumbs-up to the driver and held out the keys for her to take.

Roxie looked in no hurry to take them from him.

"Should I turn it around for you?" he asked, eying the curved and rather narrow driveway.

"Please," she said with relief.

He did so, then climbed out, handing her the keys again.

"Now, you just point it, and it'll get you there... Mostly." He was joking, but then again, he found himself wondering if he was indeed joking. On the way over, he thought the engine had a bit of a beat there?? He shrugged inwardly. His lot was to obey. He also had firm instructions not to ask for selfies or autographs, he reminded himself. Bummer. Up close, it was Roxie Tanner alright, and grubby or not, she was hot!

Roxie took the keys from him, filled with trepidation. The car was too damn big! She buoyed herself with the thought it was a holiday weekend, the roads were quieter than normal. She eyed the car balefully.

A movie about this? Men were so frigging peculiar.

She waved the young man off with a smile. She went inside to collect her things for her dance class, stuffing her purse, her phone, and her travel makeup bag in a well-weathered old Gucci leather hold-all, and squaring her shoulders, Roxie headed for the door. Her phone rang as she reached the door. Trish, again.

"Roxie hon, if anything in the script that gives you pause, hon, today's the day to speak up!" Trish said. "Needed to tell you that!"

"Okay, I hear you... thanks, gotta go now, busy day!" She still felt hungry. She set her phone down, eying the bowl of apples on the kitchen island. She should take a couple. She might be hungry after dance. She carefully selected two apples. Satisfied she had the right two, she left, thinking about the script.

Outside, she stood for a moment, getting the measure of 'the Beast' as she had dubbed it. She took a deep breath: all or nothing.

The driver's window appeared to be stuck in the open position, so her Dodgers cap would be useful. She tossed her bag onto the back seat. What if it rained?

You're being stupid, and panicking for nothing, Roxie Tanner, she scolded herself. It never rains in California, ask the Mamas and the Papas.

She slid behind the wheel, feeling ridiculously petite on the enormous bench seat. Seated behind the giant steering wheel, her bravado vanished. Her Bentley convertible felt like a toy, a damn cocoon, compared to this. She turned the key.

The engine took immediately, and the car lurched. Roxie shrieked and released the key. The engine died, and she sat for a moment, wringing her hands.

Think, think.

Was this a stick shift?

Squirming down in the seat, she peered owlishly into the gloom under the dashboard. She could see nothing at all. Her sunglasses fell from her face and it was as if someone had turned on a light. She stared into the well. Two pedals. An automatic.

See. Simple.

She was in the movie biz now, she reminded herself! Stunt people do these things all the time.

She wiped her perspiring palms on her jeans and adjusted the lever according to the diagram. Gingerly, she turned the key again, her foot hard on the brake pedal, just in case. The car moved jerkily out of the drive into the quiet street, and as instructed, she pointed the Beast towards the R 59.

A bonus for that guy. He must have guessed.

The car moved smoothly enough, and she felt her spirits lifting.

Great. She was doing just fine.

Dance class, here I come.

As she expected, the traffic was light. She clutched the huge steering-wheel in a regulation ten-to-two grip, and clamped like a beaver on the wheel, Roxie felt herself beginning to relax. She would stay in the slow lane. The few cars on the road flashing by seemed positively puny by comparison.

Roxie began to regard her drive in this archaic old relic as something of an adventure.

Too soon.

Ominous spitting noises came from the engine and the speedometer began to fall. She pumped furiously at the gas, and she heard an ominous crunching underfoot. Her sunglasses!!

The car was definitely slowing down.

Roxie eased the car over to the shoulder. She was unheeding of blaring horns, wanting only to get the monstrosity safely to the side of the road. The car stuttered to a jerky halt, threatening whiplash, to the amusement of passing motorists.

Stationary at last, Roxie sat still for a second. Then she pounded the steering wheel in mortification, shrieking in frustration.

Fuck it!

Here she was, on the damn highway, in some broken-down piece of crap.

Shit shit shit!

She clambered over to the back seat and reached for her hold-all. A frantic hunt for her phone left her empty-handed. Nothing. With a sinking heart, Roxie realized it was at home, on the kitchen counter, next to the damn apples!

She slunk low into the seat, trying to think. There was an emergency telephone about two miles back. She climbed back into the front seat and tried the starter again.

The engine cranked, then died. Defeated, she debated her options.

Get out and hitch, or trudge back to the emergency phone?

Roxie ground her teeth in frustration. She glanced at her reflection in the rear-view mirror. A panic-stricken urchin stared back at her. She groaned and slumped in the seat, pulling her cap low.

"Dress the part. Look like a waif, hon," Trish had said. Yada yada yada. Face it, she thought glumly, she matched this disgusting old heap!

If Roxie Tanner was spotted trudging the damn expressway dressed like this-! The thought made her shudder.

Perhaps it would be better to try and thumb a ride? Please God, let no one recognize me. Roxie groped for her sunglasses on the floor, pulling them up in dismay. The right arm was hanging by a thread, but when she settled them, taking great care, they stayed rather precariously on her face.

She remembered she had a bandaid in her hold-all, and Roxie effected a quick repair.

Disguised once again behind sunglasses, she stepped out of the car, slamming the heavy door shut. She pulled the cap low over her face, feeling every inch the hick she was meant to portray.

She stepped away from the car and assumed a pose.

In fact, she tried several poses, trying with body language to convey that the heap did not really belong to her, she herself was in fact quite fabulous, but here she was, in need of a teensy, smidgen of help.

The cars passed by, indifferent. She sighed. Screw being coy. She would surrender all pride in favor of a lift, any damn help at all.

It occurred to her that hers had been a sheltered life.

This would be her first attempt at hitchhiking! She took a deep breath and raised a tentative thumb.

BORN TO BE MILD

Case loved his bike. The fracas of the night before, not to mention the great sex, it all served to make him feel alive and vibrant this morning. He was filled with anticipation for this long overdue getaway with Laine. Just a few more hours to do his rounds, then off to La Senega.

Taking the old Harley this morning instead of the car was a spoil. He was wearing his favorite, albeit worse-for-wear aviator brown leather jacket. The jacket wasn't just for show; in the unlikely event of a spill, that same leather jacket would hopefully keep the little bits of him intact. He lacked only the biker's true joy, the wind on his face!

Laine had unceremoniously tossed his open visor helmet out, listening with wifely indifference to his detailed and impassioned explanation as to how bikes were meant to be ridden, with just a bandana, actually!

She had listened to his protests, smiled sweetly at him and stubbornly held out his new, full-face helmet. It was the ugliest damn helmet in the world. But with wifely cunning, it was beautifully gift-wrapped and came complete with batting eyes—he was trapped.

Her steely expression brooked no argument.

Still, here he was today, out on the open road, the old '73 Sportster purring underneath him.

Could life get any better!

He motored along at a fair pace, enjoying the old bike's 4-stroke throb, the city skyline of downtown LA beckoning.

Then, broken-down and at the side of the road, looking battered and neglected, Case saw his new love.

DARTH

After a few minutes of standing next to the cumbersome old relic, Roxie's chagrin changed quickly into despair. Callous and unfeeling motorists sped past.

She stabbed the air, making her thumb more assertive, as a Mercedes approached. To her disappointment, the Mercedes swept on by, but a biker slowed down immediately, stopping on the shoulder some yards ahead.

She stared as the biker approached, faintly alarmed. He was tugging at the strap of a huge black helmet that had to have come straight out of Star Wars.

Darth Vader, walking towards her? The stranger strode towards her, the bounce in his step showing his excitement.

Oh God, it's no good, I've been recognized, she thought, her heart sinking. Oh God! Oh God! Oh God!

She could see the tabloids already. She groaned inwardly. Mustering the vestiges of her tattered dignity, Roxie forced a smile, determined to be grateful for any assistance at all. Hell, she would give him some tickets to a show, whatever!

The stranger was fumbling with the cumbersome helmet as he approached. He finally pulled the clunky helmet free and shook his head like a terrier shedding water.

She took a close look at her unlikely knight. He was clean-shaven, seriously built under that jacket, quite good-looking, she thought. She would have given him a second look on any other day but today. He wore his jacket and jeans like a second skin, and he exuded that best of all aftershaves, testosterone. That whole macho thing was almost tangible. Comfortable trainers, she noted, no biker's boots.

Mental images of brute bikers with tattoos pledging allegiance to Mama had swamped her imagination, but her wariness faded in the face of this rather pleasing alternative. Deep-set faded blue eyes were sweeping over the Cadillac DeVille in abject admiration. She noticed the knuckles on his hand were bruised and slightly swollen. No ring on his left hand, she noted.

Not married. Inexplicably, that sent a little frisson through her. The day was delivering on its promise!

Roxie gave him her best 'I'd like to thank the Academy' smile and launched into her prepared spiel.

"Hi, thanks so much for stopping. I'm afraid—" Her words were cut off by the man's wolf whistle.

Really? In this outfit? She couldn't believe it.

"Whoooee. Fantastic!" But he wasn't looking at her. He was gazing in rapture at the car.

"Well, thank—" she tried to continue.

"It's been forever since I've seen one of these!

She realized he was quite oblivious to her presence. The stranger stood in silent homage before the cause of her sorry plight, chewing his bottom lip, lost in thought.

"Well, I—" She glanced at the car, then at him. Bewildered, she tried again, "Well—"

"What an old beauty," he breathed softly, his hand reverently caressing the hood.

Beauty? The Beast was a beauty?

He turned to her and shot her a curious glance. "You sure are lucky to own one of these." He seemed to notice her for the first time. "This is your car?"

"Yes," Roxie said. The lie slipped out without a second's hesitation. Where the hell did that come from? But it was too late, he was nodding, his attention back on the car.

A slight smile lifted the corners of his mouth. Nice mouth, she thought, yummy. She tossed her head coquettishly, and the sunglasses with the broken arm promptly gave up and fell to the floor. She bent down to pick it up from the verge, her face burning.

The stranger hadn't noticed. He had walked to the door and now he was reaching deep inside the car, pulling a catch to release the hood. Then he slid behind the wheel and cranked the engine, cocking his head to one side, listening. She noted he knew exactly where the release catch was. The Beast spat a few times, cranked, then... Nothing.

He drummed his fingers on the steering wheel, thinking. Then he climbed out and took off his jacket. She stared fascinated as it peeled off, revealing a brawny chest in a plain white Tee, no myriad of biker tattoos on his arms, she observed.

He stooped and peered into the engine bay, his arm outstretched behind him, holding his jacket in her general direction. There was no impatient snapping of fingers, but in Roxie's head, she could have sworn she heard just that.

Obediently, she hastened to take it from him.

It was surprisingly heavy and had seen better days. Surreptitiously she inspected the jacket. No Devils, or Bulldogs, or 'I Love LA' badges. – Nothing.

Her rescuer's torso was under the hood, and she eyed his backside with feminine appreciation. Curious to see what was absorbing him so, she stepped closer to peer under the hood with him. There was nothing to see, just an old engine, hissing its annoyance. He seemed to be busy, prodding and poking for a minute, then instructed, "Hold this."

Again, he didn't look up. Gingerly she took an oily-looking cap from him, unmindful of her hundred-dollar manicure. The stranger, warming to his task, delved still further, his forearms defined and competent looking. He tinkered on for a few minutes more, and Roxie stood back with an alien timidity.

She swept the hair off her face, acutely aware of her shabby attire., oblivious to the oily streak the gesture made on her forehead.

Trish and her genius ideas!

"Okay, hand it back."

He was absorbed in the engine, his hand was out behind him.

Obediently, she placed the filthy bottle-cap thing in his outstretched hand. He tinkered for a few moments, then he straightened up and carelessly wiped the grime from his hands on his jeans.

For the first time, he looked at her directly, his face thoughtful.

"You need another distributor, maybe plug wires, rotor's certainly shot. Don't think it's anything too serious though. Better let a mechanic have a good, long look at it." He examined his hands, satisfied they were clean enough. He looked at her, his face solemn.

"So! I guess you better start walking!" he said, hands on hips.

Roxie gaped at him in dismay. Was he telling her it wouldn't go?

Worse, he hadn't even noticed her, much less offered her a lift.

He burst out laughing at her shocked face, his eyes dancing.

Ah. He was teasing. She smiled back, feeling gauche, foolish.

"Cheer up, it'll live," he said with a grin. "And I'll give you a lift into the city. Lock up. Bring your things." He fired the instructions, clearly unused to argument. He was still grinning, highly amused at her earlier consternation.

Roxie felt her spirits soar. It didn't matter at all that she was the butt of his amusement. Her rescuer noticed the smudge on her face and stepped forward. He reached out and held her chin steady, pulling his tee up and carefully, he rubbed the oil smudge from her face, then stepped back to examine his handiwork.

He seemed satisfied and dropped his hand from her chin.

On a bright, sunny day in autumn, five miles off exit 34, on the R 59, Roxie Tanner fell in love.

Unmoved by any similar chemistry, her rescuer was already walking towards his bike. Hastily, she grabbed her bag from the back seat of the monster car and rushed to take her seat on the bike's pillion. He insisted she wear his helmet, helping her push it unceremoniously over her head. The sheer weight of it would snap her neck like a twig, she felt sure, but she offered no sign of any discomfort. She had a fleeting moment of treacherous doubt about the bike.

Did it seem to be of a similar vintage to the car?

She dismissed her doubts. She should be so lucky, him and her, broken down, together.

He waited patiently while she tried to contain her hair. He saw unruly auburn curls, but at last, the helmet had them beat. She gave an ungainly nod to indicate she was ready, and he kicked the engine into life. The bike seemed to be made for one, and Roxie found herself spooning into his back.

Up close, he smelt wonderful. She held on tight, loving the sensation of the powerful engine, and the wind racing by.

The ride felt surreal. She tried to drum up sane thoughts—perhaps he would take her somewhere and murder her? But that was impossible.

The truth was, he was a real, honest-to-God hero. Her very own knight had finally come along.

It had been a long time since Roxie had been on a motorbike. She gazed out from behind the visor. Mrs. Vader, going who knew where? It felt like a dream. Turbulent, insane emotions raced through her.

Too soon for Roxie, they stopped outside the big office block in West Lebonne St.

Standing on the sidewalk, uncaring of passers-by, she stood struggling with the catch of his helmet, gawkish and clumsy, desperate to know the identity of her rescuer.

He sat astride the motorbike, his arms crossed, apparently still in awe over the damn car and quite oblivious to her struggles with the helmet. He appeared in no hurry.

"My father had that car when we were kids," he said, addressing the bobbing helmet, "I knew all the specs, top speed, torque—! Hell, everything," he offered conversationally.

She managed a ponderous nod. The damn thing wouldn't come off!

She understood not a word of what he was saying, but she was frantic to keep him there, perhaps forever on the sidewalk. At least until he too realized he was in love.

At long last, the helmet gave in, and she managed to wrench it off.

"I've always wanted to get one, you know, to rebuild it, but that would be an indulgence, I guess. I suppose it drinks gas?" he asked.

"What?" She was looking down into the hold-all searching for the anonymity of her sunglasses. Then she remembered they were in sunglass-heaven, and she gave up. How the hell could she say `What', for God's sake?

Focus Roxie, she chided herself.

"Uh... yeah... Er, yes. It's... very heavy on gas! Actually, I want to sell it," she blurted.

So began, what she later described to her best friend Phillipa, her first ever 'out of body' experience.

Another Roxie was an incredulous observer from above, bobbing around like a helium-filled birthday balloon, listening to Crazy Roxie on the sidewalk.

Crazy Roxie was firmly in control.

Seconds were ticking by. Soon he might be gone forever. She held her breath.

"Really. Really!" He looked eager. "How much do you want for her?" He looked blown away by this good fortune.

Her? —That wreck was a woman? How much, he was asking.

"How much?" she repeated hesitantly, trying to think. Crazy Roxie had been caught off guard. Her voice sounded strangely hoarse. She cleared her throat. "I, I—! Uh, about... Five thousand??" Unconsciously she chewed her lip, fretting. Too much?

"Five thousand dollars!" he repeated, astonished. That was for nothing. He stared into the greenest eyes he had ever seen.

"Oh!" Roxie felt mortified. Unnerved by his stare, she was rethinking the price. Too much? It looked like shit, that was for sure!

"Uh... What I meant was, four thousand dollars!"

"Four thousand dol—!" He broke off, fascinated. He began to laugh. This chick had zero idea what her car was worth!

His laughter made her stomach flip. She nodded stupidly, smiling timidly back at him. "Uh, yes, that's what I meant! Four thousand..." She trailed off.

Roxie peered at him anxiously.

Case stopped chuckling. He appeared a bit confused. That car was worth more, but she looked like she needed the money. Laine would skin him alive, but—

"Well, actually it's worth more than that," he said doubtfully. "It seems ridiculously low."

Oh my God, too little, Roxie, too little! Then she remembered some of Trish's babble. "The train-drive needs fixing, that could cost four thousand dollars. Just that," she added earnestly. God bless Trish!

He looked surprised that she would know such details. "Well. Okay, I see."

"It could be as much as five thousand dollars," she added, sounding way too hopeful. You're scaring him, look at his face.

Case was studying her. The chick was clearly desperate. She was giving that old car away. She would probably be sorry she had been so impulsive later. Four thousand dollars was crazy, fix it up and it was worth maybe ten times that. He studied her, his head to the side, his chin dropped on his chest, thinking.

Dilemma. Would he be ripping her off? Suddenly he made up his mind.

"Look, my name is Case McAllister and I'm a doctor at Granger Clinic. I'll give you five thousand dollars for it, if you're sure about selling it. Call me next week and let me know."

Crazy Roxie nodded, a silly smile on her face.

Case McAllister. Dr Case McAllister.

Her knight was a doctor.

"Well then, guess I'll be seeing you." He grinned at her and put the helmet on, snapping the visor down. With a kick, the bike came to life. Roxie lifted her hand in belated farewell, watching him merge deftly into the traffic.

"Thanks again for the lift..." she called to the fading roar of his bike.

He was gone from sight. Keeping her head down, she hurried into the building.

THAT OTHER CRAZY

Sheila Delaney looked up in surprise to see a glowing, but unusually grungy Roxie walk in. Sheila was the long-suffering PA to Charles Manning, Roxie's manager.

"You're late. She's waiting in the studio," Sheila said, referring to Roxie's choreographer.

"Sheila, guess what just happened." Roxie's smile was radiant.

"You're winning next year's Grammy?" Her tone was droll.

"No no no! I broke down in that DeVille, the one for the movie. On the highway! I was stuck and with no phone either!" Roxie sang out happily, beaming at Sheila expectantly.

Sheila paused at her desk, eying Roxie. This was good news. She reflected sadly they all dabbled in drugs, eventually; it was just a matter of time.

But then again, this was Roxie before her. She decided to give Roxie the benefit of the doubt.

"Explain."

"This guy gave me a lift and I did the craziest thing—"

"Ah. I see." And she did. —A man.

Roxie paused mid-sentence. 'Sane' Roxie was back. In fact, 'sane' Roxie was now shifty Roxie. Hide the crazy, she warned herself. With an effort, she changed tack.

"Well, Sheila, we need to collect that car. They can tow it back to my house—must be my house—and I want to buy it. Correction, I have to buy it."

Now that Sheila didn't see coming! "The car?? The car for the movie??"

Roxie nodded. "Love it, shmove it. Adore it. Any price. Any price. Just buy it, that car, okay, that car—it has to be that car!!"

Sheila was taken aback. Roxie sounded quiet—! She searched for the right word. Frantic? Since when did Roxie Tanner have a passion for cars?

Roxie stopped, a thought had occurred to her, and she was suddenly anxious. "In fact, buy two! We're going to need two. We need to give Matt

Priestly another one, but this one, this one's... Uh, it's mine."

Sheila was speechless. "What the hell..."

Roxie's face closed, and she looked decidedly cagey. "Two, Shiel, that's this one, for me! Another one for Matt. For the movie, you know." She rummaged in her head for some plausible explanation to offer Sheila.

"I need to... uh," she thought fast, "feel it, you know, and the best way," Roxie explained, reaching, "is to drive it for a good while?? Grow into the role, as it were?"

"Ah." Sheila shrugged. Now that was BS if ever she heard it! But short of a skeptical snort, Sheila said nothing.

"Okay, leave it to me..."

But when she looked up, Roxie was gone.

RAMBO DOC

Case dismissed the girl with the startling green eyes and her car from his mind. As the clinic neared, reality set in. He mulled over the events of the night before. He was a damn doctor, not some hot-headed idiot, and he tried to find some feeling of remorse. Dig deep, McAllister. Nope, still none. No remorse at all.

It was pretty clear that Reichmann's nose was broken. His own rage and lack of control had surprised him. Provoked by that whole damn macho 'my woman' shit. Case remembered the shock in the man's eyes when he had punched him.

Satisfying. Not quite Boxing Association rules, but then Case doubted if Reichmann understood any 'rules' at all. But he, Case McAllister, had shocked himself.

He had enjoyed belting the bastard. Perhaps it was true there was a little bit of the savage in every man. He moved neatly into a gap in the next lane. He had 'wound it up' a few times in his younger days, there had been the odd brawl in college, but last night, well, that was something different.

His thoughts turned to Laine. She had been really upset last night... Appalled, for sure. She had never seen him in a brawl before. He sighed at the memory of her feminine confusion. Only a few guys would let a pass at their wife go by, and he sure as hell wasn't one of them. He'd tried...

But when Reichmann had smacked his wife, well, a man had to choose when to step aside. Last night was not one of those times.

When he strode through the doors of the rambling old building called Granger Clinic, he was greeted with a flurry of activity and giggling from the staff on duty at the main desk.

"Morning, everyone. Anything I should know?" He flashed a quick smile at Rita Doolly, the senior behind the desk.

"Hi Doc," she replied politely enough, then sniggered, adjusting an imagined stray hair. Case had the sensation that after six years, he was being assessed by the desk nurses anew. Doolly looked at him expectantly, her hands clasped, eyebrows raised in inquiry.

Was she deaf? He repeated, "Anything I should know?" More titters. He looked at the others, perplexed. Suddenly, he understood. The damn fight. They all knew about the brawl. It would be all over the hospital by now. And the one damn morning he chose to bring the bike into the city instead of the car.

Rambo rides again. He frowned, exasperated, and asked again,

"Anything I should know about?" His patience was fast waning. He tipped his head in the direction of the patient files, taking care to keep his face impassive.

Rita sighed. Details were not going to be forthcoming. Pity that. Reluctantly she focused on the matters of the day. Her face sobered as she remembered.

"Yes, there's a little boy in Ward Nine B. He was savaged by a dog and it's pretty bad. Dr Morris attended to him last night. He asked that you look in on the child, and then call in on him, if he's still around. The boy's name is Steven Cahill. He's asleep but stable."

Case picked up the file that she had pushed across to him and strode away down the corridor. Now and then, he was aware of curious glances and stifled giggles, student nurses gazing at him in fascination.

He was glad to close them out with the pull of a curtain and focus on the toddler in Ward Nine B.

The clipboard at the end of the cot told Case the boy was three and a half years old. His face and right arm were covered in stitches, a livid red and black web across the tiny face and neck. The child's eyes were puffy slits, almost invisible amongst the stitches. The child's right forefinger had been severed at the knuckle. No one thought to look for it at the time, put it in a bag, bring it in.

"Jesus." He whispered the word. He was glad the child was sedated, and he didn't have to pretend all was fine. Shana was only a fraction bigger than the infant lying before him. Case's dark thoughts were interrupted as the nurse breezed in, sweeping the curtain aside.

The nurse paused, noting the doctor's bleak visage. She was a grandmother of two toddlers herself, but twenty-three years of nursing had put the brakes on her sentimentality.

It hampered one's professional conduct.

She stood next to the cot and placed her hand gently over the limp hand of the sedated toddler. "Oh, he looks a lot better now," she said. "You should have seen him yesterday. So much blood from such a tiny thing!" She took Case by the arm and led him to the nurse's station.

"He'll be alright," she pronounced briskly, "-thanks to the likes of you and Dr Morris!"

Case gave a modest grimace. He excused himself and continued on his rounds. They went by smoothly enough, and in a short while, he was good to go. That was it. Done! He was free, for three whole days!

On the road home, his spirits soared with each mile the hog ate up. He opened up the throttle. It felt good to let loose and be on his way.

Maybe he would buy that old car, after all, restore it...

Effect another kind of surgery, as it were. He thought for a moment about the car and the girl with the green eyes. Strange, a young chick like that with such a beat-up old car! That being said, she didn't look as though she could afford much more.

It sure was an old beauty! If she was serious about selling, he was buying!

ESCAPE

When he got back from the clinic, Laine was packed and ready, and it took only a few minutes to load the cases into the trunk. The girls were unconcerned about their parents' pending departure, full of chatter about where Granny intended to take them while Laine and Case were away.

He shoved the suitcases to the rear of the trunk.

Laine bent over into the trunk, pretending to help and murmuring. "Mia called to apologize. She says his nose is broken," she said matter-of-factly.

Case was packing the luggage in the trunk, and he grunted, noncommittal. Judith McAllister noted the whisperings of the pair and frowned. She had been horrified to hear of the near-tragic brawl the night before, but she said nothing to her son. She had taken the usual sleeping pill, pleased to have the infrequent pleasure of two little bodies cuddling beside her in the king-sized bed Laine had relegated to the annex.

Her daughter-in-law's tepid version of the incident hadn't fooled Judith for a second. It was quite evident to her Laine had been shocked to her core by the incident.

Now, she eyed her son as he loaded the luggage.

Case had never been a rowdy child or a bully. Only once that she could recall, shortly after Jim died, he had come home from school bruised and bloodied from a fight. That had also been the start of his friendship with the motherless Kevin Daniels.

Judith refrained from comment. She resolved to bide her time, get the story from him another time.

Case was relieved when no questions were forthcoming from his mother and rightly assumed that Laine had 'taken care of it'. But sensing his mother's probing eyes, he felt the stirrings of conscience.

Abruptly, he was keen to be gone.

"Okay, okay. Line up for goodbye kisses." Laine beckoned them. Shana seemed never to fear the unknown, whilst Liesel was ever more cautious,

"Yes. You're big enough now to help Granny with Shana. And to feed Ollie," Laine declared her tone proud and admiring. Ollie's bottom swung vigorously to the left and right, as if in total agreement.

Liesel perked up. Power, unprecedented. She looked at her grandmother for tell-tale signs of deception. Was she being duped? Liesel decided not. She knew what a handful Shana could be. She would help Granny with everything.

Five minutes later, Case and Laine were on the expressway, headed for Tiger Peak. It felt good to be finally on the way. Case didn't have to look at Laine to guess that she was probably thinking— brooding —about the night before. She almost seemed too young to be a mother; maybe it was the bare feet, sandals kicked off already, the jeans, her hair gathered into a loose ponytail. She sat quietly beside him, content at the prospect of a long drive with just the two of them.

Case sneaked a sidelong glance.

"Guess what." he interrupted her reverie, his demeanor secretive.

"Surprise me." She glanced at his profile, so familiar and beloved.

"What?"

"Well... I've been thinking..." Case said slowly. Laine could help him decide.

"What if, if, mind, I bought you a brand-new car? Well, not brand new, not new at all, in fact, but... new to you, sorta?" His voice held a smile, and Laine narrowed her eyes, immediately suspicious. He was up to something.

"What's wrong with my Beamer? I like my car. I'm used to it." She eyed him, curious. She could see from the smirk on his face he had something up his sleeve. "What kind of car is this you want to buy? Will it pull a horsebox?"

"Oh yes," he said with a chuckle, "Five horseboxes at least. But it might look... Strange." He was laughing at some private joke. "I think the kids are growing up fast and I think you need something... uh... bigger. Much bigger."

Now he was laughing fit to bust.

Laine found herself smiling too. She loved it when he was like this.

"How much bigger?" she asked. Perhaps he wanted to get her a better truck for the horsebox, but honestly, there was nothing wrong with the Beamer, it towed just great.

"We-ell...you know that photo on mom's dresser of my old man standing in front of his Cadillac Coupe DeVille?" His face showed his excitement.

Laine stared at him blankly. Photo on Judith's dresser? Laine tried to picture it, frowning. Then memory clicked into place and she gasped. "Never, Case McAllister, never will I drive something like that. Forget it, buster. Every time I go anywhere, people will wonder where the hell Thelma is?" They were both laughing.

"No way, Jose." she declared.

"Well, actually, Thelma and Louise, that was a Ford Thunderbird, but I get your point. Perhaps it's more of a man's car?" he said slyly. The idea was catching fire inside his head, and he continued. "I just happened to have found the bargain of a lifetime this morning. I rescued a damsel in distress who had broken down on the R 59. She was so damn grateful, she even offered to sell me her car! The very same one as Dad's old car, for four, maybe five thousand dollars! That's a classic, it has to be worth three times that. Ten times that, if it's restored."

He was nodding his head, agreeing with himself. "Yep, that's a bargain, alright."

"Four thousand dollars??? For a classic? Does it go?" Laine was incredulous.

He thought about that. "That is, no, actually, not too well. That's why she was stuck on the highway. I stopped and gave her a lift into the city. The drive-train might be shot."

He frowned, remembering.

"She looked way too young to be driving that sort of car, but I guess it takes all sorts."

"Oh?" Laine was intrigued. "What was she like?"

Case pondered. "An urchin. A bit of a vagabond, kinda..." But quite hot, when he thought about it. "Like I said, young. And kind of... raggedy looking. She was embarrassed, broken down like that, and no one was stopping either. But she spoke like, like..."

He frowned, trying to think. What was it about that girl?

"Like what?"

"Like she didn't really belong with a clapped-out old DeVille. She also reminded me of someone. She seemed familiar??" He frowned, wondering where it could be he might have met her. "I think maybe I've met her before, but I can't remember where. Maybe at the clinic?"

"Familiar? How fam liar?" Laine purred. "Was she pretty?" Her fingers caressed the back of his neck lovingly, but he wasn't fooled.

He grinned at her. "Ugly as sin," he said promptly, and she smiled.

So! The damsel in distress was pretty! Laine smiled and reached into the back of the car for the flask. Time for coffee.

Case wasn't too sure he would recognize the woman again if he met her. He remembered green eyes. Masses of dark hair. He hadn't really noticed too much more about her. He had been too taken up with the DeVille.

He shrugged, giving up. "Believe it or not, I'm not sure I would recognize her again. All I had eyes for was the damn car. But she wants to sell it, and I said to call me at the clinic if she made up her mind. What do you think? Should I buy it and restore it? I enjoyed fixing the bike. We can get it for five thousand dollars?"

The traffic was starting to thin as they left the city behind them. Laine leaned over and ran her fingers through his hair, nibbling at his ear.

"Buy it. Perhaps we'll see more of you at home. You deserve anything you want, like this—!" She glanced around to check the traffic; the coast was clear.

Laine loosened her seatbelt and buried her face in his lap and gently bit the area of his crotch with her teeth, giggling. The car swerved ever so slightly, then sped on its way.

PHILLIPA

It was Sunday, and still, Roxie's head was full of her Darth Vader. She was on her way to collect Phillipa. Her bestie would talk sense into her. Not!

It took Roxie twenty minutes to get to Phillipa's apartment at the Quays. This time she had her Bentley, with all the usual controls in the usual places. It was heavenly, after the DeVille. At the plush apartment building, the security guard waved her through. He knew there was no need to alert Phillipa Young. Roxie was a familiar visitor to these apartments, and besides, in his lustful and unashamedly biased opinion, who would object to Roxie Tanner calling on them?

Roxie stepped outside the elevator into the private foyer of Phillipa's suite. She saw a coat flung carelessly on the floor, then a shoe with impossibly high heels a few yards away, then another, a trail leading to the bar. In all probability, Phillipa might still be in bed.

Phillipa Young had to be the most indolent person Roxie knew. Heiress to a hotel chain, Phillipa had never worked in her life, and it showed.

She was also Roxie's closest friend.

She was wrong. Phillipa was up, wearing nothing but a loose tee that had clearly once belonged to some or other man. At least she was up, albeit barely compus mentus, and more importantly, alone.

"Roxie? Is it time already?" Phillipa looked shocked. "What time is it? God, what a night I had! Be a pet and bring me some coffee while I try to wake up. I feel awful," she moaned. She paused, noticing the excitement in Roxie's face. "What's up?"

Roxie eyed her. "I have something to tell you. —But not while you're half asleep. Go and change; I'll make the coffee," she said. To show how serious she was, Roxie headed for the kitchen.

Phillipa gazed after her, intrigued. All this energy and it was barely eleven. With a little shudder, Phillipa went into her bedroom to change. A while later they were sitting in the living room sipping coffee, Phillipa's liberally laced with 'medicinal' Southern Comfort. She ignored Roxie's disapproving look as she poured a generous tot into her coffee.

"Hair of the dog, sweetie, hair of the dog!" She sipped her coffee with relish, her eyes shut. She opened them to find Roxie looking at her impatiently.

"What? I'm doing coffee yoga, darling. Breathe in-n-n, sniff!" She closed her eyes again, and inhaled the bourbon-infused coffee, then opened her eyes wide.

"Right, I'm good. Tell all," she demanded.

Roxie took a deep breath. At last.

She began, animated. "I had to drive the car they are going to use in the movie, a really old, old Cadillac DeVille."

Phillipa looked blank. "A what?"

"Like the Thelma and Louise car, sort of?"

Understanding dawned. "Ah. Yes, now I know. Carry on," she instructed.

Roxie continued, her face alight. "So Trish thought it would be good to give Matt Priestly a peek with me in it, sort of living the part, as it were. They sent the car to me, for me to drive."

Her face changed, brooding, remembering her encounter with the Beast. "What a heap! It's enormous, terrifying to drive, and guess what?" Here, her face lit up. "It broke down!" she exclaimed happily, flinging herself back into her chair and gazing at the ceiling in rapture.

Phillipa frowned, completely lost.

"Then, then I was rescued..." Roxie breathed reverently. She was still sprawled back in the cavernous recliner, gazing up at the ceiling, contemplating some fantasy Phillipa couldn't begin to fathom.

"So? I'm not following you, sweetie..." It all sounded rather distressing.

Roxie closed her eyes in frustration. Honestly, Phillipa could be so obtuse sometimes. "Well, I was rescued by this man, the man I am going to marry! He was on a motorbike..." She looked thoughtful at the memory,

"A really old bike, actually—" She broke off, remembering the bike. Was that not an omen? Him with that old bike, and she with the old car? Destiny.

Phillipa gesticulated for Roxie to continue, manicured hands flicking the story on impatiently. But it was coming into focus. A man.

Roxie was in this state because of some man!

"So," she concluded to a now mesmerized Phillipa, "It turns out that if I hadn't broken down, I wouldn't have met him!" She flopped back again into her chair, her head tossed back, her eyes closed, lost in the memory of that morning.

Phillipa eyed Roxie caustically, noting the eyes closed in rapture, the little smile playing on Roxie's lips. Then she put her cup down and reached for a cigarette. She lit it, and sat puffing quietly for a few moments.

She ignored Roxie's wrinkled nose of disapproval.

Roxie looked suddenly vulnerable.

"Oh, I know," she admitted, "I probably do need some serious therapy! It's crazy to be so damn... Smitten."

Phillipa sniffed in agreement and stubbed out her cigarette. Three puffs, that was her morning quota. "That's true, sweetie, but you need a psychiatrist, not a therapist," she said, her tone droll.

Roxie shrugged. "What's the difference?"

Phillipa raised one laconic brow. "A therapist, sweetie, is for when you blame your parents. A psychiatrist is for when you blame yourself!"

Roxie giggled. "Well, this is all me, for sure," she conceded, uncaring.

Phillipa continued; "My sweet Rox, I think a few salient facts elude you. Have you forgotten that you—much against my better advice, I have to add, you are already married! For better or for worse, I believe the patter goes..."

Phillipa gazed into her cup. It was empty. Pity. One coffee was all she allowed herself a day. Coffee was murder on the skin. Too early for another teensy tot? She decided it was. She set the empty cup down and waited for Roxie to continue.

Roxie's face was sober. "As we speak, they are towing that, that heap back to my house. If he wants to buy it, I need to own the car, for God's sake!" She sighed and shook her head slowly. "I couldn't help myself. Honestly, I couldn't. I have to see him again, even if it's just to realize what an idiot I am. He says he's a doctor at the Granger Clinic," she added, remembering.

"He's a doctor?" Phillipa looked up, interested.

"Yes. Roxie's face puckered in a frown. "His hands were all bruised, like he'd been in a fight. He's built, you know, like a bouncer, sort of."

"And doubtless been a fan of yours since time began?" said Phillipa.

Roxie jerked her head forward and sat up straight, her eyes alight.

"No, that's the best part! He doesn't know anything about me. He just wants to buy the Beast—the car," she said, "He had no clue about who I am. At all. Ignored me flat!" she declared gleefully.

"Ah. I see."

But Phillipa didn't see at all, and no one ever would, she decided, except for Roxie herself. She hid her thoughts. Hers was not to judge.

Roxie was clearly two spoons.

"Roxie, we've been friends forever, it seems, so I feel it my duty, as the older woman here, —though few could tell that, naturally!" She went on; "However, such love such as you describe—is sheer bliss." Phillipa grinned wickedly. "Go for it."

Roxie shrieked happily. Someone understood!

Phillipa brushed off her enthusiasm. "Personally, I think that being in love is a tedious state of mind. Being in lust is far more sensible. Shag, tag, release!" Her mouth curled in a knowing smirk. "It's the only way. There's no need for anything more." She leaned back and ran her fingers through her blonde bob. Her posture bespoke infinite wisdom. A thought occurred to her.

"By the way, how do you know he's not married?"

Roxie looked smug. "No ring. I looked."

Phillipa snorted. "Look, Rox, sweets, I'm not being harsh," she said, "God knows, I have no room to talk, but if you're buying hideous old cars after a five-minute conversation, imagine if you chat for an hour. You're using up your entire two spoons!"

Roxie looked confused. "Two spoons?"

Phillipa shrugged. "Your crazy! We're all born with at least two spoons of crazy. It's like, like—" She waved her hands, searching for the right words. "Like DNA. You know, like infidelity and such. Everyone has it!"

She pointed a warning finger at her friend, "He's bringing out your crazy!"

Roxie rolled her eyes, nodding. And then some.

"Oh well," Phillipa wriggled her bare toes, studying her pedicured feet in complacent satisfaction. "He does sound rather interesting, though. What's his name again?"

"Case McAllister."

Phillipa puckered her brow, thinking. She shook her head. "Never heard of him!"

Phillipa took pride in claiming she knew everyone that was worth knowing.

Roxie stood up. She felt too excited to sit still a minute longer.

"Enough of this. Are you coming to the Spa or not? I'm desperate for a massage."

"I'll bet," Phillipa murmured. She stood up, stretching languidly.

"Ten minutes and I'll be ready. I'm having a facial too."

Roxie gazed after her retreating friend, her mind in a whirl. Was Phillipa right? Of course she was, a tiny voice answered. You have finally lost your mind!

But there was no going back.

That man was undeniably her crazy.

HONEYPOTS

BAIT

Case was buoyed.

The weekend had done them both a lot of good. He was rested, keen to get back into it. He walked into the small waiting room attached to his surgery, pleasantly surprised to find only two patients waiting to see him. Do rounds, and then an early escape was on the cards. Lindy was on the phone, and he barely looked up when he entered. He nodded a greeting at the patients and went into his consulting room, closing the door behind him. He sat down and picked up a patient file.

He was about to ask Lindy to send the first patient in when she popped her head around the door. "I have a Mrs Roxie Carter on the line for you. Something about a car you're buying?"

Car? For a moment his mind was blank. Then the light went on. The DeVille! He felt a surge of elation. Game on! He knew that car had his name on it! Great, she was serious.

"Put her through."

"Hello?" The woman sounded hesitant, nervous.

Case had a curious sensation of déjà vu.

"Case McAllister here. How are you... Uh, Roxie." Roxie Carter. He scribbled her name on the pad in front of him so that he wouldn't forget it.

"Hi. Hello." Roxie was nervous.

That he didn't know who she was, that was exciting. "You gave me a, uh, a lift ?" she prompted, wincing in chagrin. What if he didn't remember her? Or worse, maybe he was just being polite? She plowed on, determined. "You said you might like to buy my car?" She was talking too fast. She took a deep breath and tried to slow her breathing.

"Absolutely."

She breathed a sigh of relief. For one horrible instant, she had visions of that heap standing in her garage forever, a monument to her insanity.

"Do you still want to sell it so cheaply? It's worth more, you know?" he asked, feeling rather like a shyster.

At the other end of the line, Roxie smiled at his words.

"Honestly, it's fine. I don't need more than that. It needs a lot of work." That part, at least, she thought dryly, was true. "Would you like to have another look at it, perhaps?" Time to go for broke: "Of course, it doesn't go at the moment?"

"I noticed," he said, amused.

The smile in his voice made her stomach dip. Get a grip, Roxie!

She took a deep breath. "Would you like to come, perhaps see it, at my place? Before you make up your mind?" She rolled her eyes to the ceiling. Oh Roxie, you hussy, you slut, you clever thing, you! She found she was holding her breath.

Would he come?

There was a brief silence. Then he spoke;

"Sounds like an idea. My hours are quite erratic. But maybe tomorrow evening?"

"Sure, I might not be there, but someone will let you in," she said nonchalantly, while punching her fist into the air.

'Crazy Roxie' was in control.

Case made up his mind. "Fine... I'll be there after six if all goes according to plan."

He was coming! Roxie let her breath out slowly. "Well, maybe I'll see you tomorrow then. Bye Case!"

"Wait!"

She froze.

"What's the address?" he asked.

"Oh!" Relief flooded through her. "Sorry! It's Lower Bay Road, Cliffside Drive. —Off the exit 44," she added. He must think her a prize idiot.

"Fine. He hung up. Case looked at the address, intrigued. A beat-up old DeVille in Millionaire's Mile!

Perhaps she was a maid? He shrugged. Didn't matter, that car had his name on it!

MESMERIZED

After her call to her doctor, —she was already thinking of him as her doctor, Roxie sat quietly in the sound booth, her heart beating a little too fast.

Well, there was no going back now. What she needed was not a padded sound booth, but a padded cell. He had to be married? Divorced? He had a kind of... aura that suggested—God forbid—a happy marriage, or at least a stable relationship.

Why the hell was she doing this? Like a rabbit, mesmerized by a snake.

Who was the rabbit, and who was the snake? Both exasperated and excited at this new, crazy person she had become, Roxie rose from the stool and picked up the cans. The noisy intrusion of her phone made her start. She was tempted to ignore it, then she saw the name. Jeremy.

Was he psychic? Sighing, she answered the call.

"Roxie? Hello? Hello, can you hear me?" Jeremy sounded agitated.

Roxie quashed her guilt about the doctor and answered cautiously,

"Hello. Jeremy? Where are you calling from? I thought you were in the middle of a war." The glib words hung reproachfully in the air, and she immediately felt shallow and flippant.

"I am in the 'middle of a war' as you so quaintly put it," he said, stung by her cavalier manner. "I'm just calling to tell you that I won't be able to make it home for a while yet. They've set up a really good interview with Krashovi, the new right-hand man." She could hear someone calling him in the background. "Shit. I have to go, Rox. I'm sorry."

Did he sound guilty too? It occurred to her there was a lot of guilt going around, and for what? For being married?

He broke into her musings. "This is an opportunity I can't pass by." Jeremy changed tack, feeling bad. He left her on her own too much. "How's your life, babe? What's with the movie deal? All sewn up?" Now it was his turn to sound insincere.

Roxie bit her lip. What to say, what to say? I bought a

Cadillac DeVille, two of them, because I think I'm in love with a stranger.

Focus, Roxie, focus, she told herself. He's in the middle of God knows where, and yet we can only exchange banalities. He's in a goddamn war zone. He could be killed at any time, for God's sake!

The thought prompted her to reply hastily; "Fine! All done! I like Matt Priestly. He's the director, and he loves that I love his movie! I'm his vehicle' within a vehicle, sorta thing. So things are looking good, real good."

What else? She drummed her fingers. Then she said, "I'm in the middle of the new album, East Coast tour looks a cert..."

Roxie could think of nothing more to say. Talk about his stuff. "Is it safe where you are?" she asked. A good wife would ask such a question, she thought, hating herself.

"Pretty much... but hey, what does that matter?" He gave a mirthless laugh. "I tell myself it's a numbers game. I've been with a pretty good unit. Krichev leads them, you may have read about him. He's pretty well educated, went to school in Britain, studied History at Oxford. His troops would follow him into hell, I think. But you can read all about that in next week's copy of Time," he said, sneaking it into the conversation, obviously pleased about that.

She was pleased for him. TIME magazine was a big deal, in journalistic terms. She was straining to hear him clearly; the signal was breaking up, thank God.

"Larry has caught some magnificent shots, which I might add, the authorities are not too happy about." Larry Barber was the cameraman who usually accompanied Jeremy on his assignments. "I'd better go. There's a curfew after eight, I have to get back to the hotel. I love you." The crackle on the line was distorting his voice badly.

"Jeremy?" But he was gone.

Roxie reflected that journalism was his compulsion, as music was hers. Did he need her? Not really, she decided, brutal but true. She remembered how she had thought him so noble when first they met, so real, a refreshing change from her world of glitter and ritz. Jeremy, braving bombs and death in foreign countries, to bring truth to the world.

Heroes, she thought glumly. She was hooked on heroes!

Roxie sat on the stool, gazing up at the suspended mike, as if it would speak to her, tell her exactly where she was going wrong.

You can have anything you want now. Anything.

I want Darth Vader, a little voice whispered inside her head.

—Him.

DEVIL DADDY

Laine was troubled, but she tried not to let it show. The children were looking at her eagerly, anxiously awaiting her verdict.

"Well, Mommy? How is it? See the one of Daddy!"

Liesel's face was beaming up at her. Laine stared down at the drawing in her hand and tried to muster a smile. Liesel was impatiently tugging at her skirt. Shana had her finger buried deep in her nose.

"Stop that, Shana!" Laine said, buying time to think.

She didn't quite know what to say. The picture that stared at her was grotesque. A five-year-old could doubtless draw grotesque pictures, but the garish face had horns and a tail, really huge hands.

Underneath, in a childish scrawl was the single word, ` Daddy'.

True, Case had biggish hands, but the horns?? If what she had learnt at CSU had any meaning, the implications were sobering. She looked down at the sweet faces smiling up at her, expectantly awaiting her praise. She knelt down to meet Liesel's eyes. Eye to eye, the books said...

Shana toddled closer to view her sister's drawing.

"Explain why you drew Daddy like this, darling?" She pointed at the horns. Liesel peered at the picture curiously and stepped back, peeved.

"Oh, Mommy! That's not mine! That's Kira's drawing. The little voice was exasperated. She snatched the papers from Laine's hand. "Under that one!" She impatiently swept Kira's picture to the floor, to reveal the one underneath. "That's Daddy. That's his ` scope"

A smiling, big-eared, figure dominated the page. 'Daddy' stared back at Laine. Relief flooded through her. Big ears she could live with! But horns?-Another story.

Dangling from the eyes or ears-it was difficult to decipher which-was apparently a stethoscope.

"So that's yours! Ah. Darling, you're so very good! Isn't she talented, Shana?-Take your finger out your nose, young lady. Now!"

Reluctantly Shana ceased investigations.

Her children were 'normal'. But this other drawing... Kira? Kira had probably forgotten her drawing on the back seat of the car. Laine stooped to pick up the drawing.

"Liesel?" Be careful how you approach this, she cautioned herself. Don't alarm the child.

Liesel was looking up at her, curious, waiting.

Laine knew she sounded tense and she forced herself to relax. "Liesel, honey, why does Kira draw her Daddy like that?" she asked, feigning playful surprise.

Liesel hesitated. The child looked uncomfortable and secretive.

"It's a secret, I can't tell anyone. I promised Kira."

Laine was taken aback. Her girls told her everything, she thought, but, apparently not.

Liesel was thinking about the rules too, and she added softly, "Her daddy hits her Mommy, and—" The child broke off and looked away.

"And what," Laine's voice was gentle, but insistent.

"I want to go and play!" Distressed, Liesel turned away, ready to bolt upstairs.

Laine hesitated. Don't make this a big issue in the child's head, said the textbooks. Respect their privacy.

"Fine, run along," she said. "Tonight when Daddy's home, we'll show you all the things we brought back from our weekend She shooed them out of the living room. There was another load of laundry to do, but right now, she needed to think.

Should she discuss this with Mia? They weren't that close, but they were friendly, and the children were the best of friends. Laine sighed. She would have to apply herself to her neighbor's ...Problems, and sooner rather than later.

Domestic abuse. How could she protect her children from such things?

The reality was, she couldn't. Not every couple had a marriage like her and Case. The children would eventually encounter dysfunctional homes.

They would have to deal with it, but she would be there to guide them.

Laine felt heart-sore for the two little ones next door. What hellish home life did they have, she wondered. There was one meager comfort; Mia adored her children, that was plain to see.

But that husband of hers...

Laine shuddered. Suddenly, she was glad Case had punched the sonovabitch!

She would have to talk to Mia, make time.

THE OLD COUNTRY

Mia Reichmann watched her two little girls eating their lunch. Eager little Bernadette needed no encouragement, but as usual, Kira was away in a world of her own, her food hardly touched. "Eat your lunch, babche, then you can go and play." The child seemed listless and Mia wondered if she was coming down with something. She was always glad when they came home. Everyone said kinderschule was a good thing, but she was lonely in the mornings when they weren't there. Mia had every modern appliance, and the housework was always quickly done. Rudolf insisted his house be spotless!

She sniffed in scorn. He came from such a pigsty himself! She frowned at the memory of her mother-in-law's home. It was always untidy. And gloomy. Curtains always drawn.

Her house was modern and airy, clean! Rudolf's business was not the biggest, but they were very comfortable. He had done well for himself in America, although he was contemptuous of Americans. He thought them weak and foolish.

Mia liked it here. Belgrade had always depressed her. Her mother had died just after Kira was born. There was nothing left for her in her homeland.

Her mother never did get to see her grandchild. Rudolf had insisted her mother be sent to Serenity House, a home for the infirm and elderly, and he refused to allow Mia to return to Belgrade when they heard she was dying.

He insisted flying was bad for their unborn child.

Mia submitted to his will without argument, secretly relieved to avoid Heuerstrasse and all its ugly memories, but ashamed to be a bad daughter.

Kira was born in June. Two months later her mother passed away. The letter said she passed 'peacefully', and was gentle in its tone.

Mia had tried to feel some real sorrow at her mother's passing, but memories came flooding back, her own friendless childhood. In the end, all she could muster was relief, intoxicating relief that that part of her life was buried at last, forever.

Now she was in America, with a new life!

She had her own real family, and her children would never, ever endure what she had endured. Her children had a mother who would protect them!

Mia felt herself beginning to shiver. She must force herself to think of good things. Or soon, she would get one of her headaches.

"Mama, are you cold?" Bernadette was staring at her, her big blue eyes worried. God, she was a beautiful child! With her blonde and curly hair, she reminded one of the fat little cherubs on the stained-glass windows of their church.

"I'm fine, babche. Drink your milk. Mama has to go out. Mrs Costaz will be looking out for you till I get back. I must do a few things for Papa."

"I want to come too!" Bernadette's tiny face was belligerent. "I don't want to stay here with Mrs Costaz." She looked forlorn. "Why can't we come?" She looked to her older sister for support, tears threatening. Tears were usually sure-fire with Mama.

"Don't be such a baby." Kira wasn't at all keen to go to Papa's workplace. "We will stay here, make Mommy something nice, with Mis' Costaz. A present, something out of paper. You can make your own." Kira slid off the chair and walked around the table to take her little sister's hand. "Go Mama. I will look after her." Kira looked infinitely older than her seven years.

She always tries to help me, thought Mia, and her heart contracted with love.

Mrs Costaz entered the kitchen, her arms laden with a basket of laundry, the sole of her right shoe gaping a little at the toe. They liked Mrs Costaz. She greeted the children cheerily and they answered with smiles, Bernadette's tears momentarily diverted by Mrs Costaz' smiling shoe. She stared fixedly, her tender three years denying the woman any dignity. Mrs Costaz helped Mama, sometimes she made Mama laugh. She was fat and old, but she liked children and children liked her.

Mia picked up her purse and headed for the door, showing a cheery smile.

She hated leaving her girls, but Mrs Costaz could be trusted. Mia knew she was over-protective, but she didn't care. She sighed. The accounting books were waiting for her at the factory. For a couple of days at each month-end, Mia did the books at Rudolfs engineering firm. She looked at her watch, making a mental note to get the strap adjusted. She was losing too much weight. It dangled like a bracelet on her arm.

She had dallied too long. Doubtless, Rudolf would rant when she arrived. Her head began to pound with the familiar headache as she started the car.

ALL HANDS ON DECK

At Reichmann Engineering, the staff were treading warily.

The boss was in a foul mood. He had been sour ever since that doc had rearranged his profile. Word of his beating had spread swiftly in the factory thanks to Tina Marshall, his personal secretary, who knew all. Gleeful smirks were exchanged when he was safely out of sight. Today, however, he was worse than ever. Tina was out to lunch and it was now nearly two hours past her lunch hour, and she still wasn't back.

Tina hardly ever took lunch, and an enraged Reichmann was pacing in his office, contemplating firing the bitch. He grunted at the paper-work before him. He couldn't find anything at all!

Where was she? He would show her when she got back!

He jammed a grimy thumb on the desk intercom and buzzed through to his wife. "There are invoices here to capture! Estimates too. Fetch them!" His voice was curt and clipped. It sounded particularly harsh, amplified through the intercom.

A couple of moments later Mia walked in and took a stack of papers wordlessly from his desk. He leaned back in his chair, hands folded across his belly, eying her behind hooded eyes. What had possessed him to marry this scrawny bitch? She was so spineless, not the woman he had thought she would be. They met in Serbia–he was still an apprentice then.

He, and no one else, had rescued her from her crazy-bitch mother. She wasn't the virgin he thought she would be, but after a few beatings, she had learned a thing or two! You would think by now she would know how to satisfy a man. Instead, she lay there under him and hardly moved a muscle, as if he were something dirty.

She was the slut! He was convinced she had been her uncle's whore until he came along. Bah! He almost spat in disgust.

He turned his thoughts to the absent Tina.

At least she was a real woman. Too fat, perhaps, for popular taste, but he liked a bit of meat on a woman.

Like his little pudding, Kira.

Aware of his eyes boring into her, Mia looked at him for a brief second as she took the papers from his desk, then averted her gaze. Her hatred would show.

He stayed silent, clearly there were other things on his mind.

Probably Tina, she thought, feeling only relief.

Tina's contempt for Mia was undisguised, almost on a par with Rudolf's, but Mia didn't care at all. Mia guessed her husband and his secretary were lovers, and the thought brought her nothing but relief. Better Tina than her!

Back behind her dilapidated desk, she opened a drawer and took out some pills. She had been feeling really lousy lately. Menstrual cramps but no menses? Could it be that she was pregnant again? It had been known to happen . The pill could fail. Her heart started hammering inside her chest at the mere idea.

Mia took great gulps of air to calm herself. Fervently, she sent up a prayer that it wasn't so. Rudolf would kill her!

Tina's shrill voice in the corridor banished her worries.

Good, she was back.

That would put Rudolf in a better mood before he came home to the children. Mia had long ceased thinking that Rudolf came home to her. She glanced at her watch. It was only three o'clock.

Another hour to go.

Tina Marshall had heard Rudolf yelling, calling her to his office, but she ignored him flat and carried on freshening her lipstick. So unprofessional, that dick!

Imagine if there were customers here.

Finished, she replaced the lipstick in her purse and snapped it shut. Let the sonovabitch wait.

Men, they were all sons of bitches! Tina had spent the whole afternoon at the hospital, having test after fucking test! At first, she worried herself crazy, convinced she was pregnant, but that had to be impossible. She'd had an IUD fitted when she was seventeen, she was nobody's fool! Then she stewed about cancer. Her mother's friend had died of cancer of the cervix, old Alice Schlossberg. Alice complained of dizziness, headaches, a vaginal discharge–she'd lost a fortune of weight in no time at all.

She, Tina, was also dizzy and was also losing weight. Only nine pounds though, worse luck! The curious thing was, she wasn't enjoying sex like she used to. Tina knew she was a great lay, the best, but now she had these damn little sores.

They put her off her stroke, so to speak.

Larry was her latest boyfriend. He bragged to his friends about how good she was in bed. He had finally moved in with her, after weeks of promising. He was a barman at the Bagleyston, downtown. Sure, it was a bit of a dive, but he made good money in tips. There was also a shitload of whores there, but he kept himself clean, or so he had always told her, the lying prick!

Her doctor had diagnosed the clap. That sonovabitch had given her an STD! And, worse, they were testing her for fucking HIV!

That doctor at the Center tried to keep the rebuke out of his voice, but Tina could read it in his eyes. He thought she was a whore. Sanctimonious fucker.

Tina scowled to herself, but now, back at her desk, and having had some time to think about it all, she felt an uneasy sensation of dread.

What if she did have HIV?

"Tina!" Reichmann was howling now. She drummed her fingers in irritation, feeling resentful and not at all eager to see his ugly puss.

Bastard.

He probably had it as well now! That would be one for the books. And his wife, too, if he was still screwing her, although he swore he wasn't.

The doctor had asked her to tell 'all her partners.' warn them. All her partners!

Tina sniffed in disgust. Like she was a whore, the arrogant fucker! What exactly did he think she was, telling her to tell 'all the people' she had 'relations' with to come in for a shot!

It was no big deal nowadays, he said. With regular medication, they could clear it up.

Filled with resentment, she ignored Reichmann calling her. The staff were all skipping out of the office, and going home, everyone glad the day was over, happy to get away. Tina would handle him, she always did.

Fuck them! Fuck him! She, Tina, she was the one who felt sick. Angrily she stood up. She wasn't in the mood for his shit today! When they had all left, she made her way to his office.

Reichmann was fit to be tied.

Tina closed the door behind her, her eyes rolling skyward.

"Yes," she snapped, asserting herself.

"Where have you been?" he asked, his voice filled with menace.

He sounded as mad as hell. Well, she didn't care! She fluffed her hair in the mirror behind his door, deliberately taking her time.

"Where have you been all fucking day!" he repeated, his face contorted with stifled fury. Tina turned to glare back at him.

"I've been to the doctor. All afternoon." She eyed him defiantly. The prick didn't even ask what was wrong with her. She was just someone to screw and to do his work. He and Larry, they were just the same. Well, did she have news for him!

"Has everyone gone?" he asked.

Tina stared at him angrily for a minute, then stalked out into the corridor to check they were alone in the building. She sniffed in irritation. That's what he wanted! Then he could go home to his mousy wife and children and be a big deal! He didn't give a damn if she was sick or not!

She fluffed her hair, debating. Well, no screwing, she decided. It was too painful. Perhaps it was even him that had given her the clap, and not Larry? She debated whether or not to tell him now, at this very moment, everything that know-it-all prick doctor had told her. She decided against it.

Nah. Not in this mood. Let it kill the prick! She wouldn't tell Larry either. Just kick him out! Serve them both right. One of these bastards had given her the clap!

A glance up and down the corridor convinced her they were alone. She entered his office again and closed the door softly behind her. His face was still all banged up from the beating he got from some doctor, and he was clearly still mad at her. He waved his podgy hand, beckoning her towards him, then pushed his chair away from the desk, the tiny wheels of his chair protesting underneath his bulk. He had his cock out already.

Even his dick looked angry, all purple and distorted, like his shitty face! She hid her malice behind a fawning smile. Obviously in a hurry today. No jump-starts! Pig. Bastard.

Well, she had a little something for him too!

Without a word, she knelt in front of him and took his penis into her mouth.

IN THE SHALLOWS

WITH NEW EYES

Case squatted on his heels, his chest heaving. Kevin had beaten him today as if he'd stolen something. Their weekly racquetball was as near a 'routine' a game as Case could swing. Today, he didn't care about the game. He was excited about that damn car! It was just after six and he and Kev were going out together to see that old Cadillac deVille at Roxie-?? He searched for her surname in his mind. Carter. That was it. Roxie Carter, with the green eyes.

Kevin scooped up the balls from the floor of the court and walked towards the door, his satisfaction at the outcome of the game undisguised. Victory over Case was always hard won.

"C'mon. Let's get going. I have a date—, uh, an appointment." he corrected himself. "Let's get to this wreck and meet the waif who drives a Caddie."

"I doubt it's her home," Case replied. "The address is in Millionaire's Row. Not likely."

Kevin pushed the squatting Case with a nimble foot as he sauntered past, shoving Case onto his ass. He was heading for the showers. "Move yourself, buddy! Our time's up and they want the court."

Case swung at him with his racket, but Kevin was already at the door. He picked himself up off the floor, wiping sweaty palms carelessly on his shorts. Kevin sure was on top of the world!

Twenty minutes later, they were in the Aston Martin on their way to the address that Roxie Carter had given him. Cliffside Drive in Malibu.

Case was spruced and fresh after a stinging shower. Everyone knew the suburb. Big money. The houses cost megabucks, sea views, tennis courts, all the trimmings and Case found himself wondering what on earth the connection could be. His banger in the midst of all this opulence!

Kevin was obviously wondering the same thing.

"What did you say her name was? A few of my clients come from around here. In fact, as a divorce attorney, I'm kinda well known in these parts!

Serious money here!" he indicated expansively at the homes they were passing. "Curious, though, to find an old car like that around here!"

"I'd say, from how she was dressed, she probably works around here. But I'm surprised they would let her keep a heap like that on the premises!" Case was looking out for the number. "Here it is. Turn in here."

They turned into a narrow driveway that twisted down an incline to stop outside the rear facade of a large, villa-style home, whose front would look onto the Pacific. A double garage door was open and Case saw the banged-up old Cadillac DeVille immediately. It was parked alongside a gleaming white Bentley coupe.

Lady and the Tramp!

"Well, I'd guess they're pretty kind to their help, parking and all?" Kevin said laconically, indicating the two cars parked side by side. He gazed about him, more than a little curious. "Fortunately, you have Uncle Kevin with you to save the day. At least we didn't arrive in that tacky heap of yours, and bring shame on the fam!" he said smugly.

"Hello down there!"

They both looked up in the direction of the voice, to a balcony on the upper right side of the house.

"I'll be right down," a woman called.

Both Kevin and Case squinted up at her, but the sun was behind her, and her features were indistinct. She disappeared from sight.

"Nice," murmured Kevin, "The help clearly feel right at home!"

In a few moments, the owner of the voice came out through the front door. Case swallowed and stared hard. It seemed to be the same woman. But gone were the faded old jeans and sweatshirt. Instead, here was a gorgeous, very chic and very groomed woman. He struggled to reconcile the sorry-looking waif he had rescued with this vision!

Who the hell had he seen when last they met? He felt confused. The eyes, the eyes were the same, though. The same vivid green he recalled clearly.

An Italian silk shirt hung casually over a pair of snug jeans and he could sense the swell of her breasts underneath the sheer fabric. She held up her hand politely to shake his, the bracelet on her arm jingling musically.

That she was quite at home here was undoubted.

When last he had seen her, her hair had been tightly gathered above her head. Now it fell to her shoulders in a tawny mass.

"Hello again! My rescuer." She was smiling at him and Case realized with a start it was the urchin.

He also realized he might be gaping!

Kevin coughed politely, awaiting an introduction. He was sniggering. Something was amusing him.

Kevin was enjoying Case's consternation. The prince was staring at the woman as though he had never seen her before, his face openly showing his confusion. Like it was possible to forget this package! Honestly, there was no hope for Case.

Kevin had recognized her instantly.

With a jolt, Case picked up on Kevin's polite cough and the snicker. What was amusing Kevin?

"Sorry, I forget my manners. How are you, Mrs... uh... Carter?" This had to be her husband's home. He shook her hand, wondering just how hung-over had he been that Saturday morning! How could he not have noticed this?

Oh well. He shrugged it off and turned to introduce Kevin.

"This is my friend, Kevin Daniels. Kevin, this is—" He was interrupted by Kevin, whose eyebrows were raised in mock ridicule as he turned to Case.

"I know exactly who she is, Case. You live under a rock!"

Kevin turned to smile at Roxie. "Forgive my friend," said Kevin. "He lives under a rock!" He shrugged. "He's essentially a peasant. Art and music are quite foreign to him. I would suggest you ignore him completely," he said airily. "I, however, am delighted to meet you!"

The Daniels charm was on full blast, the thousand-volt smile fully switched on. He turned to Case. "Case, allow me to introduce you to one of the finest talents in the country today. Case, this is Roxie Tanner!"

Both Case and Roxie flushed with embarrassment.

Of course! That's why she looked familiar! Case groaned in mortification. "I'm sorry. I thought maybe it was the PTA... Or something," he mumbled, cringing at how inane that sounded.

They all burst out laughing.

"Was wondering if you perhaps were one of my wife's horsey friends?" He ran his fingers through his hair, a dopey grin on his face. "I didn't recognize you. My wife is a big fan of yours!" he said. "I suppose Carter is your married name?"

For a moment, Roxie said nothing, distracted. What was he asking? Wife? PTA? Shit. Phillipa had been bang on the money! Her heart sank, but he was waiting for an answer.

"Yes, absolutely," she said.

The intensity of her disappointment surprised her. It was also a long, long time since she had felt self-conscious about her fame. Momentarily lost for words, she took refuge
behind a smile, "Well, it's nice to meet you. Again! Better circumstances, today," she said lightly.

Case stared at her, his eyes unwavering, quite fascinated. There was something about her.

Roxie felt uncomfortable, gauche even, in the face of his unflinching gaze, and in an effort to distract him, she pointed to the car.

"There it is. Why don't you both have a look, then come in for a drink? Please."

Kevin shook his head. "Case can do that. I'll come up and join you, and he can join us when he's kicked the tires, or whatever one does with a heap like that—"

He stopped short, apologetic. "Sorry, it's your 'baby,' I suppose," he said, perplexed. What did Carla Tanner want with a car like that?

"Hardly." she said, "It's sort of a prop. —From a movie. Long story."

Kevin nodded. That made sense.

Case was grinning, amused at the idea of Kevin looking at engines. That smile Roxie remembered well, and in an instant, the butterflies were back.

Case waved them away, and walked towards the monster car. It was huge. He was impressed that she managed to drive it at all! "Okay, no hassle, you go have a drink, I'll join you later. Give me a few minutes..."

Case addressed himself to Roxie. "Kevin has no interest in real cars, he's just a poser!" he said, indicating the Aston Martin in the driveway.

Kevin turned to Roxie. "That's settled. Let's have that drink. I'm just along for the ride, anyhow. Lead on." He stood back to allow her to lead the way. Roxie led the way up a few stairs to a magnificent custom-built bar that lead off the living room, and spilled onto a deck that overlooked the ocean. Everything was tasteful and stylish. He noted the muted opulence. Money, reigned in. Good sign.

"Gimlet for me..."

"Good choice." She poured them a drink, studying Kevin out of the corner of her eye. This man was incredibly good-looking, but, oh, the doctor! The mere sight of him—! He wasn't as patently handsome as this guy, but oh my God, the chemistry—

She found herself wondering, hoping. Did he feel it too?? For the first time, he had really looked at her. She hoped he was pleased with what he saw, but she half-suspected he was merely surprised at the big clean-up.

"When will you be doing another live show?" Kevin asked her, sipping his drink, looking at the gold discs suspended on the far wall. Impressive.

"Next week, actually. There's a big charity bash for the Wartime Orphans Fund. I head the line-up. It should be good. Hell, it better be. They're charging a fortune for the tickets!" she said dryly.

Kevin found himself warming to her. She was natural, approachable.

"Yes, I've read about that in the papers. We may come and see you." He swirled his glass. "Now Laine would love to come! She's a big fan of yours, from those days with the Skye."

Roxie winced. "God, I hoped the public had forgotten that! I was awful back then. Who's Laine?" she asked innocently, but she already knew the answer.

"Case's wife. Perhaps Case should take her. Hell, take us all!" Kevin grinned, eying her, wondering just how myopic his pal had to be. This girl was a stunner, never mind a damn pop icon! There was a sensuality about her that was palpable. He noticed her eyes were shining, with what—?

Excitement? Energy?

The olive skin spoke of possible Mediterranean heritage, and defined cheekbones framed cheeks that appeared at this very moment to be quite flushed. Her nose was perfectly formed above a wide, sensual mouth that would never need Botox.

Trust Case to only notice the car! What a schmuck, he thought, smiling inwardly. Typical Case.

They chatted easily.

Kevin was curious about the car. "How did you come to own such a car, much less drive it?"

Suddenly she looked embarrassed and began to giggle... "It's a prop, I'm preparing for a movie, and I took it to the extreme, as usual. I was—" she was choosing her words carefully, "intending to drive it. For a while, you know, kinda grow into the part." She shrugged, "—as I am sure you heard, easier said than done!" Roxie giggled. "But I had a hero rescue me. So, it ended well."

Kevin laughed. The prince, as ever, the damn hero!

Case walked in on their laughter. Kevin was looking quite at home, Case thought. Then again, he shrugged inwardly, this was Kevin's thing.

"Sorry to keep you both." He glanced toward the well-stocked bar she was indicating, her face expectant.

"Thanks, I'll have a Scotch," he said, in answer to her inquiring look. She was still smiling, apparently at some private joke between her and Kevin. He wondered how he hadn't noticed her looks before. Scruffy she might have appeared, but still—

He had been too taken up with the car. The thought reminded him, "That Caddy needs some attention right here and now, to get it mobile. I'll be happy to take it from you, but I doubt it'll make it back to my home. It needs a new distributor, a few odds and sods. I'll need to work on it for an hour or two before it goes anywhere! I'll arrange to get it towed." He looked puzzled. "You had it towed here? Why? You could have taken it to the agents from the get-go—"

She shrugged. "Never even thought of that," she said smoothly. "Can you get it going from here?"

"Well, I would need a couple of hours," he said thoughtfully.

She could see he liked the idea, the challenge appealed to him. Her heart skipped a beat.

"Feel free to try that here. Anytime. I'm not often here, but Juanita, my housekeeper, will let you in" Or call me, I'll set it up, she thought of saying, but held her tongue. That might scare him away. Instead she handed him her phone. "Punch your number in there, if you need me for anything, call."

Case took her phone, and obediently tapped his number, then handed it back.

Roxie Tanner's house! Laine would blow her mind!

Kevin appeared in no rush to leave. Case sipped his drink and looked around him. She had a great home, elegant, yet comfortable. He was suddenly aware he was in faded sweats.

Kevin, always slick, looked quite at home. Case gathered from their conversation that Roxie and Kevin had mutual acquaintances. He listened quietly while they chatted on about some or other showbiz eccentric, enjoying both the view and the lilting timbre of her voice. He watched a dozen different emotions flash across Roxie's face as she spoke. She directed most of her conversation to Kevin, yet Case sensed she was as aware of him as he was of her.

Time to go home, Case McAllister.

"Well, Case, I gather you love that old heap?" She was addressing him directly, breaking into his reverie, jade eyes gazing disconcertingly into his own.

"Love it, I'm crazy about it!" he returned easily. "Been dreaming about a car like that for years, so thanks. Maybe I'll return the favor someday, and give you something you really want?" he joked.

"I'll try to think of something," she replied with a teasing smile.

Kevin sipped his drink, his eyes first on Roxie, then on a bashful Case. Hmm. So the prince was not made of stone after all!

Roxie changed the subject. "I'd like to comp you some tickets for next week, a small token of my appreciation for my rescue..."

"Not necessary!" Case hastened to assure her.

Kevin wasn't having any of that!

"Balls!" he interjected. He frowned at Case. He turned to Roxie his face eager. "Great idea! Terrific!"

Case looked at him, then back at her and said uncertainly, "Well, if you don't mind? He saw an empty glass in Kevin's hand and he quickly drained the last of his Scotch, signaling to his pal it was time to go.

"Thanks for the drink." Case stood up. "I look forward to seeing you again."

Roxie smiled at him. The roadside stranger was back. "I'll send you the details for the tickets!"

"Sure," Case said. "Thanks. We'll love that."

His eyes locked on a large, framed photograph. "Is that your husband?" In the photo she had her arms around a slender, wiry kinda guy. She was laughing, either at him or with him, he couldn't decide.

"Yes. Well, he was. —Is. Was—"

Which was the truth? She was floundering. "We're getting a divorce, but it's not public knowledge, yet." She grimaced, gave a little these-things-happen shrug.

Ah. Case kept quiet. Not his business. Kevin's maybe? But Kevin too, kept silent, which was strange for him. There were other photos, of her with various celebrities, but he hardly recognized any of them.

When they left, Roxie strolled with them out onto the driveway. Up close, she could smell his cologne. It was subtle, masculine.

He was so different. She liked how his friend teased him, and he didn't mind at all. They probably go way back.

"Actually, it's really good to meet people outside of my industry. Not easy to do," she ventured. Suddenly self-conscious, she addressed herself to Case, "Don't let him bother you," she said softly, glancing at Kevin. "You got to see the real me first."

"I doubt that! Possibly another side, but definitely not the real you," he grinned at her. "'This 'you' is pretty good!"

Kevin listened to their banter, intrigued. Was the prince flirting? No, he was just calling it as he saw it, as ever. Pointless flirting with Case, he had no capacity for guile and cunning.

That was his domain, Kevin's, that's why they were the perfect pair.

Still, time to take him home! Roxie Tanner looked quite taken with his pal.

"Bye, Roxie," Kevin cut them short. "I'm glad I met you. And I, for one, look forward to seeing your show."

On the way back, Kevin gave Case a brief resume of the singer's career. He appeared to be quite an authority.

Case, usually indifferent about such trivia, was unexpectedly curious. By the time Case had been safely delivered to his car, he felt quite an authority on Roxie Tanner.

Wait until Laine heard about today!

DISTURBED

At home, his arrival was greeted with the usual happy squeals from the girls. He scooped each child up under each arm and marched indoors, ignoring their happy struggles to get free.

Laine was in the hallway, the handset of the telephone buried in her neck, pencil and pad in her hand. He leaned over to kiss her cheek. She returned the gesture absently, with two fingers on his cheek, a finger kiss. She was concentrating on what the caller had to say. He went through to the kitchen and dumped the girls unceremoniously on the floor.

Judith was there, placing food on the table.

"My, you're home late!" she admonished him, pecking him on the cheek, hardly checking her stride. He refrained from comment. He wanted to save his news, blow Laine's little mind!

He lifted the lid of the casserole dish to sniff appreciatively.

A short while later, the three adults were seated at the table, eating and chatting about the events of the weekend. Shana and Liesel hovered around, having long since eaten, dividing their attention between the kitchen and the television in the living room.

Case turned his attention to what Laine was saying.

"Ashley was on the phone just now. She's invited me to lunch on Wednesday," she said, her expression thoughtful.

"Oh! Why do you sound so hesitant?" he asked.

"Because in all the time I've known her, Ashley has never asked me to lunch! We're good friends, but we're not 'lunch' friends! She's too busy." Laine shrugged, but her face was pensive. "I told her it's fine, we'll meet at the Gazebo–have a so-called 'Health Lunch', you know, plenty of wine, no dessert!" she joked.

"Well, that's nice." Case said, dismissing the matter. He had his own news, and he was keen to see Laine's face.

"I have some news too. I bought that car," Case announced as he rose from the dinner table. "But, you won't believe who owned it!"

"Oh okay. Good. We'll see more of you here at home, even if it's just your backside under the hood." She grinned at him. "No, I probably won't be able to guess. Put me out of my misery and tell me." Laine put her arm around his waist as they made their way to the living room.

"Well, crazy as this may sound, the car belonged to—" He made a poor drum-roll noise. "Wait for it! Drum-roll! Ta-raaa!!"

He was teasing her, deliberately titillating her.

"Case, tell me!" She punched him playfully, smiling expectantly. The girls were in the living room, yelling impatiently for their parents to hurry up.

"'Roxie' turns out to be Roxie Tanner!!" he said with a flourish, grinning broadly.

Laine gave a satisfying gasp. "The singer!" she squealed in disbelief. "What on earth was she doing with an old car like that!"

He was gratified by her reaction, but the question caught him short.

He looked flummoxed for a second.

"Quite honestly, don't really know. Something about a movie prop?" he dismissed it. "Anyhow, it's mine now. They towed it to her house—which was dumb. They should have just taken it to a dealer. Anyways, I intend to do some simple surgery to get it mobile, then I shall bring our newest baby home!"

He hugged her gleefully.

"Are you going to fiddle with it there? Doesn't she mind? What's it like?" Laine was thoroughly intrigued, her mind spinning.

"Well, I need to replace the rotor, then she should fire up. A couple of hours, I'm thinking. It's pretty banged up but I think the engine is good!"

Laine rolled her eyes. "The house, Case, the house!"

He laughed. "Oh. It's lovely. And no, she doesn't mind, not at all. She's really very nice!" He frowned, thinking. "Oh, apparently, Kevin schmoozed some special tickets to her benefit next Friday. Do you want to go?"

"Do I want to go? Terrific! Absolutely." She stopped and pouted, "Case, she's stunning. You said she was no big deal! Roxie Tanner herself!" She looked at him reproachfully.

He grinned at her. "She did look better today, I'll grant you, but you're still much prettier!" He tweaked her nose playfully, then turned his attention to the children's art.

Laine sniffed, appeased.

"Good save, McAllister. Time for coffee and bed."

Later, in bed, Case sensed she was awake. She was ceaselessly twisting a strand of hair around her finger, a sure sign that she was agitating about something. He turned over to face her, propping himself up on an elbow. He was right; her normally serene face was pensive. The moonlight shone brightly through open curtains, bathing the bedroom in soft light. Her forehead was puckered in a frown.

She squeezed his thigh distractedly with her free hand, still twisting the strand of hair endlessly around and around, deep in thought.

"Okay. What gives?" he asked.

"I'm not sure..." she said thoughtfully, "I feel a bit silly."

Case kissed the tip of her nose. "Try me."

"Well, it's Kira. She's in the same group as Liesel at nursery school, and as such, they're set the same tasks. Today they had to draw 'Daddy.' Case, you should see the drawing that Kira drew of Rudolf Reichmann. It was bizarre!" she said with a shudder.

"How bizarre? Liesel isn't exactly Picasso," he offered reasonably.

"Don't patronize me, Case!" Laine's tone was unusually sharp. "I'm telling you, if I learned anything at college, it's how to recognize a disturbed child." She sighed. "Perhaps I am being silly." She nodded her head, talking to herself... "Yes, I am."

"Where's the picture?" he asked.

"I threw it away. I didn't even want the children to see it again, though I suppose all they see is a monster."

"Kira is probably angry at Rudolf, which God knows is not hard to be. Don't worry about it anymore. She was venting her feelings in a healthy fashion!"

Laine turned to face him. "Do you think so? I guess you're right," she said.

But still, she had that nagging anxiety. She allowed herself to be distracted by the way the fine hairs on his chest glistened in the moonlight. Like the little lights on the floor of an aircraft, leading somewhere...

She traced a small circle around his nipple, her expression changing.

"I need to relax, don't I? Kinda unwind more!" she agreed. "What to do, what to do?? Hmm..." Her tongue was peeping through her teeth, the drawing forgotten. "Any suggestions?"

Case kissed the top of her head, sighing in pleasurable anticipation. He wanted to feel her mouth close around his nipple. He felt that familiar awakening as slowly, slowly, she put her tongue out to tease him, a secret half-smile crossing her face when she felt a slight spasm jerk his body.

"Here, I'll show you." Her mouth closed around him, warm and moist. Her hand came up to his shoulder, and gently, she pushed him onto his back. He groaned in pleasure. She stroked the familiar contours of his body, then closed her hand slowly around his erection. Laine swung her leg over him, and hovered there for a tantalizing moment while he lifted himself underneath her. Then slowly, oh so slowly, she lowered herself and began to rock in that age old rhythm of surrender.

COMMON FOLK

"Hello Lyle, sweets! How are we today?" Phillipa flashed her special smile to the elderly doorman. It paid to bestow loveliness to the minions, because all, absolutely all of God's children had their uses. Most of the patrons of the gym were well-heeled, and for most of them, the staff were invisible. For these myopic members, tennis courts were usually 'fully booked' or the restaurants 'quite packed, madam!'

Phillipa, on the other hand, never had a problem. Her manner was confiding, sharing. She peddled her largess, and the minions bought it happily.

Lyle smiled back. " 'Lo Miss Phillipa! Good to see you," he said. "You off to the salon? You sure don't need it!" he said, oozing his own brand of charm. He also knew a thing or two about winning people over!

Mentally, Phillipa agreed with him, she didn't need it, but prevention was the name of the game.

Lyle gazed at her in frank admiration. Some of these dames were just pigs with lipstick, but Phillipa Hughes, she hardly needed any fancy beauty parlor, what with her looking like a movie star herself! She jingled when she walked, and Lyle had no doubt her bling was the real deal. Her silky white blouse was unbuttoned irreverently low, the perfect olive skin attesting to the excellence of the Spa's tan cans. The molded gold necklace around her neck was fashioned after a serpent, with a bejeweled head hissing down her cleavage.

For Lyle, she was the epitome of glamour. Here was the real thing.

Phillipa lowered her Armani sunglasses to look him in the eye, her gaze a heat-seeking missile, and he was grateful for his dark skin which hid the crimson hue. She lowered her voice, and leaned in closer;"You are too, too kind, Lyle, too kind!" she whispered, "But a girl can never have too much help, and that's the truth!"

Lyle nodded, masking his total disagreement. "Sweets, I'm looking for

Roxie, has she arrived yet?" she asked in a whisper.

Lyle nodded. There were rules for the common folk, and before him stood no damn commoner! Plus, he figured, Phillipa Hughes and Roxie Tanner were good friends!

"She's in the MJ wing. Room A-5, just past the ladies' weights room. She arrived 'bout an hour ago."

"She would've," Phillipa murmured dryly, waving to an old paramour. He sheepishly returned her wave and rushed off in the opposite direction. She watched his hasty departure with a sly grin.

Married men. They could be so tedious.

She applied her thoughts to the day's demands. "Thanks, Lyle. What would I do without you!" She turned and sauntered down the corridor towards the wing of smaller studios. Lyle gazed after her, marveling at how she managed to make the long, carpeted corridor her own personal catwalk.

The workout studios were sound-proofed and the sudden blast of music was deafening as she pushed open the door, unassumingly marked A-5. Roxie had some hideous hip-hop music in the player and was dancing energetically, focused on her workout, unseeing, her back to the door.

Phillipa rolled her eyes. It made her weary just watching her!

She closed the door behind her, pausing, watching, marveling at the abundance of energy Mother Nature saw fit to bestow on the less fortunate. She personally loathed any form of strenuous activity, bar one. Sex was about as hectic as it got for Phillipa Hughes, and even then, it was on her terms, which could induce an embolism, depending on one's degree of commitment and servitude.

Roxie stopped short when she noticed Phillipa standing just inside the door, panting. "It's about time you got here!" she called enthusiastically, "Aren't you a bit late for your appointment?"

"I'm sure... Probably." Phillipa said, unperturbed. She slipped off her heeled shoes and padded across the sprung wooden floor towards Roxie. She curled herself into a plush easy chair, waiting for Roxie to kill the music, admiring her own coiled reflection in the mirrored wall.

Vanity was such a comfort!

She noted the perspiration on Roxie's face with distaste. "Gross! You're so sweaty!"

"Good!" Roxie replied brightly, "That means I've done some work this morning." She looked pleased with herself.

Phillipa sniffed. "I just thought I'd pop by and hear what's happening in the doctor saga. I am so, so curious! Any news? What was he like, the second time you saw him? I take it you have seen him again?" she asked, firing the questions. Her head bobbed up and down expectantly, inviting conversation.

"For God's sake, stop that nauseating exercise and talk to me!"

Roxie obligingly stopped her leg-stretchers and stood still, her attention caught by something through the window. At one of the tennis courts, she could see a woman coquettishly playing up to her tennis instructor.

There was a lot for sale at the Spa.

"Well, don't just stand there! What happened?" Phillipa demanded impatiently.

Roxie turned the music off completely, reaching for a small towel to wipe the perspiration from her brow.

"Well... He came." Roxie paused, thinking.

"That's an ambiguous statement, darling!" Phillipa said with an impish grin. "Do tell more!"

"He came with a friend of his, a guy called Kevin Daniels."

"More ambiguity." Phillipa examined her perfect nails for flaws. "

Who?"

"Kevin Daniels."

"Well, well! What a small world. I know Kevin Daniels! Well, at least, I know who he is. He was Jillie Brewster's attorney when she divorced her rat! He's a great divorce attorney! I believe they stripped old Ray Brewster positively bare! Jillie got the house, a new car, half the business! She did ever so well!"

Phillipa looked forlorn and sighed. "Of course, she had to take the children too, but I suppose one can't have everything! She put out for the Daniels chap, too, who she says is utterly divine! But I gather he doesn't play. Perhaps he's gay?" She shrugged. "But whatever, he's an excellent wallet-surgeon. How marvelously timely that you met him! A girl can never ever have too many friends." Phillipa looked at Roxie, her eyes dancing.

But Roxie was miles away, deep in thought.

Then she shook her head irritably. "Sometimes I seriously question your head, Phillipa. I mean, they're friends! I hardly think Case McAllister thinks in terms of cut-rate divorces! Exasperated, she walked to the window and gazed outside.

The tennis pro and his pupil were definitely cutting a deal.

"Besides, he's happily married and, —and I can't understand what's got into me! I've never behaved like this before," she wailed, her eyes shut in confusion. Sighing, she plopped onto a couch, pulling her knees under her chin.

Phillipa cocked her head to one side.

"Actually, I meant a divorce attorney for you. That is where you're headed, isn't it?" She gestured with her hands in dismissal, disallowing further talk about divorce. She focused again on Roxie.

"But you're not finished. Now, tell Mummy exactly what happened," she said with a conspirator's whisper.

Roxie paused, agitated. "He loves the car, and he will remove it when he can get it to go, all by itself! He suggested getting it towed, but I persuaded him to—" She waved her hands. "Well, you know, do the 'mechanic' thing at my place. He's singularly unimpressed by who I am, which suits me."

Roxie scowled. "I think he thinks I'm rather sweet! He also appears to be very happily married, but—" she broke off and looked away, avoiding Phillipa's eyes.

"And what?" Phillipa pressed, but knowing what was coming.

Roxie looked back at her, shaking her head slowly from side to side, her eyes troubled, "I'm crazy about him and I scarcely know him!" She looked confused. "It's worse than that. I don't know myself, acting this way! He probably has children!"

"We can't all be perfect, darling," Phillipa said, deliberately misconstruing Roxie's last remark, but Roxie didn't smile.

Roxie's face brightened. "Anyhow, they're coming to the benefit, and I've arranged VIP seats, which should be fun for them." She grimaced, emphasizing the word 'fun', managing somehow to look both dejected and excited at the same time.

"VIP seats! That must have taken some arranging." Phillipa raised her eyebrows, impressed. VIP seats were for LA royalty.

"Well, I'll meet your hero there, and I confess, I can't wait!" She scooped up her purse."We're having lunch later, aren't we? I'll catch you at the restaurant." Phillipa glanced at her watch. She was definitely late. That poor pet of a Maurice would be wild with her!

She left hurriedly, leaving Roxie to her adrenalin, shuddering as a blast of sound hit her departing ears.

Roxie halted her workout when the door closed behind Phillipa.

After a moment she turned the player off, needing to think.

God, how would this end? She felt uncharacteristically glum. She was fed up with herself, acting like some love-struck teenager! She switched the player back on, determined to rehearse until she was exhausted.

She would sweat the damn man out of her system!

BAD DOCTOR

Case exuded energy as he pulled into the parking lot of Granger Clinic. It was Monday morning, five after six, the parking lot was relatively empty, but he knew it would fill quickly. Inside, the hospital would be buzzing. Within the old gray stone building with its hundreds of tiny, almost jail-like windows, Case knew that the tempo of the hospital had stepped up from as early as five am, and by now, it would now be pumping.

The ugly building offered Case McAllister his daily validation, his raison d'etre. The drab old hospital looked nothing less than beautiful to him and he felt the familiar pump of adrenaline as he walked through the doors.

He exchanged greetings with colleagues, nodded his head in thanks as the desk nurse handed him a folder, clearly marked with his name in bold black lettering. He scanned the contents quickly, frowning when he came to the report on the Cahill boy. The lab report was back, and it held no surprises, which was good.

Case felt a nudge at his elbow and turned to find Morris there, hands shoved into deep white-coat pockets, his eyes questioning.

"Good weekend?" Morris inquired innocently. He had a fondness for this young man, not just because he was one of the clinic's most promising surgeons, but because Case was a disciple of his discipline, reconstructive surgery.

Morris beckoned to Case to follow him, and they moved out of earshot of the general milieu.

Morris was a rude bastard with scant respect for cosmetic surgery, and he had ruffled many a conceited feather in the course of his career, opinionated and blunt, with no time for what he brusquely called 'tit and clit stitch-ups!' He wordlessly claimed a moral high-ground, and few challenged him —to his face. Although only in his mid-sixties, his spare frame had shrunk at an accelerated pace through the years, an unkind by-product of aggressive osteoporosis, aided by a workload that would have buckled most. The white coat hung loosely on the man they called the King of Second Chances.

Today, Morris clearly had something on his mind.

Case looked at him curiously, "You wanted to say?"

"Is it true?" Morris's expression was hard to read.

Shit... That. Case shrugged. "Chinese whispers. Depends what you heard? Did I deck a guy? Yes. Storm in a teacup? Yes." He was irritated and it showed.

Morris nodded slowly, absorbing. Then he shrugged, switched gear.

"What do you think?" He dipped his head, indicating the file in Case's hand.

Case was pleased to discuss something that was relevant.

"I saw the child for a few minutes on Friday morning. He was heavily sedated, but I saw enough. Nurse Lazara was there, and she told me that he took a lot of blood, but no evidence of hemorrhagic shock? Good sign?"

Morris nodded. "Children are tough. The parents will take this worse than he will. I believe the father is fighting unsuccessfully to get the dog destroyed. Go figure."

"Unsuccessfully! Jesus, if they could see that child's face!" Case clipped off his words. Doctors weren't supposed to be emotional, but his scowling face belied his detachment.

"Well, that's not our business, is it?" Morris declared. "Doubtless, they'll resolve it one way or the other. The parents are with him now. Be careful what you say to the parents. They're spooked as hell. My guess is, she's the stronger one. The child is still in an induced coma." The shaggy brows furrowed deeper. "They were here at five this morning-here till late last night. Damn nuisance."

Case hid the faintest of smiles. Heartless old bastard. But he knew that wasn't true at all.

"Okay. I'll see you during lunch, in your rooms and we can compare notes." Morris turned on his heel and called out to hold the elevator.

Case watched his retreating back, breathing more freely. Definitely no more fisticuffs for him. No thugs to head-up surgery. Bad for business.

In Ward Nine B, the parents of little Barry Cahill were still there, sitting in somber silence near his cot. At first glance, the man appeared far too old to be the father of such a young child. He was a balding, thin man whose face, upon closer inspection, looked years younger than the balding head. His eyes were puffy, bloodshot with fatigue and his chin had pronounced stubble. His suit hinted he was probably a businessman of some sort, the tie carelessly tucked into his shirt pocket. Mrs Cahill clutched her husband's hand, looking near collapse. Show-time.

"Well, here's a tough little slugger!" Case's words were determinedly upbeat, but they seemed to echo in the ensuing silence. He introduced himself to Barry's parents. They politely returned his greeting, then lapsed again into silence, He studied the chart at the foot of the cot for a few moments. Little Barry Cahill appeared to be stable. Unlike the parents.

He hid a sigh. Panicked parents wouldn't do.

Case gave them an encouraging smile, but they stared back with unhappy stoicism, bracing themselves for the worst.

"He's going to be okay, really." He gestured around the infant's face.

"That's what I've come to discuss with you. I'm Dr McAllister, I'm the surgeon who will be doing the operations to repair your youngster's face and arms. Let's step outside. We don't want to disturb him."

That wasn't quite true. A bomb wouldn't have disturbed the child, but they didn't need to know that.

The Cahills glanced at each other, conveying some private, silent message that excluded him. They followed reluctantly, loath to leave the child's side. Seated in the stark, uncomfortable chairs in one of the many waiting areas in the hospital, Case explained patiently to the anxious parents what surgery lay ahead for their son. They listened intently.

In the background, orderlies were noisily gathering up the dirty breakfast crockery from various wards, and against that noisy backdrop, Case explained the surgery that was needed, in layman's language, taking his time to elaborate on what he guessed might alarm them.

They said little, holding on to each other's hand, each drawing comfort from the other. Case noticed Mrs Cahill's knuckles were white as she gripped her husband's arm. She looked drawn and haggard in the harsh fluorescent light of the corridor. Her skirt had deep creases from the hours of sitting motionless at her son's bedside. When he was done, they looked at each other; there was another silent exchange.

After a moment, Mr Cahill cleared his throat and addressed himself to Case.

"Are you telling me that when all this surgery is over Barry will be... okay?

No significant scars?" he said, disbelieving.

"That's the plan," Case replied cautiously. "Of course, as I've explained, he has a complicated tissue type. That could cause some problems, but we'll take every precaution." He smiled at them, a small smile, "But all being equal, yeah, we'll fix him up!"

Mrs Cahill cupped her face in her hands and allowed herself the luxury of tears. Nathan Cahill drew his wife close, clumsily patting her back.

He addressed himself to Case. "I was so worried." Heavy tears began to roll down his cheeks and suddenly the man abandoned dignity for noisy sobs of relief.

Case stood up and touched the man's shoulder.

"It'll be okay. You and your wife go home, get some rest. You'll think more clearly after some sleep. We are going to keep him sedated for another 24 hours. Besides, when he is awake, it'll be better if you're both rested."

It was the wife's turn to put a consoling arm around her husband's shoulders. She looked up at Case, indicating with her hand he could go. They could cope.

Case knew they would. To be a good doctor, one had to step back, detach oneself. Easier said than done.

He sighed.

By that definition, he would always be a bad doctor.

BACKSTAGE

Friday had arrived. Case was showered, shaved, and looking forward to the concert. Sunset Boulevard traffic was crawling, and he was grateful to finally hand the Chevy over to the valet when they stopped outside the Hollywood Palladium.

Inside the packed foyer, he allowed himself to relax.

'Dr McAllister' was gone, Case McAllister was back.

He stood still and allowed Laine to adjust his jacket before they pushed their way through the crowd to look for Kevin and Ashley. They had arranged to meet at the bar to the right of the main stage. The foyer was teeming with the city's finest, resplendent and preening, eager to pose for the many photographers who were there to record the event. It amused Laine to see how they were scrutinized, then summarily dismissed. Nobodies.

They eased their way through the throng and eventually found Kevin and Ashley seated at the crowded bar.

Ashley looked faintly under the weather.

Case and Laine glanced at each other, hiding their surprise. Laine, bubbling with excitement, dismissed it immediately.

Case shrugged inwardly. Enough thinking, she's a big girl, time to relax. He ordered a round of drinks but Ashley was obviously in sync with his train of thought because she asked for sparkling water. Kevin, apparently, noticed nothing amiss.

Case surrendered himself to the energy and excitement in the air.

Is this what it's like before every live show, he wondered. It must be exhausting. Everyone looked as if they belonged in a magazine, but then again, he thought dryly, the tickets were two hundred dollars a pop! He was thankful Laine had insisted that he dress up, 'make an effort, Case!' she had instructed.

He took the whiskey Kevin passed to him over immaculately groomed heads and sipped it appreciatively.

"In ten minutes, we have to meet someone called Manning outside the theater manager's office, which gentleman, I gather, is Roxie's manager. He will then get someone to take us to our seats," announced Kevin, beaming.

Case smiled to himself. Kevin and Laine were relishing the buzz.

"Great. —You look good, Ash," Case addressed her, his admiration sincere.

Laine nodded in agreement. Ashley did look fabulous tonight!

Case turned to Laine, "You too, my darling. I feel proud to be with two such lovely ladies," he declared, raising his glass in a toast. Laine gave a gracious dip of her head, a la one well used to the boot-licking masses.

"Why, thank you, kind sir." She adopted a southern belle accent and murmured to him, "You look quite the picture yourself. There's something about a rough-looking fellah in a fancy jacket that sure gets me every time!" She licked her bottom lip suggestively, playing the femme fatale, but succeeding only in looking cute.

Even Ashley joined in the laughter. Case eyed his wife lovingly. Rough-looking indeed. Trust Laine to bring him down to size!

"I don't know, I thought I looked very suave tonight!" He stroked his recently shaven chin.

"You do. You look like a real man," Ashley said. Her tone was harsh, almost jarring.

Ashley definitely sounded faintly inebriated, and Kevin glanced at her, his expression bemused, but then he gave his wife a quick smile and squeezed her shoulders.

Laine looked at Ash, frowning. What was up with Ash?

Ashley was now smiling benignly, but the smile never quite reached her eyes. She looked away from their surprised stares.

"There's Sting. He looks old," whispered Laine, excited.

They all looked in the direction she indicated, but Sting was no longer to be seen.

Kevin checked the time, excused himself, and went off in search of the management offices and the eminent Charles Manning. He was back in a few minutes with a stout, dapper man, whose courtly manner and accent oozed genteel British charm.

Introductions were made all around, the Americans, as ever, charmed with the newcomer's accent.

Charles Manning was in his fifties, and his hair was thick and white. Clearly well used to all the pomp and ritz of the evening, he set about charming Case's party.

Ashley seemed in a world of her own, missing the general conversation.

Case had the niggling idea that the man was observing them all far more closely than it appeared on the surface.

Oh well. He supposed the man had to vet everyone and protect his star!

Manning looked at Kevin and Case and asked innocently, "Who is the car enthusiast?" The two men looked at each other blankly for a second.

"I think he means you, Case?" Kevin grinned, indicating Case. Case looked puzzled, and then his eyes lit up in understanding.

"Oh, the DeVille? Yes, that's me.—Though I haven't got it going yet. But soon enough..." Case drained the last of his drink. "I rebuild old wrecks for fun. It's good to do something where the outcome is guaranteed. I'm a surgeon, for my sins," he offered in explanation. "Seems I am a compulsive fixer."

The chimes sounded, interrupting them. They needed to take their seats.

Bullseye! thought Manning. So! This was the one! —Phillipa's friends, my eye! His face showed nothing of his thoughts. He said breezily, "Follow me, please."

Manning cut his way through the throng of people, his mind working furiously. A married man, clearly, and a damn doctor.

This was another kettle of fish.

Not good. Not good at all.

He resolved to keep a close eye on his car-buying Roxie.

Case and the others settled in their VIP seats, soaking up the pizzazz and excitement of the evening. For all of them, except Laine, who had seen a much younger Roxie Tanner years ago at a concert in San Diego, this would be the first time they would see her perform live.

An expectant hush hung over the crowd as the house lights dimmed. A pulsating drum began to pound, and a faint pin spot of light on the stage grew steadily into a pool of light, showing her backing band. The tempo increased to a swelling crescendo of music that had the audience cheering and whooping in a frenzy of anticipation.

The first acts came and went and while Case enjoyed them, he was waiting for her part with eager anticipation.

At last, it was Roxie's turn.

A single spotlight found her stage right, and the audience yelled and cheered in ecstasy. Roxie Tanner moved confidently to the center of the stage, her hands up and clapping rhythmically with the music, the first notes of the song obviously familiar to her audience. Case felt his heart skip a beat at the sheer sensuality of the woman.

Beside him, he felt Laine give his arm a squeeze of excitement, her face enraptured.

They grinned at each other in delight then turned their attention to the stage. Roxie Tanner came to the fore of the stage, swaying, cajoling the audience, controlling her subjects like the queen she was. The adulation from the audience was her drug, and she sang her heart out. Delicate silver chains kept her top almost closed, throwing laser-type reflections from the different spots. The lights bouncing off the flimsy harness appeared to be emitting an electrical energy of their own. The audience roared.

Abruptly the music softened, and she started slowly into the next song.

Roxie Tanner treated her audience to a roller coaster of emotions and song. At times, the hairs stood up on Case's arm. She was magnificent! Totally in control of her audience, she lifted them out of their day-today existence and shared with them her world, every inch the diva.

Some of the songs were composed by herself, and Case marveled at her creative talent. He found himself struggling to recall the scruffy girl on the roadside. There was no sign of that girl here onstage tonight, nor in the charming woman who had offered him a drink the other night. Instead, there was this sensual enchantress who wove a spell around the masses.

And him.

When the last note faded, he found himself up on his feet, clapping, cheering, and whistling with the rest of the audience. Laine and the others were also up, applauding mightily. Laine was quite speechless in her awe and excitement. Case smiled at his wife's excitement.

Roxie Tanner sure was terrific!

He was surprised to feel a strange emotion. Pride.

Backstage, the passages and rooms were spilling people out from every door. Roadies, muso's, backup singers, dancers, the techies... All were whooping, laughing. They had kicked ass!

Caught up in the throng, Case, Laine and friends followed the guide

Charles had sent to them, with his invitation they should join the backstage party.

Kevin was intercepted along the way by an old friend, and he waved the others on, saying he would catch up later. With his arm around Laine to protect her from the crush, his other hand holding Ashley's, Case followed their guide backstage.

Mountains of equipment had been pushed back to make way for the revelry. A deejay had already set up, and the music was pumping. He spotted Roxie instantly on the far side of the room. She was surrounded by a bevy of people, smiling, laughing, and listening to a deluge of opinions and congratulations. Behind him, Laine and Ashley were comparing notes, eying the fashionistas with fascination.

Their guide left them there, urging them to partake and be merry, and hurried off. Case cast a look about him. There was a table laden with overflowing champagne glasses, a pyramid of Moet.

He found a relatively quiet niche for Laine and Ashley and edged his way in to grasp three full glasses of champagne. Case glanced at Roxie as his hand closed around the stems of the glasses. She was looking straight at him. She flashed a quick smile, and he raised a
glass in a silent toast, with an answering smile. She turned her attention back to some bearded chap who was with Manning. She looked decidedly distracted.

The din was overwhelming. He was hardly back at Laine's side when they were joined by Kevin.

Case noticed Ashley's manner with Kevin was cool. He made a mental note to find time to have a one-on-one with his pal.

A short while later, Roxie Tanner made her way over to greet them, accompanied by a beaming and expansive Charles Manning.

Kevin introduced the wives to her, and Case stood quietly to one side while Roxie was showered with praise by the girls and Kevin.

Laine with her arm tucked under her husband's jacket and her arm was around his waist, was effusive in her praise.

Roxie smiled back graciously at them all, saying all the right things, but noting the intimacy between Case and his wife. Oh God, this was hopeless!

"I, for one, will forever be your devoted fan!" Kevin was saying grandly, and Roxie flushed, pleased. Well-used to praise, somehow his good wishes meant a lot.

Spontaneously, she hugged him.

Case smiled at them all benignly, impressed at her modesty, as was Laine. The star seemed genuinely delighted they had enjoyed her performance.

Roxie turned to Laine. So, this was the wife. Laine looked radiant, happy. Quite lovely, in fact. Well, it was to be expected. Roxie rallied herself. She addressed Laine directly, her face showing nothing of her thoughts; "I believe you enjoy my music; Kevin tells me. Thank you for that." She smiled at Laine. This was no soccer mom! A damn cheerleader, more like!

Laine smiled back, oblivious to the singer's close scrutiny, delighted to meet the star. "I am a fan! I remember seeing you at a fund-raiser in Austin in! What a show that was! I've been a fan ever since," she said, laughing.

"Were you there?" Roxie exclaimed. "God, what a disaster that was. The drummer was drunk, and his tempos..." Roxie laughed at the memory. "Do you remember that student who climbed buck-naked on the stage?"

For the next few minutes, the two women laughed together as they swapped memories.

Case watched them together, Laine familiar and beautiful, brimming with her usual warmth, the other sultry and captivating. His thoughts returned to that morning on the highway, and he shook his head in disbelief.

"What's up?" Kevin was looking at him curiously. "Why are you shaking your head?"

"Nothing..." Case felt foolish at his naiveté of that day. "Enough of the bubbly stuff. Need to find some Scotch and get some food. I'm starving. C'mon." He excused himself from the girls and went to gather snacks without waiting for a reply.

Kevin followed dutifully.

Roxie, her attention on Laine, sensed him leaving and she felt her energy dip.

"Time for me to change, catch you later girls!"

She left them with a smile, urging them to 'have fun.'

A while later, the rigors of the day began to make themselves felt. The lights had been dimmed, but the music was still pumping. Case found himself alone at a makeshift bar, ordering his ABF, glad Laine was the designated driver.

Roxie took her role as hostess seriously and was making sure they were all having a good time.

He noticed her here and there, all evening, constantly in demand. He felt a strange mixture of disappointment and relief that there was no time for them to chat, really. He searched for Laine's familiar blonde head on the dance floor, smiling when he saw his wife gyrating in the middle of the dancers. He heard Ash's distinctive cackle and he turned towards the laughter, smiling.

Ashley was standing near the fire exit. She was listening to an animated, rather sleek woman with a distinctive blonde bob. The woman appeared totally at home in all the music and chaos.

"She's very pretty. You must be proud of her." Roxie's voice was right in his ear, and he looked around in surprise. She was looking at Laine who was laughing with some man who was twirling her around.

For the first time that evening, she was alone.

"What were you smiling at?" she asked, curious.

He gestured to Ashley. "That woman over there is Kevin's wife,

Ashley, and it looks like it's time to go home," he said, grinning at Ashley laughing uproariously with the blonde bob.

At some point, Roxie had changed into a dress that showed off all her curves and not a little of her bosom.

Case found himself acutely aware of the sensuality of the woman. It was a long time since any other woman had pushed his buttons, and the sensation caught him by surprise.

Roxie looked towards Ashley, then back at him. Now her eyes were on him, and it was mildly disconcerting. "Well, that's Phillipa Hughes she's talking to. She's my best friend and a certifiable nut." She made a face, smiling back at him.

"Oh." He looked at her, and she couldn't read his expression.

Rabbit and snake, that's us, she thought. with a tummy-churning frisson of excitement. But who is what?

"Tonight has been special. I thought you were great," he said sincerely.

"I think so too." she said, and broke off, blushing at the ambiguity of her words.

He was amused, and he grinned at her embarrassment.

"I mean, not me, tonight... " she spoke quickly, flustered. "Tonight has been a success! I mean, it's been an extraordinary night. You know, the audience were so... so responsive," she managed to get out at last.

Case was smiling at her floundering. She was so modest. He liked that. "Absolutely they were responsive," he agreed. "How could they resist you?" he teased her.

Yet again, the vivacious singer was lost for words. Suddenly the music tempo changed, and the sultry notes from a sax filled the air.

She loved this song, but—

He read her mind. "Care to dance?" He held out his hand, indicating the throng on the floor. Tongue-tied, Roxie held his arm and allowed him to lead her toward the dancers. Up close, she could smell his cologne. She closed her eyes briefly, light-headed.

For the first time in a long time, Case was aware of another woman in his arms. She felt pliable and feminine and her perfume was quite intoxicating. He felt his pulse quickening, and when he felt her relax into his arms, a charge went through him.

She said nothing, smiled up at him, content to be dancing. All too soon, the song was over. They made their way back through the crowds to where a playful Laine was coming off the dance floor, assuring some eager suitor she was indeed 'very married' and 'meet my husband!'

The man, one of Roxie's regular roadies, glanced at Case, unimpressed. He gave Laine a quick peck on her cheek. "If you get bored with him, luv, ye call me!" he said cheekily, in a broad Scottish accent.

Case and Laine laughed together at his impudence.

Roxie's pal was there, chatting to Kevin. Roxie introduced Case to Phillipa, who gave him a long, speculative look that was not lost on a bubbly Laine.

"He is lovely, isn't he? Such a noble brow!" Laine teased, amused at Case's discomfort. She slipped her arm around his waist and hugged him, kissing him lightly on the lips. He returned the kiss, kissing her on the top of her head.

The intimacy of their gesture cut through Roxie like a knife.

"Yes, he is, rather," agreed Phillipa, with a smile. "Lucky you! Well," she looked at them all with a warm smile. "Super party! Lovely people! —Must dash!" She took Roxie by the hand. "Come, sweets, introduce me to that producer you've been titillating me with!" She linked her arm through Roxie's and led her determinedly away.

"What producer?" Roxie asked her, looking puzzled. Phillipa was positively dragging her along. "Stop! What producer?" She wriggled free, half laughing, half irritated.

Phillipa stopped short and turned to look at her, making sure they were out of sight of Case McAllister and his party. Phillipa's face was unusually grave.

"Roxie, honey. Listen to what I'm going to say, and smile. People are watching," she instructed, smiling sweetly herself.

Obediently Roxie smiled back at her and said nothing. She waited for the lecture she knew was coming, resigned.

"He's lovely, I'll grant you," Phillipa said. but her eyes flashed in warning, "But so is his friend, and so are half the other men here. Latch on to one of them. He's not only married, he's happily married!" Phillipa's voice softened. "My sweet, he's from a different world! You'll never fit in with his world, nor he with yours." Her smile was fixed, her eyes willing Roxie to take heed.

Roxie looked at her, then looked away without reply, crestfallen.

"Oh, stop worrying!" Roxie shrugged. "I saw how he looked at his wife. He loves her," she said. "But," she looked wistful, "there's just... Something. I can't believe the feelings I feel when he's near me," she said miserably.

"Roxie —!"Kevin's voice interrupted them. Both women jumped.

"Sorry to disturb you," he said, "we're on our way. Just wanted to say thanks. Great evening."

Both women smiled at him. Case and Laine were a little way behind him. Case had his arm around his wife, he was grinning at her as she said something to him.

Roxie dragged her eyes away, addressing Kevin.

"Well, it was great to meet all of you." She gave him a radiant smile, thinking that for her too, the night was over.

After they had left, Roxie became aware Phillipa was watching her closely, a strange look on her face.

"You were saying—?" Roxie said, absently. She glanced at her watch; it was time to go.

Phillipa shook her head slowly, it was pointless. The doctor was in Roxie's sights, and Roxie Tanner was used to shooting fish in a barrel. Whereas the doctor, Phillipa suspected, that might be a whole different ball game!

She shrugged. "It doesn't matter. It's too late anyway."

WHEN IT'S GONE

They sat in silence on the way home. Every now and then, Kevin would sneak a quick peek at his wife. She had been strange tonight, moody, then too excited, over the top.

In fact, he reflected, for some time now, Ash hadn't really been herself. All the way from the theatre, she hadn't said a word more than necessary, and he wondered what was up.

Ashley was lost in thought. When would be the right time to tackle this thing. What would he have to say? Would this end their marriage? Was it already over? How would he react if she told him she knew?

She closed her eyes and leaned her head back, remembering that shitty, dreadful night, now more than a week ago.

Her job as a fashion buyer for a large chain of stores took her to Europe, the Far East and all over North America. On her last trip she had finished two days ahead of schedule.

Weary of Tokyo, Ashley was happy to make arrangements to return home a couple of days early, well pleased with the business concluded, and eager to surprise Kevin.

What ensued was a cliché. Unable to get hold of Kevin to advise him of her early return, Ashley took a cab from the airport straight to her office to collect her car. She transferred her luggage to her car wearily, eager to get home, see Kev and soak in a hot tub.

It was a quarter after eleven when she finally drove up the drive of their Beverly Crest home.

Ashley was happy to see Kevin was home. There was another car in the driveway, another car that was unfamiliar to her. He had parked in front of her garage door. Ashley lifted her hand to the horn, exasperated, when it occurred to her it might be rude.

She used her latchkey to let herself in. In the living room, unfinished drinks stood on the coffee table and her startled eyes fell on a discarded shirt lying in a crumpled heap on the floor. Kevin was meticulous to a fault. The shirt was not one of Kevin's.

Curious, Ashley made her way up the stairs to the bedrooms. Upstairs on the landing, she stood transfixed, his name dying on her lips, listening to the unmistakable sounds of two men making love.

Fucking. Kevin and some other man!

For what seemed like an eternity, she stood, frozen. Slowly, her thoughts became coherent. Retreat. Do nothing. Escape!

Ashley fled. She found a hotel where she checked in and shut the door behind her, to sob and wail in solitude. There she stayed, waiting out the extra days, unable to face anyone or anything. Through her numbing despair, she decided eventually that the best thing to do —was nothing!

So it was that Ashley returned home, full of pretense, shamming all was well.

He, of course, had been his usual caring self, then and now.

In the car on their way home, Ashley sighed softly to herself. Perhaps he wasn't gay? Perhaps this was just some flash-in-the-pan thing? Once, their loving had been passionate, and she would make it so again. He was still loving, affectionate.

But still her Kevin?

She didn't think so.

Would he be okay on his own? Would she? They were best friends, dammit. She needed to make an effort, pull out all the stops... She looked at him, his profile driving. As if he sensed her looking at him, he reached out and took her hand, his eyes never leaving the road.

Ashley leaned over in the passenger seat and kissed him softly on the cheek, her hand caressing the back of his neck.

Kevin was surprised but gratified. Good. Her foul mood was gone. He was growing weary of the mournful creature she had become lately. Ashley was seldom moody, but these past few days had been challenging, to put it mildly.

At home, Ashley made her way upstairs, her mood determined. She was foolish to despair so easily, she told herself! Kevin loved her, of that she had no doubt. This— thing was obviously something a sensitive man like Kevin had to experience! Tonight she would take him to heights that he had forgotten.

Like an eager bride, Ashley fussed and prepared for bed. She would take control tonight. She slipped on a sexy, silky cami and surveyed herself in the full-length mirror in the bathroom. She had put on eleven pounds since her wedding day eleven years ago, and looked the better for it, Kevin assured her. She still had her looks, appeal.

Satisfied, she turned off the bathroom light and padded through to the bedroom. Kevin was already in bed, apparently asleep. Ashley dimmed the bedside light almost to nothing and climbed in beside him, her heart pounding nervously, but determined.

"Kevin?" He stirred sleepily, "Kevin, darling... hold me." Half asleep, he obligingly rolled over and drew her to him. She began to kiss his face softly, while her hand slid down his torso to close lightly around his limp penis. She felt it stir, felt him awaken. Almost automatically, Kevin began drowsily to kiss his wife back with the same soft kisses she was bestowing on him.

Ashley was making little groaning noises of pleasurable anticipation when Kevin, wide awake now, felt that familiar feeling of desperation begin to creep over him. His pajama top was open, and she pulled up her cami to cover his bare chest with her warmth.

Kevin felt himself drowning in a well of shame. Recognizing her urgency, he began to masturbate her gently, frantic to disguise his failure.

For a short time, they both feigned their role in a futile ritual that gradually overwhelmed them both with despair.

Kevin felt a wetness on his cheek, and he twisted his head to see the tears streaming from her eyes. She was biting her lower lip in a vain bid for composure.

With a choking sob, she rolled away from him, defeated.

The misery at the pit of Kevin's stomach was like a slow burn, and he tried to wipe the tears from her eyes, feeling clumsy and a coward. Tucked in like spoons, he held her while her body shook with convulsive sobs, the silk top a crumpled flag of defeat. Finally, the sobs ceased. At last she turned and looked at him, little hiccups of misery stabbing her breathing, her puffy eyes a visible rebuke.

"Kevin," she whispered, "why do you want... men? Is there something wrong with me?"

Kevin was stunned. She knew!

He didn't know how, but she knew. And here she was, asking what was wrong with her! Not trusting himself to speak, he shook his head dumbly.

Ashley lay in his arms, praying he would reassure her, and tell her it was all a mistake. But the naked misery in his eyes had told her it was all real, this thing that was disrupting her life, leaving her abandoned and barren.

The guilt and misery on his face was unbearable, and she pulled him to her bosom, hating to see him so distressed.

Ashley whispered to him, "Tell me, Kevin. Please try. Explain it to me."

Faltering, his body close up against her as if to shield her from the pain of his words, Kevin tried wretchedly to explain to his wife of eleven years how he had fallen in love with another man.

SLIPPING THE NOOSE

FLEEING

Laine's head was reeling, and unconsciously, she pulled out a chair and sat down, glad there was no one around. She needed to focus on what Ashley was saying.

She was glad they were talking on the phone and Ashley could not see her face. Her mouth set in a thin line as she listened, trying to understand what it was she was being told.

It almost defied comprehension.

She felt inordinately heart-sore for Ashley, and Kevin too. Her eyes were scratchy from threatening tears and when she tried to talk, she found her throat was closed and tight.

But Ashley was still speaking...

"—So we've talked it out, over and over again, but the truth is, he says he's gay. I figure we both need space, time to think." Ashley sounded flat, resigned. "I'm going away for a while, on a combined business trip and vacation, sort of, to South America."

Ashley sounded bleak. "So, Laine, rain-check on that luncheon?"

Laine heard herself croak "Fine." Jesus, what can I say? —I don't know what to say. I'm speechless," she admitted. There was nothing–no glib platitude, absolutely nothing that would offer comfort.

Ashley seemed to understand. She continued;

"When I return, I guess we'll talk divorce. Figure out something." For the first time, Laine could hear a tremor in Ashley's voice. And more frightening to Laine, a note of resignation. She could picture Ashley in her hi-tech office downtown, unruffled on the surface, breaking up inside.

"I wish I could suggest something more positive or constructive, but what?" Laine said, twisting a strand of hair around and around her finger, quite overwhelmed. "And you honestly think I mustn't tell Case?" she asked doubtfully, not at all convinced she should keep something this big from him.

But Ash had extracted a promise.

Ashley sighed. "Case is as much his damn hero as his best friend, and I honestly don't know how Case would handle this. Kevin is sick, sick with worry about his reaction."

Laine was silent. How would Case react? Perhaps he already knew. He had been distracted lately, moody, unlike his usual self. They were doing the first big op on that Cahill child next week, the one mauled by the dog, and she knew he was worried about the tissue fusion.

"Laine?"

Ashley's voice jerked her back to the present.

"Sorry. I'm here. Was thinking... Honestly, I don't know about Case. He's so distracted lately, and I'm wondering if it has anything to do with Kevin?" Then she answered her own question. "But no. I absolutely know he would have discussed it with me!" she said with total conviction.

"In any event, he'll be shocked, but not appalled. Case hasn't any hang-ups about gays."

On the other end, Ashley bit her lip, thinking. She wasn't so sure. Her mouth felt dry. "God knows it was hard enough for me to swallow. Perhaps I still haven't absorbed it, not really. Anyhow, thanks for being my sounding board. I'm grateful," she said softly.

Laine felt a rush of warmth. Strange, they had been friends for years now, but she had never felt closer to Ash than now. Why was that?

Because they're us, a little voice answered. Their marriage was solid, like ours. Until it's not. Laine felt inexplicable goosebumps. Stop it! This is about Ash, not you.

"Feel free to call me anytime. Anytime," she entreated. "Safe travels, and try not to worry too much." Her words sounded trite.

What did one say? Kevin-gay?

Kevin and Ashley, over?? It was impossible.

Laine shuddered.

"Okay," Ashley was saying. "Give the fam a kiss from me. Look after yourself, hon." They exchanged farewells. Laine had a lump in her throat and she found it difficult to speak.

After the call, Laine felt inordinately distressed. She had given her word to keep silent, but the thought lingered there, inside her head.

Perhaps Case already knew? No, that was impossible. They had no secrets. It would be hard to keep this from him, but Ashley was right.

Kevin needed to tell him himself.

Her cheek felt wet.

With some surprise, Laine realized she was weeping.

Next door, Mia Reichmann shushed the children and strained to catch more of Rudolf's conversation. He was talking about Doctor McAllister.

"Thanks, that's what I needed to hear. When will he be served? Good, I wish I could see his face. Bastard." Then silence.

The call was obviously over.

"Mama, you're not listening to me." Bernadette tugged at her mother's skirt.

"Hush. Mama is thinking about serious things. What is it?" Mia looked down at her child, who was pointing to her sister's dessert bowl.

"She's not hungry. Mama, can I have her ice cream, please Mama?"

Mia glanced at Kira. The child sat at the dinner table, staring apathetically at her food. She had hardly touched her dinner and now she sat staring stonily at the ice cream Mia had hoped would tempt her.

Mia was concerned. Her normally plump and jolly little Kira, lately had to be cajoled to eat. The chubby seven-year-old had always delighted in setting the example for her younger sister when it came to 'eating up.'

For a while now, the child's appetite had been poor, and Mia debated with herself whether the child needed to see a doctor. Perhaps just a tonic? Maybe she would take the child with her when she went to the doctor. Her cramps were getting worse and worse, and of late, she had noticed a foul vaginal odor.

Rudolf strode into the dining room, interrupting her bleak thoughts. He looked pleased with himself.

"Now I'll show that bastard," he crowed. He resumed his meal and Bernadette fell silent, reluctantly giving up on the ice cream, cowed by her father's presence.

"Who?" asked Mia, knowing some response was expected. But she knew exactly who. "What have you done?" She feigned nonchalance, but he eyed her suspiciously.

"I've laid a complaint against him with the Hospital Board! By the time my lawyer gets through with him, he'll be a missionary," he crowed, his eyes gleaming in malice. His eyes fell on Kira, who was eying him uncertainly. He looked at her untouched dessert. "What's wrong? Eat your dessert. It will make you strong and healthy and fat." He pinched her cheek affectionately. "Daddy likes his fat little girls!"

Kira gazed stonily ahead. She ignored him, and the ice cream.

Bernadette offered to eat her sister's ice cream. Rudolf shrugged, indifferent, his mind elsewhere.

"Go on then. It's good for you." He stood up from the table and went to watch television in the living room.

Mia felt helpless. It was time to leave, or she would be late. She wanted to argue with him., make him see reason. The children were friends. She and Laine, they were friends. In fact, Laine was her only friend, really. At the PTA meeting tonight, perhaps she could warn Laine?

"I'm leaving, are you sure you do not want to come? Mrs Costaz will be here in a minute if I call her." Mia stood, waiting for his reply. "Go. I will watch the children. I haven't got time for shit." He snorted, then sneered at her, "That's why I have you!" He turned the television's volume up, dismissing her.

Mia felt the hate well up like a living thing, and for a moment, everything swam before her eyes. Her breathing felt short, and she forced herself to calm down.

A short while later, Rudolf heard the car door slam, and he grunted in satisfaction. Stupid bitch!

What did a man want at a nursery school, looking at stupid drawings? He tried to focus on the television program, but his thoughts kept drifting back to Tina. He ought to get rid of her, find someone new. There was always some whore ready to take her place.

He felt the familiar burning in his groin and began to rub himself gently. He wondered what the children were doing. His crotch was hard, and he tried to hear what the television announcer was saying, but he was distracted.

"Bernadette, Kira." There was no reply, and he called again, louder. This time he heard their faint voices from the back porch, and he went outside to find them playing in the dark, on an old swing. "Bedtime. Come, Daddy will tuck you in." He scooped Bernadette up, and she squealed with delight. Kira skipped nimbly out of reach and ran ahead, upstairs to her bedroom.

It took a few minutes to tuck the smaller child in, ruffling her hair and smiling at her excited giggles under the blanket.

In Kira's room, he found her already in bed, in her pajamas, eyes huge and round above the covers. He sat down with a heavy sigh on the bed beside her. "Why didn't you eat your food? You know if you eat your food, you will stay strong and healthy." Concerned, he stroked her soft hair, then her satin-smooth cheeks. He took the bed-covers in her grasp. He saw that she was trembling.

"Come, don't be frightened," he said tenderly. "You know how Daddy loves his special little girl." The small bed groaned under his weight as he swung himself onto the bed.

GRACE

At the PTA meeting, Laine lifted the teacup to her lips and tried hard to focus on what Myra Egglington was saying. The school principal was explaining her hopes and aspirations for the school. Normally attentive to such matters, Laine found her attention drifting. She wished Case was with her.

Tonight, she was giving him rare time alone with his mother.

Laine knew most of the mothers and usually, she enjoyed a chat, but the recent bombshell from Ashley made every other thing appear frivolous.

What would Case say when he found out about Kevin? They both had no particular adversity against gay people, but Kevin!? Their very own 'Superman', bursting out of the closet? And keeping it from Case all these years?

It was all too much.

She noticed Mia Reichmann near the papier-mâché models and excused herself from the group politely. Laine wondered if Mia was deliberately avoiding her. These days, when it was Mia's turn to run the kids to school, she always seemed distracted, in a hurry, as if the day's demands were always overwhelming her.

Mia was friendly, smiling when Laine approached her.

"Hello Laine," Mia pointed proudly to a papier-mâché cow, "this is one Kira did. It's good, yes?" she said with quiet pride.

Laine admired the cow. It was very good indeed.

"She's a talented girl," Laine agreed. "How are they?" Psyche 101 coming to the fore. "Fine, they are very fine," Mia said firmly.

Laine found the tone of her reply curious. She seemed defensive about the children. She eyed Mia's bare arms surreptitiously and noted with relief there was no obvious bruising.

"And you? You're good?" Laine asked, nonetheless.

"Yes. No. Maybe." Mia looked uncomfortable. Then she blurted out, "I have to tell you that Rudolf has taken legal action and also, he has approached the Hospital Board. To make trouble," she finished miserably, unable to look Laine in the eye.

So! That was it. Damn that man to hell. Laine kept her expression inscrutable. It was obvious the woman was distraught enough. And Mia certainly would have nothing to do with this! Laine squeezed the woman's hunched shoulders. She felt bony to Laine, far too thin, fragile.

"Don't you worry yourself about it. Case can take care of himself," she replied with conviction. Laine's unease returned. The woman's complexion was quite gray.

Mia looked relieved. "I'm so sorry. He never listens to me. This is all my fault," she added miserably.

"Nonsense." Laine waved her apologies away. "There's no point in getting upset about it. Case will be fine."

Other parents were approaching the art display. "We'll talk in the week," she whispered. Laine excused herself and went to find Myra Egglington, the principal. She wanted to get home to her family.

Case must ensure Kevin had the matter in hand.

The Kevin thing could wait. Case already had too much on his plate. She could shield him from that, at least.

PROTECTION

Mia felt better when she drove home. Her little Kira was so talented, such a gentle child. It was Bernadette who was the mischievous one! And, thank God, Dr McAllister wouldn't be getting in any trouble because of her. Laine was not worried at all! She would know about these things...

At home, all the lights were off, except the one in the main bedroom and her heart sank. That meant he was still awake. She entered the bedroom, relieved to find Rudolf fast asleep. She washed and changed quickly, trying to make as little noise as possible, willing him to stay asleep. She pulled back the bed-covers, taking care not to touch him as she crept into the bed.

As her head touched the pillow, she recoiled in alarm. Her cheek had touched the damn pistol, carelessly pushed under the pillow. She pushed it cautiously back under his pillow.

He was far too casual with that gun, a .22 Beretta he insisted they needed for 'protection'.

Protection. Mia stared up at the ceiling.

The only protection they needed was from him, she thought bitterly. Her thoughts turned to Kira. Now that was a real worry. She would try a tonic on Kira for a while, to see if that stimulated the child's appetite.

But no doctors.

They knew nothing.

TINKERING

Case had twice been to Cliffside Drive to tinker with his new toy, the Caddie DeVille. The first time Roxie was out, and he applied himself to detaching the rotor, feeling curiously disappointed she wasn't there. On the second occasion, they connected. She drove in just as he was about to leave.

Juanita had tipped Roxie off, as instructed, and the Bentley had showed its mettle as she flattened the accelerator to get home before he left. She stepped out of her car, took a deep breath and walked towards him, smiling. They exchanged greetings, both suddenly feeling rather shy.

"How far are you with the car?" Her tone was deliberately bright and cheery, and Case felt his reserve dissolve.

"Quite far. I can drive it away, as soon as they deliver a new rotor." She looked blank, then her face flooded with feigned understanding. "Ah," she said and snapped her fingers. "I knew that was the issue!"

They both laughed. Suddenly, he flushed. "Are you getting tired of it? Is it in the way? If so, I'm sorry. I can always get it towed."

"No, no." Impulsively she put her fingers to his lips to stay his words of apology, then withdrew them hastily. "What I mean is, it's no bother. Really."

She took his arm determinedly and led him to her front door.

"Come, stay and have a drink with me before you leave," she instructed. He hesitated, but only for a split second. Hell, he was here now, and it was the polite thing to do.

He allowed himself to be ushered inside. They sat out on the redwood deck with that soul-soothing view of the ocean. She poured him a drink, and he sipped his Scotch slowly, enjoying her company. They chatted easily about their day, but mostly about being in the music industry. His curiosity about her career surprised him.

"You really are a bit of a technophile," she said after she had tried, rather unsuccessfully, to explain how tracks were laid down, one over the other.

"It's completely alien to me, but it sounds intriguing..."

Looking out at the beach, he saw a speck, a lone swimmer in the ocean, and it occurred to him that perhaps the swimmer was out of his depth, way past the shallows. The undertow could be treacherous. Dangerous. Dangerous. The word floated in his head, bugging him, a mosquito buzzing around his conscience. His thoughts swung to the here and now. Why was he so curious about her life? He had his own life, and it was a great life! Her show (he thought of it as `her show') had been on his mind too often lately, and really, what the hell was he doing here?

Never mind the damn swimmer, he was getting out way past the shallows. His wife was waiting for him, at their home. Case swallowed the last of his scotch and stood up abruptly.

He had no business being here.

Roxie was taken aback at his sudden, palpable change of mood. He stood there, silhouetted against the setting sun, his features in shadow and indistinct, but she could feel his abrupt cooling. She sat in her chair, one legged tucked under, and looked up at him, confused. What was going on here?

For a moment, neither said anything, the air between them charged with... what? Case began to say something, offer an explanation, then thought better of it. He thanked her politely, almost formally, for the drink, urged her to stay seated, insisting he could see himself out.

He promptly did so.

Roxie watched him leave, feeling numb.

Just who the hell was he, anyway? A myriad of emotions churned through her, unfamiliar emotions, defying understanding. Angrily she flung the last of her drink out. Unfamiliar tears pricked her eyes, and she blinked them away furiously. Everything had been fine. Damn him to hell! Arrogant sonovabitch!

But what the hell had just happened? She felt bleak. This teensy, tiny bit of time with him, and already, damn heartache? She banged her forehead with the palm of her hand, confused and unhappy.

Then she understood, and her tears abruptly stopped.

He felt it too!

Crazy Roxie, meet Crazy Case.

GIFT HORSES

Case tried to sort out his jumbled thoughts on the drive home.

He couldn't understand it. He and Laine had terrific sex, she more than satisfied him... He was a family man! Confused at the feelings Roxie stirred in him, he increased his speed. This thing with Roxie was like a brewing storm, this hunger to possess her, to own her.

She knew. She was waiting for him, he knew that for sure.

She was waiting for him to claim her. Case found he was fully aroused, and he forced himself to think of other things, anything to slow down the adrenaline coursing through his body and heading straight for his dick.

He turned on the radio, seeking distraction, and like an answer to a prayer, Bananas in Pajamas plinkety-plonked out, bringing his girls to the fore, banishing these unsettling, alien emotions.

Nearing home, his erection was once again flaccid. as if to taunt him into thinking he was in control, when he and his dick knew all the while, it was there, just waiting for some clandestine thought to bring it back, demanding and in charge.

At home, the clamor of the children claimed his attention. Laine and Judith were in the kitchen, caught up in a noisy debate with the children as to whether carrots were 'adult' vegetables and not meant to be inflicted on children. He called a greeting, and they all chorused back. Glad they were preoccupied and he could avoid scrutiny for a few minutes, Case escaped from the family and went straight to the bedroom. There, he peeled off his clothes and stepped into the shower.

Immersed under a stinging stream of hot water, he allowed himself to relax, let the water wash away any trace of her.

He heard Laine enter the bedroom.

"Here are some clothes," she called. He heard the closet door being opened as she took out fresh clothes for him to wear.

"Thanks, hon." How normal his voice sounded. He walked into the bedroom, still damp from the shower, looking clean and refreshed.

"That's a new dress. You look delicious." He was smiling at her as he toweled himself dry. This was his wife, this was the woman he loved. Suddenly his expression changed, became intense.

"How long did you say it was before dinner?" He let the towel fall, naked before her now, his hand stroking his penis. Laine looked taken aback at this unexpected desire.

"Wow, you are hungry," she said, surprised. She began to protest there wasn't much time at all, then cut her words off and quickly flipped the latch on the bedroom door. A gift-horse was a gift horse, and here before her stood a whole lotta horse! She was still giggling in surprise at his urgency, her laughter fading quickly as he pushed her down onto the bed and lifted her skirt up. He slid down and his lips caressed her teasingly through the fabric of her panties, and with each warm breath, a shock went through her body. His tongue teased her through the fine fabric until she felt frantic.

"Tear the damn things off. Now!" All the time she could feel his warm breathing on her crotch. "Please. Now. Now," she begged, writhing under his mouth. She felt her panties being removed and his tongue began probing her in earnest, reveling in her readiness. When he could contain his own need no more, Case climbed up over her and eased himself inside her, savoring her urgency. His own need was great, and he thrust himself deep within her, once, twice, feeling her come, and gratefully he let himself go in welcome, shuddering thrusts.

Spent, he lay on top of her, listening to her murmurs of pleasure.

Mercifully, there had been no childish banging on the door. See, he told himself, it's best with Laine, she's all I ever need.

She trusts me. I can't see her again, he resolved, ever. But when he closed his eyes, Roxie's face was there.

TOO MANY HEROES

HOMECOMING

"Your seatbelt, Sir?"

He felt a gentle nudge on his shoulder and tried to focus on the smiling face a few inches above him. She was a pretty heart faced brunette, smiling down at him with professional concern. He thanked her, his words catching in his throat. His throat felt dry, despite his solid drinking. He had barely spoken to anyone in the last ninety hours. Satisfied his croak was one of obedience, she rewarded him with a light pat on the shoulder and minced her way down the aisle of the airplane.

Jeremy Carter longed for a cigarette. Thank God, they were about to land. He sat back and closed his eyes – he tried to think of pleasant things, like his wife, a hot bath, a single malt Scotch. But instead he saw Larry's face, blood oozing from his mouth, his eyes very wide, so very shocked, questioning him, incredulous.

This was a Bad Thing. They had discussed the possibility of Bad Things happening, but neither ever believed they would fall victim. Not really. Strange that, he thought, they documented death so regularly. But it was always other people. And death, dying, that was definitely failure, and they both agreed in their line of work, failure was not an option.

Perhaps it was a survival thing, this bogus sense of immunity. That's what you needed to make this job work. He still had his camera in his hand, for fuck's sake.

Larry never knew what hit him. One moment he was clicking away, the next he lay in the mud, one hand clutching the camera in a death grip, his other hand trying feebly to push his gut back inside his belly. Not even the proverbial last word, just ...surprise.

In the hushed quiet of the plane, Jeremy felt an overwhelming urge to howl, like a dog at the moon.

They went back a way, he and Larry. They had been together in Chicago when he was still a junior reporter at the Herald, and Larry an aspiring photographer. After some nine years, they had been delighted to reconnect for Newsweek.

For the past three years, Jeremy Carter and Larry Barber had done many assignments together. Tin gods, safe from bombs and bullets, shielded from all harm by a monogrammed flak jacket that said PRESS, and the sheer nobility of their profession. After all they had witnessed, they believed in no God, no Allah, just good old Bacchus.

Alcohol was the great soother, there was oblivion in a bottle. It shielded and protected them from their thoughts, thoughts often more dangerous than the reality of stacked cadavers. Larry and Jeremy, party animals, laughing, even weeping together when the self-medication of whiskey didn't work.

Long evenings in grimy bars and pubs in the festering countries of the world, too often surrounded by illiterate peoples, both driven by an exaggerated sense of noblesse oblige.

That was how it used to be.

Until now.

Larry had allowed himself to be killed and his untimely death left Jeremy outraged and cheated.

By now the magazine would have informed Larry's Puerto Rican wife. Jeremy thought of Larry's son, Julio. He was nearly six years old, or was it five? Whichever, it was a shame he would never get to know his father. Christ. He ran his tongue cautiously around his mouth. Jesus, what he wouldn't do for another drink. But the trays were up, they were landing.

He too, was wounded, but no one could see. He slumped back, waiting for the plane to land so he could get a drink, and when that was done, get another.

It was a full hour before he cleared customs. His seedy appearance rankled the customs officer, who then proceeded to search every item of baggage with suspicious zeal. Carter didn't blame him.

He looked like hell, and he knew it.

Christ, he probably even stank. Too weary to even feel indignant, he stood quietly by until the official finally gave in. Reluctantly, he waved Carter on. He trudged outside the terminal buildings, glad to see lines of cabs, and no delays. It would be just after seven when he arrived home. Roxie might be out. He wanted to call her, hear her voice, but his phone was flat. She would be glad to see him back in the States. He let the cabbie take his luggage.

He sunk back into the worn seat, exhausted. Nearly two days without proper sleep. He would kill for a drink.

INCH BY INCH

"Hi. How ya doing?" said a familiar voice.

Case turned from the coffee machine.

Kevin. It was unusual to see Kevin here, especially at this time of day.

"This is a surprise! What's up?" Case indicated the coffee machine with an inquiring lift of his brow.

"Not on your life. No, thank you. Revolting." Case grinned at Kevin's expected answer.

"What brings you here?" He asked the question but already he knew. "I suppose that crap with Reichmann?"

"That," said Kevin, "and we need to have a chat! You're too busy even for racquetball lately," he paused, then he spoke, his face neutral, "Ashley left this morning for Rio."

Case looked at him in surprise. So soon? Laine had mentioned that Ashley was going away, but so soon after the last trip.

"So, I thought I'd look in on the esteemed healer of the sick. Got some time?" Kevin said casually, hiding the maelstrom inside his gut.

Ashley understood. Forgave him. Now, there was just Case.

Apprehension swamped him. Perhaps the clinic wasn't the best venue for what he had to say. Too late. Case was nodding.

"No problem, give me a minute." Case gave him a friendly pat on the back. They entered his consulting room and Case gestured to one of the two leather chairs in front of his desk, and he sat down in the other.

Case stirred his coffee with a throat-stick and studied Kevin with a practitioner's eye. Kevin looked jumpy beneath the cheery veneer. Off-color, even. He waited, saying nothing. Over the years he had learned when Kevin was good and ready, he would speak.

Kevin felt himself shrinking under Case's scrutiny. "Stop staring at me like that, it's annoying," he said irritably, his courage slipping. He stalled, playing for time. "Are you worried about this Reichmann thing? It's crap!" he said with conviction.

Case scowled. "I've been summoned to appear before the board next Wednesday, to 'explain' the circumstances. As you know, I'm up for tenure, so I need to come out of this smelling like roses. The truth is, I'd slug that bastard again. And that's just what I'll say to them. Drucker is on the board and it's common knowledge that he more or less has the post earmarked for his nephew. Nepotism is alive and well." Case lolled back in his chair, legs outstretched, looked at the ceiling.

"The whole damn thing's political," he said sourly.

"Is he a better surgeon than you?" Kevin asked.

Case grimaced. "Nope. But he's a good politician. Like his damn uncle."

Kevin nodded. "Well, that settles that then. You handle the board. Leave the legal shit to me!"

Case shrugged. Kevin wasn't worried, and if Kevin wasn't worried, then neither was he!

"Well, you let me know when you need a little surgery, maybe get that little dick of yours extended? I'll do the same for you!"

Kevin was looking at the distributor on Case's desk, his face curious. "What the heck is that?"

"That's the baby I had to have specially tooled for my DeVille. I'm hoping to hear the sweet sound of her motor today." "Oh." Kevin looked intrigued. "Are you still busy with that? Taking a bit of time, I'd say. And Roxie doesn't mind?"

But Kevin knew she wouldn't mind. He sensed that the sultry Roxie was more than a little attracted to his myopic friend. He wondered if Case was even aware.

Probably not. Not for the prince, torrid affairs of the heart.

Case's face had closed at the mention of Roxie Tanner. Disapproval? Suddenly, Kevin knew his visit was a crappy idea. The timing was off, the venue wasn't right either. Sure, they were close, brothers even, but Case would be underwhelmed at anything out of the ordinary, challenging his predictable life. Nowhere in the Case McAllister Master Plan would he have allowed for homos, that's for sure!

The thought laid him low, and Kevin felt abruptly depressed. He was rescued from his funk by Lindy, returned from her lunch. She popped her head around the door and informed Case apologetically she had an urgent call from a colleague. "I'll call him back in minute." He looked at Kevin.

Saved by the bell, Kevin thought. He stood up to leave.

Lindy and Kevin exchanged some light banter, and Case smiled at the pair of them. Kevin and the damn women.

"Dunno what they see in you." Case said, rising from his chair. "You're essentially a prick."

"A nine-inch prick!" Kevin said, sanguine. He was smiling, and yet Case thought Kevin looked a little despondent, perhaps? Glum about Ash going away, maybe.

"Anything else?" he asked Kevin, lifting his eyebrows askance.

Kevin shrugged. "I know when I'm being dismissed." Yet, for a couple of moments more, he lingered, seeming uncertain, wanting to say something, then abruptly he seemed to make up his mind, greeted them both and left.

Case watched him leave, feeling vaguely as if he had missed something. He shrugged. Oh well, when Kevin was ready, he was always here. He reached for the phone.

His eyes fell on the rotor and his pulse quickened. He would pop by Roxie's place later in the evening, and see if it worked. He had made up his mind, he wouldn't call. He felt lousy about how they left it last time. He needed to apologize to her in person.

If she wasn't there, so be it. He was a married man, she knew it, and that was simply that.

A LITTLE HOMEWORK

The cabbie gave a soft appreciative whistle as he turned into the drive at Cliffside Drive. He never figured the fare as loaded. The guy stank, hell, he even looked like a bum. He glanced in the rear-view mirror at his passenger. The fare also looked ready to pass out. These days you never could tell who had money and who didn't.

Jeremy was too tired to look up. His eyes opened when the engine stopped. Although he was expecting it, he was disappointed to see that Roxie's car was out. Perhaps she was parked in the garage. He climbed out of the cab, stumbling a little. Behind him, the cabbie shook his head in disgust. He watched Jeremy unload his suitcases from the trunk, not offering to help.

"That's eighty-one dollars you owe me, friend." He picked his teeth and leaned against the cab, watching the fare rummage through his pockets. It took all kinds. He looked around him. Yep, this was money, right here! He slouched against the cab, waiting, having no expectation of a decent tip.

Jeremy Carter tugged a hundred-dollar bill from a roll and gave it to the cabbie, who took the proffered bill, taken aback.

"Keep it!" Jeremy dismissed him, weary and wired. Where was she?

The cabbie gave Jeremy Carter an ingratiating smile. Carter ignored him and grabbed the handle of his luggage. As he turned, his eye swept past the open garage door and he stopped short in surprise. Parked in the garage was a monstrous old car, a clapped out old Caddy DeVille? Roxie had homework?

It had to be for that movie. Near the car stood a bucket of water and a rag, someone was obviously washing down the car. Jeremy forgot about his fatigue and strolled over to the car. The Cadillac DeVille, in near original condition, was as beat up as hell.

Vincent, the gardener and handyman, appeared through the interleaving door from the kitchen. He looked startled to see Jeremy suddenly there, looking at the doctor-fella's car!

Juanita had filled Vincent in.

The Vietnamese gardener gave him a gappy grin. "Missy Roxie say you come only in some weeks!"

Carter nodded, too distracted to respond. He looked at the old car curiously. Apparently, it required some mechanical attention. He could see some parts on the seat, and an overall was slung casually across the back seat. Somebody was fixing the car, right here? Roxie was sure living her role.

"Whose car is this, exactly?"

Vincent shrugged. "This some Doctor-fellah's car. He good flend of Missy Roxie. She asked me to wash it, 'cause it velly velly dirty." He stepped back, looking at his handiwork. "Washing no help," he said dolefully, picking up his pail. "Dis car a big heap clap!"

He had that right, Jeremy thought.

Jeremy gave up and went inside the house, looking about him for further signs of change. It was just the same. Juanita had already left. He dropped his luggage wearily at the foot of the staircase, then went upstairs to the piano room, where he mixed himself a stiff drink, then lined up a second in anticipation.

He settled in an easy chair, and sat morosely in the fading evening light, embracing the deepening gloom, taking strength from the bourbon warming his gut. He would give Roxie a call soon, tell her to come home, tell her about Larry.

He felt his stomach knot and he emptied the glass.

Who the fuck was the good flend doctor-fellah?

MELANCHOLY SELLS

Seated next to the sound engineer, Roxie listened intently to a replay and threw her hands up in disgust. Maxime was the best sound engineer money could buy, but this was crap.

He looked at her and sighed. "It's good," he pleaded. "It's good, it's good, it's good! Why are you still unhappy? I'm telling you, it's great!" He groaned in exaggeration and threw his head back, his eyes closed. Today, they planned to 'tidy up' last night's song and they had been at this for over two hours. Up with the horns, down with the horns, up with the percussion, down with the percussion, more bass, less bass–he was going nuts!

It sounded just fine to him. Roxie looked at him, dismissing his opinion in that infuriating way that she had when things weren't to her satisfaction.

She turned to her producer.

"What do you think?"

"I think it's good," Brandon ventured cautiously. "But if you're not happy, let's keep at it. But to me, it sounds real sweet." He sprawled back in his chair, crossed his arms and legs, well-satisfied with their efforts so far. This song was going to be a mother of a hit. It was a happy song. People needed to hear happy songs today. Roxie was frowning, unconvinced. "I don't know..." She sighed. "Maybe we should give it a miss for today, at least with this song. I'm not in the same mood I was when I wrote it." Her face was gloomy. "So much for heroes."

"Are you feeling blue?" Brendon looked at her speculatively.

Roxie sighed. Blue was how she felt alright.

"A little," she replied shortly. Roxie was not the confiding type.

"How about we try set down guide vocals for 'Another Day Gone.' That's a blue kinda song," he suggested.

She hesitated, then she shrugged. "Why not." He turned to the engineer. "Maxime, load the track."

"Sure..." Maxime nodded. Anything rather than another fucking take!

"You can do it justice, feeling as you do," Brendon smiled. Authentic was good, and if she was blue...

Roxie hesitated, guessing his angle. Idiot.

"Okay, might as well do something positive tonight."

"Great. Grab coffee while we set up the feeds."

She ignored the invitation to coffee and sat back in her chair while they set up. She was morose. Brendon was pleased, because he could capture mood now, and mood sold. He doesn't give a damn what the problem might be, she thought despondently. And even if he did care, you wouldn't tell him.

You don't even know yourself, the little voice inside her head taunted.

But she knew. Since she had last seen Case and they had parted so abruptly, she had been unable to shake off a constant cloud of gloom around her.

Brendon's voice interrupted her. "Are you ready?" he asked.

They were ready, waiting on her.

"Sure, why not." She went out of the control room into the booth and stood quietly for a minute while they took a sound balance.

She thought of him, feeling an energy borne of frustration replenishing her. She could let this–this whatever it was, out.

Brendon signaled to her through the glass all was ready, and the first bars from the song flowed through the cans. These were to be "guide" vocals to which the rest of the accompaniment was set. She had intended to do the master vocals tomorrow, when her voice was fresh, but what the hell— She listened to the sax, sounding steady and strong and tugging at her heart with its haunting cadence, waiting for her cue.

Roxie began to sing, her eyes shut tight. Mental pictures of a smiling Case wiping oil off her chin, straddling that big black bike, in old jeans, images of his wife slipping her arms under his jacket with an air of proprietary intimacy. His smell when she was close to him. All the images danced in her head, tearing at her heart.

At the sound desk, Maxime raised his eyebrows. She was sounding great.

He saw the sound engineer had lost his bored expression and was sitting up straight in his chair, his hands hovering over the slide controls on the mixing desk, flitting from one to another in swift, practiced movements.

"Jesus," Maxime said softly. "Look, the hairs are standing up on my arm!"

Brendon raised his hand, quieting the other's enthusiasm, but pleased, nonetheless. That was Maxime's "hit" test. He boasted that every time the hairs on his arm stood up, they were looking at gold. The song was moving and melancholy. Roxie was baring her soul.

When the last few notes had faded she opened her eyes slowly and looked up, wondering if Brendon would give her the okay.

He gave her a huge grin and beckoned to her, apparently well-satisfied. She was surprised. They were done? She joined them at the sound desk.

"I guess that's it," she said wearily. "That's me for today. If it's wrong, I'll do it again tomorrow." She picked up her purse to leave.

"Wrong?" Brendon grinned in delight. "That's the best damn thing I've heard in a long time," he exulted. He called after her, to her departing back. "Don't you want to hear how you sound?" "Nope. I'm beat!" Roxie called back over her shoulder.

The two men stared at the closed door in surprise, then at each other.

Brendon shrugged. "I don't know what's eating her, but please God, let it last."

BROKEN GLASS

Roxie fumbled with the key in the front door, pushed it open and dropped her purse on the prized Claudio Bitetti table which graced the foyer. The room was softly lit, and welcoming, and she felt glad to be home. She didn't notice the luggage behind the stairs, distracted by the gloom upstairs. She wondered why Juanita had left the upstairs lights off.

She went upstairs into the living room and flicked on the muted overhead light above the bar counter. She was mixing herself a martini when a voice came from the gloom;

"Hey Rox..."

She let out a shriek, dropping the bottle of Vodka in her hand. It smashed on the travertine floor with a noisy crash.

"Jeremy! Fuck! You scared me!" Her fear was instantly replaced by the nervous anger that follows a sudden surge of adrenaline. Her hand shook, and she set the glass down.

Jeremy was sitting just out of the circle of light, watching her with an unblinking stare. Her eyes slowly adjusted. He looked exhausted and very gaunt. She noted the dark circles around his eyes, the stubble from days of not shaving.

He had obviously been dozing in the chair. He was holding up an empty glass and Roxie realized he was also very, very drunk.

"Jesus. You scared the hell out of me," she said again. "How come you're back? You didn't let me know–I would have collected you?" she said.

It occurred to her she hadn't greeted him, and she walked over to him, stooping to kiss the top of his head.

She wrinkled her nose. "God, you need a shower. You look beat," she added. She needed to get ready. Phillipa would be there in a short while.

He didn't answer. His eyes were fixed on her breasts, eying the low-cut blouse, making her feel oddly self-conscious and uneasy. Why was he leering at her like that?

"You look good, babe. Been keeping in shape?"

Her brow furrowed at the sneer in his tone. She sat on the arm of his chair to embrace him but found herself flinching at the ripe smell of him. He needed a bath badly, and he reeked of booze. She got up and walked back to the bar.

"How long have you been home?"

Jeremy had seen her flinch and it had riled him. "Not long enough, by all accounts."

What was he talking about? Irritated, she stood up and went back to the bar to pour a fresh drink. She eyed the broken glass on the floor. Where did Juanita keep the dustpan? He was probably exhausted, if he's just flown in from God knows where.

He needed to eat. Coffee, at the least. They could talk in the morning.

Jeremy was sprawled in the chair, his limbs at odd angles, like an abandoned marionette. Roxie tried to recall the feelings that had prompted her to marry him. Nothing. A sense of loss stole through her.

She didn't love him, probably never had. Tomorrow, when he was sober, she would discuss their divorce. Then she would speak to Charles about that tour and get the hell away for a while, get Case McAllister out of her system!

She should feel sad, she chided herself. Divorce was a Big Deal.

She could ask Kevin Daniels to handle it, then dismissed that thought. Too close. —Can't move on, if you hold on!

"You look disappointed. Sorry it's me? Not the doctor," he taunted her, with a drunk's intuition.

Bingo. Her expression was shocked. And guilty? He thought she looked guilty.

"Christ, Jeremy!" Roxie was shocked. How the hell did he know about Case?

Jeremy sneered. So. He was right. Something was going on. Inflamed by jealousy, he struggled to his feet and walked to the bar, feeling stiff and achy. He needed another drink.

"So, who the fuck is 'the doctor'?" he demanded.

"What are you talking about?" Roxie was struggling to make sense of it. Could he see inside her damn head?

"Did I spoil all your plans?" He was deliberately goading her. He was angry with her, with the world, with fucking everyone. And he was good at extracting the truth. He dealt with better liars than her every day! It was pointless to try and get one over on him.

Roxie felt her anger growing. Scene One, Take Two, she thought, hiding her irritation. He was tired, he was drunk. Ignore it.

"I don't know what's eating you," she said evenly, "but I'm going to take a bath. I suggest you do the same. Sleep in the guest suite." She eyed him coldly. "Forget the damn drink." She took the glass out of his hand and put it on the counter, next to a near-empty bottle of Scotch.

Angered by her indifference, Jeremy swept the glass and bottle off the counter-top and for the second time in a few minutes, there was the jarring sound of glass breaking, and the pungent smell of booze filled the room.

Disbelieving, Roxie stared slack-jawed at all the broken glass on the floor.

"I don't know what's eating you, but you're in no state to discuss it now." With a supreme effort, she controlled her temper, forcing herself to speak calmly. Her face flushed with rage, she tried to brush past him. She needed to change; Phillipa was collecting her in just over an hour. Jeremy could sleep it off and they would sort this in the morning.

Jeremy grabbed her and pulled her up against him, pinning her between him and the bar counter.

"Where's the wifely kiss?" He pushed his unshaven face in her bosom. Roxie pulled away from the rasping discomfit of his beard, quite nauseated by the sour smell of him. Her rejection merely seemed to arouse him, and he thrust his right hand between her legs, fumbling at the zipper of her jeans, almost amused at her outrage.

She shoved him away with more force, infuriated. He was acting like an animal. What the hell was up with him?

"This should feel good." he jeered. "Or has someone else been screwing you while I'm away? Maybe the owner of that piece of crap out there?"

So that was it. That was how he knew about the 'doctor.' Vincent. Momentarily, Roxie stopped her exertions to get away from him, glad to make sense of it.

Jeremy took her pause as acquiescence and tugged at her top, ripping the buttons from the fine fabric. He grabbed her breast and pulled it from the flimsy brazier.

Had he lost it completely? Roxie was stupefied. This was not the Jeremy she knew! He placed a rough mouth over her nipple. His two-day stubble was painful and she winced. All the while, he was rubbing his hand in her crotch in a crude attempt to arouse her.

"Jeremy!" A myriad of thoughts tumbled around in her head, from wondering if she should crack his dumb-ass head open with a J&B bottle, or kick him in the fucking balls, but there was no room for that! Her mind skipped frantically from one bizarre option to another, all the while trying to find some explanation for this crazed behavior.

Finally, fury won the day.

"Who the hell do you think you are, some soldier, home from some stupid war!" she burst out, slapping his head hard, away from her bosom. He jerked his head up, his face a mask of fury.

Roxie looked into his eyes, and for the first time, she felt afraid.

This was not someone she knew.

"You bitch. We risk our necks for you, and you sit at home and screw some joker," he snarled. He saw her fear and it pleased him.

"Well, I'm home now, so let's see if you've been practicing while I've been away." He fumbled with his belt, one-handed and clumsy, the other hand holding her trapped between him and the bar. His trousers dropped to his ankles and he tried in vain, hopping in clumsy steps to try and rid himself of his shackle. His erection swayed drunkenly to the left and right, as if it too, had had a tipple.

He lurched forward to pull her towards him again, still struggling all the while to step out of his pants. He was clawing at her belt, cursing the skin-tight fit and the intricate fastener. Fumbling and panting with thwarted effort, he suddenly gave up.

There was always Plan B.

Jeremy yanked at a clump of her hair and pulled her down.

Roxie yelped in pain and she fell clumsily to her knees, revolted to feel the moist tip of his penis knocking against her cheek. A cold fury rose within her and abruptly, she abandoned her struggle.

"That's better," he responded, breathless from the grappling. He reached down and guided his penis towards her mouth.

Roxie closed her mouth around him and bit down, hard.

Jeremy screamed in pain and fell back on the floor. He rolled onto his side, curled up in agony, cursing and groaning. Shaken, Roxie stood up slowly, holding onto the bar counter for support. She spat out saliva from her mouth, her stomach heaving violently, and for a minute she thought she would surely vomit.

"Get out," she managed, between rasping breaths. "Take my car and get the fuck out of my house, you sonovabitch." She lunged for an unopened bottle of vodka and she raised it over her head, prepared to cave his damn head in if that's what it took.

But Jeremy had had enough. He held up his hand in defeat, gesturing she should stop. He looked dazed.

"I'm sorry," he wheezed. "Really... I am sorry." He pulled his hand away from his penis and she saw there was blood. Quite a bit of it. She felt quite faint.

Jeremy staggered to his feet, pulling his trousers up with care, all dignity forgotten in his efforts to spare himself further pain. He limped to the bar and took up her car keys. His hand was covering his crotch and his face was grimacing in pain.

It took everything she had to keep her nausea in check.

"I'll call you," he managed to gasp. He hobbled toward the door, hunched and grunting in pain at every step. Moments later she heard the car start up and drive away. For a small eternity, she stood perfectly still, with only the sound of her ragged breathing breaking the silence. She thought of nothing or no one, just standing motionless for what seemed like the longest time.

She heard another voice, someone calling...

"Anyone home? Roxie?"

It was Case McAllister, his voice sounding far, far away. The light from the hall cast a square of light into the sitting room and yes, it was definitely him, there in the doorway, silhouetted against the light. He was gazing around him, his face incredulous.

He was looking at her, then glancing around the room, taking in the floor with its carpet of broken glass, the overwhelming smell of booze everywhere.

Then the lights went out.

MEN ARE BEASTS

Earlier that evening, Case had tried telling himself the little metal part lying on the floor in the passenger foot-well, that was the reason for his good mood. Now he would get that car going. As for this 'thing' or whatever it was, he was only human, and it meant nothing. He had it in hand, not to screw up his marriage for bullshit!

Yet, his heart skipped a beat when he saw her car in the driveway. She was home.

He promised himself he would give himself fifteen minutes to hear that damn engine crank. If there was no joy, he would get the car towed to his place. Absolutely no more jaunts for him to Cliffside Drive.

It was just on eight, and the full moon cast a warm dappled light over the street. He glanced at his watch. He could be home by nine.

He killed the engine, electing to park in the street, in case she was going out again and he parked her in. He was leaning over and reaching down for the shiny new part lying on the passenger floor, when he noticed a man weaving drunkenly out of the house, his shoulders hunched, his face contorted. The man almost collapsed into the driver's seat of Roxie's car and he watched with a measure of alarm as the driver reversed too quickly out of the drive, the tires squealing in protest. He winced as the Bentley almost clipped his parked SUV, then it roared off down the street.

Case gazed after it, troubled by the guy's odd behavior. The man behind the wheel looked crazed, dirty and unshaven, like a bum! But it was the husband, he could see that.

He climbed out of his car and started walking towards the house. The front door was wide open.

He stood at the threshold and called her name.

"Roxie!" There was no answer. "Roxie!" he called again, disturbed.

Case took the stairs two at a time and on the landing he paused. He was drawn to the living room by the overpowering smell of booze. He paused in the doorway, taking in the broken glass, and some blood on the tiled floor.

Roxie was standing at the bar, her hand grasping the neck of a bottle, clutching it like a weapon. She saw him, then gazed with dismay at the broken glass on the floor.

She was trembling. She's in shock, he thought. He moved towards her as her legs gave way and he caught her as she fell. Her teeth were chattering and her blouse was torn. He noticed abrasions on her breast.

Case guided her gently to the sofa and sat her down. He went to the bar and opened a Coke, came back and sat down next to her, urging her to drink. The sugar would help. She sipped it gratefully, and once again, he found himself wiping her face. The blood on her mouth did not appear to be hers, he saw with relief. His arms went out and he found himself drawing her close.

"You always seem to rescue me," Roxie whispered into his neck.

Her shock was fading, and in its place, there was this, this miracle happening. Her man was here, holding her close, loving her. He was kissing her hair softly, stroking her with infinite tenderness.

For Case, there was the insane reality, of her, here, in his arms. Did euphoria bring about surrender or did surrender bring euphoria? He didn't know, and at that moment, he didn't care. Didn't think. There was just her.

It all seemed inevitable. She was his, for the taking.

"Roxie, " he heard himself saying her name softly, over and over again, feeling the softness of her face beneath his lips. Up against him, she felt warm and fragile. In an easy movement, he pulled her onto his lap to hold her more closely against him.

The trembling had stopped, replaced by a quiver each time his lips brushed her face.

Gone was the terror of minutes before. Now there was only ecstasy from the sheer miracle of having him here, kissing her softly, making her crazy. She wanted him to kiss her, hard, on her mouth, but instead, his lips just brushed her face, his tongue lightly tasting her lips, as if he was savoring her. Guided by that basest of instincts that will always fell mere mortals, she pressed her mouth hard to his. His lips closed on hers with an urgency that made her stomach lurch. His kiss was demanding, probing, crossing a threshold to that point of no return.

For Case, this lust, this carnal need for domination was new and strange to him. Intoxicating. He wanted ownership.

Roxie was lost, consumed by a fire spreading to every part of her, and she straddled him, pressed herself onto his lap, desperate that he should make her his.

Suddenly, a loud, insistent honking horn shattered the moment. It was harsh, jarring, as loud as if the car was there, with them in the living room.

Confused, almost in a trance, Case drew his head away, his eyes on hers, and the hunger he saw in her eyes made his senses swim.

But the insistent, blaring horn was not going away. He lifted her off his lap and stood up like a drunkard, leaving her on the sofa, watching him, dazed.

Was that a car horn? What-? Roxie tried to think.

Phillipa!

Case drew in a few deep breaths and walked away to the other side of the room, vainly trying to separate himself from this maelstrom that was pulling him down.

The damn blaring horn was impatient, relentless, making him crazy.

Roxie tried to move, stand up, but she had the strength of a kitten and she gave up, utterly spent. They heard a car door slam. Case tried to focus, gather himself, but he had to be content with merely standing on his own two legs. His shirt was unbuttoned, his chest was heaving, damp with perspiration.

"Hello... Roxie? Roxie, are you here, darling? We're late sweetie!" Phillipa's clear voice floated up the stairs. "I've been hooting and hooting! Your door's wide open, sweetie!"

Befuddled with lust and adrenaline, both Case and Roxie froze as they heard her ascending the stairs.

In a moment, Phillipa Young was standing in the arched doorway, peering in. She stood rooted, stupefied at the sight that met her eyes. She took in the broken glass on the floor, Roxie, slumped in a chair with her blouse torn and rumpled, her bare breasts heaving, and finally, there was Case McAllister himself, his shirt unbuttoned, his chest dewy with perspiration, and his expression almost as vague and unfocused as Roxie's.

"Good God!" She gaped at the broken glass, then again her eyes traveled from one to the other, her face awed. "Good God," she breathed again reverently, her eyes saucers, her hand to her lips.

"The man's an animal!"

His thinking unclear, Case nonetheless understood that Phillipa had misconstrued the recent events. From nowhere, he began to laugh at the sheer absurdity of it all. On the other side of the room, still seated on the couch, Roxie too joined in, at first with a weak giggle, then with more and more mirth, tinged with hysteria. Laughter kept rolling over him, rendering him weak. For the second time that night.

He walked to the stairs and looked back at Roxie. "You're in good hands. I'll call you." Then he was gone.

Phillipa turned and peered down the stairs at his retreating form, then turned back to the ravaged-looking Roxie.

"God! You lucky, lucky thing!" she said in awe.

It took Case thirty-eight minutes to get home.

Thirty-eight minutes to think about what he almost did.

Almost? Hell, did it matter? He had already betrayed Laine, and his gut churned at the thought. His head and senses swam with images of Roxie and what he wanted to do with her, so, so badly.

At a deserted part of the road, he stopped the car and got out, and shielded by his car from any passing motorist, he unzipped his fly. In seconds, his ejaculation spattered the tire.

There– That was all it took. No need to fuck up his marriage.

Case forced himself to think of his wife, his children, his life. A life that would surely be over if ever he went down that path.

He could never, ever do that to Laine. Never. There was nothing for it–tomorrow he would end it before it began. Get the damn car towed.

In time, he would forget about her.

THE RIGHT THING

THAT SLOW SLIDE

His rounds dragged on forever and foremost in his head was the pressing thought; he had to make that call.

At long last, he was back in his rooms, and for a long while, he sat, his mobile on the desk, taunting him. He could hear Lindy's keyboard through the closed door, and the familiar noise irked him.

He needed silence. He needed to think.

He had to end this ...crazy thing before it started. He didn't even know what had happened last night; why the hell had her husband attacked her?

Her husband. She was also married, goddammit! His gut was a tight knot. Patients were waiting out there, but he needed to phone her first. Case called her, half hoping she wouldn't answer.

His mouth was dry, and his heart was beating too fast. God, I'm like a goddamn kid, he admonished himself, but that didn't stop his heart from lurching when he heard her soft ` Hello'.

"Roxie, it's me, Case." He shifted the phone to the other ear. "Are you alright today? I mean, that joker—"

"—Was Jeremy, come home from the wars. I think perhaps he has PTS, or something, because he's never been like that before. He was very, very drunk," she added, rolling her eyes. Understatement. "I'm meeting him in a short while, then I'll find out what the hell was up with him."

There was a pause.

"How are you?" she asked hesitantly.

Case swallowed. If she just knew the effect she had on him! Jesus.

"I'm fine," He plunged right in, nothing else for it, "Uh... I took advantage last night. Can't even really say I'm sorry, I guess, but, Roxie, this.... This has got to stop." He plunged on, "There's no future in this." He was faltering, the stumbling words belying his emotions.

Roxie stayed silent. The pain in her heart was intense, and she found it impossible to speak.

She had just found him, and now he was telling her it was over! He was married, she understood that, but didn't he know, she would've been content to see him whenever she could?? She had to have some of him, didn't he understand that?

She wanted to explain all of this to him, but the words wouldn't come.

"Roxie? ...Are you still there?" she heard him asking.

"Oh Case," she managed to say at last, a world of heartache in those two words. Then she pressed the kill button, and, as an afterthought, powered her phone off. She saw with a curious detachment her hands were shaking. Through the fog in her head, she could hear Juanita's muffled singing. Juanita was working in the linen closet in the passage.

Roxie went to find her, feeling inexplicably that everything was suddenly urgent. She needed to get away, and get away now, save herself!

Juanita looked up and saw Roxie in the doorway. She looked hard at her young mistress. Something was wrong.

"Juanita, I'm going away for a few days, to—" Roxie hesitated. Juanita waited. Obviously, Roxie wasn't too sure about where she was going??

"—To my brother!"

Juanita waited, there was more, she was certain. Roxie looked upset. What was up?

"Oh, I don't know, but I'm going away. I'll figure it out!" Roxie wailed, giving up. "Look after things while I'm gone." Juanita had stopped folding towels and stood hands on hips, studying her Rox. Roxie was going away, but didn't know where??

"You don't know?? What is wrong?" Juanita demanded.

Roxie's face was bleak. She shrugged. "It doesn't matter, I just need to get away," she said, her voice shaky. She left Juanita to her chores and Juanita heard her bedroom door close. She listened and yes, there it was; Roxie was crying. For sure it was about all that broken glass. What had happened? Men, they were all bastardos!

Vincent had told her that Mr Carter was back, and he also said Roxie's car was gone. And now Roxie was just 'going away?

Juanita crossed herself. There was evil in the air.

She'd hung up on him!

Case felt bleak, almost desperate. His impulse was to rush out there to Cliffside Drive, but that lunatic thought was nipped in the bud by Lindy, whose whole bearing oozed frustration.

"Case, let's get going on these patients or we'll be here all night!" She noticed his glum face, and stopped short;

"What is it? What's wrong?" Immediately her manner changed and her face filled with concern. He looked as though his dog had just died. What was up?

"Nothing. Nothing." he snapped. Lindy flinched at his tone. "Send the first one in." He looked away from her, his attention apparently on something on his desk.

She hesitated, then marched out, her back rigid with indignation. Case gave himself a mental shake. This was bullshit! A tow company could collect the damn car.

He called Roxie again, but still there was no reply. Okay. He would end it personally. As soon as the day was over, he would go there. Sort this out.

* * *

When Case pulled into the driveway at Cliffside Drive, there was no Bentley there. He remembered–the husband had her car.

A terse Juanita answered the door. Roxie was 'out'. Her usually friendly face was closed, guarded.

She kept the door ajar, preferring to peep around it, signaling there was no way she was going to invite him in. "You come for the car?" Her face was inscrutable.

He shook his head. "Is Mrs Carter, uh, Roxie in?"

"She left this afternoon, for the airport" She was eying him with suspicion, and Case felt uneasy. Where was Roxie?

Juanita was deliberating. Was this Mr Broken Glass? He didn't look like a bastardo? Still, there was no telling, these days. "She will be back," she pronounced. She started to close the door.

Great. A mine of information. Case tried to curb his frustration. "When will she be back?" He heard the agitation in his voice.

"She not know. She not certain." The woman looked quite despondent at her words, making Case feel worse. "She very unhappy!" she said balefully. "She just," she waved her hand, "run away!" Her eyes were accusing.

"Where? Where has she gone to?" Case knew he was asking questions he had no business asking.

The housekeeper hesitated, looking concerned. "She not know that either." Then she realized she might be talking to the enemy, and she started to push the door closed.

Case found himself facing a closed door.

So. She was gone. He tried to tell himself that it was just as well, as he made his way to the garage. Good news. He was off the hook. On his way out, he glanced at the battered old Cadillac, trying to rekindle his interest in the car. Better get it towed. He wished he had never laid eyes on it

Roxie took a cab to the hotel where Jeremy was staying and made her way up to his room. He answered the door promptly at her soft knock, wearing the complimentary hotel robe, and now, she was relieved to see, clean-shaven. Hollow-cheeked, and his eyes were still too sunken, but gone was the bum from the night before.

He waved her in, looking more than a little shame faced. Roxie tried to act suitably injured by last night's debacle, but two things prevented her; One, Jeremy's behavior last night was so totally and absolutely out of character, there had to be a reason! Two, she felt so miserable about Case, nothing else really mattered.

They greeted each other awkwardly. He indicated the bar fridge, but she shook her head.

"Order more coffee, perhaps." she said. She kept her sunglasses on. Something to hide behind.

"I'm afraid I've scratched your car," he began ruefully. "I'll pay for the damage. It's not too serious. I was very pissed last night. Let me say again, I'm so sorry," he said, genuinely mortified.

She noticed the hand holding the coffee mug shook slightly, and from the way he was walking, he was obviously still in some pain. As if reading her thoughts, he added, ""Though, I do think your reaction was a bit extreme! What happened to a kick in the balls, like normal people do!" He mustered a little smile, but Roxie bit her lip, ashamed. She removed her sunglasses and her walls went down.

"I'm sorry too. Does it still hurt?" she asked, cringing within. "Jeremy, what the hell was the matter with you, anyway? Who was that, last night?"

He shrugged. Who indeed. His voice flat, Jeremy told her about Larry's death and she listened in shock, her hands reaching out to take up his hand in sympathy.

God, everything was such a mess! Damn!

Jeremy saw tears threatening and he squeezed her hand. He sighed heavily. "You weren't to know. I was so hyped up on uppers and booze, I'm relieved I didn't kill you! Life goes on, I'm told," he said, with a wry grimace. He leaned across and gave his wife a brief, tentative hug.

"Can I come home now?" he asked. "I promise —no more caveman stuff." Roxie hesitated, blinking away tears, thinking of Larry. She knew him, not well, it was true, but she had met his wife a few times. They had a child, she remembered. Oh Christ. That was real. Her and Case? What was that?

Everything, came the reply from her heart. Absolutely everything.

Jeremy was talking to her. Roxie shook herself out of her funk, tried to focus on what he was saying.

Ah. The 'home' thing.

Now was the time to tell him, but it seemed cruel.

Instead, she said, "Yes, sure, but I won't be there. I'm going away for a while." She saw the surprise on his face. She shrugged. "You can use the house for a couple of weeks. But Jeremy—" Bite the bullet, Rox, tell him it's over.

She looked him squarely in the eye, "I want a divorce," she said quietly.

His eyes widened in surprise, but he said nothing, his face inscrutable.

He was in fact wondering why her request didn't surprise him, not at all, really. He was silent for a moment. "I've often wondered why you married me in the first place?" he said softly. "Although I do love you, you know. I always knew that you didn't love me, but I hoped that would come." He grimaced. "We are pals, you know. We always will be, babe. I guess these ...absences of mine haven't really been conducive to nurturing any serious relationship, have they?" He sighed, looked away, then his expression changed, and he was looking at her, his eyes questioning; "But there is someone else. Of that I am sure." He mustered a smile. "So go ahead. Tell me about the doctor."

He had figured it out. Vincent. Roxie felt relieved. This was the Jeremy she knew. She remembered how he was always her rock, her haven. Impulsively, she lifted his hands to her lips and kissed them lightly.

"I wish, wish, wish I could tell you I've been having this torrid affair, but I can't, because," she said, her face glum. "I haven't! Not that that makes me happy, in any way," she said. "He's married. Worse, he's happy with his wife, and I, well, I love him! I hopelessly, and completely utterly fucking love him!"

She sighed, looked wretched. "It was love at first sight, just like the damn movies." She lowered her eyes, avoiding his gaze. "I know it sounds crazy, Jeremy, but I knew he was the one from the first moment I saw him. Can you get that? Crazy, huh?" She slouched back in the easy chair, defeated, the green eyes despondent.

Jeremy was thoughtful. This was an unfamiliar Roxie. Such intensity from his 'always in control' Roxie?

"Love at first sight." He rubbed his chin, thoughtful. "Yes, yes. I've read of such things," he said thoughtfully, "It's well documented. Snow White, Rapunzel, Cinderella. I assure you the stories are endless!"

He smiled at her. "But, of course, as a journalist, I tend not to believe the things I read! However, I'll take your word for it." He was pleased to see a small smile playing on her lips at his foolishness.

"Tell me how you met him. In fact, why don't you tell me the whole story." Jeremy leaned forward, his attention on the unhappy woman before him, his soon-to-be ex-wife.

Faltering at first, her voice strengthening as she relaxed, Roxie told him everything

SCOUTING PARTY

Kevin Daniels studied the man sitting opposite him. The man's mouth was saying one thing, but you just knew he was thinking another!

At first, he hadn't made the connection. The man introduced himself as Jeremy Carter. Then he remembered; Roxie's journo husband! That got Kevin's interest, or was it disinterest? He didn't want to be the lawyer opposing Roxie Tanner. Bad, bad idea.

It also seemed personal, now that they knew each other. There was other business out there, he didn't need this.

However, his curiosity piqued, Kevin waited to hear his story, mentally preparing practiced excuses for declining the business.

Carter's eyes were cool, his rather long face relaxed, the prematurely gray head of hair neatly cut, as if he had just left the barber. Which, in fact, he had. Kevin guessed he couldn't be more than five-nine, maybe five-ten? His visitor sat quietly, his legs crossed, his foot jiggling across his knee, in no apparent hurry at all. He was choosing his words carefully, his fingertips forming a pyramid, all the body language of a man comfortable in his own skin.

Carter's eyes were deceptively sleepy, but Kevin had the feeling he was missing nothing, taking every last thing in. He wondered how this rather ordinary-looking man had bagged someone like the exotic Roxie Tanner.

Kevin repeated himself, keen to be done with this interview. "Well, as I told you on the phone, I, in fact, know your wife. Only casually, but I liked her. She's not what one would expect..." Jeremy Carter seemed to smirk at that, and that bugged Kevin.

Carter looked at the attorney, sizing him up. So this was the best friend of Roxie's new love. What did one 'expect' of a so-called rock star, Carter wondered? Drugs and debauchery, no doubt.

Kevin knew he had sounded gauche, and he flushed. "What I mean is, candidly, I like her and I would hesitate to act in an action against her. Call it a conflict of interest, as it were. Perhaps you should consult another attorney?"

The man smiled agreeably, shrugged. "I was told by Roxie to contact you... "

Roxie told him! Kevin's face showed his surprise.

Carter leaned forward. " I just want it to be over with, if that's what my wife wants?" He looked remarkably unfazed. " I leave for Ukraine in a month, so if I can get all the paperwork done beforehand—? " He leaned back, nonchalant.

Kevin wondered if there was a good prenup? Probably.

"Your wife suggested you use me?? " he asked, surprised. This appeared to be a slam-dunk, except for one small thing-when it came to divorce, there was very seldom a 'slam-fucking-dunk...'

Carter shrugged, nodded.

He tried to picture Roxie married to this man. Was he the dull night sky to offset her shining star? He shrugged inwardly. Some marriages worked better that way.

"My wife has met someone else." There was no rancor, just fact.

Kevin kept his face bland, trying to look neutral, professional. Really? That was a surprise! Well, there's the nub of it. Obviously, the lady had an eye. He remembered how she had sized his pal Case up, like a damn Thanksgiving dinner!

Carter added brusquely, "Oh, that's not the reason. -Perhaps we never should have married in the first place."

For the first time, Kevin saw some emotion, a fleeting resignation in his eyes.

Carter spoke; "Honestly, I think she's comfortable being 'married." He did air quotes with his fingers. "But I guess there's more to marriage than being comfortable??" Carter was matter of fact again. " Anyhow, all I want is to cut the strings. There'll be no hassles, no settlement disputes, or anything of that nature. I've got money of my own, enough for me to retire gracefully, as it were," he said sardonically. He appeared disinterested in the details, and Kevin decided he probably was.

Still, Kevin was thoughtful. Why did this conversation not gel?

It felt like the guy had an agenda?

He resolved to ask her himself, find out.

"Do you intend to obtain a divorce on grounds of infidelity? Do you know who the other man is?" Kevin felt as if he was prying, and that was ridiculous.

"Yes, I do know who the man is," Carter said, scrutinizing Kevin. Nope, the dope knew nothing. "Roxie's a big girl."

Carter too, questioned what perverse streak had made her ask him to come to this guy? Probably wanted the doc to know she was serious, poor bastard.

His face showed nothing. "We're just not...compatible, let's say. Absolutely straightforward, don't you think?"

Kevin found himself agreeing, albeit hesitantly. "It certainly sounds that way," he said. "Who will be acting for your wife?" Everything looked on the level.

"Crompton has been her lawyer from way back, handled her last divorce, so I daresay he knows the routine." he said cynically. He pulled a card out of his pocket. "This is where you can reach me. I'm staying at my wife's house in Cliffside Drive until she gets back in a couple of weeks. I'll be in town for a while, then I leave for Ukraine." He scribbled a number on the back of a card.

Kevin took the card and nodded. Crompton.

It should be a doddle.? Still, he would think about it Talk to Roxie first.

Jeremy extended his hand, smiled politely and left.

Outside on the sidewalk, he looked up the building, glad to be out of there. Roxie was waiting for his call. He was to call her the minute he left Kevin's office! That she was playing a game of sorts, he had no doubt.

He shrugged. Oh well, he had done as she asked.

Kevin would undoubtedly tell his doctor pal that her divorce was going ahead. The trap was set. The question remained, would Roxie get her way?

Jeremy didn't doubt it for a second.

CLOSING DOORS

After Carter left, Kevin tried again to call Case. Case was always busy these days, and the thought plagued him; was there a reason for that, any reason that involved him? Had Case guessed? The mere thought was enough to make him break out in a sweat!

Would those blue eyes blaze with scorn, or worse, disgust.

He sighed. No use avoiding it, he would see if they could schedule a game of racquetball. In fact, he too, never had time lately. Corey was keeping him busy. After Ashley left on her trip, Corey had all but moved in. The genie was well and truly out of the bottle and the genie was dying to meet his friends, Case, Laine...

The people who mattered to Kevin.

His love for Corey had crept up on him, but now, Kevin had no doubt. Corey was truth. With Cory he could be himself. Always a giver to those he loved, for the first time in Kevin's life, the shoe was on the other foot.

And it was a great fit.

He had tried to tell Case about Corey, a few times, in fact, but somehow, the timing was just never right. He frowned. He needed to get this over with. He drummed his fingers on the desk while the phone rang, hoping Case would take his call.

Case was full tilt at Granger, and he hesitated when he saw it was Kevin calling. He decided to answer.

"Case? How are you?"

Always upbeat, that was Kevin.

Case grimaced. What would Kevin say if he knew about Roxie? He'd be horrified.

"I'm good. You?" Case replied, thinking how to answer Kevin's second question. Because I'm screwing around with Roxie Tanner...

He sounds distracted, Kevin thought, but he pressed on. "Join me for a game today, maybe a beer or two after?" He paused, expecting the inevitable excuse. This is me, cheery chump, waiting for the sword to fall.

"Have you time for your pals, in that ordered life of yours?"

He pondered, weighing his options. Laine, ever understanding, was wearying of him being so scarce at home lately. Twice recently, he had spent all night at the hospital. Just this last Monday, he'd operated at two in the morning on a suicide attempt, a guy who had taken a swan dive out of a building and landed on a parked car.

Case sighed. It would be good to win at something. He looked at his watch. Perhaps talk to Kevin about Roxie? He dismissed that idea immediately. That would be insane!

"Can we meet at six-thirty?" he asked.

"You got it." Kevin said, pleased.

He called Laine, bracing himself.

"Don't expect me too early, for dinner tonight," he said, feeling lousy.

"Oh, Case," she said, disappointed. "Are you in theatre?"

He felt shitty. "No, actually. It's just— I never seem to have time for Kevin lately, and he wants me to play racquetball. Do you mind?"

Her reply was instant. "No, of course not."

And she didn't. It was good that he was finding time for Kevin. Perhaps it would all come out and things would return to normal? She bit her lip. Case didn't seem to have much time for Kevin lately, but then again, he didn't seem to have time for anything these days. He was moody and tense, and perhaps a game would do him good.

"No, I don't mind. I'll miss you, but I don't mind," she said, berating herself. She did mind, just a little bit.

Case breathed a sigh of relief. "Thanks, hon. Give the kids a kiss for me. I'll make it up to you."

"You better believe it. Send Kevin my love. Better go, Shana's hair is wet. Love you." The call ended.

Case sat motionless, feeling shitty.

He stood up. He would have to get a move on if he wanted to meet Kevin on time. He stood for a moment, thinking, unseeing, wondering how suddenly, time seemed to be his enemy.

"Sssshit," he muttered to the empty office.

SECRETS

Kevin was already changed and waiting when Case came through the doors. He accompanied Case to the locker rooms to change, prattling all the while about everything and nothing. Case was happy to let Kevin do the talking.

They made their way to the courts, where quietly and clinically, Case took his revenge for his last drubbing at Kevin's hands. At one point, Kevin asked Case if perhaps the punching bag in the gym would not serve him better. Case smiled, but in truth, he felt as if he could do with a spell at the bag. When the game was over, they made their way to the steam rooms.

Kevin's energy seemed to dip and the conversation slowed. They were alone in the steam room, save for one elderly raisin, dosing in the corner. The pair raised their eyebrows at each other in lofty amusement at the wrinkled flesh. Aging was a bitch.

They lolled lazily on the benches, eyes shut, enjoying the steam, the quiet. Case's thoughts turned, as they always did lately, to Roxie.

Kevin, on the other hand, could hear Corey's voice in his head, berating him for his cowardly vacillations. Tell him, tell him not, tell him, tell him not —

He glanced at Case. He would listen for any gap that would allow him to unburden himself. Case had his eyes shut, but far from looking peaceful, he looked almost grim.

Case was allowing his thoughts to wander. He felt increasingly unsettled and agitated about his last conversation with Roxie. He'd thought of phoning a couple of times, but that that was a bad idea. It had been nearly two weeks since that last miserable call, but instead of dissipating, his preoccupation was growing. He told himself it was because there were "loose ends."

He needed to speak to her, and explain.

Explain what? He wasn't quite sure himself. He loved his wife, but what was this ...thing with Roxie? His dick was at the heart of it, plain and simple.

He sighed heavily. It crossed his mind to say something to Kevin, maybe talk it over with him, but he dismissed that idea as crazy. Kevin would freak out, he adored Laine. Nope, bad idea. He shook his head.

"All the sighing and the head-shaking? What's up?"

Case opened his eyes to find Kevin was looking at him, his face curious. He felt sheepish. "Nothing," he muttered. "Work stuff."

Kevin nodded. He stretched out on the bench and propped himself up on his elbow. "You'll never guess who came to see me the other day. Out of the blue." His voice still held some surprise at the mystery caller's visit. "Jeremy Carter."

" Jeremy— ?" Case repeated, knowing instantly who he meant. Carter went to see Kevin?

"Jesus, I don't know how you ever found the brains to graduate! Roxie Carter, as in Tanner?? Kevin hissed, his voice low, aware of the old man in the corner. "Carter is her married name, remember?"

Kevin shook his head and leaned back, rolling his eyes. Honestly, nothing registered with Case!

Case forced himself to portray a nonchalance he was far from feeling. "Oh, yeah. What did he want with you?"

Kevin shrugged. "The usual. One divorce coming up, this time it would appear without the unkind attention of the paparazzi. Apparently, they're both amenable and the good Mr Carter, " Kevin glanced in the direction of the dozing old man in the corner, then satisfied he was either dead or asleep, he continued, "he has no desire to claim any of her not inconsiderable fortune —probably a good prenup—but I gather they mutually want out!" He glanced at the gauge. The heat was too high. The old boy in the corner must be preparing for hell.

Case tried to collect his thoughts. "Did she send him to you?" he asked, incredulous, and Kevin looked at him, affronted.

"Why such disbelief? I'm the best in the business, I like to think!" Kevin retorted, miffed.

Case punched him softly on the arm, a tactile apology. Kevin against Roxie? No, not good.

"No, I don't mean that, it's just— " Case paused, a "WARNING" sign flashing inside his head. He shrugged. "She's like a friend now, is all." He knew he sounded lame. "You say it's mutual?"

"Apparently," Kevin was tuning out. His eyes were closed. "Anyhow, I told him I like the good lady, and if the case was messy, I would rather forgo, but he assured me they're both cool about it. Seems a nice enough guy. I'm told he's a damn good journo," Kevin sat forward again, opening his eyes and massaging his temples gently.

He looked at Case, who was clearly disinterested.

"Anyhow, she gets back next week. I'll chat to her then, make sure we're all pals, on the same page. If she objects, I'll can it. I don't need his business. In fact, something doesn't quite add up, but I guess that will come out in the wash." Kevin said, looking thoughtful. "Anyhow, I need to think about it, hear what she says." He waved his hand, dismissing the matter.

She gets back next week was all Case heard. Kevin seemed to be waiting for a response.

"Oh, so she's away?" he said nonchalantly. You fake bastard, Case McAllister. "How do you know?" he asked, with studied calm. He stood up and busied himself with adjusting the gauge.

Kevin shrugged. "It's in the papers. She's got another huge thing on next week, for some charity or another. I'm thinking of going. He was chewing his bottom lip, his gaze fixed on Case. 'With Corey Hayes, uh, a colleague of mine. I don't think you've met him, but I'd like the two of you to meet. You'll like him," he said, hoping for an opening. But there was the raisin dozing in the corner, and besides, Case was clearly not listening.

Case was telling himself to dial it back. He was being too curious about Roxie. He tried to focus on what Kevin was saying. Something about meeting a friend?

"Don't think so? Name doesn't ring a bell. But maybe soon, see how it goes," he said. His thoughts were racing. She was coming back next week!

He glanced at Kevin.

Strange, Kevin looked quite crushed.

BEWARE THE TIDE

GAL PALS

Laine would have tried the door handle, but her arms were holding the cardboard box containing the old clothes. She leaned forward again, straining to reach the doorbell. She could hardly see over the box to find the bell and fumbled blindly to find the buzzer. As her finger found it, her grip gave way and the box crashed at her feet, spilling the contents all over the floor.

"Crap." Exasperated, she gave the buzzer another angry push and dropped to the floor, gathering up the scattered contents. She was still stuffing old clothes into the box when Josie opened the door. She looked out, then down to find Laine on her knees behind a large cardboard box, stuffing old clothes into the box.

"Hey! At long last, she visits!" Josie stooped to help Laine with a welcoming smile. Laine grunted and stood up, clutching the box. "Where do you want this?" She stepped inside and waited to be instructed.

"Oh. Just put it down and I'll sort it out later." Josie closed the door behind her, her eyes merry. "First, I have to see what I need for my family, then I give the rest to the welfare. Charity begins at home, and all that jazz. So, if you see me mincing around town in your old dress, do be kind."

"As if it would fit!" Lain teased.

They both giggled but Josie was eying her friend. Her normally unflappable Lainie was looking decidedly harassed. Josie turned on her heels and walked down the passage towards the kitchen, calling out behind her, "Come on, come and talk to Auntie Josie over a nice cup of coffee." Laine followed her friend into the kitchen and sat down at the old table.

"What's up?" Josie demanded. "Spill."

Laine shrugged, nonchalant. "How are you, how's the family?"

Josie looked stern. "No small talk. Something's up. Speak!" she demanded.

Laine gave her a wan smile. "Not sure, really," Laine knitted her eyebrows and shook her head.

"Case, I guess. He's so moody lately, and I think it's because of Kevin." There, it was out.

"Kevin?" Josie looked puzzled.

"I was sworn to secrecy, but I have a feeling that this secrecy is eating away at Case, but, I'm not sure—"

"Laine, for God's sake, tell me what's worrying you?"

Slowly, Laine told Josie all, and Josie listened closely, with the appropriate gasps. At the end of the sorry tale, Josie leaned back and sighed. "I always thought those looks on a man just weren't fair!" she said with a half-smile. She spoke again, thinking aloud.

"He doesn't act gay."

"How do gays act?" asked Laine, with a hint of annoyance.

Josie flushed. "You know what I mean! I adore the man, gay or straight, we all do!" She looked thoughtful. "Poor Ash. She must be devastated." She looked confused. "So, you still don't know if Case knows?"

"No. Or even suspects." Laine said, waving her hands helplessly. "There's a few problems he has at the clinic, and he's been working too hard lately, and when he's home, there just seems to be so little time for me," she ended with a wail.

Josie reached over the table and touched her hand gently.

"Laine, don't tell Case, or even ask him if he knows. They go back a long way and Kevin will find the right moment. It's between them." Josie reasoned.

"I know. It's just-well, I'm not used to him being like this!" Laine looked troubled. "He's as loving as ever, but, well, he's really remote, wrapped up in his own little world. They've had a young man in a coma for two weeks now, a botched suicide attempt. He jumped off a damn building and Case has done two ops. He's got kids, apparently, and I think sometimes Case is willing him to wake up," she finished miserably. "Maybe that's what's bothering him??" Her face darkened. "Not to mention that ... That bastard next door," she added fiercely.

Josie shook her head slowly, pondering. She suddenly made up her mind. "Come into the living room. We need a drink!"

"It's two in the afternoon," Laine protested, but obediently she followed Josie out of the kitchen.

"Tell me about Reichmann. What's happening?" Josie asked as she poured them both a glass of wine.

"Oh, that!" Laine waved her hands in exasperation. "He's suing Case. Kevin says it's crap, but the hassle is, that bastard has laid a complaint with the Board of Trustees. Case is in line for tenure, so this might not look too great."

Josie poo-pooed that. "His reputation precedes him."

"Probably. Hopefully, that's enough. Laine looked unconvinced. Her thoughts switched to Judith. "I think Judith is also cheesed off with him because he comes home late these days, and they seldom have any time together. You know how she dotes on him. She's never been crazy about his career. You would think that with his father a doctor, she would have been thrilled, but I always get the feeling she hates his career."

Laine twirled the stem of her empty glass, surprised. She was either thirsty, or this glass had a hole. "That's an interesting thing, that," Josie looked thoughtful. "The whole thing smacks of Freud. You know, mother-son sort of thing. Psyche 101. "

Laine flung a cushion at her and they both giggled. "Do you know what the true meaning of a Freudian slip is?" she asked Laine, smirking.

Laine shook her head.

"It's when you say one thing, and you mean your mother!"

They burst into gales of laughter.

Josie was pleased to hear Laine giggle. "It's so seldom we sit like this and chat, like in the old days. You're so busy with Case, and now with your own career. I'm thrilled you're getting back into showjumping seriously. At the party, Ballard was saying that with Donatés, you might very well be Olympic material!" Josie said, looking chuffed at the notion.

Laine smiled. "Maybe. Showjumping takes two athletes, the horse and the rider. He's certainly good enough, and as for me, I think so." She trailed off. "But it takes time, I could be away for one, maybe two, weeks at a time for the bigger shows. It also takes a huge amount of money, unless you get a sponsorship, so—."

Josie waved away Laine's doubts. "That could happen! Ballard says that horse is already worth a small fortune."

"Yes, he is, now," Laine said, her face pleased. "He'll prove to be the bargain of a lifetime, I am sure." She shrugged. "It's over to me now, I guess, but," she looked troubled, "The kids are still small, and Case is so busy. "

Josie leaned in and hugged her. "Go for it! It's your turn!"

Laine hugged Josie back, smiling. "And leave him to the wolves! Okay, I'll think about it."

"Pah!" Josie was scornful. "He's had nurses throwing themselves at him forever. He doesn't even notice."

Laine was thoughtful. "I guess Judith would always step in, and help with the girls. Car-pool?

"Which reminds me..." Another shadow crossed her face.

"What now?" Josie tucked her knees under her.

Laine looked uncertain. "The little Reichmann girls. Psyche 101— We learned about fear-association, manifestations of the subconscious, warnings of psychological disturbances, that sort of thing. Well," she said, and began to speak.

Josie listened quietly to Laine's appraisal of the Reichmann child. She looked quite grave when Laine had finished. "If it were anyone else, I would say that you are being paranoid, but I know you, and knowing that sonovabitch, so the child may have a problem. But what to do about it, that's the thing. Have you spoken to Mia?"

"Yes. And no. I saw her at a parent's evening a couple of weeks ago. I tried to broach the subject, but she's so damn fierce about those children! And she looked so damn miserable herself. I feel very sorry for her. I think that husband of hers is probably in need of help. Or another damn pounding."

She half-smiled but she was clearly worried. "The little ones come over and play, often, and I worry whether something—!" She grimaced, "God knows what, well, it may rub off on my two! They're too young to know about the world's nasties." She sighed, feeling shallow and selfish.

Josie frowned. "Keep an eye on them, that's all you can do. For now. Speak to Mia and see if you can get her and her husband to consult with someone professional. You don't need to be a shrink to see he needs help."

"Well, I'll try..." But Laine was doubtful. She conjured a mental image of the timid Mia taking on that brute! Somehow she doubted it.

Josie pressed her for a second glass of wine, domestic duties forgotten with the pleasure of talking shop, but Laine hastily declined. Feeling more relaxed than when she arrived, they chatted for a while longer, then Laine took her leave, her mood a lot lighter.

On her way home, she passed the entrance to the Reichmann residence, and she wondered whether she stop this very minute, reverse, drive right up there and tackle Mia!

She decided against it. Mia knew she was there, right next door. Her days were already jam-packed with being a mommy, with Donatés' training, and of course, with being the ever-understanding wife, the last sticking in her craw these days, if she had to be honest.

Laine sighed. Her marriage had always run like a train on track, the route certain, safe. Yet these days, there was this unnerving sense the 'train' could jump the tracks. Was it her? Too much time with Donatés, the circuit? And it wasn't just the physical training. Chunks of her day these days were filling in paperwork for the shows, arranging the horse boxes, months in advance, preparing her Plan B's, fine-tuning all the details, like getting someone to care for Ollie. Someone had to feed the dog. If it was just a weekend, fine, but what if she was away for a couple of weeks at a time?

Case? He might be with her. Judith was invaluable, but how would they cope, when she returned to San Diego? There was a lot to think about.

There was hardly time for anything. Perhaps she was neglecting her husband? She would just make it very clear to Mia that she was here, if she needed help. But a nagging thought persisted.

Perhaps Mia was past helping...

HIDE AND SEEK

Two hundred miles away, at the Lake Serenity Health Spa, Roxie sat alone at the lake's edge, deep in thought, the beauty of the setting sun's reflection on the water lost on her. She had seen it all before, she was an infrequent visitor here, but usually, it was just for a weekend, to charge her batteries.

Seven days of self-imposed exile, and she still felt as if she could damn near record her own country album!

The thought brought a wan smile to her lips.

Perhaps the time had come to go home?

Roxie decided the most courageous thing she had ever done in her life was to run away from Case. She had no qualms about lurking wives. This thing with him, it was her drug, her damn heroin, there was no controlling it.

Then, she met the wife.

Not for long, but long enough to see. There was no avoiding it. He was happy. The damn wife was happy too, and gorgeous, in a toothpaste-commercial sort of way. Better to stand back, leave them to it, she had resolved.

Then, that night. That changed everything.

He felt it too. She knew it.

The sky was darkening, and she stood up, stretching, ready to take a slow walk back to the hotel. The phone vibrated and she fished it out of the deep pocket of her jacket.

It was Charles. For a moment she toyed with ignoring the call, then with a sigh, she answered.

"Hello..."

"Rox, hon, time to come home... " He crossed his fingers and waited for her tirade. But the show was next week, and they needed to rehearse. That damn doctor was behind this, he was certain of that.

To his surprise, there was a brief silence, and then she agreed.

"Don't fret, I'm on my way."

She sounded calm, flat, even. He frowned, then he shrugged.

Whatever.

NO GETTING UNDER

Roxie felt glad to be home. There were traces of Jeremy's recent presence, not least of all a huge bunch of yellow roses and a note telling her he was off to Ukraine for a month or so, maybe more.

He had signed it 'Love Jeremy.' That made her feel better. She saw another message in Juanita's scrawl. She stared at it for a long time. 'Doctor was here. He was looking for you.' She felt her heart leap, then immediately berated herself.

Screw him. She screwed it up angrily and after a moment's deliberation, fished out her phone, a determined look on her face.

Phillipa was delighted to hear from her.

"Roxie, darling. I was so worried about you. If I was the insensitive type, I would say I told you so, I absolutely and positively told you so!" But-" Phillipa said, " turns out I'm the sensitive type, after all, so I'm saying nothing, darling, nothing!!"

Roxie sighed. This was a bad idea.

Phillipa heard the sigh and ignored it. "I must gall and provoke you, my darling, in case there's the teeniest chance you'll change your mind and ... succumb again." Roxie heard sound of ice in a glass. "I'm like your sponsor, darling! —Is there a chance?" she demanded.

"Chance of what? Succumbing? " Roxie replied. "Absolutely not. "

"Liar." Phillipa said. "Bloody liar. Let me be your sponsor darling–every addict needs a sponsor. If you feel yourself ... succumbing, call me, sweetie. I, Phillipa, shall rescue you!"

Roxie could picture Phillipa settling down on the bed or settee, eager to hear all. Well, she would have to wait. Roxie was in no mood to discuss history.

"I'm fine," she said. "What I need is a night on the town. What do you say? Let's go to Duano's or someplace, cause a scandal."

Phillipa was approving. "Now I know you're on the mend. I spoke to

Jeremy, by the way. He tells me you're divorcing the poor pet.

Roxie winced. "Let's not get into my boring life," she pleaded.

"No problem. But methinks that had there been just the teeniest, weensiest bit of, let us say, ...um, rumpity-pumpyity between you and the good doctor, you'd be a happier woman! But there, I've promised not to say I told you so, so, of course, I won't! "

Roxie wondered whether to hang up.

Phillipa went on. "Actually, I know the perfect man for you, as it happens, and I'm going to arrange a wonderful evening. I'll be with divine old Pottie. That man is so good to me," she murmured, admiring the new Tiffany bracelet on her arm.

"Pottie' was Andrew Potts, an industrialist billionaire from Toronto. Phillipa treated him like a pet Corgi, as she did most of her men-friends.

"Please don't fix me up with a date," Roxie warned. "I'm off romance in a big way. I intend to bury myself in my career."

"Nonsense. A girl needs a shoulder to cry on. And if you don't want to cry, men have other uses, and what with you coming home from the wilderness and all...."

"Phillipa,-for God's sake! Let's just go out and have a night on the town. Bring Pottie, but I'll be rude to any other person! Do we have a deal?" Roxie was fast losing enthusiasm.

"Alright, darling, whatever you say. Meet us at Duano's at around ten. Phillipa rolled her eyes. Failed relationships were too, too draining.

"And darling Roxie, wear a good mood, there's a darling! Broken hearts are boring, darling!"

She hung up before Roxie could reply.

GUT FEELING

Laine waited patiently as the four little girls sorted themselves out.

Mia sat quietly behind the wheel, avoiding Laine's eyes.

Laine frowned, thoughtful. It was Mia's turn to car-pool and her usually friendly albeit timid neighbor was rather strained with her of late, and frankly, Laine felt disinclined to breach the gap. She couldn't help feeling that the ridiculous board hearing was part of the reason for Case's moodiness lately.

She noticed that little Kira was taking no part in the high jinks of the other three. The child was sitting back and staring out the window, lost in a world of her own. Her heart softened.

She leaned in at the window. "Hello, Kira. How are you, hon?" She gave the child a warm smile, but the grave little face didn't change. The child looked away.

"She's well, thank you," Mia answered for her daughter.

But something in the demeanor of the child made Laine's heart catch. Kira looked so solemn, so tiny, as if she were keeping a space around her no one should breach. Hesitantly, Laine withdrew her head and turned to Mia, who was drumming her fingers in a nervous tattoo on the steering wheel.

"Is she alright, Mia? I mean, she looks a bit ...listless?" Laine asked, keeping her voice low. She frowned , remembering the drawing.

"She's fine!" Mia said defensively. Laine's face peering in at her looked distorted and out of focus. Laine raised her eyebrows a fraction at the other woman's tone. She eyed Mia. Mia looked too pale. No, actually, quite ashen.

"Mia? Mia, are you okay? You look very pale." God, she looks about to pass out at the wheel. There were faint beads of perspiration on Mia's top lip. "I think you better come inside, drink some water. You look dreadful." Determined, Laine opened the car door and put her hand under Mia's arm to assist her out of the car.

Mia was feeling too nauseous to offer resistance. "I'm a nuisance," she said weakly, but she allowed Laine to help her out of the car and lead her inside. The other three children stopped their play and looked on, wide-eyed.

Kira watched her mother stumbling out of the car, unmoved.

"Go into the kitchen, you girls! You too, Kira!" Laine instructed,

Kira ignored her, but Laine's attention was wholly taken up by her now near-swooning neighbor. She led the woman inside, then sat her down in the living room. Laine left her lolling drunkenly in Case's favorite chair and went off to fetch some water. In the kitchen, she explained briefly to Judith that Mia was ill, and asked her to keep an eye on the girls. She returned quickly to the lounge with a glass of water.

Mia drank gratefully, and slowly, some of the color came back into her cheeks. An image flashed through Laine's head, and she was reminded of, again, a fainting Mia, just weeks ago.

Mia said nothing, and Laine let her catch her breath, fretting. This woman could drive kids no longer, that was for sure! Mia Reichmann looked really ill. Concerned, Laine sat down on the sofa and waited quietly until she thought Mia's dizzy spell had passed. Then she spoke; "Mia, have you seen a doctor?"

Mia hesitated, and looked evasive. If only she could tell someone...

"Mia," Laine probed gently.

"No. I keep meaning to, but then I put it off... I think I am afraid of doctors, really."

"Afraid?" Laine looked nonplussed. "Why?"

Mia shrugged. "Just crazy, I guess." Her accent seemed broader than usual. "My mother was a sickly woman, the medicines the doctors gave her always seemed to make her worse. Then they took her away. But I suppose that was a long time ago, and things are different now, more modern."

Laine nodded. "I would say so, yes. What's wrong? Are you having dizzy spells? It could be something as simple as low blood pressure. They can fix that in a heartbeat!"

Mia looked shame faced. "I think I need a, a, how do you say, a doctor who is just for women."

Laine nodded. "A gynecologist. That's what you mean. I have an excellent one. He's a colleague of Case's at Granger Clinic. Let me phone right now and fix an appointment for you. Please. You need to go see him." She added with sudden insight; " The girls need you to be well!"

Mia nodded at that. "Thank you." She looked too sick to argue, and Laine stood up and went through to the kitchen, found her phone and called her doctor. Dr Sarazin was pleased to hear from her, and as a favor, he agreed to see Mia the very next day. He would rearrange his schedule.

Laine returned to the living room, pleased.

"He's agreed to see you tomorrow. Two o'clock. Will you do that? I'll fetch the children, of course!" Laine hesitated, thinking.

"Is there a problem?" Mia asked.

"Not really, but I wonder if perhaps Kira shouldn't have a check-up too? I think that child is too listless. Maybe it's nothing, but there's no harm in being sure. I could even ask Case to look at her, if you like."

Mia shook her head. "No, that I wouldn't ask of you. Perhaps a special doctor for children, but there is nothing wrong, I'm sure. She is sensitive and I am sure she understands, Rudolf, and I, we are not—good." She looked down. "You know, with each other." She gestured, fluttering her hands helplessly, embarrassed. "The child sees..."

Laine nodded. It could be exactly that. What a burden for a kid!

"She is losing all her puppy fat, that's why she looks thin. She says it's evil to be fat. I think maybe the children tease her a little at school?" Mia said, looking unhappy at the idea.

Evil to be fat. The words played on Laine's mind, and again that damn drawing sprang into her head. She shook her head involuntarily, becoming aware of Mia's stare. "Sorry. It's just ... Sometimes I tend to analyze too much. It's a curious choice of words, evil to be fat."

Mia wasn't listening. She desperately wanted to get home and lie down. Assuring Laine she was feeling much better, a hesitant Laine allowed her to drive away. insisting that until Mia was better, she would take the kids. Mia looked relieved at the suggestion and acquiesced without any argument. She watched the car disappear, troubled.

Laine just couldn't shake the nagging thought that there was definitely something amiss with Kira.

POINTLESS

"Oh crap, Phillipa, you didn't." Roxie looked at an unrepentant Phillipa in exasperation.

"I did. And I'm not sorry. The man is a hunk! You need distraction! He's single, rich and straight. That's a rare combination. Not to mention he's quite good-looking, what more do you want?"

Roxie didn't answer. Steve was pleasant, it was true. They had enjoyed a pleasant lunch at Sparrows on Sunday, and he hadn't made a single pass or even overture–so far. In fact, the IT geek was almost pleasant company.

Phillipa eyed her, her face thoughtful.

"It's that macho thing he lacks, isn't it? I remember how your place looked when I found you two—" She sniggered. She knew actual story now, although she pretended not to believe it. "Well, darling, simply tell Steve you want the caveman approach, and he'll oblige you with a few good slaps!" She departed, chortling.

Roxie gaped at her retreating back. A few light sla—! She started protesting, then gave up.

"What's up, you look lost in a world of your own. Are you nervous? You're nearly on?" Charles appeared in the doorway. He walked towards her, rubbing his hands in glee. "So, all's well out there. Terrific audience. He sounded positively smug. "Play to the center right, the Press are out in force tonight." He sighed. He could see she wasn't listening.

Roxie nodded absently. Was Charles saying something?

I wonder what he's doing right now.

CAUGHT

SLICK

The show went well. Sensual, and in complete control of her audience, Roxie seemed to exude pent-up energy on stage that was palpable, and the crowd lapped it up. Charles spent a moment wondering; what was the difference between this show and the last.

It came to him.

Slick. That was the difference. The last show, she had sung her damn heart out, passionate and connected, this one was pure professionalism, from start to finish. Her voice and body had performed like a well-tuned machine, none of the passion of a few weeks ago, and the audience, they lapped it up. But he, Charles, he knew her too well...

Heart and soul, that was Rox, and tonight, the soul was missing.

Charles shrugged. He was sure only two people in the world knew that, himself and Roxie. Afterwards, he congratulated her, and she thanked him, her eyes holding his for a second, daring him to criticize. But Charles kept his face bland, and she turned away with an imperceptible shrug. If he was happy...

Manning was happy. The crowd loved her and that was what mattered. She would get over her 'unhappiness' and life would go on, and he, for one, would breathe a sigh of relief. Charles Manning felt the simmering energy she exuded of late, and God knows, energy was a positive thing, but a sixth sense prompted him to handle her these days with kid gloves, which was rather tedious.

But it would pass. Music was her first love, not any damn doctor.

In the main dressing room, amidst the usual backslapping and sniping, Roxie was detached, aloof. She was thinking of the last time. He had been here, right here, even danced with her. If she closed her eyes she could feel him holding her. God, if only she didn't feel so cheated.

"Roxie? Roxie?" Roxie opened her eyes to see Steve smiling at her. "What can I say? You were great. Fantastic." He did a little jig and pranced backwards, showing jazz-hands, lauding her, a beaming, blonde Al Jolson. Charles was offering a brimming champagne glass, but she hesitated. Everything was too noisy and too loud tonight. She yearned for home and bed.

"C'mon. This is your night!" Steve coaxed. He took the glass from Charles, who discreetly slipped away, but not before he had cleared the room. His star would join them in a few minutes. Eagerly, Steve pressed her to drink up, celebrate! After a moment's hesitation, she accepted. The champagne was icy and tasteless. It was too damn hot in here. She looked at the Silicon Valley wunderkind, finding a practiced smile He looked so damn keen. Encouraged by her smile, unmindful of her silence, Steve Davies wondered if his moment had come. She looked as if she needed to be rescued.

"Do you want to leave? We can collect your car in the morning." His meaning was clear.

Roxie thought about it. She tried to think about what sleeping with Steve would be like. Energetic, no doubt. Everything about the man was energetic. He was pleasant enough and he would hold her close and make love to her, and it would be passable. She could close her eyes and try not to think of anything but her own gratification.

Perhaps—just for a while—he would ease this dull ache inside of her? Impulsively she made her mind up.

"I'll follow you," she said. Not to leave her car. Bad idea. Any surrender would be on her terms.

Pleased, he leaned forward and kissed her lightly on the forehead. "Good.-We can go to your home if you like?"

Take him home? God no. She shook her head firmly.

"Your place is fine. Let's go." She quaffed the champagne with the enthusiasm of a child drinking medicine, and he took the empty glass from her and placed it on a nearby table. He leaned in to kiss her but she turned her head away, and he had to be content with a cheek.

"I'll see you at your place. I need to have a word with the band. You go on ahead." He looked disappointed for the briefest moment, but then, with a mental shake, he was himself again, hearty and agreeable. In a moment he was gone.

When the valet handed her the keys, she toyed briefly with the idea of driving straight home. Running away. But the cards had been dealt, and life needed to go on.

A dogged Roxie found herself pulling up outside his apartment block. She handed the keys to a fawning concierge and stepped into the elevator, her heart sinking lower as the elevator went higher. When it stopped, Roxie stepped into the penthouse foyer. It was predictably beautiful. The decorators had obviously had a field day, and her eyes searched in vain for any traces of the man himself. There were none, except a silver-framed photograph of an elderly couple. Roxie guessed they had to be Steve's parents, Mr and Mrs Energetic, Senior.

She sighed inwardly and summoned a bright smile when she saw him approaching, a delighted smile on his face.

"Are you weary, babe?" he asked solicitously, taking her jacket with one hand, and leading her to the patio with its stunning view over downtown LA.

"I'll get you a drink," he murmured, brushing her ear in a light kiss. He issued an instruction to an invisible ear in the room, and the music changed. Norah Jones. Roxie found herself smiling–this boy had it all figured out!

The music was soft and soothing.

And yet, why this overwhelming urge to scream. He was so damn predictable; it was making her crazy. She pushed her fickle and unkind thoughts away, telling herself that this ...tryst was necessary. Anti-Case medicine.

She looked around her, feeling like an actor in a poorly staged play.

He was back in moments, holding a martini. She took it gratefully, wondering how long they would have to make small talk. Where were the bedrooms?

Her perfunctory glance in the direction of the living quarters was not lost on Steve. He circled his arms around her waist and pulled her to him. Inwardly, Roxie winced. Show-time. She lifted the glass so as not to spill her drink and stood still, unbending, while he moved in to kiss her. She felt his mouth close on hers, delicate and tentative, his cologne too pungent.

Suddenly she pulled away, knowing that this was all bullshit, a giant, giant mistake. Huge. Her martini slopped on the tiled floor, and she looked down at the mess in dismay.

"Oh shit! I'm sorry." Steve waved away her apologies, but Roxie was done. "This is no good," she said woefully.

Steve smiled at her doleful countenance, hiding his disappointment. "I'm nuts about you. Let me help you forget him. I can see there is a 'him', somewhere, " he said, a half-smile lifting his mouth. She looked at him blankly, then, after a moment, she smiled back.

This time, her smile was genuine.

"Can you get them to fetch my car?" she asked, all indecision gone.

He sighed. He could see from her face it was pointless to argue. He walked towards the intercom on the wall. He instructed the concierge to get her car.

A subdued Roxie had little to say as he escorted her downstairs and walked her to the driver's door of her car. She kissed him lightly on the cheek, aware of the concierge looking discreetly the other way.

On the way home, Roxie floored the gas pedal, reckless and miserable. It had to get better, she told herself miserably.

It just had to!

DEFEAT

Back in his rooms, Case planned for the first operation on the Cahill child for the following Wednesday, and then put in a call to Morris. "I've had a look at the Cahill boy, he's coming along famously. I think he's ready for the first operation. I've booked OR three next week on Wednesday at 2 p.m. Can you assist? This is going to be tricky..."

"I remember. He's the one with the odd tissue type. No sweat, count me in..." There was silence while Morris checked his schedule. "I have something on but I'll see if I can shift it," he said.

Case's eyes fell on the calendar.

November 6th. Roxie was performing tonight at the benefit concert. Kevin was going with some-or-another Roxie Tanner fan.

Corey somebody or another?

He fought the temptation to call her. And say what? She obviously didn't want to see him.

He told himself it was a good thing. There seemed to be reminders of her everywhere, on posters, in the papers, and the other day he heard her new song on the radio.

He switched off the radio off before it ended.

Time to have his hair cut. Laine was threatening blows if he didn't.

At the barber's, he picked up a tattle magazine with Roxie's face on the cover. Compelled, he found himself reading the article. Rumor had it she was getting a divorce, and was dating a tech billionaire. They had been spotted and there it was, a smiling Roxie next to a blonde guy who needed ears just to stop his goddamn grin wrapping around his head!

He tossed the magazine down in disgust, muttered that his hair was still too long, and left.

He felt as if he were drowning. This shit with Roxie was an obsession.

Laine was becoming agitated lately. Oh, she was her usual sweet self, but for sure, she sensed something was amiss. Thank God, she put it down to the hearing and too many patients. She tried to be as supportive as possible, which made him feel even worse. Fortunately, she was also training hard for the Seattle Grand Prix preliminaries and apparently, Donatés was living up to the promise he had shown.

In all, Case felt dejected. He had never been unfaithful to his wife, never even come close, and these sudden feelings from nowhere for another woman had thrown him, left him in a cloud of gloom.

He knew Laine would never, never forgive him if he betrayed her. And his children, they were so happy in their world. He had grown up without a father.-And fatherless was what they would be if he ever betrayed his wife. An alien sense of despair engulfed him, and impulsively he reached for his mobile to call his wife, needing to hear her voice, banish these treacherous thoughts.

"Hi hon, how's things? How you doing?" Case could picture her, hair swept up in a loose knot, untamed strands of hair falling across her face.

"Case, honey? What's up?" Warm and caring. Always. Damn.

"You sound tired. Will you be home soon? I miss you," she added, feeling a little forlorn.

"Sure. Had my hair cut, and I'm on my way home. I just called to say I love you."

"My, my, this is a pleasant surprise." Her voice was soft, affectionate. "I think I'll fix you something special??" Case felt some of the tension leave him. Suddenly, his beeper sounded. Carella.

"Fuck! " He muttered, under his breath. "Honey, I have to get back to the hospital. It has to be Carella. I'll call you later." He hung up.

Damn it to hell. That meant he would be late. Laine rolled her eyes at the silence, pouting. Damn!

Case worked too hard. Tonight, she would do the whole works. Maybe he would be too tired, but she would make him untired, come hell or high water

MORE DEFEAT

Case stood still while the theatre nurse wiped the perspiration from his face. The overhead lights gave off their own heat, but Case knew that had the theatre been freezing, he would still be sweating blood. This was the third operation on Carella, and he knew it was make or break time.

The man's system wouldn't take much more. He had gone into cardiac arrest thirty minutes ago, but yet again, the surgeons pulled him back from the edge. Case scowled. The man was a leaky boat, and at regular intervals, a gage, or warning monitor beep, would alert them to a new leak...

So far, they were winning, but only just.

At last, Case stepped back and motioned to the assisting surgeon to close up. He made his way through to the scrub room, where he peeled off his gloves and mask and gratefully washed his hands and face. He let the cold tap run and turned his face into the icy stream. He glanced at his watch. It was just after eleven. Laine would be asleep. Outside, in the waiting area, he wasn't surprised to see the woman he now knew to be Carella's mother. She hardly relented in her vigil at her son's side. She appeared somehow older than when Case had last seen her, and he was silent for a moment, as he stood before her, mentally preparing his words.

Her eyes were rheumy, glistening with tears she held in check.

Case lowered himself into a chair next to her, and took up her hand in both of his. Her hand was dappled with liver spots, the skin dry and too loose. They had once been hands that were younger, fuller, stronger, but now, like the life force in her son, they were shrinking.

He stifled his sigh. This was the part he hated.

"We've done everything, everything that it is possible to do," he said softly. Her hand looked so tiny in his hand, he thought. They sat, saying nothing, for a few long moments, their silence broken by the clattering of distant meal trolleys, and purposeful footsteps clatters echoing in the long, scrubbed corridor.

He stood up. Time to go, but her face was despairing, and she was talking, softly, more to herself than to him.

She nodded, her eyes understanding.

She reached into her purse, looking for her phone.

"I will call the priest. In case—" she said, almost apologetically. Then she turned and walked away.

Case gazed after her, hating to see her bowed shoulders. He got to his feet. There was nothing more he could say or do. He needed coffee.

The doctor's lounge was deserted, and some inconsiderate bastard had switched the coffee machine off. The recliners in the lounge were worn and rather shabby, but they were comfortable, the lighting was muted and a TV screen flickered, the sound off. He switched the TV off, there was no one there but him. He switched the coffee machine on. While it was heating up, he called home. After a couple of rings, Laine's voice came on, croaky with sleep. "Hello?"

"It's me, hon. I've just come out of the theatre, and I'll spend the night here. The next few hours are make or break. I'll see you for breakfast."

"Oh, honey..." He could hear her concern, then she sighed. "Okay, I'll be waiting. Everything's fine here. I love you. You've tried your best," she added, sensing his dejection.

"Yeah, I guess so. Sleep tight, honey." He hung up, weary. He could do with a Scotch to bolster the coffee. He sprawled out in a comfortable chair next to the machine and closed his eyes. He felt mentally and physically exhausted. The coffee machine gave a little belch to indicate the water was boiling. He ignored it and tried to think if there was anything they might have missed with Carella. No, not at all.

It was over to Carella now.

As surely as a compass needle points North, so his mind drifted to Roxie. She had her show tonight, it was probably nearly finished by now. He wondered if they held a party after every show. Would she be on her own, or —

Damn! He ran his fingers through his hair, wanting to ease the tightness around his skull.

The unblinking red eye of the coffee machine grabbed his attention and gratefully, he poured himself a coffee, black with three sugars. He sipped it slowly and felt better. He settled back in the chair again, kicked up the footrest, and fell into a fitful doze.

It seemed to Case he had no sooner nodded off than his pager was calling him rudely into wakefulness. Another Code Blue in I.C.U.

Carella.

He was instantly awake. The clock on the wall said five after midnight. He couldn't have been asleep for more than fifteen minutes.

When he burst through the swing door of ICU 13, it was to find the staff already in motion. It was a well-choreographed dance, and they knew their steps well. Jennings already had the electro-cardiogram hooked up and was running a strip. -No rhythm, cardiac asystole.

They were losing the father of three.

"Charge the paddles, let's buzz him," Case snapped. "Clear the bed–stop ventilating." He took the paddles and applied them to Carella's chest. The discharge button, sent a wave of electrical charge through the inert body which heaved in a sudden responsive jerk. Everyone's eyes turned hopefully to the electrocardiogram. Flat line. He glanced at Jennings, who was holding Carella's limp wrist, feeling for any pulse. The intern shook his head, timid at his meager role in this rescue.

"Increase the voltage to 300," ordered Case.

Eleven minutes after entering the ward, Case stepped back and shook his head. Like toys winding down, everyone slowly stopped what he or she was doing. Only the inexperienced Jennings gazed expectantly at Case, willing him to pull another ace from his sleeve, unfamiliar with any ratios of victories or defeats, and a little disbelieving that they, the healers of the sick, had lost. Then he looked away, his shoulders slumped, shaking his head.

Case pulled himself together with an effort. Fuck.

They had tried everything.

He had put in nearly eleven hours of theatre time on this shell that had once been Antonio Carella, and the hospital staff hundreds of hours. The man had seen fit to take his own life and despite their best efforts to thwart him, he had succeeded.

Case felt an unreasonable anger, cheated, as if he had lost an opportunity to personally blast the man for his damn thoughtlessness in diving out of a seventh-floor window! He hadn't noticed the man's mother before, but now he saw her in the doorway, and he was relieved to see she was in the company of a priest. The priest looked too young and inexperienced, but his face was calm. He knew what he was there for.

Good. Case approached her, his emotions numbed in the aftermath of this defeat.

He began to speak, wanted to explain how they had tried everything, but she touched his arm, and squared her shoulders. The moment she dreaded had come, and she would not be found wanting. She sought to console this crestfallen doctor, and she spoke with surprising strength.

"You did all you could, I'm sure. I know this. Can I see him now?" She stood at the threshold, waiting to be allowed in. At the sight of her inert son, her voice wavered. He looked at the priest who nodded at Case's unspoken question. She was okay to say farewell to her son.

"For a couple of minutes. We have to take him away." Case put his hand on the woman's stooped shoulders.

She nodded, then guided by the priest, she made her way into the ward.

Case walked through the near- empty corridors of the hospital, out the door and along the walkway towards the deserted doctors' rooms. He unlocked the door to his rooms and flicked the light switch on. He went straight to a filing cabinet and fished out an almost untouched bottle of bourbon. He poured himself a stiff shot, sipping it slowly, savoring the burn, glad of the absolute quiet.

The wall- clock indicated it was ten to one, for those who were still alive.

Jumbled images flitted through his head. Laine, bending over the bath on the night of his birthday, the old Deville on the side of the road, Roxie, trembling and afraid in his arms. Kevin, teasing him, he was the prince—. A kaleidoscope, until they all faded, and there was just one face.

It was no use. He stood up.

He had to go.

SURRENDER

He couldn't tell if she was home or not. He could see through the gate the garage doors were closed. It was one-twenty-three in the morning. He could see a faint light burning somewhere within the house. Now that he was actually here, on her doorstep, he could feel his stomach squeezed by some giant powerful hand, and his nerve ends quivered. What the fuck was he doing here?

He stood with his hands jammed in his pockets, struggling, knowing this was the point of no return. But there was no going back. He pressed the buzzer. There was a long silence, and he pressed the buzzer again. She was probably out. And that would be a good thing, he told himself.

Upstairs, reclining in the bath, Roxie's eyes widened in surprise. It must be near two, who could be calling on her at this hour? She frowned. Steve. He had thought twice about his gentlemanly behavior and had decided to give it one last try. Damn him. Idiot! Hastily she climbed out of the copper oval bath, and dripping water onto a heated floor, shrugged on a pale blue toweling robe, tying it carelessly at the waist.

To hell with this! She went into the landing and flicked the switch to activate the gate light, then stared at the closed-circuit TV. It was a man alright, standing with his back to the camera mounted above his head, hands on his hips, looking out towards the ocean.

Roxie's mouth went dry. From any angle, she would recognize that cropped, almost untidy hair. He appeared unaware of the camera, and she pushed the button to release the gate lock, her hand trembling. Case heard the lock click back, and he pushed the gate open and walked towards the front door. She was home. As he approached the front door, he heard the click of the electronic door release.

He pushed the door open and stood hesitantly in the hallway, his heart pounding. He closed the door behind him.

What could he say? What the hell was he doing here, at this time of night?

There was a light at the top of the stairs that led to her living room and he walked slowly to the foot of the stairs. His heart was that giant, drum that leads the parades, and he was doomed.

He was almost at the top of the stairs when he sensed her. He paused and looked up.

She was standing there, watching him, waiting for him. Her robe was pulled loosely around her, and her eyes, those incredible green eyes, were searching his face.

God, she was beautiful. It was inevitable. He was finally here, standing before her, her presence washing over him, quelling all the doubts.

"I want—" ...he tried to speak, his voice sounding thick, hoarse. Roxie was staring back at him. He was here. Finally, finally here. "I know what you want," she said softly, and held out her hand.

The touch was seismic, yet still they stood apart, allowing the contact to sear through them, burn them, brand them. Fuse them as one.

She turned and he followed her into the bedroom. It was almost in darkness, save for a muted light from the adjoining bathroom, where the door stood ajar. She led him to her bed, then turned to him.

Case closed his eyes and inhaled her, not touching her, feeling her removing his jacket. There was no resisting her. He knew he was lost.

Slowly, she undid the buttons of his shirt, one by one. First jacket, then shirt fell in a careless heap on the floor. He stood immobile, content for the moment to let her have control. Her breath was coming in short, ragged pants and he knew her ache matched his own. Her hand moved to his belt, but swiftly, he stopped her hand. She was his now.

He pulled the robe from her body, and pushed her gently onto her back, savoring every inch of her. It was happening, and he was in no hurry. Roxie lay back, passive, watching him loosen his belt, step out of his trousers, his socks.

Their eyes devoured the other's perfection. There was nothing to disappoint. The desire in his eyes was as tangible as his erection, and she closed her eyes, her legs wrapping around him as she reached up, impatient now, pulling him onto her, desperate to feel him deep, deep inside of her.

She felt his probing, his toying with her. and her first orgasm broke over her, impatient, shuddering. But she wanted him inside her, dammit, why was he tormenting her. Hungry impatient lips sought his mouth, and at last, at last she felt him claim her, rough, almost uncaring, driving her into a frenzied writhing underneath him. Roxie screamed aloud in her ecstasy, again and again, all dignity abandoned as she begged him to take her yet again, offering any and every part of herself to him.

Case had waited long, and he took his time, exploring her, taunting her, inexplicably harsh in his thrusts, driving her to a pinnacle she had never thought she would ever find.

For him, it was about possession, conquest, and it would be absolute.

When she thought she could, would surely die, he was done, and she lay panting beneath him, utterly spent.

Yet it seemed to take mere minutes, and he was entering her again, uncaring and carnal, sure of his control over her, confident of bringing her to life again. There seemed to be almost an anger with each thrust, as he roughly sought his own release. His climax that swept through them, an erotic force that left them both wet and clinging to each other, survivors in a storm, exhausted and spent.

Case rolled away from her, panting. It was done.

She was his.

There was no going back.

IN THE WEB

Four hours later, Case found himself in his car and driving home, as if the world hadn't stopped, and everything was still the same. He should have felt exhausted, but instead, he felt alive, intoxicated in the aftermath of those stolen hours with Roxie.

Not a lot had been said.

There would be another time for speaking.

Case had heard her whispering 'I love you' over and over again, and he wondered that such words could come so easily to her lips, so soon. Was this love?

Where to from here?

His mind felt ready to explode with the enormity of it all. When he stopped outside the old house, parking between Laine's car and the old bike, he felt as if he was back in another world, a world which was sleepy and sane and familiar. And lost to him.

A world where he had squandered his right to be there....

The October air was sharp and crisp. Dawn was breaking, normally so beautiful and soothing, but now the curtain was going up, it was time to act his part!

He let himself into the sleeping household and made his way upstairs. In the bedroom, Laine's huddled form under the blankets looked strangely defenseless. She half-stirred, then went back to sleep. Case went through to the bathroom and turned on the shower faucets to the maximum, peeling his clothes off and wondering whether anything of Roxie clung to him? His senses still filled with her, he stepped into the shower and gave himself up to the memory of the past four hours. Showered and replenished, Case wrapped a towel around his waist and went through to the bedroom.

Laine was awake, eying him, stretching languidly, like a cat. "Hello, my darling, an all-nighter?" She pouted; "Come, climb in with me for five minutes before the household wakes up." Suddenly she was looked at him keenly, tilting her head to her shoulder, examining him with narrowed eyes, and for a minute his heart stopped.

She could tell!

"I like it," she said at last. "Your hair looks good, better!"

Case let his breath out slowly. The haircut! She patted the bed beside her. She looked warm and familiar. He felt a violent, nauseating tide of guilt, but he pushed it back. He padded over to her, and sat down next to her, dismissing her invitation into the bed. He reached out and drew her close. Gently, he stroked her hair, sickened with remorse.

"How was it at the hospital?" She nuzzled into his neck.

"Carella died." There was no point in saying more.

"Oh Case," she said, distressed. "Oh Case." He held her, quiet, tense, his thoughts a maelstrom of recriminations and guilt, his heart beating faster when images of Roxie writhing underneath him, came to the fore, unwanted, ...unstoppable. I think I'm going crazy. Here I am, this is me, holding my wife close, loving the feel of her, and an hour or so ago I was in Roxie's bed, and God help me, I don't regret it. Laine's holding me like I'm some kind of hero, Mrs Carella looked at me like I'm a God and Roxie— !

Yet, my face is normal, nobody can see what a shit I am. This is the mother of my children, she would go through hell and die for me, but if she finds out I have been unfaithful then I will lose her, and maybe my kids-and I want Roxie more than anything.

"Case, don't look so grim, my darling. You know you did all you could." Laine stroked his face, enjoying the feel of his stubble against her fingers, wanting to banish the anguish she could see on his face.

But I am angry, he thought miserably, because I am about to deceive you and I know I will see her again.

Laine cupped his face in her hands, her eyes perturbed. "Darling, what is it? You look so serious and angry. What is it, tell me?" Her face was troubled, and Case looked at her for a long moment, then kissed her, a long, slow, loving kiss.

"I love you," he said, and he meant it with all of his heart.

She leaned back on the pillow, breathless. "I should say so, after a kiss like that. And I love you too, my precious baby!" She pinched his cheeks in her fingers and waggled his face playfully from side to side, her mouth a moue.

"Now, do you want some breakfast, or do you want some breakfast." She gave him a sultry wink and rubbed her breasts invitingly. He smiled at her.

"No time for a big breakfast, so I'll settle for something to eat." The fake playfulness in his voice amazed him. How easy this duplicity was.

"Okay. But tonight, I demand my rights," she teased. She sat up, wriggling her feet into her slippers.

"I need to shave, then I'll see you in the kitchen." He fell back on the bed and stared up at the ceiling, hearing her open the closet for her dressing gown. With his eyes shut, he knew she would be running a hasty brush through her hair and sweeping it up into a loose knot on top of her head. He lay there, staring at the ceiling, listening to her humming softly, happy.

Unafraid.

SLIPPERY SLOPING

SWALLOW WITH WATER

In the household next door the Reichmanns were also up early. Rudolf liked to be gone by seven. In the kitchen, Mia went about her usual breakfast chores, but she was perspiring heavily, and she felt feverish. The breakfast smell of frying eggs and bacon was making her quite nauseous. Rudolf insisted on his full breakfast every morning. There were seldom any variations. Bacon, three eggs, fried tomato, three pieces of toast.

Mia pulled her wrap closer and shivered, her eyes watching the swirls of an early morning fog dancing in a smoky cloud over the grass. She needed to think about spectacles, her eyes were deteriorating at a remarkable rate.

God, the smell of food nauseated her. Even the aroma of his coffee made her queasy.

Lately, she could barely face the thought of food.

Mia knew she was ill. Three weeks ago she had gone to that doctor, who had prodded and poked her and taken a scraping of her insides. She had given him a urine sample, just as Laine instructed her beforehand. There was something about the doctor that unnerved her. Oh, he had been friendly, quite chatty in fact, ignoring her silences, but as the consultation continued, his chatter seemed to wane. He stopped talking and became quiet. When he was finally done, she was glad to escape, stumbling past the knees of other patients waiting in his reception, aware of their curious glances.

She hurried to the drugstore, exchanged shy pleasantries while the script was filled. A great believer in tonics, Mia bought a large bottle of a caffeinated tonic, the label promising instant energy and guaranteed pep!

She sighed, despondent. Neither the medicine nor the tonic seemed to be helping.

She was shivering uncontrollably, a physical state that was becoming increasingly familiar. She stood resigned, knowing that in a few minutes, it would pass. The early morning sun spilling through the windows afforded little warmth and she felt chilled to her marrow.

The worry that had been playing in her head these past weeks came to the fore. What if she were seriously ill, like her mother? She shuddered at the very idea. God forbid, she would kill herself first!

She felt a pang of guilt. This was her own fault. The receptionist for Dr Sarazin had phoned her four times in the last week, urging Mia to return to the consulting rooms. In the messages she left, she addressed Mia as if she were talking to a child, explaining they had the results and 'would Mrs Reichmann be so kind as to call in again, for Dr Sarazin to have 'another little peep?'

Well, Mrs Reichmann wouldn't let them have another little peep!

Doctors, they were useless. They gave you medicine that made you feel worse. It was all guesswork.

Now as she clutched the kitchen counter, her head spinning, Mia feeling so thoroughly wretched, Mia was of a mind to give anyone a 'little peep.'

She rubbed her temples, trying to massage her headache away.

She heard Rudolf coming down the stairs and hastily she served the eggs up into his plate, affecting an energy she scarcely felt in order to prevent a tirade. He hated to be kept waiting. She saw with dismay that from her wretched daydreaming, the yolks were hard. There was no time to cook more.

Perhaps he wouldn't notice, he too, was unusually preoccupied lately.

Rudolf entered the kitchen, his countenance surly.

"Where's my lunch?" he demanded. He took his lunch with him every day, plain sandwiches of beef or salami or sausage. He preferred sausage. He didn't hold with so-called store-bought food. She pointed to his pail on the counter.

He grabbed the pail and walked towards the door.

"Aren't you having your breakfast?" Mia asked, disbelieving of her luck.

"No," he said tersely. "Not hungry. I feel as if I'm coming down with the flu." He marched out the door and minutes later, she heard his car start up. She stared unseeing at the closed door behind him. Better see to the children. They would be late for school.

Laine fetched them now, sometimes the older lady, Dr McAllister's mother, Judith. She was a nice, quiet woman.

She was like herself, Mia. That Judith didn't like all the talk-talk.

Feeling weary and exhausted before the day had even started, Mia made her way listlessly upstairs to the girls' rooms. She would have to pull herself together. She needed more of her special pills.

DUSTING OFF DREAMS

Laine watched the children scamper through the gates, calling out cheerful greetings to their friends. They loved school, but for her part, she relished that all too brief time of day when they were safely at school, and she had the day to herself.

She started the car and headed in the direction of the stables. There was time for a really long ride this morning. Donatés was coming along well. At first the brick wall had bothered him, but slowly he was getting used to it. Yesterday he cleared it beautifully.

Jason Ballard believed that Donatés was good enough for the San Diego qualifier, but Laine was stalling.

The strange thing was, she wasn't afraid of losing, rather, she was nervous about winning. Victory would come with a whole bunch of decisions to make, and Laine wasn't sure her family was ready for them.

Jason insisted she was ready to take on the big guns and she was flattered at his faith in her, but she understood too well that the path he was proposing would not end with that one particular show. If she won, that would be a tremendous feather in her cap, and certainly, she could ride Donatés as well as anyone, better than anyone, in fact, but did she have the time to pursue her dreams?

It was a consequence she had to consider.

If the horse was really that good, he deserved to be exhibited to the max. That would mean big money, big rewards. And a great big chunk of her time. Laine frowned. She was a mother, and a wife.

Everything would change. She would have to rearrange her life, the lives of Case, the children. Winning could change everything. The idea was both thrilling and daunting.

Stratton had his eye on Donatés.

Perhaps the right thing to do would be to sell him, but Laine shied away from the notion. Besides, deep down she knew that if the animal was as good as he promised to be, she wanted to be the one to take him to the top. Donatés was her birthday present from Case, after all.

How could she possibly just 'hand her baby over'?

Laine felt torn.

'If not now, when?' came the treacherous thought.

Her fingers drummed on the steering wheel. The truth was, she would have to make up her mind. And soon. Relinquishing her amateur status and take on the challenge of the A-Grade shows, that was a big deal. She would need to talk it over with Case. Maybe call Lindy and book some time, she thought dryly. The next qualifier was Marlborough gymkhana in Lester county. It was 10 days away. The same weekend as Case's medical seminar in Phoenix. She always went with Case to the medical conventions and annual seminar.

Still, she had to see, simply had to see, what Donatés could do with some real competition! Use another rider?

Stratton? The idea made her bleak.

Still debating the issue in her mind, she turned into the winding dirt track that led to the Ballard Equestrian Center. There were only a few cars parked in the members' yard, and she could see Jason busy with the new Stratton colt in the far paddock.

Luke Stratton was a competition rider who had paid a small fortune for his roan warmblood called Majestix. The horse had a huge stride in the ring and was already clearing the jumps with ease.

She walked to the fence, watching Stratton put the beautiful animal through its paces. He was having difficulty with was the combination jump. The horse seemed unable to measure his stride, despite a brisk flailing from its rider. He was clearing all the other jumps without objection. Laine watched, critical, but holding her tongue. Stratton was calling it too early.

Imagine her and Donatés placing in the San Diego qualifier! It was an exhilarating thought. With training, Donatés could get to that, she felt sure.

"Donatés is a better horse than that." The voice was so close behind her, it made her jump. Startled, Laine turned to see who it was that was reading her mind. Scott Boyer stood a few paces from her, his hands on his hips, challenging her to disagree.

Laine recognized him. He was the young groom who was helping out at the stables for a while. Apparently, he was studying to be a veterinarian.

Laine had heard his sister was married to Jason's brother, or was it his brother married to— ?

Whatever.

She looked at him with some interest for the first time. Thick-set and tall, with a burly neck and shoulders, he looked older than his twenty-two years. His face was earnest as he regarded her, his eyes challenging her to disagree. The air of quiet confidence belongs to someone older, she thought.

He was wearing chaps, the leather dark and well worn, accentuating the pale blue denim crotch. He looks quite sexy, she decided, amused at the thought. He probably thinks I'm some rich bitch who sees Donatés as a toy, and with some of the members here, I can't say I blame him, much. She smiled at him. He reminded her a little of Case, at that age. The arrogance of youth.

She was pleased nonetheless that he shared her unspoken opinion.

"Thank you for the compliment. Do you think so?" He was, the other riders said, very good with horses. He was also very patient with the youngsters, a valuable attribute in Laine's eyes.

"Sure I think so! You're very good too. You've got great hands." His smile was impudent. She smiled, amused at his sass.

"I've been riding for a long time. I daresay I've learned a thing or two," she said dryly.

He nodded. "Donatés has the ability. And you're the one to bring it out." He crossed his arms, thinking. "But, the competition is tough—" He shrugged, as if he could understand the challenge might be too much for her.

His blasé attitude needled her, just as she was sure it was meant to, so she refrained from comment. She gave him a nod and a polite smile, and turned and started walking in the direction of the South stables.

To her surprise, he trotted after her. He caught up with her in a few strides, his face earnest.

"I mean it. I've watched you and I think you're by far one of the best riders I've seen. It's talent. You should take it seriously, not like the other women who ride just for kicks and stuff," he broke off, lifted his hands in a dismissive gesture.

Laine knew what he meant.

She knew all the stories about the randy Jason Ballard. Common sense and an observant eye told her there was more than a semblance of truth to them.

Jason had hit on her when she first joined the stables. The others teased her was a rite of passage. Laine took his misguided attention in her stride, brushing him off with ease, as happily married women do.

However, as a trainer, and an ex-Olympian, Bollard was undoubtedly the best rider she knew.

She glanced sideways at the young man who was skipping sideways as they walked, so he could watch her, unblinking. He seemed in no hurry to leave her side and was clearly waiting for some sort of response.

"Don't you have things to do?" she asked him mildly. He grinned at her polite rebuff.

"Absolutely. It's my job to get horses ready." He shrugged. "Well, they're ready". Laine found herself thawing. She knew he found her attractive, and it was mildly flattering. She was like Mrs Robinson, in The Graduate!

She was smiling at the idea.

"What's so funny?" he inquired, half-smiling too, sensing somehow she might be laughing at him, but content to be in her company.

"You. Just you. Yes, Donatés is good. I'd be pleased if you'd get him saddled. I'll be at the stall in ten," she pointed to the far paddock. "I need to pace the new course," she called over her shoulder as she walked away. Boyer looked disappointed, then nodded and turned away. The conversation was over.

Pity that.

A FINE LINE

The note on his desk had reminded him he was expected at the boardroom at eleven a.m. Sharp.

If he took on Morris's post, he would need to attend a meeting with those stuffed shirts once a month. He wondered, for the first time ever, if Morris's job was what he wanted. He shook his head to dismiss the treacherous thought.

He had more serious things to think about than this.

Like his affair with Roxie.

For that's what it had become.

Once used to a calm, ordered life, suddenly everything was different. Life was upside down. Fucked up, in fact. On countless occasions, he made decisions, promises to himself, this must end. Then, Roxie called him, —and bam.

His life was now a soup of endless worry, anticipation, guilt, failed promises, and broken, oh so very broken, vows.

He was amazed at how easy it had become to deceive, and he despised himself for it. Whenever he could sneak the time, those stolen hours with Roxie were his addiction, passionate, frenzied. Carnal even, to a degree he had never known, but then, there were tender moments, and it was those tender moments, he instinctively knew, that was quicksand!

Try as he might to fight this force that drove him to Roxie, he always gave in.

She never failed to surprise him. She had no formal college education, yet she was well-read and could discuss widespread topics with aplomb. To his untrained ear, she played the piano beautifully, deriving as much pleasure from his sole audience as from any standing ovation Lately, if they found the will to get out of bed, she had taken to playing him her latest songs, eager for his comment. It was a side to her that he loved.

They laughed a lot. That surprised him too. She had a ready wit, and

Case found that she could make him smile quite easily, something which she delighted in doing, happy to play his clown, anything, to chase the shadows from his face. And sexually—

She aroused a lust in him that left him shaken at its depth. Their fucking was the union of beasts. There was no other way to describe it. He loved how she needed him, her submission was absolute, her appetite insatiable.

They would roll away from each other, drained and sated, only to feel desire come stealing back. That ecstasy was there for the taking, on tap. There was no thought of resisting. But if his capitulation was total, his conscience was alive and well! In Roxie's presence, guilt was obliterated, only to surface the minute, the very second, they parted.

If Laine found out–he would lose her, undoubtedly.

And Case knew if he lost Laine, he would lose everything.

Case loved his wife, he knew that. In fact, when he looked at her lately, his stomach churning with guilt, he felt a new fierce, aggressive love within him, a voice inside of him, yelling at him to fight, fight for her!

He knew this, this... thing with Roxie, was no good. It could never be called love because love was supposed to happen once in a lifetime, and that, goddammit, was that.

This was all about screwing, and soon, he assured himself, he would tire of it.

Soon.

But not now.

Now he was a circus performer, on the high-wire. He would ride this thing out. Laine would never know.

FOUNDATIONS CRACKING

"I'm looking for Dr McAllister, Lindy, is he here?"

Lindy looked up.

It was Michelle, Dr Sarazin's nurse.

"He'll be here any minute. He's at a Board meeting. What is it? Can I help?" Always interruptions, and she had to prepare the files before the afternoon patients started arriving.

"Oh, the hearing." Michelle looked at her, curious. Everyone knew that the fight-guy had laid a complaint. "I was told to give this to Dr McAllister– he wants Dr McAllister to have a look at it and then call him ASAP." She walked into the room and laid a large brown envelope on Lindy's desk. Lindy glanced at it. The name said Reichmann. It was probably that medical report Kevin Daniels wanted on that Reichmann oaf.

Lindy took the envelope off the counter and put it in her drawer.

"I'll see he gets it. The girl looked surprised. Why was Lindy putting it away in her drawer? But Lindy was looking back at her, askance...

"Oh. Okay , fine. No problem." Puzzled, Michelle left the room.

Lindy turned back to her work.

When Case finally strode into his rooms, the waiting room was packed. He walked over to Lindy, grinning. He spoke softly, for her ears only.

"All's well that ends well. That ends the Reichmann saga, and I want to hear no more about it. Done and dusted." He glanced at her pad. "Any news?"

Lindy gave him a glad smile. "That's great!" she whispered back. "Terrific news! They dropped off a lab report on Reichmann, and Roxie Tanner called you. She says to call her 'at the studio', no less!" Lindy said, teasing him, but he didn't smile.

Case's frowned. She shouldn't call him here. She knew that, surely. Something must be up.

"Bin the Reichmann report, it's not needed now, the Board dismissed his complaint," he said. "Give me five minutes, then send them in. I need to make a call."

In his office, Case keyed Roxie's number.

"Case, how did it go?" The husky voice was concerned. "I was worried."

"Roxie, honey. It was fine," he said, admonishing himself. He should never mention these things, she belonged to another life.

"Nothing to worry about."

He heard her sigh of relief.

"Will I see you tonight?" she said softly.

Case hesitated. He was always late home these days. Shana wouldn't even kiss him the other night. What the hell was he doing? "I think not. I need to see my kids. I'm sorry."

"I understand, I do." she said pouting, " But I miss you, God, I miss you, she whispered into the phone, her longing almost tangible. "I couldn't sleep after you left, and I just lay there, wondering if there'll ever come a time when we can have a whole night and day together. Can't you come around for just an hour?"

"I want to see you too, Rox, but—" He did want to see her. He sighed. "Perhaps for an hour, around six."

"Wonderful." He heard an audible sigh of relief. "Promise me." Her voice was soft, pleading.

"Rox, hon, I promise. If something comes up, I'll phone you."

"Okay!" She sounded delighted, excited. "I am supposed to be here till around twelve tonight. they've got the backup singers coming in after eight, so I have to be back around then. See you later...."

"Okay. Sure." Case shook his head, disbelieving of himself. Was this really him, well and truly into an affair, whispering to a lover, deceiving his wife left right and center? It was becoming easier to do, but harder to live with. How long would Roxie be happy with an hour stolen here and there?

How long would he be happy? Hell, he was already unhappy.

They said their goodbyes and Case pushed his chair back and stood up. He walked to the window and stood gazing out, watching an orderly help a patient into a wheelchair.

"Case?" Lindy was standing by the door, staring at him in an odd way.

Back to the real world. Sighing he walked back to his desk and sat down.

"Shall I send Mr Bertram in? I want to try and leave early, I'm on duty tonight."

"Sure, show him in. Lindy," he said, picking up Mr Bertram's file. "Oh, and get Laine on the line and tell her I'll be home around, uh, nine. Tell her I'm tied up, okay?" He was peering at the file, a frown on his face.

Lindy eyed him for a second, then disappeared. A moment later Bertram walked in, pleased to be finally talking to his surgeon.

Back behind the reception counter, Lindy was dumbstruck.

'Roxie honey.' Roxie honey!

Roxie-fucking-Tanner was 'Roxie honey'. And Case would be seeing her at six! Oh shit oh shit oh shit!

The twice-divorced Lindy's heart was thumping, this was huge, unreal.

She had been about to close his door, when she caught the first 'Roxie honey'. Then, prompted by the cunning of ex-wives the world over, she had taken seconds longer than she should have, closing his door, —and caught the second 'Rox honey!'

Her mind reeling, Lindy called his home number. The bastard! Lindy felt near tears. She knew. She just knew!

Judith answered the phone. "Hello!"

Lindy was relieved. It wasn't Laine, it was the mother.

"Hi Judith, it's Lindy here. Is Laine around?" she asked, her fingers crossed.

"Lindy, can I help? It's Judith. Laine's at the stables."

Lindy tried to sound casual "Wee-ell- Nope. Just give Laine a message, Case is busy with a patient right now, so he asked me to call. Tell Laine to expect him around nine?" Lindy said, her voice flat. There, she was an accomplice now, the bastard.

"Oh." Judith's was suddenly cool. "I'll tell her, thank you." The phone clicked dead.

Lindy stuck her head around his door. "I left a message with Judith."

"Thanks," he said, without looking up. Mr Bertram was coming along nicely. He tilted Bertram's self-conscious face into the light.

" Thanks Lindy," he repeated, vaguely aware she was hovering at the door, but he was focused on his patient.

Lindy was glad he didn't look up. If looks could kill, he would be dead.

THAT BAD IDEA

They were on the fifth round of Bananas in Pajamas when Laine swung the Beamer SUV into the drive. In her cottage, Judith McAllister smiled as she heard the shrill, happy voices approaching the house.

She stood up to go outside and greet them, stopping at a mirror to adjust a few untidy wisps of hair. Judith liked to look neat. Neatness reflected one's inner self. Satisfied with her appearance, she went outside, smoothing the wrinkles out of her slacks with her hands.

Laine opened the back door to let the children out, and they tumbled out, giggling and full of news about their day. Laine, still sporting jodhpurs and riding boots, leaned back against the car, arms folded, and watched them race across the grass to their granny

"Granny, Mommy's horse is a champion and Jason said that Mommy is a champion too and that Mommy must ride Donatés in the Mar...Mar... Gymkhana." Liesel burst out, the words spilling out in an excited rush. Laine was laughing at the children's jabber, but Judith could see her eyes were sparkling with excitement. Something was up.

Laine looked disheveled and hot, but inordinately pleased about something.

"Is that true? Is Donatés going to be a champion?" asked Judith. .

"Looks that way," said Laine, trying to play it down, her pleasure nonetheless quite evident. "He cleared the five-foot-five mark and Jason is over the moon. So I am I! He wants me to enter the San Diego Grand Prix, if he makes the qualies."

Judith looked blank.

"Qualifiers," Laine explained. "And we will, she said emphatically." She took her daughters' hands in each of hers, leading them towards the house, calling to Judith over her shoulder. "It's a big deal!"

"I'm sure it is," Judith murmured, and hurried after them. In the hallway Laine shooed the girls upstairs to run the bath water, then strolled with

Judith towards the kitchen, discussing what would suit for dinner.

"Let's fix a nice stew for dinner. Case loves lamb," she said, pulling the meat from the fridge. "He's going to be so excited when he hears!"

Judith hesitated. Damn. "Case called, or rather his secretary called and she said to expect him around nine. He's tied up at the Clinic," she said, her words rather clipped and short.

She busied herself selecting vegetables.

"Ooh, shit." Laine looked crushed. "I have this huuuge news, and lately, there's never any time to think, let alone discuss anything. Damn!" She gazed at Judith, disconsolate.

Judith looked away, busying herself with the preparation of a salad, not wanting Laine to see her annoyance.

She heard Laine clap her hands, suddenly excited.

"I've had a great idea!" she exclaimed. "Why don't I get dressed up and take my man out on the town? We need to celebrate. Until what time did they say he would be there?"

Judith looked at her dubiously. "Eight, I would think? Said he'll be home by nine."

"Do you mind?" Laine asked her. Judith looked doubtful?.

Judith rallied herself. "No. No, of course not! Actually, that's a very good idea! See if you can get him to relax a little. I'll take care of the children. You go on up and bathe, change into something nice." Judith waved her out of the kitchen, insistent.

Laine's eyes lit up. "You're a treasure," she exclaimed. She walked out of the kitchen humming.

Judith heard her leaving a message for Case on his phone, telling him she was on her way in. Judith stared after her, the kindly expression fading, to be replaced by a frown.

Where exactly was her son?

BUILDING WALLS

Laine took her time bathing and getting dressed. She wanted to look especially good tonight. Case was so tired, they hardly ever seemed to make love lately. Now at least that was a state of affairs she could fix. She took care, choosing a black dress from the closet that hugged her figure and accentuated her blonde hair. After a couple of moments' idle deliberation, she gathered her hair into a loose chignon, strands of blonde hair framing her face in a soft cloud. He always liked her hair that way. Case loved to be the one to pull the pins that held the delicate knot together and watch her hair cascade down.

And she loved what came after.

A while later she descended the stairs to squeals of approval from the girls.

"Mommy, you look so pretty. Like a princess." The little faces shone with approval and Laine smiled over their heads at Judith.

"Well, I'm off to seduce my husband, get him away from his work for an hour or two. Do you think I'll succeed?"

"Undoubtedly. You look fabulous!" Judith's face echoed her granddaughters' admiration. Buoyed, Laine took up her car keys, filled with purpose.

Time for some real romance.

Forty minutes later, she pulled up and parked in the doctor's parking. She fixed her lipstick quickly, snapped her purse shut and climbed out the car. She heard someone give a loud wolf whistle. Her heart racing, she looked around, hoping to see her husband. "Laine, hold up there." She turned to see the burly figure of Mark Tomlinson rushing up to her, his eyes admiring. He was an obstetrician, and a good friend of Case's. He was puffing, face red with exertion. He caught up to her, beaming.

"My, but don't we look delectable! Are you meeting Case? Going out?" He fell into step beside her.

"I'm surprising him! Going to take him out for a quiet meal. We have something to celebrate." She gave his arm a conspiratorial squeeze.

He smiled back at her. "He's a lucky guy! Enjoy it." With a wave, he left her and headed for the Path Lab elevators.

At the main desk, the duty nurse looked surprised to see her.

"Hello Rita? Is Dr McAllister around? Can you page him?" Laine was glowing, clearly excited.

"Hello, Mrs McAllister." The woman smiled at her. "It's ages since we've seen you here! You're looking good! Are you meeting Dr McAllister here?"

She liked Laine McAllister. She was friendly and didn't hold herself above you, unlike some of the wives. And didn't she look like a movie star tonight!

Laine looked suddenly shy. "Yes, well that is, I'm surprising him! I got a message from him saying he would be here till late, so I thought I'd surprise him and treat him to dinner. Can you page him for me please?" Laine asked, waving goodbye to Mark, who was backing into the elevator to gaze at her that while longer, nodding his head, holding his thumb up, his face full of exaggerated admiration. Both women laughed at his clowning, then Rita replied, her face regretful.

"I will, but I don't believe he's here, I saw him leave a while ago."

Laine felt her heart sinking. All this, for nothing. Where was he?

The duty nurse put out a page. Perhaps the doc had returned?

There was no response.

Both women felt awkward.

'Call Lindy, she will be able to get hold of him, I'm sure," suggested the duty nurse.

"Good idea." Laine reached for her phone and called Lindy, walking away from the counter.

The phone rang and just as Laine was about to give up, Lindy answered.

"Laine, hello..." Lindy sounded wary.

"Lindy, I'm at Granger. I'm looking for Case, I thought I would surprise him, take him out for dinner. He's working too damn hard these days. Anyhow, they can't seem to raise him?"

Lindy's mind was working furiously. Of course they can't! He's with that slut. What to say, what to say??

"Didn't you call and leave word he would be here till nine?" Laine was asking. She sounded dejected and Lindy's heart went out to her.

Lindy's mind was racing. Shit! What should she say—?

"Sorry. I think he's been called to Mercy Memorial for an emergency consultation. Is his phone off? Did you try to call him?" Of course, the phone will be off, dumb bastard. "Oh Laine, I'm so sorry."

Lindy sounded mortified, thoroughly distressed.

Laine hastened to reassure her. "Oh, don't worry! I just wanted to surprise him. I'll call him now on his mobile..."

Sonovabitch, thought Lindy. That sonovabitch!

"Okay, sorry I can't help more." Lindy said, genuinely mortified . She had her pager out and was tapping out a frantic message to Case.

LAINE LOOKING FOR YOU AT GRANGER, SAID YOU AT MERCY ON A CONSULT, WTF!!!

She could hear Laine was pissed, despite her brave words.

"Thanks, hon." Laine killed the call, turned and walked towards the glass doors, her eyes stinging, all too aware of the duty-nurse's eyes following her. It was humiliating. Damn Case! His priorities were screwed up lately. He was always late home. It was too much! Her good mood vanquished, Laine started the car, distressed and angry.

This bullshit had to stop!

When Case arrived home just after nine, his mind was on the message on his pager. He had winced when he saw that, understood instantly. Lindy was covering for him.

The house was mostly in darkness, save for the upstairs bedroom light. Strange that she had retired so early. The children were already asleep, and he hesitated outside their door on the landing, filled with contrition. He made his way to the main bedroom, feeling drained and guilty, hoping against hope she would be asleep.

Instead he found her sitting propped up in bed, a book on her lap, her face stormy.

Case braced himself. She looked as mad as hell.

"Hi hon. Why so early to bed?" He asked, deliberately casual as he removed his jacket. He knew her well enough to know when she was in a temper. There was silence for a moment, and then she snapped, "Case, have you forgotten about us, your family?

Case stood perfectly still. He kept quiet, wondering how to respond. Infuriated at his silence, she flung the book at him and bounced out the bed, her eyes blazing.

"There's a limit to how hard you can work and neglect your family, and I will stand for it no longer! I felt a perfect fool at that damn clinic, all dressed up to take you out to dinner. Your damn phone is always off. Goddamn you." She looked near tears.

Overcome with guilt and remorse, he moved towards her to take her in his arms, but she flung off his embrace, livid.

"Go to hell. I want a husband, not some lodger. The word snapped out like a blow.

"Laine, honey, I never knew you were coming in." he protested lamely. "It would have been great to go out, have a bite to eat. I'm truly sorry." And he was.

Deeply sorry. She looked hurt and angry, and it was his fault and now the whole thing was growing–even Lindy was lying for him? What was that about? Doubtless there would be texts on his mobile. It was off, flat.

Having a battery that was 'flat' was one of the first tricks he learnt in this new world of lies and deception.

The tears were streaming, yet he hesitated to reach for her. She looked ready to strike him.

He hadn't spent much time with the kids these last weeks, even played with them, or even spoken to them. Jesus, this had to stop. He loved Laine and he could never hurt her.

"Case, you're too tired even to make love lately. Is your work really so important? What about us?"

She sat on the edge of the bed, defeated. "I was so excited this afternoon, I got dressed up, and...." She sank back on the bed and began to cry, inconsolable, her face in her hands, furious with herself for being so damn needy, but unable to stop the tears.

Oh Jesus, oh please, don't do that. Case felt his heart contract. His head was a storm of recriminations. Shout at me, hit me, throw things at me but don't, don't be so hurt, I never meant to hurt you, I'm sucked up in something and I feel crazy with guilt, and I feel love, and all sorts of things I shouldn't feel.

Case took her hands in his, and angrily, she tried to shake him off, but he held them firmly. He climbed into the bed beside her, pulling her into his arms, and stroking her hair until her sobs subsided.

"I'm sorry, honey," he told her over and over again, feeling impotent. And he was. Undressed and in bed, she curled her back into him, a spoon within a spoon. She seemed not to feel the soft kisses his lips made on her back, and he could find nothing to say to draw them both together as before.

Finally, distressed and seeking to make her one with him again, he began to caress her from behind, willing her to respond to this, his clumsy overture of apology. Laine lay still, feeling her body awakening to him as it always did. He entered her swiftly, anxious to bring her to that point where she was his again.

He was gratified to feel her slowly start to grind herself against him, hungry now for oblivion. At last, she shuddered against him, and he kept on, holding her fast while she writhed against him, felt her orgasm building again.

Laine hated herself for succumbing, but God, she needed this, it had been too long. When it was over, a strange thing happened that had never happened before.

She found herself weeping.

BRAVING THE STORM

IT'S ALL LOVE

Kevin eyed the screen with more than a little trepidation. There it was, in the inbox. Finally an email from Ash.

What now? The ongoing rift between himself and Case laid him low, and the idea that Ashley too might be lost to him was something he could not bring himself to contemplate.

He tapped on her email and began to read:

Hey Kev I am in Rio at the Palazzo, which as hotels go, is supposedly one of the better hotels, but frankly, it leaves a lot to be desired. Maybe I'm missing the States. I know I'm missing home. I miss you, of course, most of all. But, I am having a bit of fun too. Which surprises me, but there it is, life goes on.

Keven felt his spirits lifting..

The question I've asked myself over and over again, is will you be there for me when I get home? Life without you at my side seems impossible to imagine. But at last, I find I can face the answer. You won't be there. Not by my side, but hopefully, still a big part of my life. (As you can probably gather by now, I'm a bit lonely, and a LOT mellow. But whatever, it just seems very important tonight (did I mention I'm a bit drunk) that I tell you I love you.

It's a different love, but love it will always be. I want you to be happy. Hell, I want me to be happy!!! I'm working on that. I guess it will take time. I'll be home on Wednesday, and we'll figure it out, like we always do.

Be happy Kev. Ash

Kevin sat absolutely still for a long while.

Ash didn't hate him. The Mrs Sheppards of this world didn't matter.

The people that mattered, they would understand!

He straightened up in his chair, reaching for his phone, filled with purpose. He would tackle Case. Come clean.

They were closer than brothers, goddammit!

It would all be okay.

DOGGY PADDLE

Someone was calling his name. Case looked around and saw Doctor Sarazin bearing down on him.

"Case. Hold up there. I need to talk to you." He fell into step next to Case.

"Have you got a minute? I think I have a rather delicate problem." Case slowed his walk, looking at the man in surprise. Their medical suites were two doors apart, but their disciplines seldom overlapped. Sarazin was a gynecologist. He looked after Laine, in fact.

Laine? Case stopped mid-stride.

"Is it about Laine?? Is there anything wrong?" he asked, concerned.

"No. Nothing like that," Sarazin hastened to reassure him. It has to do with another patient Laine referred to me, a neighbor of yours, I believe. A Mrs Reichmann."

Case breathed a sigh of relief. Mia Reichmann. What could be up with her? Also, how was her business his business? But he reserved his comments and waited for Sarazin to explain.

"I have to get to Ward 20, and it's fairly urgent, can you come by and see me in my rooms, say around one?"

Case glanced at his watch. That gave him an hour to finish his rounds. Everything was dragging today.

"Sure, I'll be there."

With a thumbs up, Sarazin turned and strode in the opposite direction, leaving Case gazing after him. Mia Reichmann? He shrugged, well he would find out later, although he doubted he could help in any way.

When he finally made his way to Sarazin's room, it was ten after one, and Sarazin's waiting room was full. He flashed a smile at the young nurse behind the desk, who smiled back shyly. 'Doctor is waiting for you." She looked barely old enough to be out of school, he thought, feeling old.

Sarazin looked up when he entered, indicating Case should sit. He launched into his 'dilemma' without preamble, pushing a file across his desk to Case.

"Plenty of people waiting out there, so I'll get right to it. I sent a copy of this report to you a couple of days ago, made Michelle take it personally to you as a matter of fact, but I haven't heard from you?"

There was the faintest reproach in Sarazin's voice. Case opened the file curiously. "It's confidential, but there are circumstances... " He raised his hands in a helpless gesture.

"You need to see this. The woman is your neighbor. Plays with your kids." Case's eyes widened. Sarazin had his attention.

He looked at the file. What the hell was he on about?

He hadn't seen the file before.

Lindy must have forgotten to give it to him. Case frowned, peeved. He waited for the other man to continue.

Sarazin was looking decidedly uncomfortable. He indicated the file. "As you can see, the woman has tested HIV positive," he coughed. "I hoped for a mild infection, and I prescribed antibiotics, but her tests are back. It's worrying, to say the least." He sat back, pensive. "You can read it at your leisure. It goes without saying that her husband needs looking at too."

Case said nothing, his face stony. The sonovabitch, pawing Laine. A crimson hue rose in his neck.

Sarazin got to the point; "Contrary to ethics, I'm disclosing this because I have a real problem. She refuses to come in. She's clearly terrified of doctors and hospitals, but she needs treatment, Case. Urgently. I know she's your neighbor, probably Laine's friend, because Laine sent her to me." Sarazin paused, looked uncomfortable.

Case had a feeling there was more to come. He was trying to process it. Sarazin should never share this with him, but he would've done the same, and Case felt grateful to the man.

Sarazin sat silent, waiting for Case to say something. Case stood up and paced the surgery, his hands in his pockets, thoroughly perturbed. Those little kids. "Shit, " he breathed softly, and Sarazin nodded.

Shit indeed.

"What is it you suggest I do?" Case asked at last.

"Call on her. Convince her she needs to come in; she has two kids to think of. It's unlikely she's the spreader." He looked thoughtful, then shrugged. His patient was the woman. Her husband was another matter.

"It has to be the husband. —Fast-growing demographic, married men." Sarazin was bleak. "Whatever. Fact is, they both need treatment. She needs to be hospitalized for a week or so, not longer, and she needs to start dealing with this."

Case eyed him. Call on Mia? He didn't embrace the notion at all. Still, there were the kids to think of. He had no choice.

Sarazin was standing up, signaling the matter was now in Case's hands.

"The woman is so damn panicky. She won't take any calls from the rooms. I even tried calling her from my phone, but no joy."

Case nodded. It didn't take a lot to frighten Mia Reichmann. That bastard was to blame for this, he was sure of that. His mind was racing. Exactly who the hell was living next door? "I'll call on her on the way home."

Sarazin looked relieved.

Case turned to go "Thanks," he added, sheepishly, as an afterthought.

Sarazin could have kept this quiet and that might have compromised his family. He had hardly left Sarazin's rooms when his phone began ringing.

It was Kevin. Again.

"Kev?" There was a world of impatience in that single word and his tone threw Kevin.

What was up with him? Mentally, Kevin crossed his fingers, "Do you think that you could find time to have a drink or two with me tonight? I need to, uh, talk something over with you?"

"—Out of the question, Kev. No can do, sorry. I'm snowed under. Can we make it some other time?"

Shit. Kevin hesitated, "I guess so. He felt his confidence ebbing away. "It's not that important. Perhaps on the weekend?"

Case sighed. "Sorry Kev, I'm away this weekend–a Medcon in Phoenix. Although Laine isn't coming this year, she's showing Donatés in Lester County.

Kevin raised his eyebrows. Maybe that was why Case sounded so peed off. Laine always went with Case to these things. She called it their mini honeymoons.

"It can wait. No biggie." Kevin kept his tone light, hiding his disappointment.

"Yeah, thanks. Maybe give Laine a call, wish her luck." Case said, and Kevin could tell his mind was elsewhere. "Talk soon, Kev."

The phone was dead.

Case had no time to dwell on Mia Reichmann and her problems. He was running late and, he shook his head gloomily, the damn day was just getting worse.

Lindy glanced up when he entered his rooms, muttered a greeting and turned back to her computer. There was a chill between them, ever since Lindy had covered up for him a couple of nights ago. She handed him his messages, exuding silent reproach.

He took them, feeling awkward and uncomfortable. He would have to face the music with Lindy soon.

In an unexpected lull at his rooms, he found time to call Roxie. She answered after the first ring. He felt the familiar rush at hearing her voice.

"Case, I've written the most beautiful song. You inspire me." She sounded pleased with herself. "Can I see you tonight?" she asked, her voice wistful.

"No," he paused. He was taking too many chances. "I'm afraid I have something to attend to on my way home. Sorry," he ended lamely

"Oh. Okay!" she answered blithely. "I'll just give you double loving when I see you! Do you know when that will be?" She was trying hard to sound casual, not be a pain. Don't chase him away.

"Uh, let me call you." He was hurting Laine, this had to end.

They were both silent for a couple of moments. Roxie felt the awkwardness and forced herself to change the mood. "Case? It's okay. I understand."

Did she know what he was thinking? His frown deepened.

"I love you," she said, her voice was soft.

"Sure," he responded, a gauche and uncomfortable philanderer. Sure!? Mentally he kicked himself. Could he possibly sound more lame? "I'll call you," he muttered, frustrated with himself.

Why didn't he just end it? That was the right thing to do. Because I can't, came the sorry answer. Not now. I'm in too deep.

Lindy ushered in patient after patient, maintaining her frigid wall of disapproval. He wondered if she had overheard his conversations with Roxie. Clearly. The idea should have bothered him more, but in fact, it was almost as if the load lightened.

One less person to bullshit.

For the first time in his life, Case felt out of control.

All the remorse in the world evaporated when he heard Roxie's voice. She was always sweet and loving, a welcome contrast to the cool atmosphere which lingered at home lately. Laine had forgiven him, yet there was a barrier.

She had informed him, rather than told him, that she would be taking part in a qualifier this weekend, and announced he was 'on his own' for the medical conference in Vegas.

In truth, he was relieved Laine wasn't coming. The weekend would be a good time to clear his damn head. Distance. Perspective. That was what he needed. Far away from both women.

Still, it was a qualifier for the Seattle Grand Prix and he felt churlish for wanting her at his side, rather than him being at her side. It was a big deal, this qualifier. However, she didn't seem to particularly want him there.

Rather, Laine had been quite assertive.

"I want to go. I'm damn good and I want a little ribbon to tell me so!" she said, her tone challenging him. "I can take the kids and Judith, we'll stay over at a hotel. It'll be fun for them."

"Okay, it's just you always come with me." He shrugged, ostensibly absorbed in his iPad. He failed to see the hurt in her eyes at his casual acceptance.

Fight me on this, Case. Cancel your trip, she thought. She looked at him, willing him to speak, but he remained engrossed. Defeated, she turned went to the study.

Case listened to her finalizing arrangements for the weekend, and he felt oddly excluded. He would have liked to have seen her ride in her first A-grade qualifier. Still, there would be many. This was only the beginning. If she really wanted him there, she could have asked him to come!

He couldn't help feeling aggrieved.

When he left her, her kiss was perfunctory, distant.

On the way to the clinic, he felt quite sorry for himself, managing to conjure up feelings of slight, the way adulterers tend to do.

It was his doggy paddle in this sea of betrayal.

Anyhow, he told himself, it was better they had some time apart.

He needed to be alone, to think.

NO LUCK

Case buzzed Lindy, "Have you confirmed my flight to Vegas?"

"Yes." Click. Intercom: Off. Attitude: Definitely off.

Case sighed. These days, Lindy was cool, downright frosty. He tried again.

"Did we get a file from Sarazin? He said he sent it to me and he was rather acid that I hadn't seen it?"

The intercom crackled into life again. Lindy bit her lip to control her temper. Now he was accusing her of negligence. Really, it was too much.

"You told me not to bother you with any more of the Reichmann nonsense. I have the file here in my drawer. I'll bring it through now." A few seconds later, she marched through the door, slapped the file down on his desk and flounced out.

"Lindy! —Talk to me!"

She paused in the doorway, her back to him, debating. Then she swung round, closing the door behind her, her round face beet-red with anger.

"You. You're having an affair with Roxie Tanner!" she said. Almost immediately she put her hand to her mouth, shocked at her audacity. There, it was out. Her words hung in the air. But she stood steadfast, her eyes unwavering.

He stood up from his desk, and walked to the window, saying nothing, looking out, hands in pockets.

She sighed. "C'mon Case, talk to me. This is so unlike you. If Laine finds out, she'll be destroyed. Have you thought about that?"

He turned to look at her, his brow furrowed, his mouth a tight line. He was moved by her concern. He looked at her, his blue eyes were unhappy, his brow furrowed.

"All the time. But, like a moth to a flame, off I go. Maybe I'm in love with her..."

Finally, he had said it. That 'thing' that was worrying him.

He saw the shock in Lindy's eyes, and she walked to the visitor's chair and sat down heavily, disbelief in her eyes.

"Case!" Lindy was shaken to the core. "Laine adores you. You've got children, a career. This woman is also married," she reminded him, trying to reach him.

Ashamed, he turned away from her distress.

"Roxie's getting a divorce," he said, his voice flat.

Why the hell was he telling Lindy all of this anyway? He continued, "I know. I can't believe this is happening to me, I thought I was the guy with everything, beautiful wife, family. Then pow! Out of the blue, I meet someone..." His voice trailed off.

"Case, it's a cliché. You can't love two women at the same time. It's crazy!" she implored, praying he would listen to reason. He looked away, knowing she was right, knowing it was impossible.

"I know it's not my business, but—" she floundered, searching for the right words. "It's a lie," she burst out, feeling quite desperate, "a lie of the heart! It's all just —just bullshit !"

He felt both lousy and touched, seeing her agitation. He walked over and sat down next to her. He reached over and gave her shoulder a quick squeeze, his face glum.

"I know you're right. I'll sort it out, this weekend."

Her eyes searched his face for a moment, then she stood up, shaking her head.

She didn't believe him! Call it a woman's instinct, whatever. He was in too deep, and Lindy's heart felt heavy.

"Roxie Tanner!" she muttered. She seemed to mulling something over, then, hesitantly, she spoke; "You were always the lucky guy, but now, Case," her voice steadied, hardened, "Make no mistake, now you're shit out of luck!"

NEIGHBORLY

It was the first time Case had turned his car right instead of left, and the Reichmanns driveway was unfamiliar. He felt ill at ease, but he had promised Sarazin he would speak to Mia, and after reading her file, any delay seemed folly, so here he was, in the Reichmann driveway.

Peering through the faux stained-glass door, he saw shapes moving inside the house. Judith had called ahead and assured him Rudolf was away on business, according to his wife. He waited patiently for one of the shadowy figures to answer his knock. After what seemed like an age, Mia Reichmann herself opened the door.

Case was shocked at her appearance. She looked gaunt and haggard, thinner, if that was possible.

The dark eyes, always huge and timid, widened even more when she saw who it was.

He managed a smile, hiding his shock. "Hello Mia. Can I come in? I need to talk to you for a moment or two?"

"Oh, Case," she said, her voice flat. "You looked like Rudolf through the glass. I wondered why he was knocking. I thought I must have locked the door."

For a moment she looked inclined to refuse him entry, then she stepped back reluctantly and ushered him to a neat but sterile living room. It had none of the familiar clutter of a home with small children.

"I take it Rudolf isn't home yet?" Better make sure.

"No. He is away." Her eyes were bright, her pupils dilated and Case figured that could be barbiturates? Maybe taking too much of them? Not good.

She indicated a chair, her face resigned rather than curious.

Case sat down, sitting forward, feeling ham-fisted and uneasy. He got to the point without preamble.

"Mia, Dr Sarazin has asked me to come and see you. You've been avoiding his calls?" Case said. He wondered where the girls were. Probably around the back, playing.

"I already got the medicine from him. It doesn't work," she said. She tried to summon a smile. "I'm afraid I am not a great believer in doctors." She was twisting her wedding ring nervously, her bottom lip clenched between her teeth so hard Case thought she would draw blood.

She's on the verge of hysteria, he thought. He ran his fingers through his hair, wondering how to reach her.

"Why won't you let the doctors treat you?" he asked. What was behind that?

Mia avoided his gaze, her eyes downcast, wondering if this man could be trusted. The eyes that held her own appeared kind?

"My mother was always sick, ever since I was a tiny girl. The doctors always came to our house to visit her, but still, she remained sick. After they left, she always felt worse," she said with a shrug as if that was the end of the matter. Her shoulders were hunched, and to Case, it was as if the woman was shrinking before his eyes.

"Children need their mothers..." she said firmly. "I can't be sick, they need me. God will take care of us," she said, resolved, "I must always look after my little girls. I can never, ever abandon them." Her expression was mulish.

Case hid his impatience with difficulty. "Mia, no one wants you to abandon your little girls. But you are ill, you need treatment, for at least a week or two. No longer," he promised, trying to placate her. "If you don't do anything, you could get very sick, you could be in hospital for a long time, which will be worse. Better get this fixed now?"

"Need treatment for a week or two!" She looked up, alarmed. "What's wrong with me?" Suddenly, she looked frightened "-Do I have cancer?"

He shook his head quickly. "No, no." He hesitated-there was no easy way to say this, "You have tested HIV positive."

She stared at him, not believing what she was hearing. The room was swaying for a moment and then it righted herself and her neighbor was still there, looking at her, his face worried.

"HIV positive?" she whispered, aghast.

"It's very treatable now," he said calmly, "But it will eat away at your health unless you get the proper treatment. There are a few other complications. Dr Sarazin wants to remove a cyst as well. For that, you need to spend a short while in a hospital..."

She just stared at him, dumbstruck.

Mia was trying to focus. He was still talking, and she was trying to make sense of it. What about HIV? That was a death sentence, was it not? She tried to focus on what he was saying.

Case felt desperately sorry for this timid little woman, but to show any pity would frighten her. Play it down as best as possible. He continued; "Mia, it's not the terrifying thing it used to be! But you have to have treatment. You cannot let it ride."

"HIV, " she breathed. "I am HIV positive??"

For a moment Case thought she was going to swoon. He took one of her hands in a mute gesture of comfort. It seemed ridiculously tiny, like a child's hand.

"Rudolf! " She spat out suddenly, "It is my husband who did this, this thing to me." She was having difficulty breathing.

Case bit his lip. Of that he had no doubt. Still, Mia was the pressing problem. "He can also be cured with treatment. Has he said anything to you?" Case asked, but he knew what her response would be. Of course that bastard would say nothing, if he even knew.

"I hope he dies!" Mia hissed. "He would never tell me. He probably got it from his whore." Her eyes glittered. "Good. Let him suffer. I hope it kills him!" Her rage was giving her strength, and perhaps, Case thought, that was a good thing.

He said nothing, allowing her time to digest it. What could he say? Sorry, I should have clobbered him harder. Sorry? Dumb word! He felt empathy for this bird-like woman, who would almost certainly face the battle that lay ahead alone.

Mia tried to control herself. She reminded herself the doctor was right there, in front of her. His eyes held concern whereas another's eyes might hold only disgust.

Mia looked at him, careful to mask her thoughts.

She knew what to do. In fact, it felt as if she had known what to do for a very long time, but now, it was clear in her head. Her face closed. It wouldn't do to alarm her neighbor and friend, alert him.

"Case, don't worry. Please." She appeared calm, although her words were barely audible.

Case breathed a sigh of relief. For a moment there, she had looked quite demented.

"I cannot go to the hospital, not immediately, I must make arrangements. I will go in and see Dr Sarazin. And I will tell Rudolf to see his doctor."

She stood up, anxious that he should leave. She had to think about everything. Prepare.

He stood up too, his face doubtful. "Are you sure? You won't let me down? Promise me. This is most important." He searched her face, looking for signs of deceit. She was almost too calm.

Mia saw him to his car, her manner polite and distracted. She assured him, promised him she would be in touch with Dr Sarazin first thing in the morning.

Case started the car, and with a last quick smile of farewell, he drove away.

She watched him for a minute or longer, and even when the car was no longer in sight, she stood still, thinking. At last, Mia gave her head a shake and went around to the back garden to find her girls.

They were in the huge dollhouse Rudolf had bought for them last Christmas, wholly absorbed in their play. "Come children, we must get ready for supper." She took Bernadette's unwilling hand and led the toddler inside, calling for Kira to follow.

"I'm not hungry. I'll stay here." Kira sat on her haunches in the doll- house, unmoving. "Bernadette can have my supper." The little face was mutinous. Kira turned her attention to her dolls, ignoring her mother.

Mia dropped Bernadette's hand and marched back to the dollhouse. She grabbed Kira and dragged her out, the child squealing in fright. Mia slapped her hard and the child began to wail.

Mia felt instantly remorseful. Ashamed.

It wasn't the child's fault. Rudolf was to blame for this. Mia felt hate well up in her so intense she thought she would collapse from the potency of it.

"Momma?" Kira's howling had stopped and she was watching her mother's pale face, her eyes frightened. Momma looked so sick. With a mixture of relief and dread, the child heard her father's car in the front. He would know what to do.

Mia also heard the car. He had just missed Case! A pity.

She would have liked to see him bloodied and bleeding again. She dropped to her knees and clasped the child to her bosom.

"Alright, stay here. Momma has to talk to Daddy. Come back here Bernadette." She beckoned to the toddler, who was standing uncertainly a few yards away. Obediently, Bernadette came closer, her little face puzzled.

Mia ushered them back into the dollhouse. "Play a while longer, I need to talk to Papa."

Mia went upstairs and groped around her lingerie drawer, feeling for the gun. In the distance she could hear the car door slam.

Soon he would be coming up the stairs.

She found it and took it into her hand, gripping the barrel, playing with it, getting a feel for the weight of it. The irony of it almost made her smile; he was right. It would protect her.

She heard his heavy tread on the bottom stairs and her fingers closed around the cold smoothness of the pistol. She swung around to face him as he walked into the room, the gun in her hand.

He stopped short, gaping in surprise. He stared at Mia, noting the wild eyes, and how the hands that held the gun shook.

"What is this?" His eyes narrowed and he took a step toward her.

"Stop. If you come near me, I'll kill you now, I swear!" It was hard to breathe and her hands wouldn't stop shaking.

Reichmann hesitated. He eyed the gun. She knew how to shoot it; he had shown her.

But would she use it? No, she didn't have the backbone. He asked her again,

"What is this about?"

"You bastard! You and your whore have given me HIV. I have a filthy disease because of you and that, that whore!" she spat, her face contorted with hate. He could beat her, but she would kill him first! He blinked, then swallowed at her words. His usually ruddy face had paled. So that was why he had felt so lousy. That bitch, Tina.

He didn't know!

Mia watched all the emotions flit across his face.

"Your whore has murdered you," she hissed.

He turned away from her and walked to the bed and sat down heavily, his back to her. He spoke over his shoulder. "Put the damn gun away, we have children to think of–kill me, and they lock you up!"

He swung round, looking at her. "How do you know this for sure?"

He was right. She lowered the gun. Not now. There were still things to do.

"I went for tests," she said, her voice wooden. She flung the gun in the drawer and walked out, leaving him staring after her, unseeing.

Rudolf tried to collect his thoughts. HIV? Could this be true?

From that bitch Tina, for sure. For the briefest moment, his mind flashed to Kira. No, that was too crazy.

Tina. First things first.

CHARADES

When Case came down to breakfast the next morning, he raised his eyebrows at the suitcases standing packed and ready in the hall. His luggage stood next to hers, packed and neatly tagged, ready for his trip to the medical conference in Phoenix.

He found the family in the kitchen. They were all seated around the table having breakfast, the children agog with excitement.

"Hi hon," he bent and kissed the top of Laine's head, and she reached up and caught his hand for a second. Her smile was warm, and he breathed a sigh of relief. Storm over. She stood up to get his breakfast from the warmer.

"Hi, Mom. Looking forward to the trip?" Case addressed his mother, who was wiping the remains of Liesel's breakfast from her chin. He felt refreshed for the first time in a long time. He had finally had an early night and slept like the dead. It was just after eight. He wondered what Roxie would be doing now.

Damn, it was a sickness.

Immediately repentant for the errant thought, he turned his attention to the children. Judith stood up, pushing her chair back from the table.

"Hello and goodbye. I'm off to take the children to school. I won't see you till Monday." Judith felt pleased. Case and Laine looked as though they had resolved their differences, and she gave him an unexpected beam of approval. Good.

"Okay. Bye, kids. Be good. Don't give your mom a hard time." He turned around from the table and hoisted each child in turn into his arms, planting kisses all over their faces.

'Bye, Daddy. We love you and we'll bring you something nice from Jim Kana." they chorused as they rushed out, keen for the day to move along so this new adventure could begin. Judith pecked her son fondly on his forehead.

"Bye, son. Enjoy the conference." She picked up the car keys off the key rack near the door and strolled after the children.

"Alone at last." Laine sat down next to him and smiled at him, her chin cupped in her hands. She watched him eat, relaxed. "I feel a bit nervous too. This is the first time I've been away without you, and I feel so—.grown-up," she said, smiling.

He grinned back at her. For a moment, time moved back, and things were exactly as they used to be.

"How far is it? How many hours' travel?" Case asked, loving her naivety. He ate heartily. He hadn't realized he was this hungry.

"Four hours, not more. Donatés left yesterday with the Stratton horse. It was very good of them to take him in their box. I hope he's okay?" Laine's said, fretting. "But Scott Boyer is with them, so I guess they will be fine. Jason promised he would see to Donatés personally."

"Who?" Scott Boyer, that was a name he didn't know.

"That new stud that's joined the stables. He's great!" she teased, with a mischievous grin.

"I'll bet," he said dryly. He put the last of his pancake in his mouth, winking at her.

Laine laughed. "And you? Will you miss me?" she asked, and the sudden wistfulness in her voice made his heart catch. "I wish we were going away together. I'll miss you!" She stood up and walked round to his chair, then wriggled down onto his lap. "I'm sorry I was such a grouch." She ran her fingers idly through his hair, kissing his forehead lightly. "Maybe this is a good thing, give us a chance to really miss each other."

Case nuzzled his face into her bosom, happy that her anger had at last dissipated. She smelt familiar, felt soft, womanly. He hugged her close, savoring her.

"Case, will Mia be okay?" she lifted his head back, out of her bosom, wanting a serious answer to a serious question. Laine had been distraught to hear the real cause of Mia's illness. Distraught, then outraged, then sorrowful.

"Sure. Sarazin is good. He'll sort her out," he reassured her. "Get going..." He lifted her off his lap, then stood up. "Drive carefully. Stay off the gas."

"Okay." Laine pushed her worries about Mia to the back of her mind. Case had the matter in hand.

"Kiss me a kiss to last the whole weekend," he demanded, because it was a farewell ritual they had, and it was expected.

Laine looked at him, pride in her eyes. He looked spruce and fresh this morning, eager, even. He stood there, waiting for her embrace. Impishly, she pulled his shirt out from his trousers and slid her hands up his chest. God, she loved the feel of him.

Case kissed her, a long, loving kiss. Then he straightened up and tucked his shirt back inside his pants. The intimate gesture made him feel uncomfortable, and it disturbed him that it was so.

She was his wife, dammit.

He waved them goodbye, and they all seemed happy and excited to be on a road trip, it was an adventure! When he could see them no more, he walked back inside the house to collect his luggage. He needed to get to the Clinic–he would leave from there.

Every fiber in his being said 'go to her', but he couldn't do that. Enough was enough. The wild idea had crossed his mind Rox could meet him in Vegas, but that was insanity, and he dismissed it immediately.

In his inbox was his return air ticket to Phoenix. He thought about it. That's exactly what he needed, a break from everything. Everyone. No Roxie, no Laine–just distance, and time to think.

As if on cue, the phone rang. It said Pathology and he winced at how devious he had become.

Roxie.

"Hello." Her voice was husky, as though she had been fast asleep, was still in bed, and he wondered what she looked like, all drowsy with sleep. He felt his loins twitch at the thought.

"Case?" Roxie lowered her voice. "Have they left? Can you talk?"

He smiled. "Sure I can talk–for a couple of minutes, but I have to leave soon, need to look in at the Clinic, then off to the airport."

"About that," she said, "I had an idea. Want to come away with me?"

His pulse quickened, and he slapped his forehead hard with the palm of his hand. No, you dumb bastard, no!

He kept his tone light. "Would be nice, but impossible! Couldn't do that!" He said firmly. "Out of the question."

"Oh, Case, darling," He could hear she was disappointed. "Why not? No one will know?" she cajoled. "I have two tickets for Acapulco, it's an hour's flight–and we are there! No interruptions, we can wake up together. Please, darling, this is such a golden opportunity!"

Just the thought of a whole weekend, with just him and her was making him hard. And it was true, who would know?

No one.

She could sense him weakening, and she said softly, " When will such an opportunity come again? Do you do these seminars often? I just want a little teeny piece of you. Please my darling." She gave a low chuckle. "Do you want me to beg? —You know I can beg! she teased, her voice low and sultry.

He chuckled. Suddenly, he made up his mind.

"Okay, let's do it!"

"Case!" He heard her shriek with delight, and at his end, he grinned. An entire weekend with her, just one weekend, then this had to stop. He would tell her that on Sunday night, when they returned.

Mexico. It was close, yet far enough away.

"We can go to tiny, smoky little clubs and dance, cuddle. Oh, darling, I can't wait." She sounded giddy with happiness.

"Okay. The tickets?" he said, uncertainly. He was thinking about the logistics, and a thought crossed his mind; he couldn't use his card! For anything. Laine reconciled their accounts.

"Leave it all to me! God, I can't believe this is happening. I'm so excited!."

Case rang off. He had a dumb grin on his face. They would have this weekend. After that, he would definitely end it.

They never swam in the ocean, they never ate in a restaurant. The only thing they needed was each other. Once, they took an evening stroll.

Case pondered, was it possible for his dick to fall off?

They found a rather grubby-looking bar in the backstreets and went inside for a drink. The place was dimly lit, the tables pushed on top of each other, and they found a table almost hidden at the back of the room. Roxie kept her sunglasses on. She could see him clearly, and that was all she needed to see. Slightly elevated on a make-shift stage, a battered piano and a karaoke system held pride of place. There were a handful of locals watching an impassioned version of a woman wailing, "My hut will go onnnn—" To make sure the patrons understood exactly which song it was, a man jumped up behind her and held her tight. The woman lifted her arms up and out wide, a la Titanic. Her diminutive companion peeped out from behind her, smiling from ear to ear, basking at her talent and the whistles of appreciation from the scattered patrons.

"You sing something for me, please... Anything..." Roxie begged. He snorted, "You have to be high! There is no way," he said firmly.

But if she was high, so was he. There was just no saying no to her. In the end, he did a passable version of Johnny Cash's Ring of Fire. He was just hitting his stride, when poof, the song was over!

Roxie noted he got his fair share of whistles and cheers, mostly from the women. She also knew it had not a lot to do with his vocal prowess.

'Johnny Cash' handed over the microphone to the next contender, wishing she could sing too, but that was tempting fate. Incognito was the order of the day.

She put up no resistance when he pulled her onto his lap.

They ordered tostadas, surprised to find when the food came, they were both ravenous. Roxie admired and clapped the aspiring singers on, waving shrimp at them in encouragement. Case paid them scant attention, having eyes only for his gorging lady love.

"Stop staring at me. You're putting me off my food," she complained, smiling, and reached across, pushing his chin, trying to turn his head away from her.

"Can't help it," he said. "I've never before seen food dribble from a mouth as sexy as yours." They were laughing, happy.

As weekends go, it would be one of the best in their lives.

But he felt awkward when it was time to settle up and he had to stand back.

Roxie laughed his discomfort away, and told him to organize their cab while she settled up. He left her, glad to be able to do something.

Roxie handed the receptionist her credit card. The woman glanced around, then reached under the desk and pulled out an envelope and handed it to Roxie. Roxie opened it quickly and looked inside. There were beautiful glossies of the two of them together. She was laughing up at him and he was smiling down at her, his arm around her. That they were lovers was undoubted.

"Terrific," she said with a bright smile, and popped the envelope into her bag. She slid two hundred-dollar bills across the counter.

"Now I have to have something to remind me," she said to Rosita with a wink.

The weekend was just wonderful.

LOST AND FOUND

IT'S JUST BAGGAGE

Josie was pleased to be going home. Breaks were good, but home was better. Visiting his brother in Las Vegas had been fun, but Vegas was too hot and living out of suitcases was definitely not her thing! Plus, she missed the kids. She inspected herself in the mirror. This blue dress was very flattering. She looked about ten pounds lighter.

"I'm ready, let's blow this joint," she said. "Home! Here we come."

It was a bumpy flight back and when they touched down at LAX, Josie felt quite frazzled.

She hated flying. 'If God had wanted them to fly, he would have given them tickets!'

The couple trudged towards Baggage Claims and Ivor took up a position near the carousel, ready to dive for their luggage and haul it off. One suitcase. Good.

Second suitcase —gone!

Josie's lime-green suitcase, hard to miss, was nowhere to be found. The other passengers trailed off, and the carousel was definitely empty. They looked at each other.

Josie felt peeved, but not unduly worried. These things happened. "Go to the Starbucks, I'll meet you there. I have to report it." Grumbling under her breath, Josie turned to seek out the Lost Baggage counter.

Ivor pecked her on the cheek and walked towards obediently towards the sliding doors.

At the LOST BAGGAGE counter, a weary clerk pushed a tablet toward her and instructed her to fill out the form, which should have been a simple matter, but as it turned out, it wasn't. It was a good thirty minutes before it was done.

Thoroughly wound up by the delay, and aware that Ivor would be fretting by now, Josie began the long walk to the far end of Terminal 3, toward the Starbucks where Ivor would be waiting.

Suddenly she spotted Case and Laine, although Laine was mostly hidden behind a kiosk. They were obviously still in honeymoon mode. Laine must have changed her mind after all, and gone to Phoenix with Case. So much for her career coming first, Josie thought, sniffing.

Case was smiling down at Laine, who was reaching for him, pulling him towards her for a kiss. Case was shielding her from the eddying crowd.

Josie hesitated. She should say hello, but Ivor was waiting, and her sister would be keen to hand back their kids. No, better to run! She would tease Laine about it tomorrow.

Then she froze. No way was that Laine. It was Case, alright, but this—

This was a brunette. The woman's sunglasses were tilted off her face and when they stopped their lingering kiss, the woman pulled her sunglasses back onto her face immediately.

In a blind panic, Josie nipped behind a pillar, trying to regain her composure.

After a moment, she peered out. The woman— Who the hell was the woman? The sunglasses might just as well have been a ski mask.

Josie gasped. God. Could that be the new bestie, Roxie Tanner? With her goddamn tongue down Case's throat.

Josie turned and fled. She was still running blindly when she cannoned into Ivor.

"Whoa. What's the rush? Where've you been? You took so long?" Relieved to have found her, he kissed her on the cheek. "You were running right past me!" he exclaimed, rolling his eyes.

Women!

"Oh, Ivor. Oh God oh God oh God!." Wild-eyed, Josie glanced over her shoulder. There was no sign of Case. "I need a drink," she blurted. "Is there time for a drink? Please, c'mon, let's have a drink." She slumped against her bewildered husband. He patted her arm soothingly.

Really, she was in a state.

"Ivor, do you love me? Do you really love me."

"Of course," he said, feeling guilty. He always hated filling in forms, he should have done it. And even if they never got the baggage back, so what? It was one of those things, shit happens.

"Would you ever be unfaithful to me?" The demand was so left field that he began to laugh, but her unhappy face stopped him short.

"Be serious, Ivor, I need to know!" she said, her eyes fixed on his.

Ivor drew his wife close and sat her on the stool he had just vacated.

"I promise you, I have no intention of being unfaithful" he looked at her, curious. What on earth was this about?

He tried to lighten her mood, "Whatever you heard, it's not true about the hookers in Vegas. You know I stick to roulette." Josie was two inches taller than him, but with her seated now on the stool, and him standing, they were the same height. It was a good feeling. He stroked her hair.

Josie looked at him blankly. What the hell was he on about? Oh. Las Vegas.

Then, to his amazement, in the midst of her smile, she burst into tears.

Case, of all people, that—that rat-bastard! And Laine, her best friend! Bewildered and at loss, her husband held her close.

Women. Sometimes they were such children.

HIGH NOON

Case had seen Josie.

He sat in his sitting room, his mind still reeling. Of all the people—Laine's closest friend! It was over. He was fucked.

Deep down, there was a part of him that was almost relieved. Now this insanity would end. Would have to end. And that would be a good thing.

Then, reality took hold, and suddenly he was drowning in absolute and utter panic. Laine was a Texan at her core, and she wouldn't take any crap, not ever. His mind ran through the scenarios.

She would divorce him, and certainly, she would never ever forgive him. He would lose his family. She would probably move back to Austin! A myriad of scenarios flooded his thoughts, each of them a little more unpleasant than the one before. Frantically, he tried to think of a solution, a way out.

Perhaps, if he spoke to Josie—?.

Now, it was just before midnight. He had showered and was in his old Levi's and a faded plaid shirt, waiting up, dreading the distinctive sound of the BMW's diesel engine pulling into the drive. She would be home any time now. Doubtless tired from the trip.

What to do...?

An untouched Scotch stood on the table next to his chair, the ice almost all melted.

Before the weekend, he had resolved that this thing Roxie would be the last. They had spent a glorious weekend in Acapulco, hadn't seen much outside of the hotel room and that dingy little night club. Case had waited for the right moment to tell Rox, 'Never again, it was over...'

Finally, he realized that the right moment would never come. She was his addiction.

Roxie had been appalled as he when he told her they had been spotted. And that it was Laine's best friend, who had spotted them, that made her even more upset!

Roxie was upset, but not for the reasons Case assumed.

Roxie always knew there had to be a day of reckoning, in fact, she would welcome that day, but not now, she was not ready just yet for a high noon with the wife. Not just yet... Case was torn. She saw that. No matter how great a time they were having, he had refused to turn off his phone, in case Laine needed him, and he always called her in the evenings, walking out of earshot.

Alone with his thoughts, Case waited for his family with turbulent feelings, his gut in a knot. Things were coming to a head. Perhaps it was as well that Josie had seen him. This guilt was crushing him.

He would simply have to tell Laine. He tried again to picture how she would react, but it was impossible. They had never even come close to anything like this before in their marriage. And he loved Laine, it was just...

Fuck it.

His self-flagellation was interrupted by the sound of her car coming up the driveway, and his stomach churned.

Case went outside to greet his family, making a concerted effort to hide his turmoil. Tomorrow, he would talk to Kevin. He had to talk to someone, and who better than Kevin?

Kevin would know what to do.

The children were fast asleep in the back seat. Laine jumped out, holding up her ribbon at his approach, a huge smile on her face. She looked dog-tired, but triumphant.

"Hail, the victorious heroine returns," Case exclaimed, feigning a lightheartedness. She gave him a long hug.

"Case!" Her smile was ear to ear. "It was such a wonderful feeling! Oh, why couldn't you have been there! The children were so delighted; I think they even had a vague idea of what's at stake!" Judith exited the car on the passenger side, and she paused, beaming at the two of them.

"She rode beautifully, Case. You would have been very proud of her," Judith smiled fondly at her daughter-in-law. She looked back at her son. Was something amiss? She gave him a long second look, her eyes narrowed.

"Anything wrong, son?"

"No, not really," he said glibly, "But it's after twelve. and I worry," he said, managing to look pained.

Laine stepped away from him and gazed up into his face. He did look rather drawn.

"My darling!" She looked at him in surprise, "You were worrying? She tweaked his cheek playfully. "—Don't worry so. We're home now." She hugged him close, nuzzling into his neck. "Don't be a grouch, I've missed you. -Here, take one of the children."

Case leaned inside the car and took up his oldest daughter in his arms. The little face was both grubby and angelic, and she lay limp and trusting in sleep. Holding her close, he carried her up the stairs to her room, placing her gently down on her bed. She stirred a little, opened her eyes to give him a sleepy smile, then drifted off again, content.

Case removed her shoes, then covered her with the duvet. He switched on the night light and crept out of the room. Laine was coming out of Shana's room, her tread furtive so as not to awaken the infant. She read the question on his face and nodded with a smile.

She was asleep.

Case crept into his youngest child's room. Shana looked cherubic in sleep. He looked at her, his heart filled with love, but it was aching, too. Would Laine ever forgive him? Was he about to lose everything?

Laine was all-in, or nothing. It was her ability to sever the 'crap' from her life that he always admired. It was the thing that made her serene, made her so focused when it mattered.

Shana slept on, oblivious to her father's struggle, blissfully unaware she was a contender in a race for his love, his loyalty.

Case sat on the bed watching his sleeping child for a while, his arms crossed, thinking. At last he crept away to join his wife.

Laine was in the shower, and he stripped quickly and climbed into bed, intending to wait for her, but physical and mental weariness overwhelmed him and induced blessed sleep. He was only vaguely aware when Laine crept into the bed beside him, stirring with pleasure at the warmth of having her nestle into his side. She too, was spent, and within minutes was sound asleep.

He slept fitfully, awakening in the night to feel Laine's familiar body and glad of the comforting warmth of her. Other times waking, thinking of Roxie, the glorious weekend, sharp and clear memories to torment him.

In the end, he overslept, a thing he never did.

In the early morning kitchen hubbub, Laine more like a traffic controller than a loving wife and mother, and grateful for her preoccupation, he took his leave and slunk away.

Afterward Laine berated herself, she had barely noticed Case this morning. It had been bedlam and the phone never stopped, with people calling to congratulate her. Case was happy for her, but he could have stayed just a few minutes, she thought with some chagrin, just a short while, so they could at least exchange a few words.

She grimaced. She was being petty. There would be time enough tonight.

For a brief moment, her happiness at her recent victory with Donatés was clouded by the horrible thought that she and Case were fast becoming ships in the night.

And try as she might, she couldn't seem to stop it.

SAVED BY A KNELL

The next day, a multiple-car pile-up off the 101 spared him from crippling guilt and introspection.

The victims were being wheeled in, one after the other. There were already three DOA's. Priority was saving a young biker in his mid-twenties, who had flown through the windscreen of a swerving car. As yet, they had no identification, and the John Doe was rushed into O.R 2

He and a fellow surgeon, Abe Ludlow were quickly at work, beginning with extracting slivers of his cranium from John Doe's cerebrum. The time stretched into four tense hours. Twice, their patient went into cardiac arrest, and twice the theatre team revived him. In the seventieth minute, they heard their patient was one Felipe Sanchez, married, twenty-eight years of age, the father of three sons. His wife was trying frantically to find someone to look after the 'two little ones' and she would be on her way.

It made no difference to their endeavors, but there was a renewed intensity to give Felipe Sanchez another chance to see his sons.

They finally wheeled Sanchez into the ICU a little after nine. Sanchez proceeded to live for another forty-three minutes before his failing heart gave up for the last time.

As he made his way across the parking lot towards the doctors' suites, Case saw a woman that he guessed had to be Sanchez's wife. She was pelting across the parking lot, her shoes clattering, as if she had not had a chance to put them on properly, her face agonized. She had a toddler in her arms and clutched a young boy by the hand, half dragging him behind her, yelling at him to keep up.

He stopped and gazed after her, feeling infinitely grateful that this time, Ludlow had drawn the short straw. Ludlow would be waiting in O R to greet the woman, break the news...

Case turned away. He felt exhausted. Everything these days seemed overwhelming. He hadn't spoken to Roxie the entire day. Or Laine, for that matter. And dammit, where was Kevin when he needed him? He glanced at his watch. He would try one more time to get him.

When he walked into the rooms, only Lindy was there, her eyes glued to her screen. She called a polite greeting, her fingers on the keyboard keeping up their tempo, but she sneaked a sidelong peek at him as he walked by. He sure looked beat!

Case closed the door between them and walked to the window and stood there, gazing out at his bleak view of the parking lot, seeing nothing, trying to think, sort out his jumbled thoughts and feelings, hyped by his recent marathon in O.R 2.

There was a tentative tap on the door. Lindy peeped in, hesitant, loath to interrupt him. He looked as if he had the world on his shoulders. She quelled a sense of foreboding. He looked so... despondent.

"Lindy?" His manner was questioning.

"Oh, nothing!" she said. "I was wondering if you would like some coffee?" She saw him relax a fraction, lower his guard.

"Please. That sounds like the best suggestion all day." He moved to his old chair and sat down, and it creaked beneath his weight. He stretched back, legs straight out before him, his arms crossed.

"One coffee coming up." She departed, thinking he looked curiously vulnerable today. Lindy had already heard they had lost the John Doe. Aggie, her pal in O R had told her.

He looked so damn down. Case took all losses to heart, despite all the veneer of professional detachment. That's just how he was.

When she returned a few minutes later, he was on the phone, obviously talking to that stuck-up cow, Kevin's secretary. He flung his phone down as she walked in and it skidded across the desk. Clearly not happy, she thought dryly.

"Damn that woman! I have to get hold of Kevin, and you would swear she's never heard of him! His damn mobile is always off. I've left messages, if he calls, put him through!" He sat up straight and pulled the cup of coffee towards him, muttering his thanks, clearly wanting her to leave.

Case felt bleak.

Kevin wanted to see him, not too long ago, and he remembered all too well his own brush-offs, and it made him feel crappy. One more thing to feel lousy about, he thought.

Well, now he would make good. He needed to see Kevin, really talk. He needed to come clean, tell him everything. Kevin would know what to do. He himself—!

Well, he was in too deep to think straight.

His dark thoughts were interrupted by the insistent beeping of his pager. They needed him in Surgical Four. Hastily, he downed his coffee. Time to focus on real problems.

BAD

Anthony Sarazin's bland face revealed nothing of his anxiety. He looked at the sad, pathetic woman that was Mia Reichmann, and tried again;

"Mrs Reichmann, I tell you it is imperative, imperative that you make arrangements for someone to take care of your children and allow us to take care of you for a couple of weeks. Your body is weak, you need all your strength to fight this disease." He sighed, "I assure you that oral medication, tablets, are not as effective as the treatment we can give you here at Granger."

"Not now." Mia's face was set, stubborn, contrary to her usually meek and mild demeanor. "Not now," she was emphatic.

"When then?" He struggled to hide his impatience.

"I must find out from Mrs Costaz. She is a good woman. I will ask her if she will stay with the children while I am in the hospital. I must have someone to look after my babies." she said tremulously.

He tried to be gentle; "Your husband—" he broke off. If the bastard could do this to his wife, he surely wasn't the type to look after children. "Is he seeing his doctor?" he finished lamely.

Mia nodded.

Defeated for the time being, Sarazin sat down and pulled his script pad towards him.

"I'm prescribing some tablets that will keep this in check, but I expect to see you back here soon. Now, there are some things you must do to safeguard the children." Mia sat silent while Sarazin lectured her.

She understood him perfectly. She was a danger to her children.

Rudolf did this.

She tried to concentrate, but she had one of her headaches again. At last, he was finished, and he pushed a small booklet toward her. Living with HIV.

"Here, take this," he said kindly, "basically it outlines all I have been saying."

Dumbly, she took the booklet from the desk and put it in her purse. She needed another tablet, like those the unwilling Polish doctor had given her. At the drugstore, Ivor had pressed her to see a doctor. A nerve doctor. Doctor for this, doctor for that.

None of that mattered any longer.

"Dr Sarazin, please. I feel very nervous, and I wonder if you could prescribe some more of these for me?" She held up an empty vial of Varetium, and he frowned when he read the label.

"Under no circumstances. These will react adversely to the other lot of tablets I've prescribed." Not to mention it could cause psychotic episodes, but he kept that to himself.

He was sympathetic but firm. "I'm afraid if you have headaches, you'll have to stick to aspirin." His tone brooked no argument

Chastened, she left from his surgery. She was aware of the young receptionist's eyes, boring holes into her back as she made her way out of his reception. She knows, Mia thought.

Her face burned with shame as she made her way to the parking lot, and her hand shook as she tried to unlock her door. Safe from prying eyes inside her car, she sat quietly for a while until the fear subsided. She had to have some of those tablets. They were the only thing that saw her through the day.

Mia opened her purse to check how much money she had. Two hundred dollars. It would be enough. She started the car and headed towards the Clairmont mall.

In the drugstore, a bored young man that ambled forward to serve her. He raised his eyebrows when read the label on the empty vial. He looked at her. "Strong stuff." He set the vial down on the counter.

Mia looked around her. There was no one near them, within earshot. Nervously, Mia counted out a hundred dollars. The young man's eyes widened in surprise.

"I'd like some more of these." She pushed the empty Varetium bottle toward him "Got a fresh script for this?" He was smirking now. What a lulu.

You never could tell.

"Keep the change," Mia whispered, her eyes imploring him.

He glanced around. Rosa was on duty in the dispensary. She would play. "Coming up," He was now brisk efficiency. He disappeared to the back again, and came back a short while later with a full vial. He took the empty container and flung it with a flourish under the counter into a bin.

"Don't need that. Pleasure doing business with you, miss." He peeled forty-six dollars from the pile and pocketed the rest. "Call again, anytime," he called over his shoulder as he made his way to the till.

But Mia had already left.

RETRIBUTION

Tina Marshall fixed her lipstick, her pinkie gently dabbing each corner of her generous mouth. She deftly slipped the lipstick cap on, her eyes locked on her reflection in the small mirror suspended on the side of her filer. He was waiting for her. Let him wait. It wasn't often that the bastard took her out to lunch She could feel him eying her, but she ignored him and fluffed up her hair one last time

"Come, Tina," Rudolf said impatiently.

Satisfied, she popped the lipstick into her purse, and smiled coyly at him.

"I'm ready." Perhaps he was finally sick of that mousy wife of his. They sat silently in the drive to the restaurant, and she wondered where he was taking her. They were passing the better parts of town, the cheap bastard, and she began to protest.

"What is this? There are no restaurants here." She looked around, nothing but old factories and warehouses, mostly empty

"I'm moving to bigger premises. I want your opinion on a new place." Rudolf reached over and patted her knee, smiling, his eyes on the road.

Tina sat back, mollified, sniffing in satisfaction. He was finally recognizing her worth. She wished she had worn something more modish, but the first she had known of this unexpected treat was when he had asked her early this morning. This outfit was good enough for work, but she had better at home. Like the new red one with the fine silver leaf pattern running through it. Now that was real pretty. —Set off her new blonde hair.

She flipped the sun visor down, remembering the roots. Yessir, her roots needed doing again, the blonde was growing out. The car came to a halt outside a deserted factory and she looked around.

Christ. What a dump.

Rudolf was already out, unlocking the big double doors of the warehouse. Tina waited in the car impatiently. No way was she getting out, it was too dirty. The big doors swung open. He walked back to the car, climbed in, and drove the car inside.

She began to feel uneasy. The place was filthy. Vandals had broken most of the windows. Rudolf killed the engine and glanced at her, smirking.

"Well, what do you think?"

"I think it stinks," she said, emboldened by this new confidence in her opinion. "It's too far, for one thing."

He nodded, as if in agreement. "Well, that's not the real reason I brought you here. I have something for you. A little gift, you might say. Wait here." He wagged his finger at her playfully, motioning for her to sit put.

Tina stared at him in surprise. A gift? That was new. He climbed out of the car again and she heard him pop the trunk and take something out. She drummed her fingers impatiently on the door rest.

His voice in her right ear startled her. He jerked her door open roughly.

"Get out. I don't want blood in my car," he said evenly.

For a moment the meaning of his words was lost on her. Startled at his abrupt manner, Tina gaped at him in surprise. Her surprise slowly became paralyzing fear. Wrapped tightly around his fist was a thick, studded leather belt.

"What is this?" Her voice was hoarse with fright.

"I'm going to teach you a lesson. You have given me a disease,

I am told, by my doctor. And my wife, too." Tina started to bluster, her mouth dry.

"They can cure it, easy, dead easy. Please Rudolf-"

So she did know. His rage spilled over. His hand lashed out and caught her in the mouth. Her head snapped back from the blow and she felt too dazed to even scream. She could taste blood. Roughly he pulled her out of the car and she fell in a heap on the concrete floor.

"Raise your arms!" He swung the belt and it caught her with a loud smack across her bare legs and she screamed in pain. "Raise your arms," he roared again.

She saw he had a piece of rope in his other hand. Was he going to strangle her? She began to scream, but he struck her again in the face, this time with his fist, and her scream died with the thud of his fist in her face.

"Stand up, raise your arms!" he instructed again, his voice menacing.

Terrified, she stumbled to her feet, her arms in the air.

"Good, now we undress you. Don't struggle and don't scream. Or do, as you please. No one will hear you here." Swiftly he bent and pulled her skirt up over her head, fumbling and clumsy. "Raise your damn arms!"

Stuttering and begging, a sniveling Tina raised her arms. He took the rope and looped it above her head, around the skirt, effectively blinding her, muffling her pathetic pleading.

She looks like a sack of potatoes with legs, he thought with grim satisfaction. Roughly, he yanked her pantyhose and panties down to her ankles, effectively hobbling her.

Terrified, Tina tried to hop away. Rudolf watched the futile hopping, smiling at her bare buttocks quivering with each hop.

He kept silent and still, allowing her to go a few yards, enjoying the spectacle. Then he stooped and picked up the heavy leather belt and walked softly towards her. She could hear his breathing and the sound terrified her.

"Please Rudolf, " she begged, but her please were muffled in the folds of her skirt. He raised his arm and lashed out with the belt, catching her squarely across the buttocks. She screamed in pain, her body jerking in a tortured spasm. There was an angry weal across the white expanse of her bottom. He raised his arm again.

He beat her mercilessly and carefully, cursing if he drew blood. He took care to avoid the parts of her people might see. He never said a word, grunting with exertion, smiling grimly when he saw a wet stain of urine spreading over the dusty concrete.

At last he stopped, exhausted. He knelt down and untied the knot to release her arms. He walked to the trunk and carelessly tossed the rope inside. Tina watched him, prostrate, incoherent with terror.

"Get up. I will take you home now. If you say a word of this, next time, I will kill you. Do you understand?" Dumbly, she tried to nod.

Rudolf took out a cigarette and lit it. He leaned back against the car, exhaling smoke, watching her. "I'll give you two minutes to get straight, otherwise you walk back," he said calmly.

PANDORA'S CHILDREN

EXPOSED

From Granger Clinic, it was a good thirty-minute drive to Kevin's elegant home in Shelton. Case was determined to talk everything over with Kevin.

He would know what to do.

It occurred to him Kevin might be out, but there was no other way–Kevin wasn't returning calls, and Case knew he had to speak to Kevin first, before he spoke to Laine. There had never been secrets between them, and the time had come to come clean.

When he arrived, he saw Kevin was home, but there were three other cars already in the driveway.

So he had visitors.

Case had hoped for a one-on-one, but he would take Kevin aside. He sat for a moment in the car, summoning his courage. Hell, Kevin would know what to do, tell him how to handle this.

He was in a bind, a big one.

He grimaced. So much for being a fucking Prince.

Case got out of the car and walked slowly up the drive. He could hear loud music coming from the patio.

Party time, while Ashley was away!?

He walked through the unlocked front door, calling a greeting.

There was no reply. Perhaps Ash had come back early? He could hear laughter outside, and Case walked through the landing to the enormous window that looked down onto the patio and garden below. He raised his hands above his head to the glass, and gazed down, cursing softly.

Nope, too many people–and they were all guys?

Kevin was standing at the barbecue, hands in pockets, talking to two men he didn't recognize.

The one guy was really making his point, waving his hands with almost feminine emphasis. Kevin was listening to him, his head cocked, but looking down at his shoes, rocking softly back and forth on his heels.

Case nodded. That meant Kevin had tuned out. He knew that stance of old. Perhaps Kevin would welcome the interruption?

Suddenly another figure appeared a younger, bearded man, bearing a tray of snacks above his head. The man set them down on the patio table with a flourish. He walked over to Kevin and slipped his arm around his waist. It was an intimate gesture, the same way Laine snuggled into him.

Case's jaw dropped as the guy fondled Kevin's hair, saying something in his ear. He watched as the man leaned forward and kissed Kevin on the mouth. A gentle, intimate kiss.

Kevin kissed him back!

The other two men were looking on, laughing at them.

Case stood framed in the huge window, dumbfounded.

Kevin said something and they all burst out laughing.

Case's breathing was suddenly ragged, and his heart was thumping as if he had been running.

What the fuck...

Kevin glanced up to the window, perhaps sensing him there, watching them.

His eyes widened at the sight of Case framed in the giant window, looking down on them, his hands up, like a wrathful archangel.

Case saw shock and dismay flood Kevin's face.

That broke the spell.

He fled.

In his rear-view mirror, he saw Kevin rushing into the street. He saw Kevin's hands drop to his sides, his image shrinking as the car sped away, until there was nothing.

Case killed the engine and sat in the car for a minute or two, trying to think, before he went inside and faced his wife. Case felt as if he was losing his mind.

Images of Kevin, then Roxie swirled in his head. He pinched his eyes shut. It was all a bad dream. There was Laine, bending over the tub, laughing with the girls, Laine giggling, blindfolded, playing zombie-zombie. Laine, stroking Donatés, smiling at him.

What the fuck! He thumped his hands on the steering wheel, needing to shout and scream. Everything, absolutely everything, was fucked up!

Lucas 'Case' McAllister knew his world was unraveling.

His wife was waiting, inside. More lies, more deceit... The only bigger liar in the world than him was Kevin, his best friend, his queer friend. How long had Kevin hidden this from him?

Why? And why had he never seen it?

He shook his head like a terrier shaking off the rain, wanting to banish all the images. He had to get out of the car, then walk inside, face her.

She was up and waiting for him in the lounge, looking at the TV although she looked miles away, lost in thought. The noise from TV was jarring, and he winced at the racket.

Laine looked up at her husband, smiling in greeting, and immediately turned down the volume on the TV. She was glad he was finally home. He looks so tired, she thought, exhausted.

"Case, honey." Her smile faded and she looked at him in concern. "Is something wrong? You look absolutely finished." She stood up and kissed him lightly on the lips. " "Sit, I'll fix you a drink. Or do you want your supper? Should I get it now?"

Case sat down in on the couch and closed his eyes. On top of everything, Kevin, gay! Fuck. It was just too much to grasp.

"A drink would be good."

He watched as she poured a scotch for him. Good. He would need that.

She walked over to Case, holding a drink out to him.

"Why are you shaking your head like that? Something you need to talk about?" she asked softly. She sat side-on next to him on the couch, drawing up her bare feet up and tucking her knees under her chin. She reached out her hand, lightly caressing his face, running her fingers through his hair.

Case sipped his Scotch, stalling. He had to tell her. Everything. But how?

"I went to Kevin's house, to talk to him, and there were these ...guys there." He said the word with difficulty.

Laine leaned forward, stroking his hand. Ah. So that's what this was about. He knew.

"And," she prompted.

"Christ, I saw him! Kevin's gay! His face was stony and his voice too harsh, rasping.

"Oh, my darling." Laine frowned, wondering what she could say. He seemed inordinately upset, and she had no doubt that was because Kevin had deceived him. Case had no time for lies. She tried to pull his head towards her for a kiss on his brow, but he sat there, resisting, not looking at her. He felt a million miles away.

"Case," she said puzzled. He was so–odd. But, then again, he had been blindsided. She sighed, took her hand away, studying him, perturbed. "He's still Kevin! -Your best friend." He shook his head, looking down at the drink in his hand.

"Case? Look at me!"

He glanced at her, then looked away, too quickly, she thought. What was up with him? His expression was sick with ...what? He was looking at her, his eyes unfathomable. Looking into those eyes she loved so well, Laine felt a chill run through her.

Case looked positively haunted.

Something was very wrong.

Case kept his gaze averted. She was seeing right through him, he was sure. He could read the trepidation on her face and closed his eyes. Oh Jesus, would there be no end to this night!

There was nothing for it.

He took a deep breath and the words tumbled out.

"Laine, I'm having an affair... "

For one wild, split second, Laine wondered if she was feverish.

Case felt her fingers freeze in their caress, and he saw the loving concern change into a mind-numbing shock. In a millisecond, the loving look was gone, and there was only this ashen, horrified face staring back at him. He wanted to take his words back, but it was too late.

Too late for everything.

Afterwards, she wondered how might she have reacted differently in that moment? What gesture or words could have salvaged their marriage? Should she have screamed more, cried more? Perhaps she should have clung to him, stopping him from ever leaving her and the children.

Afterwards, she had time to think about broken hearts, and she understood it clearly now; the heart didn't break. It just caved in, and the very essence of all that you, the you who you used to be, well that was just ...gone, in that nanosecond.

But in the moment... Well, it was all different.

She didn't think of any of those things. Instead, she scrambled away from him, as if he were an assailant,

"What? What did you say?" she whispered, barely audible. She stood up, and stepped back, staring down at his averted head.

"I'm having an affair." Is that what he had said? Present tense.

Not, 'I've had an affair', but I'm having an affair.

Oh God!

Laine felt the blood leaving her face, and she had to sit down again.

Case wanted to look away, but Jesus, she was ashen! Her color was slowly coming back. He felt sickened.

Oh God, I've hurt her like I never thought I could. I, who swore to protect and honor her, she's the mother of my children, for Chrissakes, and look at her face! You did this!

She wants me to wake her up, out of this nightmare, but I can't carry on bullshitting her, and she'll ask me any moment now 'Do I love Roxie-and what will I say? Can you love two women at the same time?

He tried desperately to keep a hold of himself, and he said, woodenly, over and over; "I'm sorry, so sorry..."

"Who?" She whispered, but she knew already.

"Roxie. Roxie Tanner," he said, his voice low.

Case looked into her eyes and he saw the door slamming shut on his life.

"Did you spend the weekend with her, Case?" she asked, her throat catching, incredulous.

He nodded.

"You bastard," she whispered. "You miserable sonovabitch." A thought occurred to her. " How long..." she asked. Her words were almost normal, the whisper was gone.

Case looked away. He couldn't bear to see the pain in her eyes. "Maybe eight weeks. —Laine, please..."

The pain fled from her eyes and in its place was something he never thought he would ever see–

Revulsion!

She was staring at him, shaking her head slowly, as if she could refute the meaning of his words..

"Get out!" she said quietly, her voice was suddenly quite clear, her eyes glittering.

"Get the hell out of this house, now!" Her voice was rising, and she was yelling now, rushing at him, flailing at him in a blind, numbing rage. "I WANT YOU OUT OF THIS HOUSE, TONIGHT!" She was screaming at him now, her fury uncontrollable.

Case had never, ever heard her like that before. In the midst of his panic and shame came the obscure, ridiculous thought she would wake the children.

Laine suddenly ceased her yelling and closed her eyes. She took a deep breath, struggling for control. "I'll send your clothes to wherever you're staying. JUST GET OUT!"

She stepped back, then ran at him, shoving him, sobbing, pushing him towards the door, again and again. There was no dignity for either of them, for her, only disbelief and a terrible soul-destroying rage, for him, abject shame and self-loathing.

Case moved backwards awkwardly, stunned he had brought her to this. He tried to find something he could say that would make things better, but there was nothing.

"Laine..." was all he could say, raising his arms to ward off her angry futile blows, pathetic in his attempts to calm her.

"Just get out!" she said, the tears were unchecked and streaming, her voice was small, defeated. "I'll explain something or other to the girls."

The rage was surging again. "Get out! GO!" She was shrieking again, waving him away, unable to bear the sight of him.

Somewhere, in between her shouting, was her sobbing, a dry, gasping sound, as if he had taken from her the very air she breathed. He turned and half-walked, half stumbled out of the house.

He could hear his feet scrunching on the gravel, mixed in with the sound of his wife's grief, and in a daze, he opened the car door.

Case drove around aimlessly for a long while, trying to grasp the reality of what had he done. At last, he found himself outside a hotel near the Clinic. He checked himself in, glad to be out of the car, within four walls, and silence.

He thought of Roxie. What would she say, would she be thrilled, guilty, what?? Would he ever feel happy again? Strange, all he could think of was Laine, not as she was tonight, but Laine of a few weeks ago, laughing in his car, bending over the bath, the night of his birthday, smiling, happy, adorable.

His wife.

Discarded.

HOLLOW

When her mother died, Laine had cried for days on end, but eventually the tears had stopped, the pain abated. This, this pain, this would never stop. This agony would never, ever leave her, she was sure of that.

She took refuge in the bedroom room, locked the door and howled and screamed into her pillow, rocking in anguish. There could be no noisy sobbing, because the children might hear, and that would never do. She had to hide, because the very essence of her being had been hollowed out, and people would see, see she was broken, pitiful, empty.

The reflection in the mirror was an imposter. She was no longer Laine McAllister, happy, adored, married.

She was betrayed, with a heart that had not broken, but had simply caved in.

There were just two things that made reminded her that life was ongoing, reminded her that perhaps, she was still alive.

Her girls. And rage.

Rage would surge, quiet the heartache and humiliation. Then it would receded, and once again she would feel foolish, humiliated, worse, confused. Where had this betrayal come from? Why didn't she see it coming? Case was hers, from the moment they met.

She was his.

She was born to love him; and he to love her. She'd known that for the longest time. How then, could he have betrayed her? How was this possible?

And inevitably came the question, what did she do wrong?

Laine had no control over the tears. Control demanded strength, and she had none of that.

For four days Laine stayed in the bedroom, her door closed to the world. Judith told the girls she had flu, and it was highly contagious. The running nose, swollen eyes and screwed up Kleenex that fluttered everywhere were the perfect props to validate the farce.

Laine simply collapsed, grateful Judith was still there. Judith would take care of the girls. She couldn't face them. What could she say? Brave face? That was impossible.

Judith tried in vain to comfort her, then finally she stole away, leaving Laine to her grieving. Grieving, that was something Judith understood. Her role was to distract the children, keep them away from this distraught stranger that was their mother. She brought Laine trays with food, then took them away again, barely touched.

She felt helpless, but she understood too well.

Laine had told her between great gulping sobs about her son's infidelity, and of course, it should have been a terrible shock, but it wasn't.

Just that dreadful sense of deja vu

Judith did not trust herself to speak to her son. She knew well that what is said can never be unsaid. So, she let the phone ring when it saw it was him calling. When he called on the home phone, she was terse, wrathful. Yes, the girls were fine, yes Laine was fine, and was there anything else?

On the fifth morning, an overwhelmed Judith resolved to call a doctor, although she knew a 'doctor' was not what was needed, but she was beginning to flounder, running out of excuses to give the girls. They demanded tremulously that Daddy had to come home now to ' fix' Mommy. Judith hid her anxiety from them, a master with years of training.

Laine stayed cocooned in her bedroom, the door closed, the curtains drawn.

Josie came calling, twice, and twice Laine declined to see her, staying upstairs, pleading illness. Jason called her on the cell phone, and Laine let it ring.

Laine was on fully automatic with the girls, grateful that Judith was there to take up the slack, wanting only to be alone, to try and make sense of what would never, ever make sense. When she at last turned her phone back on, she had a flurry of texts. She ignored them all, except for one cryptic text from Jason Ballard.

His text was cryptic:

What about Donatés? No one is working with him. Scott is doing the daily exercising, but Donatés is a one-man horse. WTF is going on!

As for Case, the mere sight of his name amongst the messages triggered a fury that left her exhausted. Delete, delete, delete, was the order of the day. On the fifth morning, she woke up to the sound of Shana crying, a miserable, forlorn wailing, and Laine knew she had to get it together.

Her wallowing had to stop, for the sake of the children.

When she made her way into the kitchen, wan and spent, she forced a bright smile and announced to the girls and Judith;

"Goodness, I feel much better at last. What's for breakfast?" She hugged her daughters, actually feeling them, and the warm little bodies broke through the ice that had closed around her heart. Shana had a plaster on her finger, a nick with the kitchen scissors.

Judith apologized, mortified that such a thing could happen on her watch.

Laine brushed off her apologies, feeling guilty. She was leaving too much to her mother-in-law.

She asked Judith; "Want me to take them to school this morning?" hoping she wouldn't have to, but it seemed the right thing to do. She wasn't ready to face the world out there.

Judith was mightily relieved to see Laine up . She was pale, but at least she was up.

"No, don't worry.," she reassured her. "Have a long shower, freshen up, and by the time you're dressed, I'll be back. Then we can talk..."

Laine winced. She had not the slightest desire to 'talk'. The house phone rang and automatically she answered, instantly regretting it.

It was Ballard, positively whining.

Donatés was restless and jumpy and did she know all her good work was being undone. Boyer was doing his best, but Donatés was playing up. The horse was missing her!

Ballard sounded quite frantic.

"I'll be there," she said curtly and hung up.

Ballard stared at the dead phone, bemused. Something was amiss. Like a hound picking up the scent, he wondered if there might be trouble in paradise. He dismissed that idea as being ridiculous and turned his mind to matters at hand.

When Judith returned later sans children, she found Laine in the kitchen, but this time, Laine was fully dressed and in her riding gear, looking rather pale, it was true, but, at least she was up and about!

Laine had her hands wrapped around a cup of steaming coffee. She looked up when Judith entered, attempting a smile, then giving up.

Judith poured herself a cup of coffee and sat down at the kitchen table.

"Talk to me..." she instructed Laine.

Laine shrugged, her face bleak. "What is there to say?"

Judith's hands were clasped before her, resting on the table. She sighed.

"I suspected perhaps he was having an affair. It was the same with his father," Judith said softly.

Laine stared at her in confusion. Case's father?? The perfect Jim McAllister? What the hell was she talking about?

Judith read the questions in Laine's eyes. She debated how much to say. How much was too much, and it was a long time ago. Buried forever, she had always hoped.

In the end, Judith decided the only thing she had the energy for was the truth.

"Laine, I know what you're going through," she said quietly, "I've been there myself. I had the same thing, years ago with Jim." She was staring fixedly into her coffee cup.

"You did!?" Laine was incredulous.

Judith shrugged. "When he told me, I screamed, shouted, ranted and raved–you name it. I even threatened to kill myself, can you imagine?" She gave a wry smile at Laine's shocked face. "That's easier said than done when you have a small child, and one on the way. First, one has to find the time," she said laconically.

Laine was staring at Judith, her problems momentarily forgotten. She found it hard to imagine Judith was never anything but cool and collected. She was such a proud woman. The thought of a suicidal Judith was impossible to imagine!

Judith continued; "He came home one day and I found him crying in the basement, this grown man, sobbing like a child." She set her cup down and was rubbing her hands, in a nervous gesture. "I had never, ever seen him cry before. He confessed to me that this 'Joanna' woman–her name was Joanna Stevens–she was pregnant with his child, and did I want a divorce?" Judith's face darkened at the memory. "Can you imagine? He left that decision to me, whatever happened, it was my decision!"

Judith's face closed, became hard. "God, I despised him for that."

Laine kept quiet, listening, her own woes temporarily banished.

Judith's tone was flat. "I told him, 'She's got one of yours, I've got two, you decide. I left him there," she said, " to his damn weeping! After a while, he came upstairs and he promised that he would end it, that day. That we would start again... "

Judith gazed out the window, her face wistful. "I believed him, you know..."

"Afterwards, I wondered why he was weeping that day, because he was giving her up, or was he genuinely sorry?" Her voice trailed off. "I never did find out, in the end," she continued, matter of fact. "She left the hospital, and for nine whole, happy years, I thought she was out of our lives, until a couple of weeks before Jim died. Apparently, he had 'bumped into her', he said, a few months earlier. He wanted a divorce."

Laine stared at Judith, her face disbelieving. Is this what Judith had bottled up inside for twenty-two years, knowing that her husband had died loving another woman? All these years, holding her head up high, pretending. Laine shivered, feeling suddenly chilled.

Judith gave a defiant jerk of her head. "I refused, of course. We fought, bitterly, but finally, he saw things my way, and promised he would end it, that very evening, tell her everything was over. He swore to me he would!" Her face sagged, as if her words were depleting her. "I'm told he left the hospital just before twelve that night, and he had a coronary on the way home." She looked resigned. "There I was, lying in bed, in the small hours, wondering if he was coming back to me, or was he just ...staying with her?"

She shrugged. "In the meantime, he was dead!" Judith almost laughed, as if this was one of life's jokes.

She dismissed Laine's horrified expression with a wave of her hand. "Oh, I've made my peace, years ago."

Laine had serious doubts about that, but she said nothing. Was Judith saying Case had a brother!?

"At five-twenty in the morning, I finally heard a car stop outside. But of course, it wasn't him. It was a patrol car, come to tell me about Jim. Apparently, he had the good sense to pull over, then he had the heart attack that killed him."

Judith took a deep breath, "Oh Laine, I was so very angry." she said sadly. "Of course, everyone thought I was so strong, but I was just angry. It's crazy how you can love someone and yet, their death leaves you so very bitter, I mean, how dare they die?"

Laine stared intently at the older woman, her own troubles momentarily forgotten. The thoughts were jumbled. "Are you saying that Case has another brother or sister somewhere?" she asked at last.

"A half-brother," Judith emphasized. "He would be thirty-six now. She moved to San Francisco, just after the funeral. His name is Josh McAllister. I heard she had her name legally changed after the child was born. The old 'up-yours', meant to hurt me."

"And Case knows nothing of this?" Laine shook her head in disbelief. No wonder Judith had never been crazy about the medical profession!

"There are just two people who know, Joanna Stevens ...And me. Now you. Funny, it hardly seems important anymore." She stood up.

Brisk, efficient Judith was back. She was late for her golf and Judith was looking around for her purse. "She wrote to me once, you know, a few years ago. Told me she was the only family the boy had, that he too, had graduated as a doctor, and if I could just find it in my heart to forgive her, it would be nice for the children to get to know each other. Naturally, I tore the letter up! Never heard any more.."

Laine found herself avoiding Judith's eyes. Nothing 'natural 'about it! Case had a brother, a doctor as well.

The whole thing was insane.

Judith sighed, and smiled thinly. She gathered up her purse and car keys.

"You're wondering how I could have done that? Hate and love, Laine, they're surprisingly close." She studied at her daughter-in-law, her face softening. "However, you're not me, thank God. You have something my son always needed. You are his haven, his rock. I doubt he will give that up."

Judith flushed, suddenly awkward, and uncharacteristically vulnerable. "I'm afraid I'm not a very good one for this sort of thing, Laine, as you can see." She sighed and looked away. "Twenty-odd years of rage are bound to take their toll. All I can say is, don't be hasty. Children are scant comfort in the early hours of the morning when you're alone in your bed." Judith smoothed non-existent creases from her slacks.

Laine stood up and reached out and pulled Judith into an embrace.

True to form, Judith suffered the hug awkwardly.

"Have you ever forgiven him?" Laine asked.

Judith had a wan smile. "It's myself I need to forgive, always prideful and stubborn." Judith grimaced. "His mistake was infidelity, mine was pride." Her voice trailed off, then suddenly she was her usual brisk self. "Carrie Lewisham is collecting me for a round of golf. Will you be okay?" She cocked her head to the side and eyed Laine, her face uncertain.

Laine dismissed her concern with a wave. "Sure, I'll be fine. I'm off to the stables to see Donatés. He's pining for me." Laine sensed the other woman was eager to escape, and Laine was just as keen for her to be gone.

She had enough on her plate! Judith had kept it all buried for twenty odd years, and it could stay damn buried, as far as Laine was concerned.

"Go ahead. I'll be fine." Laine waved her away.

For a long while after Judith had left, Laine sat at the kitchen table, thinking.

What should she tell the children about Case? How to explain his absence? How could he do this to them? And, the most troubling question of all, how long would she feel like this, a zombie, numb, going through the motions, hollowed out. But one emotion pushed through the pain, alive and strong.

Rage.

CATCHING COLD

Case was driving too fast, his mind racing, his thoughts jumbled, on his way to the Brea and his home. It had been five days. Surely Laine would to be ready to talk to him, by now?

There simply had to be a way to come through this. You want her to talk some sense into you, you gutless sack of shit, said the voice inside his head. But it's too late for that now, isn't it? You've hurt her already, now you're going to leave Roxie, destroy her too? Way to go, McAllister, fuck up everyone's life!

When he arrived at the house, the first thing he saw was Laine was out, her car was gone, and there were two suitcases standing next to the stairs in the hall.

Pushed under the handle of the one, was a note with his name on it.

Case shook his head in silent frustration, notes were no good. They needed to talk. He stooped and took the note. He felt a sinking sensation in his stomach when he noticed two cardboard boxes stacked to the brim with all his medical journals. He groaned aloud. She was serious.

"It looks as though she's serious..." His mother's words behind him seemed to read his mind.

Case swung around to see Judith in the passage, her face set in stony disapproval.

"Where is she?" he asked. He resented her presence at that moment, and he knew was being selfish.

Laine needed her. "Where are the children?"

"They're all at the stables. I believe she's told the children that you're going away to another seminar... Same address, son?" she asked, with heavy sarcasm. Case stood still, ignoring her barb, massaging the taught muscles in his face with his fingers, thinking. After a while, he looked up, rankled.

"Why are you so bitter?" But the truth was he didn't care for her opinion, not now.

Judith didn't reply. To tell him would require an energy she simply didn't have. He walked past her into the sitting room, went straight to the liquor cabinet and poured himself a drink.

Judith pursed her lips. It was three in the afternoon.

He tore the letter open that Laine had left and read it, mindful of his mother's presence. She was, apparently, disinclined to leave him to his thoughts. It was succinct and brief.

Case,

Stay away. If you need anything, tell Judith. Call the girls between 5 and 6, or not at all, as you wish.

She hadn't bothered to sign it.

Case crumpled up the note, his heart in his boots, aware all the time of his mother's unflinching gaze. He had fully expected her and the girls to be home. It was pointless calling ahead, she wouldn't take his calls. He would have to go through his mother, of all people.

Judith had sat down on the other side of the room, her legs tucked in at the ankles, hands in their familiar clasp on her lap, her whole mien challenging, demanding an explanation.

Well, he had none to give, not yet. He noticed his mother had her golfing kit on. Obviously, life went on.

"Well?" Anything to divert her attention from him.

She shrugged. "It would appear like father, like son," she said sardonically.

Case frowned at her and emptied his glass. Like father...? He dismissed it. He refused to be drawn into an argument about crap when his own life was falling apart. Had his father messed up?

Maybe had an affair too? It would explain a lot.

Judith was speaking, her tone softer.

"The girls miss you. They never leave my side, they're petrified I'll just disappear..." She was talking to him normally, now, there was no rancor in her voice, but her words cut him like a knife.

"I am so angry with you, Case, disgusted, and that's the sorry truth," she continued, her voice flat, and somehow her lack of emotion pained him even more.

He had a mental image of Shana, trailing behind him, incessantly asking, `Why Daddy? Why? Why this, why that Daddy....'

"Mom,..." he said at last, "try not to worry. We'll sort this thing out. I'll give her a bit of time.." he said, and Judith could hear his fear, and his fear prized open the smallest crack in her hard veneer. "Please, just ask her to call me."

Judith nodded. She wanted to say more to him, but inexplicably, there was a lump in her throat, and it was difficult to speak.

Frustrated at her silence, he shook his head in despair and strode out of the room. A short while later she heard his car start up. He was leaving. Judith went to check in the hall, her feet dragging.

The suitcases were gone, as well as his books.

She sat down heavily on the bottom stair, ungainly and deflated, glad she was alone in the house. There, at the bottom of the stairs, she buried her face in her hands and wept noisily for her son, her son who was losing everything.

She would explain to the girls she was catching Mommy's cold

CLEANING HOUSE

Mrs Sheppard settled herself down, pencil and notebook in hand, ready to take a letter. He had called her in, but there he was, gazing out the damn window.

After a couple of moments, Kevin swung around and looked at her. It was time to clean house. "How long have you been with me, Mrs Sheppard?" he asked her politely.

She frowned at him. "Two years," she answered. "Why?"

Kevin sat staring at her for a long moment, and she began to feel unnerved. Under the table, she began to jiggle her foot. She took off her spectacles and began to clean them vigorously. His next words took her breath away.

"Because I must dispense with your services. You are sullen, and I find your attitude distasteful. For some time now, in fact," he sat back, eying her, keen to get the matter over with.

"What? You can't do that," she exclaimed. She ceased cleaning her spectacles and fixed him with a baleful glare. "Why? I'm one of the most efficient secretaries here."

"Indeed you are. Also one of the most unpleasant. As the youngest partner here, frankly, I got lumbered with you," he said unkindly, too bleak to care. "I am tired of it. I am therefore dispensing with your services immediately, and I shall get a temp to assist until I find a suitable replacement." He looked at her coldly. "I believe that's all there is to be said, under the circumstances. Naturally, you will receive full severance," he said.

The meeting was over. It was done. Doubtless she would sue. He was ready for her. He leaned forward, Christ, his head hurt. Case still wouldn't return his calls. He kneading his brow with his fingers, his eyes closed.

Mrs Sheppard gathered her startled wits. She jumped up.

"Look at you, you're exhausted, that's why you're in this curious mood today," she exclaimed.

Kevin opened his eyes to look at her, frowning.

She smiled at him in what she deemed to be a motherly fashion. "Let me get you some more coffee and hold all your calls for a while. We can discuss this silly business later."

Without waiting for his reply, she laid her pencil and pad on his desk. "Coffee and some aspirin, that's what you need." Kevin blinked at her, fascinated. What a chameleon.

But she was right about one thing, he could do with another cup of coffee, and as for aspirin, definitely.

Next up, Case!

This rift had to end. So Case knew. So what. Suck it up, Kev, he told himself. Persist.

Case would come around! He would catch him unawares, just go there, out to the Brea, and let the damn cards fall as they may. He thought about it.

Yes, that felt like a plan. He resolved to go there, today, that very evening, when the girls were in bed. Then they would talk this out.

He would do exactly as Case did, pitch up unannounced! But the difference was, he wouldn't run away.

STEPPING UP

The sun was setting when Kevin turned into the McAllister driveway. He saw Case's car was gone, but Laine's car was there, in the garage.

Well, he would wait until Case came home.

Meantime, there was Laine to face. He winced at the sight of the DeVille Case had bought from Roxie Tanner. It seemed a lifetime ago.

Laine was coming down the porch stairs to greet him.

He could tell immediately, she knew. She looked wan and rather hollow-eyed, and the usual sunny Laine-smile was gone. But when she hugged him, it was her familiar hug, warm and genuine, and his spirits lifted a fraction.

He noticed she was incredibly pale!

"Laine?" They walked towards the house, his arm around her shoulders and he looked at her, long and hard. She looked drawn, unhappy. In fact, quite stricken.

Abruptly, Kevin realized there was something wrong here, very wrong. He stopped mid-stride and turned her to face him. She averted her face and looked away.

He was appalled to see tears streaming down her cheeks.

"Oh Kev," she said and dissolved into floods of tears against his chest. They stood there, outside the house, and she sobbed into his tailored shirt while he held her, dumbfounded. This couldn't possibly be about him!

Someone had died?

After a while, Laine pulled herself together, and even managed a shaky little laugh when she saw the consternation on his face.

"Sorry, Kev." She hunched her shoulders, covered her face with her hands and spoke through her fingers. "That's all I ever do these days–is damn cry."

"Because-?" he asked uncertainly.

"Surely- !"

They both spoke at the same time.

She looked at him, confused, and then Laine realized he was wondering if this could be about himself and Ashley. The gay thing!

Did he not know? She bit her lip and looking at him intently, her eyes still red from the storm of weeping.

"You don't know? Case doesn't live here anymore— He's with Roxie Tanner."

Kevin felt as if he had been punched in the gut. He took a step back from her, crooking his head as if to get a better look, see if she was serious.

"Well, talk about the stuffing being knocked out—" he breathed, dumbfounded. It was impossible. What the hell was she saying?

Laine saw from his stunned expression he hadn't known, and she felt shitty. Now it was her turn to reach out to him, hug him. He stood quietly in her embrace, overwhelmed. She released him and grimaced, her face resigned.

"Come on in, I'll tell you everything."

They sat in the kitchen and he listened in dismay to Laine's halting, painful recounting of events. Case! With Roxie. The prince, fallen—

His thoughts shot back to his conversation with Roxie's soon to be ex-husband, Jeremy Carter.

It was Case! Case was the 'someone' in Roxie Tanner's life. Carter had been on a fishing expedition! Kevin could not remember too many occasions when words had failed him, but this was one of them.

"Oh Laine, what can I say...?" He reached for her hand and squeezed it, then he stood up and pulled her into a hug. There were no words.

If she lived to be a hundred, Laine would always remember that hug, how Kevin's love and concern that evening vanquished some of her confusion, made her feel as if once more, she mattered.

She urged him to tell her about his new love, his life.

His smile was instant, shy.

"Corey," he said simply. "I'm in love with him. He was looking at her, wary, but determined to bare his soul.

Laine gave him a reassuring touch on his cheek, sensing his reticence.

"I think deep down I've always known I was....different, but with Case as a friend, it was easy to ignore that side of me. He's so damn macho without even opening his mouth, and I guess it spilled over onto me. Girls were easy."

He grinned, "I hero-worshiped Case. Still do. He was always so approving of me, right from the first day we met. We connected. Me with no mother, he with no father—we were different, yet the same.

He shrugged. "I don't expect you to understand, just believe me when I say that when I'm with Corey, it feels right."

Laine sighed. By rights, she should hate him, she thought. Not because of his homosexuality, that was irrelevant. But he had done to Ashley what Case was doing to her.

And yet, it was different.

Kevin was being truthful, true to himself, at last. Whereas Case, well he was just a lying sonovabitch!

"Actually, Ashley told me before she went away," she said with a small smile. "So I've known for some time. Ash begged me to allow you to tell Case in your own time. So," Laine shrugged, "I said nothing to him. I thought it best to let Case find out from you."

She looked away, chewing her lower lip at the memory of that ghastly night.

"Yeah." Kevin looked grim. "Well, things never turned out quite that way," He swung off the stool with a sigh. "I tried, many times, but he always seemed ...Closed, unapproachable. Just —distracted." His mouth curled in derision. "Now I know why."

He could still see Case's horrified face up at the lobby window, like an apparition in a nightmare. He had drunk himself into a stupor that night, after an explanation to a horrified Corey.

He thought about it.

Ashley and him coming unstuck, that was one thing. But Case and Laine, that was unthinkable.

"What are you going to do, Laine? You have to face him— perhaps even her, sometime? You have children, you can't go on avoiding him forever." Kevin frowned, worried. This was bad, that she wouldn't even talk to Case. Very, very bad.

"I don't know," she said miserably. "I feel too betrayed. "I thought we were the happiest couple I knew, he never, ever lied to me before, and to find out they've been-together, and for weeks!" She shook her head, her face suddenly stony. "It's over, I'll never trust him again, not ever."

Kevin flinched. The prince was knee-deep in shit, for sure. Laine was no Ashley. Sure, Laine was devastated now, but devastated wives became crazy, and they had this nasty habit of eviscerating their unfaithful husbands.

Kevin reflected that there also had to be something about Roxie Tanner for Case to behave as he had. His dick talking?? Probably.

Hopefully.

That would fade, but then it might be too late. He said nothing of his thoughts, and instead tried to be the voice of reason. "You don't believe that. Give him a chance to explain."

"Explain what? All the finer details? No thank you," she said flatly, her mouth twisted. "If that's what he wants, to hell with him. And if it's not what he wants, to hell with him still. We can't come back from this, and that's the part that hurts the most."

Kevin's heart sank.

"But don't worry about us," she said, thinking suddenly of Kevin and Case. "He'll come around. —It must be wonderful for him to have someone to punish!" she said, with a sudden shrewd insight.

Kevin frowned. Laine was one in a million. Case had to be insane, no other explanation. The faint beginnings of an idea stirred in his mind, slowly taking hold, and it lightened his mood.

"Laine, things will work out, you'll see," he said softly. "Some marriages are all the stronger for troubles like these." He flushed when he caught the full blast of her withering look. "It's true," he insisted. "I've seen the worst of breakups come right back from the dead. Remember, I'm a divorce lawyer. I see these things!" he said with a smile. He tilted her chin up, making her look him in the eyes. "And I tell you, it's true."

The withering look changed to one of doubt.

Good. It was a start. They chatted for a while longer, and when he was sure she was feeling better, he stood up to leave. "Remember, you've got me. Anytime you need me, call me. Anytime," he emphasized.

"Thanks, Kev," she said. "Perhaps you can come and rescue me one evening, take me out to dinner, let me meet Corey."

She linked her arm in his and walked with him to the front door.

"I'd like that, you're my family and It's important to me that you like him," he said, touched. "I'll maybe check in on you on the weekend?"

Laine hesitated. "Thanks, but I just about live at the stables lately. Donatés has developed into something of a wonder-horse. It seems to be the one thing I can still do well. I have him up to five foot eight in the jumps, and I'm going to enter him in the San Diego Grand Prix. Sundays are mini-competition time. We jump against the counties."

For the first time that evening, she appeared animated, exuded a different energy.

Kevin was relieved to see a glimpse of a life beyond heartbreak. "So you think you have the makings of a champ?" he said with a smile.

Her face was serious. "It takes horse and rider. We have to be the perfect pair."

There was a pause and the words 'perfect pair' seemed to hang in the air, mocking them. Laine shook her head quickly, as if to banish her demons. "Anyhow, Jason seems to think so."

She looked up at him, her face grim. "Training keeps me sane.-Well, not much," she said ruefully, "There's two me's. One that gets on with it, and the words that come out of her mouth sound sane, normal.

Then there's the other me, the one who is always, always screaming in her head, "It's not fair... It's not true!" Laine looked sheepish. "But, thank God, I can keep that me hidden. Mostly," she said with a small smile. "Have to be getting on with my life!"

"As you should," he said softly, kissing the top of her head. "Well, I'll call you, okay?"

But as Kevin drove away, his mood changed. Fuck Case and his stupidity.

The irony of it swamped him. Fuck me and my stupidity too, he thought. There we were, both hiding behind platitudes and polite conversation.

Just what was so special about Roxie Tanner anyhow?

He signed. Nothing for it. He would call on her, let her know exactly what she was fucking up!

TURNING AWAY

Kevin was already there, when Roxie turned into her driveway. He was leaning against his car, arms and ankles crossed, a man with all the time in the world, or a man with mission.

Roxie wondered which it was? The latter, she was sure. She felt uncharacteristically anxious at the sight of his Aston Martin in her driveway. He hadn't said much on the phone, just insisted they needed to talk.

In fact, he wanted to talk to both of them, so clearly the cat was out the bag.

Laine and Kevin were tight. Is that what this was about?

He smiled that Kevin Daniels smile when she got out of her car, and she allowed herself to relax a little. She smiled back, feeling that pent-up energy he always seemed to exude.

"Roxie, how are you? You're looking good." He kept his arm at his side. This was not an occasion for hugs.

Kevin sensed she was nervous. Good. She knew she was fucking up! He found himself comparing her to Laine. Roxie had none of Laine's serenity, but rather a raw sensuality. If that comes after you, he thought wryly. Poor bastard!

"Kevin." She was sizing him up as well. "Are you here on business?" she asked, referring to his formal attire.

"Oh." he glanced down at his suit. "No, not business. Business is over for today. His face was serious. "I had rather hoped to see both you and Case. Are you expecting him later?"

She shrugged. "I hope so, but it's anybody's guess. He usually calls me before he comes here." She grimaced, "With his work—" What the hell, tell the truth.

She shrugged. "With him, there's no guarantee."

"Ah." She sounds like a wife already, thought Kevin.

She led the way indoors. "Time for a drink?"

"Why not?" He was in no hurry. "I hope you don't mind me just popping by?" he asked diffidently, but they both knew he didn't care if she did mind!

"Not at all," she replied, her voice even. "You mentioned you called to see both Case and myself?" she prompted. "He's not here, but what can I do for you?" Those incredible jade eyes fixed on his, curious, showing no sign of retreat. She indicated Scotch and he nodded.

Kevin watched her pour the drinks. It seemed like a good idea at the time, but now he wasn't so sure. "I went to see Laine the other night. That's how I found out, about...you and Case." He looked bleak. "I must have been as stunned as he was that night when he came to visit me!" He bit his lower lip, and his tone was droll. "It seems we've both had our little secrets."

The irony was not lost on Roxie. She looked away, towards the expanses of the Pacific, wondering what one should say. "Yes, he told me about that evening. He was quite upset"," she said. Understatement of the year, but there seemed no point in rubbing salt...

Kevin smirked, laconic. "You think? And how do you feel?"

She was amused that he would even ask, "Kevin, in my life I've met so many gay people, it doesn't bother me in the least. Not at all. I look for talent everywhere, and when I find it, their damn sexuality is the last thing on my mind."

She looked at him, her face concerned. "But I do think the whole gay thing was a shock for Case." She gestured with her hands it was all nonsense. "Give him time, he'll get over it."

Kevin couldn't help feeling cheered at her words. He reminded himself this was the enemy. He liked her, this Roxie Tanner, from the first time they met. It would be so much easier if he didn't.

"I hope you're right. But what I wanted to discuss with you concerns Laine." He saw her flinch, and pressed on. "And his family, the family that you want him to abandon." He held up his hand, placating, preempting any comment. "I won't insult you by asking if you love him, I'm sure you do," he said, putting his glass down. He was choosing his words with care. "The thing is, Ashley and I never had the intimate sort of marriage that they had. I think we both envied them." He looked at her, his face solemn. "Most people do, you know, envy them," he said with pride. "Theirs was one of the happiest marriages I know. Nauseating, they could be," he said, a small smile on his lips. "Not that I didn't love my wife, I did, I do," he corrected himself, "But they, Case and Laine, they are in their own league." He looked her in the eyes. "I just wondered if you really, really know just what this split will cost Case! —And I don't mean money," he said.

Roxie looked away, then she looked at him, defiant.

"I've thought about all of that. These things happen every day. Case was meant to be mine. I was meant to be his. It's something neither of us can help. And I know I can make him happy. We'll just have to work it out," she said defensively.

Kevin face hardened. "These things don't 'happen every day', as you so glibly put it. Or do you fall in love with someone like Case every day?" he challenged her.

Roxie looked away.

Kevin said nothing, his heart sinking. It was something big, something special for her. It had to be. As for Case leaving Laine, that was unthinkable and yet, it had happened. He reminded himself that Laine had booted Case out, and his pal had little choice in the matter. Still, semantics.

"Roxie," he persisted, "Look at me. Do you understand, as happy as he might seem with you, he loves his wife, he's just —distracted."

If his words stung, she didn't show it. Instead she squared her shoulders, her eyes flashing. " We belong together, Kevin! I cannot let him go, ever."

Suddenly the spunk seemed to leave her, and her shoulders sagged, and she covered her face. "I just can't..." she whispered, blinking away tears.

He frowned. She really loves him. What a fucking mess!

He gave her shoulder a gentle squeeze, and then let his hand fall.

To like her, feel sorry for her, felt like treachery! But it was Case who was the bastard here, not him. He reached for his drink, finished it in a swallow, anxious to be gone. To hell with Case. He had said his piece. Whether it would help, only time would tell.

He spoke quietly. "Laine is one of the world's survivors, she'll always get by. Some guy will snap her up in a heartbeat. No doubt about that. She has the kids, a career, and if she cracks a sponsorship, well then," he sighed, and thrust his hands in his pockets, "she'll be lost to him forever, that's for sure!" He looked at her, his face hard. "Then, Rox, you will have to put back the pieces. And that's what you'll have, Roxie, pieces. Laine, she'll be okay. —Case is the one I worry about!"

He was at the door. "Tell him I was here, will you? I want a chance to speak to him, face to face, but not at the clinic." He hesitated, then added; "Tell him I miss him," he said simply.

"Sure," Roxie replied, her voice small. She was entitled to no kindness from this man.

"Don't mention it." He waved and left. A moment later she heard his car roar into life.

Roxie was disconsolate, Kevin and Charles Manning. Both against her. Even Phillipa, seldom daunted by social norms, had a whole bucket of reservations about the affair. The whole damn world was against her, she thought, brooding.

But perhaps Kevin Daniels had offered her a lifeline? She frowned, remembering.

What did he mean, if Laine McAllister got a sponsorship, she would be lost forever?

Sponsorship. That meant giving someone or other a chunk of money?

Roxie looked around for her phone.

THE CAVALRY'S COMING

Later that morning, Kevin was looking through his mail with scant enthusiasm when his mobile rang. Only two people had that ring, either Ashley or Case.

It was Ash. At last. He felt his spirits lift.

"Ashley? Ashley?"

"Kevin?" Her voice sounded small, tentative.

"How are you? Where are you?"

"I'm in France. And I'm fine, thank you. Are you good?"

"Yes... Great. Funny, just this morning I put on that tie you gave me, and I was wondering how you are?

There was silence, and the line hummed more loudly. She sounded as if she had something on her mind.

"Kevin, I can't talk, the reception here is lousy, but I'm calling to tell you that I'll be home on Wednesday, and I.." the line faded into silence again, and for a second Kevin wondered if they had been cut off. "I will be coming back to the house, and I was wondering— Been away for a while, so—"

Suddenly he understood, and he flushed.

She wanted to know if the coast was clear, no more surprises.

"That's good-great! Really it is," he reassured her. Another thought occurred to him, "—Or do you want me to move out?"

Reality struck home all at once, and he felt awkward and uncomfortable, instantly despondent.

"No, no, of course not." she said hastily, "I mean, we haven't really decided anything? Have we?? About the house and that sort of thing?"

Now it was her turn to sound uncertain.

"I'm just letting you know I'll be home on Wednesday, and then we'll sort out all that... that sort of thing. I just don't want to.. .to... embarrass you?" her words were halting and uncomfortable.

"Ah." Kevin flushed. "No, it's okay. Do you want me to meet you at the airport? It's no bother!" he said. "Honestly!"

"No, no, that's been arranged already thank you. My office will sort it, don't worry. I'll see you Wednesday evening. Should be home around 6 or so...

"Good. Fine, fine. Great.' He didn't know what else to say.

"Okay then... Bye. Look after yourself." She hung up.

Wednesday. She'd be home Wednesday.

He swung his chair around and tried to focus on the papers before him, but turmoil made for mistakes, and that would never do. Case and Laine. Laine had said nothing to Ash, she had pressed him to say nothing. 'Ashley has enough to deal with, Kev.'

All these fucking secrets! Still, he felt hopeful. Ash would know what to do. The cavalry was on the way.

He gave up trying to work and reached for his phone.

"Corey! Guess who's back on Wednesday! Take me to lunch, and I'll tell you all!"

BOTTOMS UP

Kevin lay back, listening to the sounds of Corey making the coffee in the kitchen. He could smell bacon too, but the truth was, he didn't feel hungry. He was in Corey's tiny apartment, champing at the bit to get home, to see Ash, something familiar, something from his other life.

At least she hasn't dropped me like a hot potato, he thought, embittered.

Why couldn't Case understand!

There had been no word from Case even after his visit to Roxie, and Case's silence cut Kevin deeply.

Ashley, she was something salvaged from that other life.

She would be devastated to hear about Case and Laine.

Well, at least Case and Laine were talking now, after a fashion. Sighing, Kevin rolled onto his stomach, hands under his chin, seeking a wisdom that eluded him.

He knew about pre-divorce shenanigans, too well, but this, this was all so different.

These were the people in his heart!

Laine had mentioned divorce to him for the first time on the phone yesterday. She said Case was going to see her on Friday night, and apparently she intended to broach the subject of divorce.

Kevin frowned, recalling the conversation;

"I have to, Kevin," Laine said, her voice wooden. "My life has to go on. Each day the children wonder if he'll come home today, and then—" Suddenly there was a catch in her voice, and he heard the vulnerability she tried to hide. "There's just nothing he can do to undo this - so why drag it out."

Drag it out? It had been a mere few weeks, he thought, but he refrained from comment. This was Laine, and perhaps one week apart was a lifetime, perhaps it was more she was from take-no-shit Texas. He closed his eyes and changed the subject.

"Ashley gets back on Wednesday."

"Oh." Her voice lifted. "Kevin, you sound quite pleased!"

"Oh, I am," he had admitted. "I've missed her. Not that anything has changed, but—, I just miss her. Everything seems to have exploded in my life lately, and then you and Case.," he sighed. "I guess I need my other best friend at this time. And that's still Ash.

Thinking of that conversation, Kevin rolled over and sat up, restless, agitated. His life had changed so dramatically, now this, this crap with Case and Laine, and none of them, not one of them, had seen through the other.

Corey entered with the coffee on a tray, saving Kevin from further gloomy contemplation.

He sat down on edge of the bed, noting the frown on Kevin's face. Case. This had to be about the damn Case guy.

Kevin took the coffee from Corey, and Cory clinked his mug against Kevin's.

"Bottoms up!" Corey said, with a mischievous wink.

Kevin's snort of laughter made him splutter coffee all over the bed!

PERFECT STORMS

She was back!

Kevin was delighted to see Ashley's car in the driveway.

"Ashley! You look good. Welcome home." He gave her a warm hug and kissed her lightly, stepping away a little too quickly. Things were different now.

Still, she looked happy to see him, and that pleased him.

"Hello, Kevin. It's good to see you too. I see you've missed me, in small ways." Non-comprehending, he stared at her.

"The coffee creamer. It's finished," she said, smiling. She looked relaxed, composed.

"Oh," he nodded. "You'll find a lot more missing before the day is out!

They smiled together and he could feel some of his tension fading. "So was it a good trip?" he said brightly, then flinched, feeling trite. "I'm sorry. It wasn't the best reason to go on a holiday..."

She was nonchalant. "The trip was so-so. I needed to run away from everyone. It did me good!"

He thought that part was true. She looked relaxed, tired perhaps from her traveling, but at ease.

"Anything out of the ordinary happen here?" she asked, making conversation. She felt tired and longed for her bed, but he looked eager to talk.

The smile left his face. He looked suddenly bleak.

"No, that is, not with me. But Case-"

Ashley sensed a discernible drop in his energy. Was Case being a bastard about the gay thing?

"There's no other way to say this, so I'll just say it. Case has left Laine. He's having an affair with Roxie Tanner." Ashley paled visibly.

Could it be true what he was saying?

Kevin saw the disbelief in her eyes. He shrugged.

"Yes, it's true. He moved out the Monday after you left! It's serious. She's crazy in love with him and he— " He scowled. "Well, I can't speak for Case."

"Jesus! Oh God, what's happening to us all?" Ashley's voice was barely a whisper. She looked winded, her hand over her mouth, her eyes wide in dismay. "I've sent her the odd message, and she's been so... disconnected. Now I understand why! Oh my God!"

Kevin crossed his arms, glum. "I remember teasing Case in the car, the night of his birthday, saying that he hadn't tasted life. Case, the perfect prince. And bam! Things go crazy!" He lifted his hands in a gesture of helplessness.

"Why haven't you spoken to Case?" Ashley demanded. "Surely, if there's anyone in the world that can talk sense to him, it's you. He can't possibly mean to leave his family. I mean, there are children—!" Ashley's voice faded. She was beyond appalled.

"I can't talk to him. That is, he won't talk to me. He found out about Corey. He wasn't pleased, to put it mildly."

Ashley snorted. Kevin's sexuality, that hardly compared! What on earth was going on with their friends!

"Laine? How's she? God, I must call her!" Panicked, Ashley looked around for her phone.

"She's devastated. Heartbroken, as you can imagine. But," he paused, searching for the right words, "She was destroyed." He had a faint smile. "But, like the good 'ol phoenix, she's up again. We all seem to be stronger than we knew."

Then he grimaced. "And God knows, so much weaker," he added.

"Anyhow, some of the anger has subsided a little, but not much. It seems they are talking, a little. I gather he's had the children for weekends. "

"For weekends! Oh, God, I just can't believe this!" Ashley exclaimed. "How does she explain it to the children?"

"Says he's working. 'Learning at Doctor school.' He looked glum. "But she's talking divorce, Ash, and she means it." Kevin looked ashamed. "Once, I remember he said he needed to talk to me, and all I could think about was my problems. I was worried, you know, thought perhaps he'd found out. We never did get to speak. He came here, unexpectedly, saw me with Corey." He winced at the memory. "We were kissing on the patio. Well, enough said!" Kevin looked dejected. "His affair with Roxie Tanner–that's probably what he needed to talk to me about."

There was no end to it! Ashley stood up, her face drawn. She walked over to him and held his face, kissed him gently on the lips. "We'll get through this, Kev. All of us. But I have to call Laine, this minute. There's some luggage in the car, can you bring it inside, please?"

"Sure." Kevin left her in the kitchen and Ashley leaned forward on the counter and placed her head in her hands. —Case and Laine. It was unthinkable. Their marriage was epic! Laine loved and trusted him so. He worshiped her too, goddammit!

But one thing Ashley knew; Case wasn't the frivolous sort, and if he had left Laine for Roxie, it was serious.

Biting her lip, she called Laine's number.

BAD TIMING

Roxie looked at Charles Manning in defiance, oblivious to the exasperation on his face. The day was warm, but she felt chilled. She crossed her arms and looked at him, her face set. "No way. No way can I do the East Coast now. It's impossible, out of the question!" She shook her head to emphasize her sentiment.

Charles stared back at her, thoroughly exasperated.

"This is the opportunity you have been waiting for. This is what you've been working for, and now you don't want to go! You need exposure there. He changed his tone, "Look, I'm not talking about a country-wide tour, I'm talking about a few concerts on the East Coast. You'll be away a month. Tops."

He huffed in annoyance and frustration. "The money guys need to see you in action, and that's all I want. That's all you want, for God's sake."

He was angry now, a rare thing for Manning, whose staple diet was a crisis a day. However, this wasn't a crisis, this was a catastrophe! What on earth could have gotten into her?

Suddenly he knew.

He sat back and glowered at her.

"It's that doctor again, isn't it? That's what's behind this."

"What do you mean, again?" she snapped, but he noted she didn't deny it.

"The last time you were unprofessional," he said, heavily emphasizing the word unprofessional, "and hared off into the unknown, it was because your head was screwed up with him. Now I finally have all the players on board to get you an East Coast tour -and you won't go!? Jesus Christ! What about your career?" he spluttered.

Sheila looked in at the door, her eyes wide. Usually, it was the other way around, with Roxie doing the yelling. He glared at her and she withdrew her head hastily.

Roxie was unmoved.

"Charles, maybe I better spell this out for you. For the first time in my life," she hesitated, "someone else is more important than my career. And the time isn't right now for me to leave and go tearing off to the other end of the world. I have to be here, nearby," she said.

"Don't care! Don't bloody care! What about me, who's been busting my butt to get you this far. Now you have a chance at unbelievable exposure, a movie in the works, and you tell me you don't care!" His face was purple with rage.

She shrugged, undaunted.

"I never said I won't do it, I just said not now. The timing, Charles, is not right. Perhaps in a couple of months' time, But not now. It's too soon." Her jaw was set stubbornly, and he sank back in his chair, weary. He stared back at her for a long moment.

"You have the chance to be the queen, queen of this business, and you're taking chances?" He could not believe what he was hearing.

She turned to leave. "Is there anything else," she asked, ignoring the voice of reason inside her head.

"No," he scowled, fed-up. "I guess that's it." He took a deep breath. "I'm going to keep these buggers at bay for a week or two, in the hopes that you come to your senses."

Roxie slung her purse over her shoulder, indifferent. "Well, I'll be on my way." She gave him a quick smile. "Cheer up Charles, it's not so bad. It's only money."

"That's what you think," he muttered. "Tell me, what can be more important than realizing the dream of a lifetime?"

"That's easy, Charles!" she called over her shoulder. "The love of a lifetime."

CLEANSING SPIRITS

It was one of those days when she felt resolute, —as resolute as one could be, with Kleenex ever at the ready. It was time to face the world and admit that her marriage was over.

Laine thought about Josie. She couldn't keep avoiding her forever. She didn't have long to wait. That evening Ollie started barking shortly after Laine put the children to bed. A car was approaching. Her foolish heart leapt.

Case??

She looked out the window and her heart sank. It was Josie's Volvo pulling up. Laine gave herself a mental shake. This was her best friend, yet Laine dreaded facing her. Where was Case, Josie would ask, and what would she reply? She rehearsed various responses in her head. He was at a seminar? Operating?

Josie was knocking at the front door, and Laine's was still scrambling for believable scenarios. Judith had retired to the annex. For the briefest of seconds, she thought of pretending she was out, or asleep perhaps?

But there was no choice, she had to open the door, or Josie's loud, insistent knocking would wake the girls.

She opened the door, flustered, still agitating about what to say.

Josie stood before her, her rounded face unusually solemn. She was holding a large paper bag. When Laine opened the door, she set the bag down carefully, and Laine heard it clink, as if it had bottles inside. She stepped forward to hug Laine, concerned.

"Laine. Where have you been? Why don't you return calls? I've been worried about you, all the girls are!" she scolded. She fell quiet when she saw Laine's drawn face. She held Laine fast in a second hug, then pushing her arms out straight, held her friend at arm's length. She stared hard at Laine and drew in her breath, alarmed. Laine looked like death!

Laine endured the scrutiny, feeling decidedly uncomfortable. Josie released her grip, picked up the paper bag, and strode inside, ahead of Laine.

Laine sighed, closing the door. What was there to say, anyhow? She turned and followed Josie and her clunking bag into the living room.

Josie set the bag down again. She swung around, her demeanor one of no-nonsense. "Laine, what's going on?" she demanded, "You look like shit!"

Laine nodded, rolled her eyes upwards, uncaring. "Tell the truth, why don't you," she muttered. She shrugged.

Josie eyed her. "C'mon Lainie, tell me, sweetie. I know something is very wrong." Indeed she did, she thought, but not for her to be the messenger! And from the look on Laine's face, Josie guessed she knew. She sat on the couch and patted the space next to her. Laine sat down obediently.

"Case left me."

There, it was out. Quite easy, really. Three small words. Three small words that meant her life was over, that her life before was a sham.

Josie stared unblinkingly at Laine, struggling to grasp the enormity of those words. Looking at her friend's pale and defeated face, she had an overwhelming desire to murder Case McAllister. She had toyed with the notion umpteen times these past days, since the episode at the airport.

Laine looked shattered, as if someone had taken everything that was the real Laine McAllister and left behind this empty, broken dummy.

But Laine and Case. Separated!

It was impossible. No fucking way! But then, Josie reminded herself, she had seen his feet of clay.

And here was the debris, the fallout. This wasn't just the failing of any marriage. This was Laine and Case McAllister. This was up there, with the fucking Titanic!

An epic fail, goddammit.

Laine and Case were supposed to be unsinkable. Didn't they know that?

Josie felt overwhelmed, and quite frantic.

Laine watched Josie's turmoil play out in her face, and she felt as if she should say something, but there seemed not a lot to say. She reached out and took Josie's hand, trying to convey with a touch she understood. She was only just holding herself together by supreme willpower. Perhaps coffee? Offer her some coffee?

Josie snapped out of her spell. "He left you. He actually left you?" She sounded dazed.

Laine nodded dumbly, not trusting herself to speak. She felt humiliated, but more than that, she felt naive and stupid. She knew Josie exalted Laine's marriage as being perfect, her husband as being perfect.

"That, that ...motherfucker." Josie breathed slowly, her brows knitting in fury.

The shock at Josie's foul language had Laine's eyes like saucers, and that pleased Josie. Anything was better than that stricken look. In any event, only rage would keep her own tears at bay, and Josie's tears were the last thing Laine needed to see!

"You heard me." she snapped. "That motherfucker. How could he do this to you? "She lunged for Laine, gripping her in a huge clumsy bear hug, outraged. Her friend, her serene, smiling Lainie, felt fragile in her embrace.

The dam wall broke for Josie. Despite her resolve to be strong, Josie felt her tears streaming. Laine was beginning to cry too, at first, softly, and then with great, gulping sobs that chilled Josie.

There was nothing she could do.

She held her friend tightly while she sobbed, hearing Laine's anguish, feeling her pain as if it were her own heart cut in two.

Mostly the lump in Josie's throat prevented any words at all. The best she could do was sit there, on the couch, enfold Laine in her arms until the storm passed.

Eventually, a stream of persistent snot coming from Laine forced Josie to let go and she burrowed in her purse for a Kleenex, chiding herself.

This was a time to be strong, for Chrissakes.

Tears were a luxury she could save for later.

At last, after an eternity, Laine looked up, wiping her nose and eyes unceremoniously with the back of her hand, drained. She noticed Josie's own red eyes and felt worse.

"Sorry," she said wanly, "I intended to be so together."

"Mmm," muttered Josie, patting her back, "Well, just in case you weren't —" She reached into the bag and brought out a bottle of wine, opening the bag wide so Laine could peer inside. There were three more bottles. "I brought medicine."

Laine looked into the bag, and then she looked at her friend, her eyes narrowed. "You knew?" she asked, disbelieving.

Josie gave a little shrug, gesturing expansively, "Eh. I sort of had an idea," she admitted, "I never dreamed he would leave you for her."

Laine stared at her, her face incredulous. For her? Josie knows?

Josie shrugged and explained, her eyes miserable, "I saw them. At the airport. They were kissing. " She squirmed at the recollection, "-Like lovers kiss. I thought I would die from shock." She leaned forward, holding Laine's shoulders with her hands, forcing Laine to look her in the eye. "Never, ever did I think he would be dumb enough to leave you! He loves you so much. This I absolutely know." She ended emphatically. Her head was bobbing up and down, willing Laine to agree.

Laine said nothing, aghast, waiting- There was more, she was sure. Josie felt flustered. There was nothing for it. Tell her all.

"When did you see them together." Laine's eyes bored into Josie's. She repeated slowly, trying to understand, "When you saw them together?? When the hell did you see them together?" she repeated, her voice rising. Did everyone know about Case and her? Was she the proverbial cliché, the last to know? "Did you know about Roxie Tanner, and you never told me?" She stared at Josie, disbelieving.

"No, of course not!" Josie retorted instantly, affording Laine some comfort, then Josie squirmed, uncomfortable. "That is, not really. I saw them together at the airport when we went to Vegas, for my nephew's bris."

Josie knew she might be babbling, but fuck it. Anyone would babble! "Anyhow, I spotted Case, and I thought he was with you, so I went rushing up, I had lost Ivor, and our baggage, you see, I was in an absolute tizz, anyhow, there I was, hurtling towards him, " she said, cringing at the memory, "only to notice at the very last minute, when he stepped back, the woman he was with, —that sure as hell wasn't you."

Josie looked thoroughly miserable. "I don't think he saw me, but I'm not sure. I think not. I just turned and absolutely flew in the other direction. Oh Laine, I didn't know what to do," she wailed. "I've been in an absolute state! I haven't even told Ivor," she added miserably. Josie was wringing her plump hands. "I've been trying to see you, but honestly, when it proved difficult, I was half relieved. I just didn't know what to say, or do!"

Laine wasn't listening, she was doing the math. "At the airport? On a Sunday?"

"Yes. A couple of weeks back. Oh shit, I was hoping he would come to his senses." Josie said wretchedly. "Now you say he's moved out. Oh, I absolutely can't believe that."

Laine's expression was stony. "Well, believe it," she said, her voice hard.

"That's probably why he came clean. He was afraid I would find out from you. Damn him to hell." To her dismay, Laine felt the tears coming again. That bastard. She bowed her shoulders and hid her face with her hands and began to cry anew.

"Oh God." Josie gave up being 'strong' and allowed her own tears to flow. The Kleenex was soon sodden, and reluctantly she left Laine and went into the kitchen to collect two paper towels. When she returned, she was relieved to see Laine had composed herself.

Laine blew noisily into the proffered napkin. Through reddened, puffy eyes she eyed a hapless, tearful Josie.

"God, don't we look a sight." Laine muttered, "That's all I seem to do lately, drift around aimlessly, looking for a quiet place to howl." She sighed," Sorry, Jos, I never meant to unload on you."

Josie shrugged. "Well, if not me, then who?" She began to open the wine. "Get the glasses. I guessed we would need serious alcohol reserves tonight, I knew it. —Told Ivor to collect me at eleven, so I don't have to drive."

Obediently, Laine went off to fetch glasses. When she returned, the two women gave each other a small smile, knowing the worst was behind them. There was a comfortable, albeit sad silence in the room, broken by the gurgling of wine into the glasses.

"Fuck him," Laine said abruptly. It was Josie's turn to look shocked. "No, I mean it. Fuck him." She tilted her glass upward, and when she straightened it, it was empty. She twirled the glass and lunged for the bottle.

Josie nodded approvingly. "That's the stuff. blot him out!"

Alcohol, the great healer. Josie filled up her own glass again. Tonight, of all nights, it was important that she keep up!

Laine vented while they emptied the next two bottles, and Josie listened, the pair of them growing more belligerent as their gills slowly filled with the Merlot. After the second bottle, bravado reigned, banishing any suggestion of defeat, or a reconciliation.

"Don't do anything ...foolish," Josie warned her, wondering at the same time who the hell she knew that Laine could be 'foolish' with! There was no one, really. No one like Case, that miserable, treacherous bastard!

Obviously, Laine's thoughts had gone down a similar path, because she answered immediately, "Oh, there's no one," she said with a nonchalant shrug. "I've thought about it.—One does, you know, it's probably the ego kicking in, but there's no one at all. Just good old Jason, "she said with a pout. "Jason's the best we've got!"

Josie wrinkled her nose in distaste. "Ah. Yes," Josie intoned. "Jason. He of the Great Dick."

"What?" Laine looked at her.

"Alice Parker banged him after she got divorced, she says he is all dick," she shrugged, "but, you know, no technique."

Laine belched softly, disinterested in this nugget. She stared at Josie, her eyes owlish from the drink. Big dicks, small dicks, they were all bastards. Although, "he's always very nice to me?" she murmured, trying to be fair.

"I bet," Josie said under her breath, but loud enough for Laine to hear.

They sniggered together.

The women sat in comfortable companionship, speaking only as thoughts entered their minds, Laine brooding, Josie overwhelmed and trying valiantly to distract her.

The wine was slowly but surely doing the anesthetizing.

Never a big drinker, Laine wondered perhaps if the wine was disagreeing with her.

It was a tad gassy. Maybe it was her? Maybe she was gassy?

Josie interrupted her deliberations while Laine tried to remember when last had she been this drunk. Not ever, she concluded.

"Music, we need music. Happy music!" Josie announced, reaching for the TV control and flipped it on, changing to a popular music channel. "Music and wine, that's what I used when Ivor dumped me for that slut, Miranda," she said triumphantly, "Music, and wine of course. Always works a treat."

"Ivor dumped you?" Laine asked, disbelieving. "When did Ivor ever dump you? That's a lie!"

Josie gestured, poop-poohing. "The man was confused, we were young. He was toying with the idea. But he lived to regret it, big-time!" she said. "I forgave him, but man, he had to grovel!" Josie eyed her pal from under her lids. She knew Laine, and Laine was from Texas, and everyone knew Texan women were full of crap! For sure, Laine would toss Case out on his sorry backside!

Fact was, she, Josie, she was a softie. But Laine, Laine McAllister was a whole other story! She had booted Case out already! Josie shook her head. Perhaps Laine thought Case would never actually go?? Her heart was aching for her friend, but Laine's tears had stopped, and it was over to her, Josie, to make sure she was fine.

"Have you thought of confronting her?" Josie asked. "I'll go with you!"

"Oh please, spare me!" Her face showed disdain. "Roxie with her boxie!"

They both giggled uproariously at that.

Laine found she had hiccups. "It's Case. He was in control, undoubtedly. Seduced maybe, but we had vows and if that's what he wants—!" She looked at Josie, and inebriated or not, Josie suddenly saw a glimpse of the Laine that would be an Olympian.

Laine shrugged. "—Then he must tell his story walking!"

A popular song came on. Josie adopted a pose, oozing sass and belligerence, and she lip-synced to the music from the TV. "I can buy myself floweeeeers" wailed Josie.

Laine began laughing. This song they knew well. Josie competed with Miley Cyrus with a heartfelt passion that had a drunken Laine in stitches.

At the chorus, a tone-deaf Laine joined in, her spirits both pickled and lifted.

When Ollie started howling, it was too much for the women and they collapsed in a hysterical heap, wiping tears of laughter from their faces.

They were interrupted by a man's timid voice.

"Everything okay here?? Josie? Time to go???" Ivor stood in the doorway, looking nervous. When women laughed like that, some poor sod was the victim. Something was up with Josie these last days, and it had to do with Laine, for sure.

But whatever it was, they looked as if they had resolved it, and then some.

"Hello," they chorused together, giggling.

Laine felt suddenly queasy. "Do eshcuse me, don't feel too good..." She tried to get up but staggered.

"Ivor," snapped Josie, "For God's sake, help her to the loo," Josie herself looked decidedly tipsy.

Ivor was appalled. "Me, help her? In the toilet??" He had seen Case demolish that tree trunk next door, and Josie was seriously asking him to help Case's wife in the loo!

"She wants to be sick," Josie gestured impatiently, "and you know I'm no good at that. C'mon, c'mon!" She snapped her fingers.

Comprehension filled his face and Ivor rushed to help Laine, leading her from the lounge with tender care.

"Just hold her hair back!" Josie called after him.

She sat back in relief. Good man. Always great timing. Her head was hurting.

They left Laine covered up with a blanket on the couch, out cold. Josie pulled the door closed behind her, feeling rather like a surgeon who had extracted a tumor. Her pleasure evaporated like mist when she climbed in the car and reality came flooding back.

She leaned against her bewildered husband and howled all the way home.

INVISIBLE

Mia stared dully at the breakfast table. Two fried eggs gazed back at her in oily reproach. She stood motionless, listening to the fading sound of Rudolf's car as he departed for work. Since her insane threat to shoot him, he was more scathing than ever, and she felt relief at the fading sound of his car. Satisfied he was gone for the day, she turned away, eager to fall into bed once more in her 'new' bedroom, the guest bedroom. The breakfast dishes she left on the table were a silent rebuke, but she felt too weary to bother. She was taking two of those tablets to help her sleep now, but sleep was at best fitful.

Certainly no preparation for the grind of the day.

Lately, she had scant energy. Just arranging mealtimes each day was a chore which tried her sorely, and she rarely ate the results of her handiwork. It seemed so pointless, this endless meal-planning. The children pecked like birds, even Rudolf, once quite gluttonous, lacked appetite.

Still, nutrition for her children was an important responsibility and Mia applied herself to her duty.

It wasn't just the cooking. In truth, everything was a challenge, and each challenge left her feeling a failure, incompetent. She knew there were some decisions to be made, but she was waiting for the fatigue to pass before she tackled the burning issue, her failure as a mother. This sickness, this fatigue, was causing her to neglect that most sacred of all duties, being a good mother to her children.

Mia's shame at this inadequacy was abiding, superseding everything else.

She glanced at her bedside clock as she climbed back into the rumpled bed. The guest room was rather small, sparsely furnished, and she wished it mattered more, that she could be a real homemaker.

But the truth was a cot in a cell would have sufficed if it meant not sleeping next to Rudolf.

She should wake the children, and get them ready for school.

Laine had been ferrying the children for some time now, assuring her that it was fine until Mia felt better. Mia, grateful to be relieved of the task, acquiesced with relief.

Laine could be trusted.

There was time for at least another twenty minutes nap, and Mia lay down gratefully. She would say a prayer, God would guide her, protect her children. Her thoughts drifted to the children.

There was something wrong at that school. Kira was reluctant to leave her in the mornings, and lately, the child was increasingly forlorn, fractious. Bernadette, naturally, followed the older child's lead and played up, not to be outdone in this matter of vying for their mother's attention.

Mia felt mortified to admit it, but the truth was her children were almost too much for her to handle. Their endless energy and demands left her spent and exhausted, and she hated herself for failing them. She closed her eyes, trying to banish the ever-hovering cloud of self-loathing. The early morning light troubled her eyes and Mia tugged the pillow over her face.

She shivered. The days were still warm yet she felt chilled most of the time.

Perhaps the children should just stay with her a while, leave this kinderschule? School meant facing other people, meetings with teachers, PTA, extra-mural functions...

She would have to be there, out and about. Being a 'good mother' was more than dropping them off and collecting, that was the truth. How would she find that energy? Better let them stay at home with her, at least until she felt better. She couldn't protect them when she felt this way.

Mia fell into a fitful doze, jolted awake by the sound of a car's horn. She sat up, startled, her heart pounding. Here was Laine, come to fetch the children and they weren't ready! Panicked, she clambered out of bed and hastily pulled on her robe and hurried downstairs. Outside, in the circular driveway, parked right outside the door as she always did, Laine sat waiting in the car, her thoughts seemingly elsewhere.

She looked up, surprised to see a bare-footed Mia hurrying towards her, her robe blowing in the breeze, sans children.

"Hello, Laine... Children." Mia flashed a smile at the McAllister girls in the back.

They thought Mrs Reichmann looked quite wild. They chorused a polite greeting from the back seat, curious.

Laine smiled her hello, wondering what was wrong this time, then immediately feeling petty. How did Mia managed to drain her of the little energy she had!

Mia swept the hair from her face. Without any makeup, the woman looked positively haggard. "Kira is ill today, and I'm leaving her here at home, I think, till she is better." she said in a rush. "Also," she hesitated, ashamed that she was wasting Laine's time. "I think that I will be taking the children to school myself from now on." She waved her hands apologetically, her eyes too bright in her pale face. "I cannot trouble you more."

Laine paused, wondering what to say. It was no bother to collect the Reichmann girls. But frankly, she felt too depressed with her own woes to argue the point, and if that's what Mia wanted—? Still, the woman didn't look well at all and Laine certainly wouldn't allow Mia to take her own children in a car.

What if the woman had one of her dizzy spells at the wheel? Jesus! Laine felt drained. She should care more, but she was too damn tired.

"Are you feeling any better lately? Honestly, it's no trouble. If you want me to take the girls, let me know," she said, determined to be polite.

Mia shook her head, adamant.

Laine gave the faintest shrug, relieved, she had her own troubles.

"What's wrong with little Kira? She's been looking peaky these past few days?"

Mia gestured, dismissive. "A little flu, nothing more." Again she pushed her hair impatiently from her eyes, edgy, wishing Laine would leave. There was nothing wrong with the child, why did Laine persist with these foolish thoughts? She was the child's mother, and if anything was wrong, she would know, she would feel it.

Laine sensed the other woman's impatience, and she felt aggrieved, in spite of herself. The child needed to see a doctor and this damn woman needed a shrink!

Still, it was just she who questioned the woman's state of mind. She was probably filled to the brim with all the psychobabble she learnt at college. None of which was proving worth a damn in the real world, certainly not when it came to her own woes. She nodded to herself. Parents, sometimes they were a menace to children, herself and Case included. She had been so full of stiff pride last night, doing her fair share to hurt everyone, the kids,

Case, punish herself. And for what?

She drove away, glancing in her rear-view mirror. She could see Mia still gazing after the car, the brisk morning wind gusting around her, her robe swirling up in the air. Laine shuddered.

It was true, she felt as if her life was over, but Mia looked dead already!

Fine pair of neighbors they made.

DROWNING

He took the bill from the desk clerk. He scanned it and winced. The cost of infidelity—

Case had been at the Meridian for nearly two months now, but in truth, his stay was sporadic. He sometimes stayed with Roxie, or, once or twice, stayed over at Granger's D-Q, not an unusual occurrence for a staffer, but unusual for senior staff. He knew the stay-overs would feed the Granger gossip mill, but frankly, he just didn't have the energy to care.

He folded up the bill and put it in his pocket. It all felt surreal. What the hell was he doing here, looking at a hotel bill, when he had a home, and a family? One minute he was a king in his castle, or a goddamn Prince, according to Kevin, the next minute, he was falling through a seismic crack in the ground called Roxie!

The familiar waves of guilt and self-loathing rolled over him. Only one person had single-handedly fucked up everyone's life, and that person was him.

But there was a glimmer of hope, perhaps...

Laine was finally prepared to sit down and talk to him, tomorrow. Friday.

He would see his wife and girls and from there. Who knew?

Reconciliation? Or permanent banishment?

Case had no idea which way the wind would blow, and worse, whichever way, he screwed up someone's life.

If Laine was still devastated, she sure as hell gave him no hint. She was aloof on the phone, distracted even. As if she were in a play, and someone had forgotten to give her the script. Every time he spoke to her, his palms were dry, and the words stuck in his throat. Not an hour went by when he didn't wonder how she was, how were the girls, were they okay.

Of course they were 'Okay,' replied the Roxie part of his heart.

Roxie was always there too, inside his head, damning him.

He shrugged off his fretting. The children were fine. Laine would see to that. He felt unreasonably sullen that she was capable of closing him out so utterly and completely. He understood that there could be no second chances with someone like her, yet the hope of a second chance never left his mind for a second.

Yesterday, they had even discussed the children on the phone, briefly. Shana was playing up. Laine was matter of fact, mentioning the little ones missed him, a lot. No bitter rebuke, no recrimination ...Nothing. She mentioned casually, as if he didn't know-and he didn't-that Judith was leaving soon, returning to San Diego.

Case was pleased to hear that. That would mean Laine would be alone, completely.

A chance to miss him? Or would he be more closed out than ever?

He climbed into his car and sat there for a moment, feeling helpless, homesick, torn, discouraged... A failure in every respect. It occurred to him that the only time he didn't feel all these things was when he was with Roxie.

There were no moments for quiet reflection when he was with her. She was vivacious and effervescent, and she almost blocked everything out.

He owned her in bed, completely, sometimes brutally, as if there was a need to punish her for this lust he was never supposed to feel. But did he want to own her in life?

He thought not.

Everything with Rox was too different, too damn fast. She was pressing him to move in with her, but he stubbornly refused, which was perhaps hypocritical, given he was there so much anyway.

Roxie was hurt by his indecision and his reticence when it came to discussing anything about 'the future' although she tried not to show it. She mentioned briefly that Charles was pushing her to do an East Coast tour soon. She sounded patently unenthusiastic, and Case understood he was the reason why, and yet again, he was drowning in a tide of guilt.

He was getting in the way of her career, and that was troubling him.

He tried broaching the subject that evening.

Roxie," he said, deliberately casual, 'Why don't you want to do this tour? I thought it was good exposure?" "It is. —The best," she replied.

"Then why are you stalling? It's only for a month?"

They were having dinner on the deck. Juanita was away, it was just the two of them, and she surprised him with a more than passable meal. He wondered idly if she had any domestic leanings.

Evidently, she did.

"A month is too long to be away from you. Not now. Not just yet. Later perhaps," she said, putting her fork down. 'Why? Do you want me to go?" She was looking at him, scanning his face.

"No, that's not it," he said, wondering if he was lying. "It's your dream. You told me that. Look, I don't pretend to understand how your business works, but it sounds like a big opportunity." He carried on eating, avoiding her eyes.

"Well, yes. Yes, it is," she admitted. She shrugged. "But it will come again. I'm not ready to leave you just yet."

Discussion closed. He was starting to know her 'stubborn' face.

He grinned. "Do you think I'll run away?" Instantly he regretted his flippant words.

"You might. Will you? Will you run back to Laine?" she asked. She could never bring herself to say your wife. 'Laine' was easier.

Case frowned. Laine. The familiar use of his wife's name rankled him. Why? He decided he was monumentally full of shit.

Roxie decided to take the bull by the horns. "That's something I've been asking myself, Case, and I can't find an answer. -Will you run back?" She pushed her plate away and sat back, studying him.

Case was glad he was eating, it gave him time to think. She had no make-up on, her hair was pulled back off her face, the dark mass accentuating lucent, flawless skin, but the green eyes were troubled. He wondered for the hundredth time why it was he had never noticed just how gorgeous she was the first time he ever laid eyes on her. Because you were in love with your wife then. You saw nothing and no one. Just the damn car.

The Deville, a goddamn Trojan horse.

He gave his head a little shake, the way he always did when he was thinking hard. "The truth is, I might... " he said at last. It was too exhausting to pretend.

He saw her flinch, but there was no point in bullshit. He sat forward, reaching across to take her hands in his. "I miss my family, my other ...Life. But when I think of not having you—! He shrugged. "I'm addicted to you," he said simply.

Roxie said nothing, just gazed back at him, those green eyes holding his.

After a moment she stood up, and pushing his chair back, climbed on his lap. She parted her robe slightly and pressed his face into her breasts, holding his head, her eyes shut, loving him, willing him to feel it.

She was caressing his face lightly with her lips. If he felt pain, she could fix it.

Case closed his eyes, soaking her in. She loved him so. Her adoration was intoxicating, and like any addiction, the stolen pleasures outweighed the risks.

But try as he might, there were the ever-present memory of Laine.

Laine laughing with the children, Laine loving him, the blonde hair tickling his skin, the smell of her, that special smell on her skin when they made love. Laine, bending to say goodnight to the children, her hair a silky curtain as she kissed them goodnight. That ridiculous snort she had, when she couldn't contain her laughter. All that serenity that used to be his life.

Now she wanted nothing more to do with him.

"So, will you run back?" Roxie was pressing him.

"I don't know," he said at last. He was touching her, making her quiver and it aroused him to know her orgasm was moments away. "Neither do I," she said thickly.

She was tugging at his belt buckle.

"Enough talk. Fuck me!"

MUDDLING THROUGH

WEEKENDS

Laine stirred, reluctant to be pulled from a fitful sleep.

The phone was loud, demanding that she answer it. She glanced at the bedside clock. It was eight a.m. Drowsily, she decided the children had probably been fed by Judith.

If the alarm hadn't buzzed, it had to be Saturday or Sunday? God, the sleeping tablets were too strong. No more, for sure. She fumbled for the phone.

"Hello," she said, her voice was croaky with sleep.

"Laine, it's me." Laine felt her stomach turn and groaned audibly. Case. The black cloud that had been shadowing her for the past weeks descended like a familiar fog.

"Laine, please...." Case sighed. He had heard her groan. She was still so angry, and refused to discuss anything, anything at all, with him. He pressed on. "Laine, I have to talk to you sometime. This can't go on. I have to see you, and the girls..."

She kept silent. She could picture him, his face agitated, running his hands impatiently through his hair. Just hearing his voice cut like a knife and her gut was instantly churning.

A pity there wasn't a pill for that. What day was it? Saturday.

"Why do you want to see me? We can make arrangements for you to see the girls.." Her voice was flat, and at his end, his heart sank.

It was useless.

"Laine, we need to talk. We have to talk. He was pleading now, and she could hear his distress, but it couldn't touch her, because she was behind her wall, protected from deceit and lies and betrayal. Her world was different now. He had left and taken away the laughter, the light, the love.

"Case, what do we have to say to each other? I will never forgive you. I don't want you back" She could feel herself getting upset again. " I don't even want you near me!" She felt the tears threatening, and she took a deep breath. Never to shed tears in front of him!

"As for the children, why don't you collect them for the weekend? Roxie has a big enough house, I'm sure," she said acidly.

Case chose to ignore the barb. But he had to know, and he voiced his pressing concern;

"Have you said anything to the children?" He had a pounding headache, and he lifted a hand to his throbbing temple. As long as they knew nothing, there was hope, of a sort. Hope for what, exactly, he couldn't say.

There was a pause. "No," she replied, eventually. "Just you're away at 'doctor school' for a while, that's something they can understand. If you want to tell them more, I can't stop you. I just don't want them to hurt. I'm not ready— But I suppose that's inevitable." Her voice trailed off.

Like you're hurt, he thought, hating himself.

However, the idea to collect the children was a good one, maybe stay at a resort just out of town? He felt like a stranger with his daughters, and it was an uncomfortable feeling.

"If I fetch the children, will you be alright?" Laine had never been entirely on her own before, in thirteen years, ever since they had been married. Certainly never without the children and him. There was silence.

She knew what he meant.

"Quite honestly, I don't know," she answered at last. "But the truth of the matter is, perhaps it's something I'm going to have to get used to. Now is as good a time as any to start." The chill in her voice pained him. "I'll get the children packed and ready, you can collect them around two. I won't be here."

"Laine, please, can't we just try to discuss this," he said, feeling helpless.

Her heart quickened at the need in his voice, a small glimmer of light on any other day, but pain, pride and anger held sway.

"Alright, " she said at last, "but not today. Not when the children are around. They must be protected from—" She thought about it, "From us, I suppose," she finished.

Case felt a glimmer of hope.

It was something, a beginning. "Okay. Next week then. Monday evening. I'll bring them back tomorrow afternoon. 'Bye.' He rang off before she could change her mind.

Laine dropped the phone and pulled the covers over her head in a child-like gesture, wanting to block out the day.

Life had become all about pretending.

The sheer physicality of her heartache surprised her. There was the day to get through, one foot in front of the other, and how to do that, when there was this ache in one's chest, this nausea that would come from nowhere, this shortness of breath born of ever-lurking panic!

She chided herself constantly, reminded herself sternly her children needed her, and forced a smile on those occasions when she found them insisting that she look them in the eye.

Of course, there was also the damn weeping. She cried after she fed the dog, because Case usually did that.

She wept while she was pouring gas into the tank, until the gas spilled all over her shoes.

There was that brash-looking drugstore lady, who squeezed her hand when she asked for herbal tranquilizers, and shot her a look of such pure kindness, Laine struggled to make it out the door, the tears were streaming so.

Rejection, it was the worst pain of all.

She had moments of sheer bewilderment when she knew unequivocally that it was all the most horrendous mistake, and then, moments of such deep and abiding despair, she feared for her sanity.

She avoided everyone.

'Laine' was in there somewhere, but the old Laine, the one too frightened to come out.

They were Mr and Mrs Dumpty, and all the king's horses...

—But there was one glimmer of light.

Donatés. Donatés and only Donatés freed her from everything, and in those seconds when his hooves left the ground, they were flying, transcending affairs and bastard husbands. They soared between heaven and earth, free. It was an avenue where she wasn't a failure and she clung to that.

The horse seemed to sense her misery, and he rose to the occasion, as if to show her that all was not lost. She thought about her chances in the Seattle show in a couple of months. Jason was pressing her to enter all the qualifiers, boosting her crushed ego at every turn, quite in awe of her dedication to Donatés.

He probably knew, she thought.

Hell, everyone knew.

Time to get up!

MOTHERLESS

If Case expected open arms and joyous squeals when he arrived to collect the girls, he was sorely disappointed. They weren't waiting for him to arrive, and they scarcely glanced up from their play when he found them in the backyard, engrossed with the new pet rabbit.

Judith's frosty reception also rattled him. Would there be no end to it, he thought moodily?

He realized his daughters were mad at him.

"How's my girls?" He fixed a bright smile on his face and knelt beside them in the sand, gathering them to his side, determined to ignore their casual reception. They gave him a polite kiss on his cheek, then stood silent and stiff in the circle of his arms. Ah. He was being punished, and a real effort was called for. "Well, aren't you pleased to see me?" He stood up, one child on each hip. He could see Shana starting to thaw a little.

"Where you been, Daddy?" she asked imperiously, reluctant to let him off the hook.

"I'll explain everything in the car. Say goodbye to Granny." Case set them back on their feet, and they made their way hesitantly to Judith, who standing silent on the porch, watching them, contriving–and failing miserably–to look happy.

Liesel swung around, facing him. "Who's going to look after Mommy? We've never left her alone before." She crossed her little arms defiantly. "I'm not going."

The bottom lip was shaky and she eyed Case solemnly, willing him to put her world to rights. Case heard his mother huffing in anger, and a moment later the squeak of the screen door as she went inside the house.

His throat closed and his mouth was dry.

How did one handle this? Shana was looking at her older sister doubtfully, then walked over to him and held up her arms, wanting to be picked up.

"Want to go with you, Daddy."

"Liesel, Mommy can't come, she has to train Donatés, and I'm taking you to the fun fair, to the zoo, everywhere. Guess what, we're even going to stay in a hotel."

"Why?" she asked, ever logical. "Why can't you stay here?" Grudging, she allowed him to pick her up again. Case sighed. Liesel never was a pushover.

"Because it's a treat, that's why. And now we have to go, but not before you hug me and tell me that you forgive me for staying away so long. I promise I'll make it up to you this weekend. What do you say? Let's give Mommy a nice rest." Liesel stared at him, and Case waited. It would be touch and go. He kept his smile fixed.

After an inner struggle, Liesel gave him a perfunctory hug, allowing him to lead her away, conceding a temporary defeat.

"Can I sleep with you in your hotel bed? I've never slept in a hotel bed before. Then I'll be good." Her little tongue licked her top lip speculatively, sizing him up, wondering if they would strike a deal.

It was a long, trying day. The children were happy to be with him, but niggledy.

That night, he lay in the king-sized bed, the children lying with him. He waited until their breathing was even and regular, then surreptitiously reached for his phone.

She answered almost instantly.

"My darling," she murmured, happy to hear from him.

"Hi, Roxie." His voice was soft, so as not to awaken the children

"God, I thought you'd never call. I feel like a teenager again, just sitting around, wishing the damn phone would ring. How's ...things?" she asked, referring to the children.

When he had told of his plans to fetch them, she had urged him to stay away, and devote time to them, displaying a shrewd insight. It sounded like good advice, and now that the day was finally over, he was grateful for her sensitivity.

"Well, I feel as though Laine deserves a medal! What I mean is, it's not easy to keep them entertained all day. They were exhausted when I finally put them to bed."

"Did you see Laine?" Laine–it was better than saying 'your wife'.

"No. Maybe tomorrow, when I take them back," he replied, aware of her nervousness at such a meeting. Never mind his own apprehension, he thought wryly.

"Will I see you tomorrow for lunch?"

"It might be a little difficult," he cautioned, thinking of Liesel.

"Forget it, you can't frighten me." He could hear the smile in her voice. "Well, I'll be there, at Thai-Thai, waiting. If you can make it, good. If it's hard, don't fret..."

"Sounds right. Bye..." he was whispering. Liesel was stirring. "Bye, hon."

He put the phone on his chest, thinking. Shana had crawled into the crook of his arm, and he gazed fondly at the cherubic face.

Liesel's clear piping voice in the silence interrupted his train of thought, startling him.

"Who's Roxie?"

Caught completely off-guard, Case was silent, his guilt temporarily scattering his wits.

"Well? Who's Roxie?" Liesel demanded again.

Busted. "Oh, her..." Case offered casually, floundering, "She's a friend of mine. She has a great house near the beach." He was suddenly seized with a flash of inspiration. "Gosh, it's too awful about her," he said mournfully.

There was silence while Liesel digested this. Curious, she took the bait and asked, "Why?"

"No kids," he said sadly, "loves kids, and has none of her own! Especially little girls, and she's always asking me about my two, so I said if I get the chance, I might bring them around to meet her." Case oozed sympathy for the hapless Roxie and held his breath.

"No kids?" Liesel said slowly, absorbing that. "No hussbin too?" she asked cautiously.

He answered sadly, "Nope. No husband, either."

"Well, she can't have you and she can't have us!" Liesel declared with crushing finality.

Case groaned inwardly and closed his eyes.

Chalk up one for the prosecution. He reached across and took her tiny hand in his.

Laine, ever-present.

CHARADES

Sunday got off to a sorry start. Case awoke feeling stiff and sore, having slept cramped the whole night within the confines of some eighteen inches of bed, whilst the girls sprawled out in splendid comfort

Before he even opened his eyes, Case had the alien sensation of his buttocks feeling soggy and damp. He realized after a startled moment that Shana had wet the bed. He had forgotten the nightly ritual of emptying bladders before sleep, imperative for Shana. He eased himself up, trying not to awaken them, but they sensed his movement and opened sleepy eyes. He fixed them both with a bright smile of good-morning cheer, cringing when he saw the horrified dawning in Shana's eyes as she realized her transgression. She began to bellow, mortified by her body's babyish betrayal.

Alerted, Liesel inspected her own pajamas, found a damp patch that had seeped over to her part of the bed, to taint her for evermore. She set up a horrified wail in chorus with Shana, holding the offending pajama part away from her small body, disgust etched into every pore. Her revulsion served to mortify Shana still more, and she stepped up her volume.

Caught up in the crescendo, Case tried hard to unscramble his beleaguered senses and to refrain from panic. He filled the tub, then ordered a coffee and two coke-floats from room service, his own strict rules about candy and junk foods but a vague memory!

His nerves were ragged, and it was far too early into the day.

Two little ones and no Laine to preserve peace. He felt inept, and the feeling was shaming. The distraction of lunch with Roxie seemed like a good idea, after all.

Thai-Thai was a small but exclusive restaurant in Malibu that Roxie favored. The maître-d was anxious to please. When they arrived , he led Case and the girls to an outdoor deck with a great view of the beach, with lattice screens offering the patrons some privacy.

Roxie was there already, waiting, looked radiant and fresh, in faded Levi's and a loose-knit white top. She was LA royalty, and everyone around knew it.

Except perhaps the harassed man with the two small girls!

Case gave her a friendly but detached hug, and a light peck on the head, aware of the children's curious scrutiny. He allowed himself to hold the bewitching jade eyes for the briefest moment.

Roxie, in turn, kissed him politely on his cheek. For a second he stood still, looking at her, feeling his equilibrium being restored. When she nudged him, he hastily introduced his daughters, mentally crossing his fingers. To his surprise, Shana clambered onto his lap and glared balefully at Roxie, while Liesel looked at her with dawning recognition.

"You sing. I know you from TV!" Case winced, but Roxie smiled at her awe.

Both adults laughed at her undisguised fascination.

Unimpressed, Shana scowled at Roxie and buried her face into his jacket.

That set the tone for the day. Shana refused steadfastly to be drawn in, but Liesel couldn't have been sweeter! When lunch was over and Case stood up to leave, Liesel surprised and touched Roxie by giving her a spontaneous goodbye kiss, while Shana blew up her cheeks and stared sullenly out the window of the car. Case thanked her politely for her company, and Roxie demurely waved them all goodbye.

Back inside her house, Roxie felt a despondency sweeping over her. She walked outside onto the balcony and gazed at the beach, deserted save for a solitary family frolicking in the last bit of evening light. They looked like stick figures from this distance, and looking at them, she felt lonely.

He was taking the children back to her. His other life.

She tried in vain to dispel the melancholy mood. The children were beautiful, as she had known they would be. Shana was a miniature Case, Liesel a diminutive Laine. Shit. She sat down on the deck chair and pulled her knees up under her chin, her eyes troubled.

Until today, his 'family' had been only a vague thing, names, not much more. Shana doted on her father, and her misery that he was taking her home, only to leave her yet again, that bothered Roxie.

They were so innocent, so oblivious. How could she be doing what she was doing, wrecking their marriage. Could she stop?

Never, and that was the truth.

Could Case?

Probably, came the unwelcome answer.

Things would just have to work out, they had to, because she couldn't, wouldn't, give him up, ever.

REBOUNDING

"Are you finishing early today? Come on, wait a while, join us for a drink in the clubhouse?" Jason said.

Laine handed a skittish Donatés over to the young groom standing by. She patted the animal lovingly, feeling a little guilty about the white foam of sweat on his flanks.

"No thanks. Enough for today, I think. I need to get back..."

She felt hot and sticky, and Case would be home soon with the girls. She thought wearily that it was as good a time as any to face him.

But not like this. Her hair was wild, and she felt grubby.

"Laine. Is anything wrong?" Jason was looking down at her, his eyes narrowed against the glare from the sun. He was mounted on Stratton's Big Heart, the horse restless and pawing the ground, eager to get into the arena. Impulsively he whistled to a stable hand and swung himself down off the horse. He handed the stallion over to the hand with firm instructions to 'warm him up slowly' and walked over to join Laine, who watched his approach with dismay.

It was time to be gone, and she didn't feel like idle chatter.

He stopped before her, hands on hips, his face concerned, and asked again, "Anything wrong? Anything at all you want to talk about?"

"Nothing at all." She gave a bright smile to prove her words and started walking towards the car park. He fell into step beside her.

"Laine, I don't want to talk out of turn, but this is a small community, and word is that you and Case have had a ...falling out."

Falling out? Laine grimaced at the quaintness of the expression. He caught her arm, stopping her mid-stride, compelling her to face him. "Is it true?" The tanned, lined face was troubled, concerned.

Laine stared back at him, her face inscrutable.

So it's out! They know. She wondered how they had found out. She kept to herself. No matter.

To hell with them all.

"Yes," she said simply. She was feeling in her purse for her keys. "Case and I have separated." She found the keys and began walking away, horrified to feel her lip trembling.

For a moment Jason stood fast, looking after her. He would never have believed it of Laine and Case McAllister. McAllister had to be nuts. He hurried after her.

"Listen, please, listen!" He caught her on her arm, forcing her to stop. She looked at his hand on her arm, then at him, her eyes cool. He flushed. "I know," he raised his shoulders, dropped them." I know I have a wolf's reputation, but I like you, really I do–aside from the fact that you're going to do my stable's reputation a lot of good when you clean up all the ribbons with Donatés, I just want to say—" he gave a little cough, uncomfortable, "I really am sorry to hear about you and Case.' He looked sorry, and Laine looked away. More kindness.

Kindness undid her.

"It sounds trite I'm sure, but if you need me?" He shrugged, "I'm here. Call me. Anytime, I mean it," he said earnestly. Someone was calling him from the paddock, but he ignored their shouts, his eyes holding hers.

"Thank you, Jason. Now, I better be going," she said. He was standing in front of her, and she smiled at him, dangling her car keys in front of his nose. She needed to be gone from here.

"Oh." He glanced at the keys. "Okay. See you tomorrow." He stepped aside to allow her to pass, waving impatiently to still the person shouting from the paddock. "'Bye." He held the car door open for her and she climbed in and adjusted her sunglasses carefully, then waved him goodbye.

She's gutsy alright, he thought, as she drove away.

McAllister had left her, said the gossip, for some bimbo pop star, go figure.

He shook his head.

What a dickhead!!

Judith was preparing supper when Laine arrived home, and after a few polite stabs at conversation, she excused herself and went upstairs . She showered quickly, telling herself it didn't matter what she wore when he dropped the children off.

Yet she found herself selecting her clothes with care, choosing a huge chunky knitted sweater that she knew he loved. She rearranged her hair twice before she was eventually satisfied. She was applying the finishing touches to her make-up when she heard his car in the drive.

It was curious. Her feelings were a kaleidoscope. Trepidation, angst, happiness. And then, swamped with sorrow, loss, anger. Anger was too mild a word, rage, rage was what she felt.

How to keep all of that under control?

She paused and took a deep breath on the stairs before she descended to greet the children and Case, summoning all her courage. She was pleased that she'd decided to take pains with her appearance, gratified when she saw his eyes light up when he caught sight of her, dissipating some of her tension.

The children rushed to greet her, Liesel clinging to her like a long-lost friend. A patently cool Judith approached the returning children from the TV lounge. She offered a terse greeting to her son, more for the sake of the children than from any softening of her attitude. Judith allowed them a few moments of boisterous greeting, then discretely led them away to the kitchen to have some ice cream, a seething Mary Poppins!

Case watched them walk away, his hands in his pockets. He turned to look at Laine and twice they started to speak at the same time. Finally, her head in turmoil, Laine walked to the cabinet and poured herself a stiff drink, offering him the same.

"Thanks. You look great. Really good. Really," he said earnestly, and for a fleeting second, she was reminded of when they met, the shy college student who had waited outside the library to waylay her, a lifetime ago. He still had his hands in his pockets that same way now, and now he stood awkwardly, as if he was waiting for an invitation to be seated. He looks, she thought unhappily, like a stranger in his own home.

The image of him and Roxie entwined made her gut knot, and she had to consciously focus on what he was saying, to try to move past the familiar stirrings of anger, but she could feel it; the wall was coming up.

Laine knew she was trapped by her rage, but it was also her rage that drove her, restored her. He looked like Case, but this man was suddenly, impossibly, a stranger.

"How were the children?" She handed him his drink and for a second their hands touched and she drew her hand away too quickly.

"Fine. It's quite a job, playing mother," he said wryly. He ran his fingers through his hair, disconcerted. "I think I rather failed at it." He looked around, as if looking for a place to sit, then sat down on the edge of his old chair.

His body language wounded her. Seeing him thus, poised for flight, made her throat catch.

Laine felt defeated. It was all useless, this talking. Her martini was burning a hole in her empty stomach and the sensation was almost soothing.

"What did you do today?" she asked, by way of conversation. In truth, she didn't want to know. He looks a little thinner, she thought, gaunt.

"We had Thai food for lunch— " he broke off, embarrassed. But the 'we' was out there, the fly on the wedding cake. He soldiered on, feeling gauche. "I thought they would enjoy it."

"I'm sure they did." she said coolly, then took another quick sip of her drink, but the ache inside was threatening to crush her. Was she screaming? It felt as if she should be screaming? No, she was sitting here, with him, playing charades.

She looked across at him, not trusting herself to speak just yet. She could see his lips moving, but for the life of her, she couldn't hear a word he was saying. "Laine, are you alright.?" Case was looking at her with concern. She looked too pale. He felt an overwhelming urge to grab her, kiss her tenderly, force the old Laine to show herself, but that, of course, was insanity.

"I'm fine," she managed to say. "Maybe I overdid it with Donatés today, I feel quite exhausted." Her voice was back and she sounded normal. Did he think she sounded normal? She wanted him to leave, go, leave her alone with her misery. Her drink was finished, but she didn't trust herself to stand up, not just yet. How was it possible to hurt this much?

It was definitely better when he was away. In future, when he collected the children, she would absent herself.

"Okay." He looked doubtful. "How are you coming along with Donatès?" He finished his drink, and he looked at the empty glass in surprise. He needed more courage. "Laine, can't we talk? I'm sorry, truly sorry about all this, but our marriage— ! We can't just walk away!"

Then come home, she thought. Don't listen to me and my hurt, bitter words. Just hold me and say that everything is fine and you'll never see her again and that you love me only, now and forever. If you're in there, somewhere, hear the words I cannot speak.

But instead, she found herself asking, "Do you love her?" Her voice was flat, devoid of emotion. And he, unseeing of the danger, duped by her calm, chose to answer honestly.

"It's a mess. I don't want to lose you, the children."

She struggled to breathe, then she heard the words leaving her lips, her voice so calm, so cold and detached. "You'll never have me again. I will never trust you again, ever." Her eyes were narrowed, and he searched in them for any sign that she didn't mean what she was saying.

She looked disdainful and beautiful, and lost to him forever.

"You don't mean that, Laine," he muttered, "you don't take thirteen years of marriage and throw it away without a discussion, or even a fight. Please." He was pleading with her, and she could hear his pain.

It surprised her.

"I don't see you fighting for our marriage!" she retorted bitterly. "Were you "fighting" to save us when you took our children to lunch with her?" she asked, her voice scathing. Anger gave her the energy she needed, the strength to push him away.

It was time for him to leave.

"Is there anything else?", she asked abruptly..

Like a tongue finding a sore tooth, she had asked him the one question she didn't want answered;"When you leave here, where will you be going, Case? To Roxie Tanner?"

Case looked at her, shaking his head, defeated. He was going back to his hotel, but what was the point.

Somehow, he had hoped, coming here, that he could fix this, that she would tell him to stay, and never ever again, leave her.

She was discarding him. In that moment, on that day, that was his perception, his personal truth.

Afterwards, when he thought about it, he knew he had handled it all wrong.

But in the moment, he was hurt, rejected and stung to provocation, so he replied, equally cool;

"Probably."

He stood up, ready to take his leave, thoroughly provoked.

"Case?"

He looked at her, wary now of this stranger he used to know so well. "Yes?"

"Say goodbye to the children," she reminded him, her voice cool.

* * *

Case drove back to his hotel, beyond bleak. His meeting with Laine had gone to hell, nothing like he planned or hoped for. She had been so aloof, so... Disinterested. He thought about her question. His feelings were different for Roxie. Were they strong enough to make him chuck up his family?

Or had he already done that?

Case banged the steering wheel angrily. This was all his fault.

Why couldn't Laine see? Why wouldn't she listen? Unhappy, he looked up and saw the overhead sign to the River's End exit.

Roxie would be ecstatic to see him. But he needed to be alone, he needed to think. The empty apartment and its silence waited for him.

Thank God.

Silence was what he craved.

JUST A KITTEN...

Later, after he had left, she bathed the children, now strangely subdued after their noisy arrival. Shana was eager to get to her bed, and turned her head away from Laine when she stooped to kiss the child goodnight.

Liesel hugged her fiercely, and when she released her, Laine saw tears rolling down the child's cheeks.

Laine struggled for composure and held the child close, stroking the soft baby hair. She knows, she thought, but could find nothing to say to comfort the child.

"Is Daddy ever coming home?" Liesel asked, brushing her tears away fiercely, trying not to cry, but desperate to be reassured. Laine hesitated. She didn't know, but right now she was the adult, Liesel the child who need protecting.

"Sure. Sometimes, grownups fight about silly things, but we'll sort it out." Laine forced a smile.

Liesel looked at her, and the doubt Laine saw in her eyes made her heart break.

"So you're not getting a divorce?" Liesel asked, persistent.

Laine was floored. "Divorce! What on earth made you think that?" She didn't even think the child knew the word, much less wonder about whether she and Case—

"Well, anyhow, I knew you couldn't be, because Vanessa at school explained it to me," Liesel said.

"Explained it —?" What the hell did little Vanessa know about her and Case?

"She told me when her Daddy went away forever, and got a divorce, she got a pony!" Liesel said solemnly. "Daddy said he's not giving us a pony."

"Of course not," Laine stammered, her thoughts in disarray, "He's just away, for a short while."

"A short while...?" The child pondered. She looked up, her face eager.

"Okay then. Let's ask him for a kitten!"

Liesel had no idea why her Mommy was laughing, but she relaxed. "Divorce" was not happening in her house.

UNIVERSE TALKING?

Roxie checked her watch for the second time in the last five minutes. All around her, there were irritating people wanting this or that from her, being tedious, when all she wanted was time to think.

Case intended to talk to Laine. How would that work out?

Roxie was apprehensive. Would it now be an open tussle between the two women? She didn't underestimate Laine's hold on Case for a second. There were the children, they had history...

She just prayed that he loved her more and realize they were meant to be.

From that very first moment when he had pulled his bike onto the verge of the road and walked over to her, with that... something, taking her breath away. Their love had been inevitable. Out of her hands, really.

But, there was the matter of The Wife. Life's Big Mistake.

All those damn promises and obligations. Case would spend his life doing the right thing. Which was fine, as long as he did it from a distance.

Her phone rang, startling her. Hastily, she snatched up the phone, her heart beating fast. Please let it be good news, she couldn't take much more of this!

"Hello?" Roxie could hear the damn panic in her voice. Dial it down.

"Roxie? Honey, it's me." Honey. Case's familiar baritone filled the line and she felt weak with relief.

"Case, where are you?"

She heard him sigh. "I checked out of the hotel and into the Meridian. They're furnished apartments. I'll be staying here a while." There was a pause, and the unspoken words were hanging in the air.

Until he knew.

"Oh..." she said, thinking; The Meridian. That meant they hadn't reconciled.

"Yeah. Well, anyhow, this looks okay." His voice was noncommittal.

"Case, we've never really spoke about everything. I need to see you. Please. Come here! Or I'll come there?" She felt frantic. He sounded too detached.

"Roxie, I need some time to think. There's just so much going down. Let's get together tomorrow for supper, okay?"

Careful. A warning voice came from within. Don't crowd him. Give him a chance to miss you.

"Sure," she soothed, " Just— I'm worried about you. And if I'm truthful, I miss you so much, it hurts."

Her words pleased him, and it annoyed him that they pleased him.

"I want to see you too, he admitted, "but I have to think things through."

"Okay. I understand, really I do. Just don't forget, I love you, please?" she said, her eyes shut, willing him to feel her love.

"I'll see you tomorrow, at around seven unless something comes up at the clinic. Bye."

"Bye," she said woefully, but he was already gone.

Case felt agitated after his call to Roxie. He wished he could talk to Kevin. Where was Kevin when he needed him? Nothing made sense, nothing. There was no way forward.

Either way, he broke someone's heart. He sighed. Time to get some sleep.

At one in the morning, he was still wide awake, tossing and turning, wrestling with his conscience, castigating himself for his weakness, when he heard a knock on the door.

His heart skipped a beat. Had Laine relented? He had messaged her he was at the Meridian, hoping she would understand his mindset. Rescue him.

Eagerly, he went to the door, determined to make it right with her.

But it was Roxie who stood in the doorway, her face pleading.

"I'm sorry. I know you want to be alone, but I couldn't stay away... Are you angry?"

He stood back to let her in, hiding his disappointment. Her joy at being with him shone in her eyes, and she hugged him fiercely. "You can't be alone. Not while I breathe.."

He hugged her back, suddenly grateful to be rescued from all his self-flagellations, this endless fucking guilt! She smelt wonderful, and they stood for a moment or two, holding each other, feeding two different needs.

The universe was talking, he thought to himself.

Maybe listen?

NOWHERE A RESCUE

When she arrived at the Ballard ranch, Laine saw a lot of activity at the northern stables. She stood staring across, her hand shielding her eyes, wondering why all the hands appeared to be there.

She noticed that new groom, Scott Boyer loping towards the stables.

"Scott," she called out to him. He looked around to see who it was. His eyes lit up in pleasure when he saw her.

"Mrs McAllister." He grinned at her with that youthful, undisguised admiration. "How are you? Come to spend some time with Donatés?" He strolled over to her. "Have you made up your mind yet? Everyone is hoping you'll enter." He was referring to the County Championships. She hesitated, then heard herself answering, "Yes... Been thinking about it. -And please, call me Laine." He made her feel ancient. Was she ever that young?

"Actually, I think I am..."

He fell in step beside her as she walked to the stables. He looked pleased at her reply.

Where the hell did that come from, asked a little voice in her head. "Need to get on with your life," answered the same voice.

"Wow. " He sounded excited, and she felt quite gratified. "Well, that's going to set some tongues wagging for sure." He grinned quickly. "I know that Jason really thinks you have a chance, otherwise he wouldn't pressure you."

She gave a short laugh. "If I win or place, it'll be great for him and his reputation, if I lose, I'll be the laughing stock of the equestrian community," she retorted.

"Is that what's bothering you?" He looked disappointed. "I figured you for a fighter, at least." Laine flushed at his reproach. She found herself caught short.

She was a damn fighter.

"It's not just the losing, really..." And it wasn't. "This is another league, A-

Grade. Donatés will need a lot more of my time if I pursue it.." "So?" he stared at her blankly.

"So.-I'm a housewife, with a family. I don't know if I have the time." She wondered why the hell she was explaining herself to him

He said nothing for a moment, turning his head to better look at her as he walked alongside, wondering if the rumors were true. He shrugged. He had heard this woman's asshole husband had left her. That meant she had time.

"Well," he said, his face earnest, "You have the talent to make a career out of showjumping and you've struck pay-dirt with that horse of yours. If you don't want to take him to his full potential, I guess you'll have to sell him. He deserves a real shot... I know Stratton's mighty keen to buy him." Laine snorted. "Stratton's too hard. He'll never get out of him what I can." She grimaced. "But I take your point. I can't keep him back, he's too good. But I will never sell him. Sentimental value, that sort of thing." Her tone was light, but her face clouded.

Scott eyed her, saying nothing.

For the second time, she was aware that there was something about him that reminded her of Case. He was a handsome young man, and he looked quite virile in those damn chaps. For no reason, she found herself blushing. He mistook the blush for rebuke and punched her arm gently, in a boyish manner.

"C'mon. Don't look so serious. You know you have to be the one. I know you could do it. There are a dozen people who would kill for an opportunity to ride in the state trials. And you've got the right ribbons to qualify." His face shone with sincerity and suddenly he flushed. He was letting it all hang out, like some dumb kid. "Well, the vet's there in the north side giving the horses their boosters, and some are pretty skittish. Guess I better go help. There are no hands on this side, do you want me to saddle up Donatés for you, before I go?" he offered politely.

"No. No, not at all. I can manage. And thanks Scott, for the encouragement, I needed it." She smiled sweetly at him and he looked bashful.

"Yeah. Well, I meant it." He strolled away, and she looked after him. He was a nice young man.

His girl was lucky.

The South stables were deserted and Donatés whinnied with excitement when he saw Laine, pawing the ground, raring to be let out. Laine led the animal around to the hitching post outside the tack room and proceeded to saddle up the horse, talking to him all the while and caressing him gently. A voice behind her made her start.

"Laine. Hi, how are you?" Jason Ballard sounded pleased to see her. She hadn't even heard him approach.

"Oh. Hi Jason. Lots of activity at North stables...?"

He smiled at her, with his perfect, pearly teeth. "Yes, well it's that time of year again," he answered easily. He'll do Donatés and the others tomorrow. How are you?" He stopped next to her, taking the girth strap from her hand and pulling it tighter around the horse's girth. Donatés moved back restlessly.

"Thank you,' she murmured politely. He was standing far too close and she stepped back, but he caught her arm.

"Laine, if you need someone, I'm there to listen. I'm a wolf, it's true," he shrugged. He knew his rep, was quite proud of it, in fact. "I genuinely care about you. So if you need me..." He shrugged, and the ambiguity hung in the air...

Laine felt a giggle rising up in her, and despite her efforts to control it, that familiar snort came.

"What's so funny?" He looked offended and stepped away, bristling.

"You." Laine smiled at him. "God, Jason, you are such a jerk," she said. He was looking thoroughly wounded and that just made it funnier. "Does that line really work with the other women?" She swung herself up onto Donatés and sat there, looking down at him, feeling unkind when she looked at his crestfallen face.

But he was beginning to smile.

"Most times." He was grinning too now, "I do have better, it depends on the occasion. I guess it was kinda cheesy. But I do like you, Laine, a lot."

"I'm hope you do, Jason," she called as she swung the horse around. "I like you too, but if you do that again," she pulled Donatés up, and looked over her shoulder back at him, "I'll kick you where it hurts, and I'll stable my horse elsewhere. Are we good?" She rounded the horse, waiting to make sure he understood, holding the rein wide to hold the restless Donatés in.

He held up his hands in a gesture of peace. Satisfied, she wheeled the horse around, urging it into a trot towards the northern ring.

"Okay. But I'm only human," he called after her.

Out of the corner of her eye, Laine caught a movement behind the tack room. She glanced over and saw Scott Boyer standing perfectly still, watching her, a small smile playing on his lips. Clearly, he had witnessed the little scenario that had just unfolded.

She gave him a conspiratorial wink, and urged Donatés away into a canter.

The bay was in fine form, sailing over the five-foot-six crossbar with such ease, it buoyed her immeasurably. They were flying, defying gravity, each time the horse cleared the jumps. He kept breaking stride at the water jump, but Laine coaxed and cajoled until he was clearing it comfortably. After an hour, he was doing the course fluidly.

The shadows from the huge pine trees were stretching long over the paddock and Laine turned the horse around and took him back at a swift canter to the stables. There was no one there, and even the clubhouse parking looked deserted. Time had crept up on her, just about everyone had left.

Darkness would settle within the hour.

She dismounted and loosened the girth and hauled the saddle off. She stood outside the stable doors, caressing the animal's face gently, then wiping down his damp flanks with a piece of sacking. The sun was setting, and the dusky evening light filled her with an almost forgotten sense of peace.

Laine felt loathe to return home just yet. The girls were fine, Judith was there. Here, astride her Donatés, it was the one time these days that she felt still intact, complete. With her horse, she was doing something and doing it well! It was the one facet of her life that still felt the same. In fact, it seemed more important than ever.

She gave an angry shake of her head. Enough. She determined not to let melancholy taint this rare, good mood. She made a quick check-in call to Judith, taking heart from the happy shrieking in the background.

Judith was her usual unflappable self, urging Laine to take her time, and 'socialize some'.

Judith's words made her feel inexplicably sad, and the unspoken message in the "socialize some," doubly so.

She wasn't supposed to socialize. She was Sadie, married lady.

Suddenly, Laine felt unwilling to lead the horse back into his stall, and impulsively, she walked him to the railings, and using the rail, hopped up onto his bare back and headed him in the direction of the dirt track that led to the equestrian trails.

They cantered along for twenty minutes, woman and beast, enjoying the tranquility. She needed this, she thought, just cantering along, feeling at one with the world for the first time in too long. Donatés knew the route well and surged forward. Laine could feel the powerful muscles rippling beneath her, the rhythmical movement and fading light soothing.

But, at last, aware that dusk was fast becoming night, she reluctantly rounded the horse and started back towards the stables, the evening quiet disturbed only by cicadas and the rhythmical sound of Donatés' hooves on the dirt road.

In the courtyard, a solitary light was on outside the stables, and Laine was surprised to see Boyer perched on the rails, tapping away at his mobile, obviously waiting.

For her??

He looked up, his face breaking into a broad grin.

"Hey!" he called as she approached. He stood up and caught the horse by the harness. Laine nodded her greeting. She felt glad to see him, comforted, in some strange way.

"Am I keeping you from home?"

He shrugged. "Have to stay and see that everyone's tucked safely in," he explained. "Was that a good ride?" he asked, seeing from her flushed cheeks it was. He led the horse inside the stables.

"Wonderful!" Laine said. She stayed mounted, allowing her horse to be led inside the barn to the tethering post. The young man kept his eyes averted, but he was drinking her in. This had to be the most desirable woman he had ever seen. One day he, Scott Boyer, he would have a wife like her. The reins secured, he turned around and lifted his arms up to assist her down. Laine swung her leg over and allowed him to lift her down, and for a second she was caught between him and the horse's flank. Even in riding boots, he was a good five inches taller than her, and she had the queerest sensation of being a girl again.

He made no move to step back. He appeared almost mesmerized. He was so close she could feel his heart pounding. Laine hesitated, then compelled by some instinct deep within her, slowly reached up, put her hand behind his neck and pulled his mouth down onto hers. There was an urgency in her kiss that took his breath away.

He responded clumsily at first, unbelieving, then quickly unquestioning of this miracle, submitted enthusiastically to her kiss. Laine slid her hand down his thighs, feeling the smooth leather of riding chaps, then pressed her hand hard on the straining denim, her eyes dreamy.

Scott felt as if he were in a dream. She led him inside the tack room, to the dilapidated old groom's sofa in the corner, with its coir stuffing protruding from two holes in the worn fabric. She pushed him on his back, but he was oblivious to the scratchy padding. All he felt was her–on top of him–kissing his face tenderly, lovingly. This was Laine McAllister herself, opening his shirt to caress and kiss his chest.

Afterwards, he tried to remember who had undressed who, but it was all a blur, just the sweetness of her remained crystal-clear, vivid in his memory, and her hunger. They made love frantically, ignoring the discomfort, Laine wanting only to couple and find release, he, determined to please her, but woefully clumsy.

Donatés gazed from his stall, watching their coupling, his large brown eyes unconcerned at this union. Once, her body still quivering from pinnacles just reached, Scott Boyer thought her sated and moved to gather up his pants, crumpled in a heap on the floor. She caught his hand, her breath still short pants. She stared at him, eyes huge and soft.

"No," she shook her head slowly.

Then she showed him what pleased her.

Afterwards, they got dressed quickly, Laine saying very little, and he was disturbed to see her eyes were sad when she kissed him lightly on the cheek in farewell. He wanted to walk her to her car, but she declined, leaving him to attend to Donatés. He tried to press her, feeling it the least he could do.

She stood right there, before him, but he could feel she was somewhere far away, out of his reach.

Shyly, he took her hands in his own.

"Laine, I– " He tried again. "For what it's worth, I think–" She touched her finger to his lips to stop his words, and he fell silent.

"Thank you", she said simply. She turned and strode away, and he watched her leave.

Had he made her happy?

No, not really, he decided.

But hopefully, for that short while, he had made her forget.

TWO SPOONS CRAZY

UNSEEING

Mia stared down at the blood in fright. It was too much.

She leaned against the bath and put her head against the cool enamel in an effort to quell the nausea that threatened to overwhelm her. Her period was sometimes heavy, but this bleeding was far, far too heavy. She felt a panic rising within her, and she clutched the edge of the bath until her knuckles were white.

"Mama? Mama?" Bernadette was knocking on the door, her little voice peeved. "Mama? Mama, I have to go." The four-year-old was hopping up and down outside the bathroom door. Mia tried to answer her but felt too weak. If she lifted her head, she would faint. And the burning, dear God, she had to get rid of this burning.

"Mama...." Outside the bathroom door, Bernadette started to wail as her bladder gave way. The puddle spread at her feet, messing the carpet. She cranked up the volume. Now she would get into trouble, and it was all Mama's fault. The child gazed appalled at her sodden feet and bellowed her chagrin.

Downstairs, Mrs Costaz stopped filling the washing machine with laundry, listening to Bernadette's wailing. She straightened up, wondering what could be wrong. She waited for Mia to attend to her.

The child should stop wailing any minute now. Mrs Reichmann was upstairs. Those children should be in school, she thought, disapproving. It was a week now, and for no rhyme or reason Mrs Reichmann was keeping them at home, and her not well at all. He was a pig, that man, a real pig. She shook her head in disgust. Anyone could see the woman wasn't well. But still, the husband was off on a 'business trip'–wouldn't be back until Friday or Saturday, apparently. How he could leave his wife when she was so sick was beyond Mrs Costaz.

The wailing continued and concerned, she dropped the remainder of the laundry into the basket and went to investigate Bernadette's grievances.

Bernadette was standing outside the bathroom door, the chubby little face contorted as she howled in chagrin. She pointed to the culprit, a soggy pool at her feet. Kira peered out from the doorway of her room, watching her younger sister's distress, unconcerned and indifferent. Mrs Costaz clicked her tongue in annoyance at the child's apathy.

Kira should try and calm her sister down. And where was Mrs Reichmann? Kira, sensing Mrs Costaz's disapproval, disappeared back into her bedroom. Mrs Costaz saw her retreat as she stooped to pacify Bernadette. That child wasn't right. Something was troubling her. Kira was so... so listless lately. Nothing seemed to touch her, or please her.

The good-natured Mrs Costaz picked up the crying Bernadette and with her free hand pushed the bathroom door handle down. She wanted to effect repairs on the hapless child, at the same time gingerly holding the sodden Bernadette away from her skirt. The door wouldn't budge and she realized with a twinge of alarm that Mia had to be inside the bathroom.

"Mrs Reichmann," she called, concerned.

After a moment came a reply. "Yes."

"Are you alright Mrs Reichmann?" She rattled the door handle, concerned.

"Yes, fine. I'll be out now." Mia sounded faint, and Mrs Costaz turned away from the door, her forehead puckered in a frown. She made her way to the master bathroom and washed the child down quickly, wondering whether she should perhaps call that nice Mrs McAllister.

Her husband was a doctor after all. She would know what to do.

Sponged down, Bernadette bounced playfully on her hip as they made their way to her bedroom for fresh clothes. Mrs Costaz was almost done when she heard the door of the bathroom being opened, and a moment later Mia stood in the doorway of Bernadette's room, her face pale, clutching her robe to her.

"Is she alright?" She indicated to Bernadette, who looked sulkily away. This accident was all Mama's fault.

"She's fine, she just couldn't make it to the toilet in time. No matter, I'll rinse them and put them in the laundry." She held up the offending garments. "Are you alright? You look so pale?" Mrs Costaz' eyes narrowed in apprehension.

"Fine, don't worry." Mia brushed off her concern, gesturing dismissively.

"It's that time of the month, and I feel a little weak today, I'm bleeding too much, perhaps." She leaned against the door jamb and pushed her wispy hair from her face, a faint line of perspiration on her upper lip. "But I think perhaps it would be a good thing if I took advantage of the fact that you're here today–stayed in bed. Would you mind?"

"No, of course not," she reassured her. Mrs Costaz shooed Mia away. "I'll keep the children happy. When are they going back to school?" she asked, masking her disapproval. She hoisted Bernadette back onto her ample hip, tweaking the child's cheek as she did so. Bernadette giggled. Mia's eyes clouded and she looked away.

"Soon, soon." She turned on her back and made her way to her room, the spare room where she was now sleeping. Mrs Costaz looked after her and sighed under her breath, her heart saddened. They were having problems, Mr and Mrs Reichmann.

Mrs Reichmann had been sleeping alone for a while now, and God knew, that was no life.

She had been married to Mr Costaz for thirty-seven years before he died, God bless him, and after five years she still missed his heavy bulk in the bed. Nowadays, she slept alone, the old mattress dipping where his heavy frame had worn down the springs over the years. He was no longer there to prevent her from rolling into the hollow that used to be him, but she refused to get rid of the old bed. At night, the sagging mattress brought its own comfort.

She shrugged to herself as she went carefully down the stairs. Perhaps, in this case, it was better. She heard how he spoke to his wife. That man was a real pig.

Grateful for the respite, Mia lay in bed, staring at nothing, listening to the sound of the children's voices as they floated up to her. What would she have done without Mrs Costaz? Perhaps she should go to that clinic, but who would look after the children? Mrs Costaz? She would have to ask her. She couldn't take much more of this agonizing burning, and now this constant bleeding. Even the pills weren't doing much lately, except to make her sleep if she took three. She needed three pills to sleep now, and another four Varetium capsules to get through the day.

The instructions on the bottle of barbiturates recommended one or two a day, but that was nonsense. She closed her eyes and allowed a fitful sleep to claim her.

Hours later, Mia was pulled unwillingly out of her slumber by a soft voice calling her, a gentle hand on her shoulder.

"Mrs Reichmann. Mrs Reichmann. Are you sleeping? Mrs Costaz's voice was soft, tentative. Mia turned over in the bed to see the kindly woman leaning over her in the darkened room.

"No. It's alright." She shook her head in an effort to wake up. "What is it?"

"I'm leaving now. I prepared a supper for you and the children, a little chicken. They are downstairs watching television, and perfectly content, so just take it easy." She smiled at Mia reassuringly. "You have been sleeping the whole day." She took her coat from over her arm and shrugged it on. "You must have needed it. Also," she delved into her skirt pocket, "Good news. I found his watch. In Kira's room."

She held out Rudolf's watch and placed it on the dresser. It was his pride and joy, a Breitling. All hell had broken loose when he misplaced it.

Mia lay back, relieved. At least that was something.

"He will be happy you found his watch, "she said, trying to muster a smile, but she felt dizzy. "Thank you, you are very kind to prepare the supper." She raised herself on her elbow and tried to clear her thoughts.

Rudolf's watch, found. Thankfully, he couldn't accuse Mrs Costaz of theft because he insisted it was on his wrist the night before.

"Do you want me perhaps to take it to the jeweler, and get the strap repaired? This is the second time he has lost it. One day it will drop off his arm and be lost forever, "Mrs Costaz cautioned, knowing that was a nightmare they didn't need. "You look as though you should be in bed for a week at least. Let me do this for you, it won't cost much. You can pay me for the repair when I give you the slip."

Mia nodded gratefully and the housekeeper picked up the wristwatch and slipped it into her coat pocket. She turned to leave with a little whisper. "Remember, if you need me, just give me a ring."

"Thank you, you are always so kind to me." Mia struggled to speak forcefully, clearly, to reassure Mrs Costaz she could leave them with a happy heart. "Where exactly did you find it, by the way? We hunted everywhere."

"Oh," Mrs Costaz flicked her head towards the children's rooms. "In Kira's bed, between the sheets. He must have dropped it there when he said goodnight."

NO MORE FEAR

Mia listened to Mrs Costaz's car leaving and closed her eyes. Kira, that was the only one he had time for. And yet, the child was always so distant with him, seemed almost to hate him. They had found his watch, which would please him. Mia lay back, grateful to have some rest.

Suddenly her heart began to pound. In the bed, between the sheets?

How did the watch get there? Did Kira take it? She closed her eyes and she heard Mrs Costaz' voice resonating inside her head, 'in Kira's bed, between the sheets' .

With a ragged intake of breath, Mia sat bolt upright up in her bed, her fists clenching the sheets. Her breathing was ragged. Could it be? Could these terrible, insane thoughts be true? Mia's heart was pounding so violently, she felt it would surely burst through her chest.

She tried desperately to think clearly, banging her fist to her forehead, to banish these terrible thoughts.

Suddenly, it all seemed so clear.

Kira, wan and listless, cringing anytime he chanced to touch her. And he, always encouraging her to eat, so affable and benign, 'Papa likes fat little girls' he would say. Kira, pushing away her plate of food. Trying to repel him with starvation!

Laine's voice floated back to her, as in a dream, 'Evil to be fat? That's a curious choice of words, Mia?'

Oh God. Mia felt faint. She sat on the edge of the bed, her body rocking in misery. Oh God, oh God, she had forsaken them. She had promised to protect them from the evil of the world, and she had betrayed them. Kira was just seven!

How long? How long had this evil been going on in her house, while she took medicine prescribed by doctors? Mia felt a visceral hate such as she had never felt before.

Rudolf, he had violated their child, but the terrible truth was–it was she who was to blame. She had let this happen. She was right there, a few feet away, and yet he had perpetrated this evil.

Well, she would deal with him. She knew exactly what to do, what had to be done. The hysteria of a moment ago was gone, and in its place, insanity summoned its own calm.

Rudolf. That was simple. He must die.

And this terrible, evil world, this world was no place for little girls to be without their mother.

There was no other choice.

They must come with her.

It all seemed so clear now, so inevitable.

The rage that had threatened to crush her minutes before, Mia felt it ebb away, vanquished by a new sense of purpose.

If God waited for her and her little ones, then the Devil himself surely waited for Rudolf!

Mia found the children sitting in the television room. watching a program about butterflies, their tiny faces enraptured. They looked happy to see her up and about. Bernadette got up and quickly scurried onto her mother's lap, her grievances from the morning's episode forgotten. Mia held the child close to her, rocking her on her lap, her eyes shut. When she thought—

"Mama, you're hurting me." Bernadette's cries broke her reverie, and she loosened her grip. Bernadette wriggled out of Mia's arms in protest.

Mia turned to her older daughter, who was watching her with expressionless eyes.

"Kira. Kira, turn off the television." She said, her voice gentle. "I must talk to you." The child hesitated for a moment, then grudgingly obeyed. She sat down on the floor in front of the television, away from Mia, her legs crossed, eying her mother warily. She hates me, Mia thought. I should have protected her, and I didn't.

She dismissed the thought. It was of no consequence. He would never hurt her again.

The television was off, the room was silent–Bernadette stopped her antics in surprise, looking first at her mother, then her sister. What was up?

"Come to me, Kira, I want to speak to you. Come, please?" Mia beckoned her, holding out her hand. The child stood up reluctantly, slowly approaching her mother, her eyes distrusting. When Mia put her arms around her, she stood stiff and unyielding in her mother's embrace.

God forgive me, Mia thought, but she kept calm, caressing her daughter's face with a mother's loving touch.

"Here, sit on my lap." She hauled the unwilling Kira onto her lap, panting with exertion. Bernadette wandered closer, her face curious at all the attention lavished on Kira. She stood patiently by, watching. What had Kira done?

"Kira, tell me, did Papa come to your room last night?" Kira's eyes flew open, and then her face closed, became guarded. Her lips started to tremble, and Mia winced at the fear she saw in her child's eyes. She closed her arms around her oldest daughter and hugged her to her, kissing butterfly kisses on the soft hair, catching her breath when she felt Kira's small frame shiver in trepidation.

"Tell me, darling, I must know. Did he come to your room last night?" Gently, she lifted Kira's chin to look into her eyes. The child's eyes were huge, filled with foreboding. She nodded.

So it was true. Instead of hysteria and rage, Mia again felt this new composure. It was all so very clear. It was as if she had known for the longest time what to do.

"Does he come often? Please, tell me? Whisper in my ear."

Kira began to weep. She buried her head in her mother's neck and spoke softly, stumbling over her words. Mia stroked her head and said soothing words while Bernadette looked on, wide-eyed.

What was Kira telling Mama?

There was one thing Mia had to know. "And Bernie, tell me, please? I must know. Does he visit Bernie?" Kira glanced briefly at her young sister. She shook her head mutely, and Mia felt a relief so intense it made her faint.

Mia tried to smile. She must get a hold of herself. Kira was looking at her, her face curious. Mama looked different, better.

"Now," Mia said, addressing them both, her face animated, her voice clear, "We are going to go away. After Friday, we will leave. We will be safe from all harm, and we will be together, just us, you, Kira, and me!" She tweaked Bernie's cheeks, smiling."

Kira looked up, hopeful. "Really?"

"Really," Mia promised. "But Mama has first to speak to Papa. "So, we will wait until Friday?" she said brightly. "Then we leave. Do you like that idea?" Mia beamed at a doubtful Kira. She pulled her daughter to her in a fierce embrace.

"Where? Where are we going?" Bernadette interjected, her face excited.

"It's a secret," Kira chided her younger sister. Mia stood up and eased Kira off her lap.

She had better see what it was Mrs Costaz had prepared for supper, feed the children. And she had things to do. She needed to prepare.

INNOCENCE

Laine adjusted Liesel's coat and stooped quickly to kiss the child. She stood back smiling, watching them proudly as the two scampered through the gates to join the other children milling around the steps of the school building. Shana stood back, a little removed from the other children this morning and Laine watched as Liesel turned to chivvy her younger sister on, ever protective.

It was good, she thought that they had each other. And it was doubly good that she had them. God knows what she would have done without them, demanding—no, insisting—that some routines stay the same.

Laine wondered just how much the children understood. Shana was increasingly fractious, and she knew it was due to Case's absence. Shana had always been Daddy's girl and the child asked after him endlessly. Laine tried her best to diffuse the tricky situations when they arose, but there were times when she too, wanted to sit herself down and wail right alongside the child.

She closed her eyes, momentarily weighed down with the enormity of it all, then turned back towards her car. She had shopping to do, there was no time for moping.

"Laine. Laine." She turned to see the school's principal rushing up to greet her, her face red with exertion. "Laine, hold up there a minute." She was shooing children out of the way, and Laine wondered what it was that had Myra agitated so early in the morning. Her turn at the bake sale wasn't for another couple of weeks. She waited patiently while the woman waddled up to her.

"Sorry to hold you up, " she wheezed, "but I need to know about the Reichmann girls! Do you know why they aren't coming to school anymore?" Myra Egglington was embarrassed by her puffing. She always felt so damn fat with these perky, skinny-bitch wives! This mother was nicer than others, but she could afford to be, always looking as if she had just stepped out of a goddamn shampoo commercial!

Laine stared back at her in mild alarm, pondering. Mia had said she would take them herself. Perhaps she still wasn't well enough?

"No," she said slowly, "I don't know. I think that Kira has been a bit off-color, and Mia Reichmann herself, well she has been rather ill," she said. "But she did tell me, when last I saw her, that she would be taking the children to school herself from here on in? Have you tried calling her?"

"I spoke to her last week. She said Kira was ill, and the little one wouldn't come without her sister. Personally, I think that's sheer nonsense. That little one is such a sunny little thing isn't she?" Myra added. "Kira is the one who is always so quiet. I've thought for some time that the child wasn't well, but we can't look after the children beyond the realms of the school, you know??" she said unctuously. "Still, I wish parents would let us know what's happening." Myra realized she was talking to a parent, and said with an ingratiating smile. "Well, sorry to trouble you. I just wondered what had happened. -And are you well, hon?" she inquired, as an afterthought. There were rumors...

"Fine, just fine." Laine gave her a sunny smile. "How are my girls faring?"

"No problem. No problem at all." The principal smiled, "Well-balanced little girls. A real pleasure." Laine nodded, glad to hear that. The separation wasn't being felt, yet. That was good.

"-Well, can you?" Myra was staring at her expectantly, obviously expecting an answer.

"Sorry, will I do what?" Laine asked, embarrassed at being caught not listening.

"Will you call on Mrs Reichmann, see what's up?" Myra repeated, thinking, 'It's true'. There was a sadness around Laine McAllister, she could see it now.

"Of course. I'll look in on her. I'll do it today," Laine promised, groaning inwardly. The last thing she felt like was Mia Reichmann. She wondered as she started the car; did the school principal know about her and Case?

Probably. Everyone seemed to know. This was a small community.

Oh, Case, what have you done. The old despair flooded through her.

She took a deep, gulping breath.

They needed milk, and sugar. Laine started the car.

NO SHELTER

Ten minutes, ten minutes is all it takes to be a good neighbor, Laine told herself. Reluctantly, she turned the car into the Reichmann driveway.

She found the children playing outside in the garden. They looked well enough and greeted her cheerily. "Hi, Mrs Klister," Bernadette lisped her fair hair a halo of untidy curls, her little cheeks grubby with leftover food and grime. She was a gorgeous kid by anyone's standards and Laine softened at the child's breezy grin "Hello," Kira added softly, her usual solemn little self.

"Is Mommy in? Can you call her for me?" Laine smiled at them, squatting to admire the dollies sitting in regal splendor before a feast of grass and mud pies.

But there was no need to call her.

"Laine," Mia was approaching, looking unusually relaxed. "Laine! How are you?" Mia greeted her neighbor warmly.

Laine stood up. "You are looking better!" Indeed she did, still a little gray, but there was color in her cheeks. Her eyes were unnaturally bright, but she appeared more at ease than when Laine had last seen her. "How are you feeling?"

Mia shrugged, her hands upturned in placid acceptance.

"As you see," she said smiling. " —A lot better! What can I do for you?" She bent to hoist up her youngest daughter to her hip, kissing her affectionately while she addressed Laine.

"Well," Laine felt foolish, "The school was querying the whereabouts of the children. They were quite worried, I think. I promised I would look in, see if perhaps you wanted me to collect them again. I've told you before, it's no bother."

"You are kind, but there is no need for them to go back there. I am keeping them with me, until Friday," Mia said, preoccupied with her infant. She looked up at Laine, smiling, "Is there anything else?"

"Until Friday?" she asked, confused with this new, serene Mia.

"Yes. Rudolf gets back on Friday night, and then, we are leaving. I am taking the children, and we are going away." She leaned forward, "For good." she whispered with a small smile.

Laine gaped at her in sheer astonishment. This was all very sudden. "Is Rudolf going too? I mean, what about the business? Or are you moving a little closer to the business?"

Laine was confounded.

In Mia's weakened state, she chose to move? Or worse, run away?? Was that what this was about?

"I'm afraid I'm not with you?"

Mia's smile faded. In fact, Laine thought, she looked rather cagey.

"I am taking the children away, for good," Mia repeated. She flicked a stray hair from her face, looked around her. "-In fact, I'm leaving Rudolf," she confided, lowering her voice.

She put Bernadette down, stroking the infant's tousled hair absentmindedly.

"We're going to meet our grandmother, in Serbia," Bernadette interjected excitedly, tugging Laine's jodhpurs for attention. Laine smiled absently at the child, her thoughts a jumble. Mia's mother was deceased, she knew that, but she supposed it was a story Mia told the children to make the trip more appealing.

Even Kira looked perkier, she thought, trying to quell her doubts.

"Well," Laine said hesitantly, turning her attention back to Mia. "And this is all happening on Friday?"

Mia nodded, emphatic. "Friday. Yes. Of course, with him, I never know what time he'll be back, but," she shrugged and smiled enigmatically, "I will be waiting."

Laine thought she heard an edge in Mia's voice. The mere idea of her oaf of a neighbor, and this sparrow of a wife having a confrontation made her shudder.

"Mia, I don't mean to pry, but does he know? Is he agreeable to this?" she asked, her brow furrowed. He was a violent man and God knew, Mia was in no condition to travel -or be beaten up by a raging husband, for that matter. Oh God.

Laine tried not to look panicked. She was wondering what, if anything, she could do.

Mia brushed off her concern, seemingly amused at Laine's angst.

"Really, don't worry. It will be alright, Laine," she reassured her. She hesitated, as if a thought had crossed her mind. "You have been a good friend to me, and my girls, and I thank you. Case too, he has been wonderful. No one ever did before, for me, what he did." She touched Laine on her arm, then quickly drew her hand away, her cheeks coloring at the familiarity. "I thank you both," Mia said, heartfelt. "I really wish things could have been different."

Laine was touched. What did one say? In truth, Mia looked to be quite feisty, in control. Yet—. Her sense of foreboding was growing. The children certainly looked happier.

Laine searched Mia's face. Her eyes were too bright, but other than that, she looked fine.

Well... Okayish.

"Mia, we are always there for you," she heard herself saying, reminding herself the 'we' is 'me', but Mia probably didn't know that. And she thinks Case is a hero!

Both their husbands, rat-bastards!

What the hell!

Spontaneously Laine stepped forward and hugged her neighbor. To her surprise, she felt Mia hug her back, even cling to her for a few seconds. The response should have made her happy; at last Mia, was reaching out.

Instead, the gesture left Laine feeling oddly distressed. This woman was so alone. Perhaps it was best she returned to the places and people she knew.

"Are you still on the medication?" Laine pressed, her voice gentle.

"No." Mia's face closed. "Nothing. I don't need this medicine from the doctors anymore. I fix myself." she said shortly. The pills, her pills, that was different.

Uh-oh. Here we go! thought Laine, but she kept her face impassive. Case needed to speak to this woman. Well, that's not possible anymore, a little voice answered. "Well, if there's anything I can do, let me know. Please call us and say goodbye before you leave."

Mia nodded, staying silent.

Laine turned to leave, but Mia caught her arm, suddenly eager. "There is something you can do," Mia said. "Please, our children have been such good friends, and I would like to give a little... a little party on Friday. For the four of them. In the afternoon. Will you bring them? Please, just for an hour or so. It is a farewell party!" She looked pleadingly at Laine.

Laine hesitated. It seemed a simple request, but she could not quell her sense of unease. And why on earth shouldn't she feel misgivings, she asked herself. The poor woman was stealing her children away, to God knows where... She supposed that took courage, escaping from a mongrel husband.

The last made up her mind.

"Well, okay, if you think you can manage four little tykes. I know they are a handful." "Wonderful. Oh, I am so glad, they have been such good friends." Mia looked delighted.

"Of course. I'll get Judith to bring them across on Friday, and I'll collect them myself later, after training. Is that okay? Around five or so?"

"Perfect." Mia clapped her hands with delight. The children looked up, intrigued at the excitement. Mia beamed at them. She explained to them there was to be a party for the four children. Their faces lit up.

"Now, I must take the children shopping, for things for the party!" She smiled contentedly, holding their hands in each of hers. They were looking up at their mother, their faces eager. Shopping for a party! Their eyes shone.

"Remember, if you need me, let me know," Laine said, turning to leave. There were only a few hours of light left and she wanted to give Donatés a strenuous workout today. Hell, give herself a strenuous workout!

She would have to get a move on.

She could feel Mia's eyes on her as she walked away.

In her car, Laine hesitated. What a damn cheek she had, sitting in judgment of Mia. Hers had been the perfect marriage, and where the hell had that got her?

Mia watched her neighbor depart. Laine also had two little girls. This world was not meant for little girls, but Laine probably didn't know that! No matter.

She did, and she could fix things

INTERVENTION

Kevin was thinking about it, rubbing his temples.

This conversation with Ashely was giving him a headache. His gut was churning at the mere suggestion, but Ash was right. He owed it to Case to do something, although God only knew what the fuck could ever fix this mess.

"Well?" She was on speaker phone and the extra volume seemed to amplify her agitation. Kevin sighed. He knew this Ashley of old. She had the bit between her teeth, and there would be no stopping her.

"So, Case is actually going there tonight? And then, they are going to talk divorce, or— What exactly?" Ashley was demanding to know, although he had already told her everything he knew. Kevin was stalling, trying to think.

Ashley sighed. She was getting testy. "Look Kev, all I know is, if it goes well, well, then we can slink off. But if it goes badly, then Laine will need us. Either way, we should be there. In need, reason with them both. Please, Kev!" She sighed, " I know you're nervous about seeing him, but someone has to talk sense into him! We simply cannot just stand by and let them screw it all up."

"You don't think we will be interfering?" he asked. It felt a hell of a lot like meddling to him!

"Of course, we will be interfering! Don't care!" She was firm. "Case and Roxie Tanner won't last, of that, I am absolutely sure, but by the time Case comes to his senses, it will be too late, for sure! I know Laine. She'll let her pride bury them. Let's not let that happen."

Kevin drummed his fingers on the desk. She was right, of course. Case was damn well caught and hogtied, in the middle of a spider's web, a beautiful spider's web, perhaps, but stuck fast. Kevin found himself nodding.

For sure, the prince was not thinking straight. It had to be all about his dick.

He made up his mind.

"Okay, I'll collect you."

"Great! He could hear the relief in Ashley's voice. "If she's expecting him around half-six, let's get there, maybe around seven-thirty, eight??"

When Kevin put the phone down, he sat quiet for a moment, shaking his head.

What a pair they were! Kevin Daniels, queer.

And Case McAllister, dumb stupid bastard.

RED MIST

FAREWELL PARTY

It was Friday afternoon, and the two girls were dressed in their party outfits, little faces aglow with excitement. Bernadette and Kira had popped in the day before, accompanied by the affable Mrs Costaz, the little ones babbling excitedly about all the goodies that had been specially purchased for this farewell party. There was to be candy galore, strawberry ice cream and games that were brand new!

Laine's two daughters stood before her, submitting to her inspection, anxious to get to party. They looked beautiful, Laine thought with a measure of pride, Shana positively preening in her party clothes.

"You look wonderful, both of you. Now remember, don't eat too much and get sick. Daddy's coming to visit tonight, and I want you both to be nice and healthy." They squealed with delight at her announcement. Yay! Daddy was coming. And a party! This was going to be a really special day.

"Is he coming to stay?" Shana asked immediately, her face eager.

"No. He's still at Doctor School. He's just popping in. But tomorrow he's fetching you for the weekend."

"Oh." Her face fell, and Liesel shot Laine a reproachful look.

Oh God. Laine sighed inwardly, feeling treacherous. She rallied herself.-Not now, no downers now.

"Okay, Granny's ready to take you. Now remember, be good, really good. I want Mrs Reichmann to tell all the people at home how good the little girls are in this country."

"In this country! -Are they leaving the U.S?" Judith looked up, intrigued.

"Apparently," Laine replied. "Going back to her mother or something." She bent to kiss the children goodbye. "Tell Mia I'll collect them around five-ish, okay?"

"Okay. Come girls, let's go." Judith intended to walk with the children to the Reichmann house, through the field. They could easily manage the walk; it was close enough. 'Allow the children a chance to burn off some energy,'

Judith ventured.

Laine nodded. "Well, I'm off. Today, five-foot-seven, tomorrow, the world." Laine tried to sound cheery. Case was coming to see her this evening, and this time, she wouldn't blow it. She would keep her emotions in check. He said to expect him around six-thirty.

She would have to leave the stables in good time to collect the children–be ready for his visit.

The children gave her a last kiss goodbye, and Laine found she was hugging them for just that fraction longer than normal. It was Mia. Her plans to run away rattled Laine. But there was nothing she could do. She watched them toddle out obediently behind Judith. Shana protesting it was too far to walk, but Judith was having none of it, and jollying them along. Impatient at her baby sister's dawdling, Liesel took Shana's free hand in hers.

They were a quaint picture, as they strolled towards the wooden gate that led to the north paddock. Laine watched them through the kitchen window, smiling at the tableau.

But time was marching on. She grabbed her car keys. Time to focus on Donatés.

FIVE CHANCES

Judith found the Reichmann girls playing outside, eagerly awaiting the arrival of their guests. They too, were wearing pretty little dresses that they proudly told Judith were 'brand new.' Judith left the four of them playing at the old doll's house in the Reichmann's back yard and went up around the house towards the back door. She tapped politely. It was slightly ajar, and she stepped inside, calling Mia's name softly.

"Mrs Reichmann, Mia? Are you in?"

She turned as Mrs Costaz came into the kitchen, beaming.

"Hello, Mrs Costaz, your guests have arrived." Judith smiled in greeting.

Upstairs, Mia heard Judith calling, and she froze. The bedroom door was locked, and no one could walk in. She told herself Mrs Costaz was downstairs, she would see to see Judith.

Mia carried on with her task.

There were only three rounds of ammunition left in the box, and she counted two in the gun. Five bullets. It would be enough. Carefully, she emptied the bullets from the magazine making sure there was nothing in the chamber. Satisfied the gun was empty, she fired a couple of times, hearing the metallic clicks, practicing. No mistakes like leaving the safety off. She nodded, satisfied. She carefully reloaded the magazine, then slid it smoothly into the gun. She was ready.

The Lord himself said, "Suffer the little children to come unto me." There was no doubt in her mind. The day of reckoning was here. This time, she wouldn't make any mistakes. She could hear the high-pitched squealing of the girls as they giggled and shrieked outside, hear the regular, oil-starved whine of their swing. Mrs Costaz' voice floated up, admonishing them, telling Kira to be careful. She walked to the window and looked out. They were all giggling, and the tableau made her smile.

Little girls. Her smile faded. Little girls had no place in this world. Well, she would take care of that.

Mia checked her reflection in the mirror.

She looked pretty today.

She heard Mrs Costaz talking to Judith McAllister. Mia recognized her voice. So, Laine was not here Better.

In the kitchen, Mrs Costaz was speaking. "So, are the guests of honor here? Well, I too, have made something special for today. But I didn't hear your car?"

"Oh, it's a pleasant walk. Don't worry, they are already playing in the dollhouse with Bernadette and Kira," Judith told the housekeeper. "Should I leave them with you? Is Mia around?"

"No problem, no problem, leave them, they will be just fine, maybe eat a little too much." Mrs Costaz waved her arms, indicating Judith could leave them with a happy heart, "But such are children. Mia is upstairs changing, but don't wait for her, they're fine with me."

Judith relaxed. "Good. Laine will collect them around five." She turned on her heel and departed, calling goodbye. She stopped to peep in at the children at play before she made her way to the field path. They all looked perfectly content.

Mia heard Judith calling goodbye. She stood at the top of the landing, waiting, wanting Judith to be gone.

There wasn't much time, she needed to prepare.

SANDS RUN OUT

Mia went quickly downstairs into the study and sat down behind the desk. She opened a drawer and removed a writing pad. After a moment of thought, she began to write quickly. The world would know about men like Rudolf. She hesitated.

It crossed her mind that she owed the McAllisters an apology.

They would never understand, perhaps. They were good people.

She began to write.

The letters took a couple of minutes, there wasn't that much to say. Her actions would say it all. Her task finished, she placed the letters in envelopes and sealed them, placing them prominently on the desktop. She opened another drawer, removing a small safety deposit box, taking care that the sharp sides of the tin didn't scuff the inlaid leather on the desktop. It was a fine piece of furniture, one of the few pieces she had selected herself.

She twisted the combination expertly, and the little padlock clicked open.

She opened the tin, staring in surprise. There was even more money there than she anticipated. Carefully, she counted it out. Twenty-four thousand dollars! Well, Rudolf would have no need of this. She shoved the money into a large envelope.

Then she closed the tin again, clicked the padlock shut and replaced it in the drawer.

With the bulging envelope in her hands, she went to find Mrs Costaz.

She found her outside, sitting in a garden chair, watching the children at play, a smile on her face. The McAllister children paused in their frolicking to greet Mia politely.

Mia beamed back at them.

"They are truly God's richest blessing," Mrs Costaz murmured, with a knowing nod. "And that Bernadette. She will be a real beauty someday." She chortled at the antics of the youngest Reichmann child.

Mia said nothing. She sat down next to Mrs Costaz, watching them. But it was time.

Mrs Costaz looked at Mia's solemn face. "Why the grim face? This is a party," she chided, jocular. "Come on, let's go inside and fetch some of the goodies." She lifted herself up from the chair, grunting. Her age was catching up.

Mia nodded. "You're right. And we have business to discuss." She followed Mrs Costaz into the house.

Inside the kitchen, Mia addressed her without preamble. "Mrs Costaz, I must dispense with your services immediately. I have here your wages, in lieu of notice." She took the bulky envelope from the kitchen counter. "You have been good to me and my girls, and for that, I thank you from the bottom of my heart." She thrust the envelope into Mrs Costaz's hands.

Mrs Costaz stared at the envelope, speechless. Was she being fired? Her mouth dropped open in dismay.

"Please, don't look at me like that," Mia begged her. "Understand, I have no choice. I'm not sure if they—" She stopped short, choosing her words, then continued, "—If you will get your wages, and I need to be sure of that. Please keep that."

Mrs Costaz was trying to give the envelope back to her, clearly upset.

Mia shook her head, refusing the envelope. Mrs Costaz stared first in consternation at the envelope, then at Mia.

"But why? Are you dismissing me? Who are you going to get to look after the children? Do all this work?? You, you are not well!" Mrs Costaz was decidedly upset!

Mia took the older woman's hand and spoke with an urgency she hoped Mrs Costaz would understand.

"Please! I am not dismissing you, but who will pay you if I am gone?" she said. "The children and I are leaving. I am taking them somewhere. Away. And I am feeling much better, really I am. Take the money, please, and leave now," she said.

Mia felt desperate. Mrs Costaz could ruin everything!

"Safe? What do you mean, safe?" Mrs Costaz was not to be appeased. She looked at Mia, her brow furrowed, questioning. "Are you running away from your husband?" That had to be it. Mrs Reichmann was running away. If that were so, she would surely need this money! She tried again to give the envelope back, but Mia would have none of it.

Mia shook her head, her voice unusually firm. "No. No, I am done running away from him. Believe me," she said "I will be waiting for him, as always, when he arrives home tonight. But then I am leaving, it's true." She patted Mrs Costaz on the shoulder, consoling her.

Mrs Costaz was beginning to weep.

"Please don't worry. We will be fine, all of us," Mia entreated her. "There comes a time when one knows what the right thing is, you know, to do."

Mrs Costaz looked at her doubtfully. It was true, Mia did not look too distressed. "I don't know," she said doubtfully. "You're like a family to me. Where are you going? Will you write to me, tell me you're all safe?" She felt sure now Mia was running away. Perhaps it was better she did not know too much, because if the police asked her, there would be no need to lie.

Mia hugged her. "Of course. Of course. Now, say goodbye to the children!"

"Now! You want me to leave right this minute?" Mrs Costaz gaped at her in disbelief.

"Mrs Costaz, listen to me." Mia was starting to feel panicked. "I am," she hesitated, choosing her words carefully, " leaving today. So are the children. That is the reason for this party. I want their little friends to remember them with love! And now," she contrived to look encouraging, reasonable, "While they have their friends to distract them, it is better if you say good-bye to them now, leave them when they are happy and smiling?"

"I—! I wanted to give them some special cake." Mrs Costaz was weeping. "Can't I look after them for you this afternoon? I can leave around five?"

Mia shook her head firmly, ignoring the brimming eyes. "No, I'm afraid not. You should say goodbye now," she said. "It's for the best."

Mrs Costaz brushed her eyes and shook her head. Who would have thought such a thing! The wages afforded no comfort at all, and she stuffed it disconsolately into her apron pocket. She shuffled out of the kitchen to say goodbye to the children.

Outside, she called out to them, but at first, they didn't hear her, above the laughter and yelling. She called to them again, and this time they stopped in their play, their little faces expectant. "Is it time? Is it time for the party yet?" Bernadette voiced all their thoughts, her face eager.

The older woman tried valiantly to hide her distress, aware of Mia watching her from the window. "No. I'm calling you to say goodbye. I'm going now, my angels. Come and kiss me." For the life of her, Mrs Costaz couldn't muster a smile. They walked slowly over to her, curious at her change of mood, the two McAllister girls hanging back.

"Your mother tells me you are leaving tonight, and I might not see you," she said., "For a while." It was too much to bear, to say 'forever', plus, it would distress the children, she knew that. They loved her too.

"Promise me you will be good girls, and you will write to me. Okay?"

"We're going to see my grandma," Bernadette announced proudly.

"And I can write, not so good, but I am getting better every day," Kira ventured shyly. Now the day of departure was here, she looked less enthusiastic than her younger sister. She suddenly threw her small arms around Mrs Costaz's neck and hugged her fiercely, clinging to her.

"We will be good. I promise!" she whispered fervently in her ear. "I'll miss you." Reluctantly, she released her. Mrs Costaz smiled at her, her cheeks wet. Now that was more like her old Kira! Bernadette hugged her too, kissing her on the cheek, anxious to resume the game, happily oblivious to any undercurrents. Mrs Costaz always went home, no need for tears!

Mia was busying herself in the dining room, finishing off the decorating of the party table with care. She had gone to great trouble and the table looked beautiful. There were four large parcels on each chair, elaborately wrapped and tied with colorful ribbons.

Mrs Costaz's special cake had pride of place.

She heard the older woman returning and sensed her watching her from the doorway. She invited Mrs Costaz to inspect her work, her voice bright, animated.

Mrs Costaz walked over and inspected the table. She looked at Mia, her eyes searching.

"It looks lovely," she said at last. "You've gone to great trouble. You must be feeling much better." This felt all wrong somehow.

"I am feeling better. Much better." Mia said. "Today is a special day. I want the children's last memories here to be happy ones." She turned, reluctant to face a final moment of farewell, but there was no escaping it. "Well, goodbye. Thank you again, for all your kindness. Your many kindnesses. There are no words..."

Mia felt herself getting distraught. Tears! That would never do. Mrs Costaz should go. She hugged the other woman. "Look after yourself, my dear, darling Mrs Costaz," Mia said softly, "One day you will forgive me, but I have to do this."

Mrs Costaz hugged her back so fiercely it made Mia flinch. She was going to run away from that brute. Well, that she could understand.

"You and the children, I will always worry about. Please let me know you are fine when you get wherever you are going" she begged. She kissed Mia lightly on both cheeks." I mean it. Please take care," she stepped away, uneasy.

"I will," Mia promised. She had to be strong. Her manner changed, became brisk. "You be on your way, we will call you, let you know we are safe. I promise!" she said briskly, taking her housekeeper's arm and steering her towards the door.

Reluctantly, Mrs Costaz gathered her things, stuffing the sealed envelope into her purse, protesting at the last minute that the ironing was still in the laundry.

Mia was firm. The ironing was not important today.

She walked with her to her car and stood and waited as Mrs Costaz's old Ford labored to start. It was always giving her trouble lately. The money would come in handy, Mia thought, pleased about that.

The starter motor turned, then died.

Mia held her breath. She couldn't have car trouble, not today. But at last, the engine took, and Mia waved after her, watching until the old car had disappeared around the bend.

Good.

She had the girls to herself. It was time to start the party.

JUST PARANOIA?

Laine took a deep breath and wheeled Donatés around to try the jump again. It was late in the afternoon, usually her favorite time of day, but the shadows were growing longer, reminding her time was passing. She was determined to get it right. She patted the horse's neck and whispered encouraging words into Donatés' flattened ear. He flicked his ear as if he understood her perfectly and was determined to try.

Reins gathered, she urged the gelding into a swift canter. The jump loomed up ahead and yet again, the horse reared in protest, baulking. He pranced skittishly on his back legs for a moment, backing off nervously, his ears flat, whinnying his distrust. Laine steadied the animal calmly. He was being impossible today and she wondered if the beast could pick up on her turmoil, her apprehension about Case's visit and the night ahead. They were one, her and Donatés, when she was astride him, and she felt sure it was so, it was her fault, this skittishness.

She allowed him to let off some steam, then wheeled him around back to try the jump again.

"It's the brick wall after this jump! The count is wrong, and it's putting him off. Try him from the west side, maybe he'll prefer that fit," called a familiar voice.

She looked up in surprise. She hadn't noticed his arrival. He was leaning against the railing, watching her. He looked, she thought ruefully, no older than damn twenty! She was a Mrs Robinson!

Scott climbed lightly onto the fence and perched atop, rubbing the back of his calf with a booted foot, balancing on the top pole with that effortless grace of youth. Unwelcome, embarrassing memories of the other night surged to the fore in her head. She shook her head in vexation. It didn't happen, and that was simply that. A picture flashed through her mind of the pair of them, literally having a 'roll in the hay' and she quelled it with an effort, feeling her color rising. Her face carefully masked, she nonetheless swung the horse around to try the jump from the other angle. Donatés approached the jump at a fast canter and sailed over with ease.

She heard Scott whoop with satisfaction, and she smiled inadvertently. Clever sod.

"Way to go," he called out, apparently in no hurry to leave. Laine trotted over to him. She sat high on the horse, he on the fence, and still they were almost eye to eye, but she was fractionally higher, and she lamented inwardly that she needed that teeny psychological edge.

She sighed, time to be blunt;

"Can you make yourself scarce, you're putting me off," she demanded.

"Seems like I just gave you some good advice," he replied calmly, undeterred.

"You did," she agreed, "But let me give you some good advice, in turn," Her eyes held his steadily. "The other night was a mistake. I'm sorry, I uh, I took advantage." To her chagrin, she found she was blushing.

He grinned, amused at her discomfort.

"Seems to me you took advantage, —twice," he said impudently.

She gave a short snort of laughter, then choked it off hurriedly. Not appropriate Laine!

"Scott," How could she put this, how do you explain such things to a twenty-two-year-old? "My husband has," Laine faltered, but she decided the time was past for vanities; "—Left me, and I was angry. That night was ," she shrugged, bleak, "It was a mistake, I suppose is the right word for it, and I am sorry. But it will never happen again. Understand?" She felt the words catch in her throat, but her gaze was steady, challenging. Damn. The pain was always there, just waiting to pop up.

Scott looked at her, considering. That woman who had given herself to him with such abandon was gone. He also could feel her sorrow. Who the hell could leave a woman like this. Certainly not him. He was besotted, nuts about her, from the first time he had ever laid eyes on her.

He shared nothing of his thinking. Instead, he replied calmly; "Your husband is a fool," his face flushing. "I would never leave you,.".

Laine grimaced. Donatés moved restlessly underneath her, as if he too, did not like the tone of the conversation, and she steadied him.

"That may be, but I love him, fool that I am," she said, startling herself.

Did she just say that! Shit!. Was it true?? It just slipped out! Shit!

Scott was gazing at her, his face closed and inscrutable. She went on, "I am sorry about everything. Scott, is this going to be a problem?"

To her relief, Scott shook his head. He stared at her, his young face open, without guile. "Well, no problem from me, you can believe that." He paused, but like her, he had passed the point of no return and candor was called for.

"I just think I love you," he said simply. He saw her color, but he pressed on, "I would never do anything to hurt you, cause you pain. If you ever need me— Hell, use me!" he ended with a smile, trying to lighten the moment.

He was rewarded with a quick smile. To Laine, he suddenly looked much older than his years. Abruptly, he jumped off the fence and was gone, striding away to the South stables.

Laine watched him go. She was a cliché, dammit, but she allowed herself a soft sigh of relief at his departure. She had to pick her battles, and Scott, thank God, was not one of them. She glanced at her watch. Four-thirty. She had to get this jump right today, or tomorrow would be a disaster. She had no desire to start the course from scratch.

Laine went to work. When she finally dismounted, it was nearly five-thirty. She would be late fetching the children. She handed the horse over to a waiting stable hand with a quick hug to Donatés' damp neck. It was her habit to oversee her horse settled for the night, but today she was running late.

The kids needed collecting.

Jason Ballard was in the feeder barn, supervising the shoeing of a mettlesome gelding. Anxious to avoid conversation, she waved to him and hurried on her way. But he was having none of it, and he leapt up to intercept her.

"Good going, today," he nodded his head approvingly, falling into step beside her. "Have you decided?" he asked. He was referring to her and Donatés in the State qualifiers.

She paused, mid-stride and turned to look at Jason.

"Yes," she said. "I think I'm going to go for it!"

"Great." Jason was delighted. 'I figured you for a trier!' Scott's words too, as she recalled.

She gave him a rueful smile. "Hopefully, that's true." She turned and walked towards the car park. "Yes, it might bankrupt me, but I'm going to give it a shot," she called over her shoulder. Ballard stood, gazing after her, his face pleased.

"Excellent!" Ballard yelled after her, "You've got a real winner there. We'll get a sponsor!" he yelled after her.

Laine rolled her eyes, wondering if she was biting off more than she could chew. Preparing Donatés would take a lot of her time. But she had time, plenty of it, and perhaps it was time to make a new life.

She'd better be good enough, she thought grimly, because the pro-circuit would take serious money.

But for now, there were the girls to collect from their party. They would probably be tuckered out when she collected them. It would be strange not to have the two little ones from next door coming around, she reflected. Where on earth would Mia go to?

To her mother or something...

And what would that thug of a husband have to say about that? God, she detested that man! Laine frowned, concentrating on avoiding the deep ruts in the road. Dirt roads were fine for horses, lousy for cars. Carefully, she picked her way around the corrugation, pleased when she swung onto the asphalt road that led towards home. It was a five-minute drive from here and she allowed herself to relax a little behind the wheel.

Something was bothering her about this move of Mia's, but she couldn't put her finger on it. The truth was, lately, Mia gave her the heebie-jeebies.

Always so damn stricken, afraid of the craziest things, taking all that bastard's crap.

Kira would be just like her mother, a timid little thing. Not Bernadette though, she was a feisty, cheerful little mite!

Mia's mother was dead, in fact. She had no other family, just the children. Laine remembered Mia telling her that.

Why would she tell the children that she was taking them to 'see her mother?' Laine tried to quell her paranoia. Maybe to keep them relaxed? Probably that, she reasoned with herself. Perhaps she was running away with the children to one of those havens for abused women?

But still— Laine pushed her foot flat on the floorboard, and the BMW's speedometer shot up in response.

At the entrance to the Reichmann property, the SUV fishtailed into the long dirt driveway, stirring up a cloud of dust as she drove too fast up the long, winding driveway. She pulled up with a sharp halt in the drive. Berating herself for her wild imagination, Laine took a deep breath to settle her nerves.

Mia Reichmann was at the front door. She came down the front steps, looking quite alarmed at Laine's noisy arrival.

"Hello Laine? Are you in a rush? You are late?" She looked at Laine, troubled.

Laine felt her fright subsiding, to be replaced by an embarrassment so acute it made her blush. Mia looked better than she had done in a long time, in a smart blue suit, her hair styled and groomed. Hell, even her nails were done!

Mentally, Laine kicked herself.

Mia was still too pale, but she certainly appeared... different? Happier? Laine felt like a prize idiot.

She heard herself floundering, apologizing.

"Yes. Yes, as a matter of fact, I am. Sorry, time got away with me?" she smiled in apology, feeling shitty. "Are the children ready?" she asked.

It was this thing with Case, it was making her crazy.

Mia smiled. "I told them to wipe their faces when I heard your car. They looked so messy." She smiled benignly at Laine. "But I think they had a wonderful day, thank you."

"Were they well-behaved?" Laine fell back on trite conversation, hiding her agitation. Now that she had a chance to really get a good look up close, in fact, Mia looked ghastly. Her make-up sat like a garish mask on her face, the dark eyes looked feverish, her pupils too dilated. A childish yell from behind the door interrupted her inspection. The girls came pelting outside and down the porch stairs.

"Mommy, look what we got!" The girls were each clutching a huge doll. Laine stooped to kiss them, admiring their gifts. The dolls were exquisite and had obviously cost a small fortune. The Reichmann children stood at their mother's side, each clutching an identical doll.

"Mia, you really shouldn't have," she protested.

Mia shrugged. "Why not? I want them to remember Bernadette and Kira with fondness." She looked pleased with herself, and Laine felt petty.

"You're still leaving then?" She didn't look well enough to go to the store, never mind run away. Laine tried to think what to do, what to say.

Mia nodded her head. "But of course. I have to wait for Rudolf, first. He said not to expect him too late. She smiled, but the smile didn't reach her eyes. "I will wait up for him."

Laine felt confused. She couldn't be running away! However, if she was, she doubted Mia would make it to a bus stop, looking as ill as she did. Laine had no doubt. The woman needed to be in a hospital. No amount of makeup would hide that!

Case would have to do something. He could fix this. If this woman listened to anyone, she would listen to him.

Laine felt sure time was running out for Mia. There were the children to think of. If Case couldn't fix this, then she would have to. How the hell she would do that, she didn't have a clue. Welfare? It was a shitty choice. But that was tomorrow's problem. For tonight, there was Case.

They walked together towards the car. Hiding her unease, Laine couldn't resist asking her gently;

"Are you taking your medicine?"

"Never. Never will I poison myself again, and betray my children." Mia said vehemently.

Laine had her back to Mia, and was stepping into her car, but at the fury in the other woman's words, she stepped back out of the car and turned to gaze at Mia in open concern.

Aware she was being too emphatic, and perhaps showing her hand, Mia changed tack. The anger left her face, to be replaced by cunning.

"Don't mind me. Don't worry, I'll be fine." She gestured Laine should leave, her manner placating.

The Reichmann children stood nearby, and they were looking anxiously at Mia, then accusingly at Laine, alerted that something was wrong by the shrill tone in their mother's voice.

Laine felt bad. She knelt on one knee to draw the two Reichmann girls to her, giving them a big hug, a flurry of kisses. Perhaps this would be the last time she would see them. She was pleased to see them smile shyly back.

She stood up and smiled at Mia. It was pointless questioning her further. She doubted Reichmann would let his wife leave, and she didn't want the children distressed at the thought they might not see their friends again.

Laine got behind the wheel for the second time. Mia called her two daughters to her side and urged them to wave goodbye. Glad to be on her way, Laine started the vehicle, the excited jabber of her girls in the back seat going over her head.

No, she was not crazy. There was definitely something 'off' with that woman.

Case. He would know what to do.

PREMONITION

Roxie was hiding her agitation. Case had refused 'a quick bite' and she couldn't think of any other reason to delay him. He never ate at the hospital these days, and he had lost a bit of weight. That troubled her. She felt unusually insecure this evening. Which shouldn't be an issue, because, God knows, she always felt insecure with him, but today the feeling was acute.

Roxie felt out of step with the universe. Her Italian grandmother would say il Machioto was about. She shivered. Superstitious nonsense.

"What time do you have to be at the reception tonight?" he was asking her.

"Around nine, ten, fashionably late," she joked, trying to appear unconcerned. She knew he was also tense about his meeting later with Laine. Hell, she was freaking out, but her face betrayed nothing. Perhaps he would come to the party by himself? Join her after?

Unlikely. Anything in the press would humiliate Laine and Case would have none of that. No matter, she would make her excuses and leave. But she needed him to know, really understand, that she needed him.

"Will I see you there later? Maybe we'll catch a late supper?"

"Maybe," he said, feeling cornered, "The supper, that is. -Party, no." He gave her a self-deprecating grin, but she could tell his mind was elsewhere. Abruptly, she wanted to press him, demand he surrender his life to her, completely commit to her, but of course, that was impossible, out of the question, so instead, she asked, "What time is she expecting you?"

"About now. I should leave. And Roxie, perhaps don't expect me tonight." Her eyes widened fractionally, but she said nothing. He saw her consternation, but he resolved to press on, regardless. He needed time to think, Jesus, just to think! That had become a luxury! Everything, everything was just too fast!

He tried to explain; "What I mean is, maybe I'm best on my own tonight; give me a chance to think things over. Do you understand?" he asked, knowing full well she wouldn't understand at all.

Roxie nodded. She felt close to tears, and there was no real reason. No reason except he was going to see his wife, probably to see if they could perhaps patch up their marriage. Where would that leave her? It won't happen, she told herself. He loves me too much, I have to believe that.

Dumbly she nodded again, and then to her absolute mortification, she burst into tears.

Case sighed. Life was a fucking mess. He was quickly at her side, holding her close, but she saw his eyes were the eyes of a drowning man. That glimpse sobered her, and she composed herself.

"I'm sorry," she sniffed, "I'm just so damn frightened. I love you so much. God, if you left me—" She made a Herculean effort to control herself, rid her voice of its tremor. He had enough on his plate.

"Roxie..." He tried to think of something comforting to say.

"Don't say anything." She put her hand over his mouth to halt his words. "I understand, really I do. I'll see you when I see you. Okay?" She gave him a watery grin and he hugged her, touched.

"Okay. Will you cheer up? Promise me?" He lifted her chin to look into her eyes and the tears threatened to flow again. He had held her chin in this same way, on that fateful day they had met. She took a deep breath, struggling for composure.

"I promise."

His glance was approving. He nodded, satisfied.

"Okay, I must go." He looked a bit more cheerful. "I'm dying to see the girls, I want them for the weekend, if Laine is cool with that, spoil them."

For the weekend. That implied he wouldn't stay the night with Laine. Roxie felt her spirits lift slightly.

"Thanks for being with me, coming here before you go there tonight. I needed that," she said softly, holding his eyes. He kissed her lightly on the forehead but didn't reply. He was champing at the bit to be gone.

Roxie sat down at the breakfast bar after he had left.

For the hundredth time, she allowed her mind to imagine what it might be like to make a family, have his child. A little Case. Be one of those families, like the ones she always saw on the beach? She wondered if she could fall pregnant, thinking of the flushed birth control pills. That had brought no guilt, rather, the idea made her giddy.

She might give him his first son! Sure, Case would be angry in the beginning, but he would be happy, in the long run.

Roxie thought of Laine McAllister and the hold she had over him, with his two daughters and she clenched her jaw. A son would solve that.

Her thoughts turned to Phillipa. Had she sorted out 'their little problem?' That would be the beginning of the end.

She could never lose him, not now, not ever.

TROJAN HORSE

When Laine arrived home, the children immediately rushed off to prepare for Daddy's visit. This was the best Friday ever, first the party, now Daddy was coming!

Judith picked up on Laine's apprehension immediately. "What is it?" she asked, anxiously, keeping her voice low so the children wouldn't be alarmed. Laine seemed distracted, worried. What now? She bit her lip and looked keenly at her daughter-in-law.

"It's just me, and my paranoia about Mia Reichmann. I want to ask Case to call on her, tonight, after he leaves me. There's something off about that woman..."

Laine marched to the fridge and poured herself a glass of milk, indicating with a dismissive wave of her hand all was good. Judith allowed herself to relax some. The kids had obviously had fun at the party, and there was no point in fretting.

Laine walked out onto the South patio with its soothing view over the valley and plopped herself down on the in the swing bench, wondering where it was exactly, that her life had blown up in her face.

Was it when Case 'rescued' Roxie? Could it be that simple? If there was no Roxie, would he have met another 'Roxie' down the line, and perhaps he would have left her some dreary day in the future? Had their happiness been a lie, their vows, a lie? She thought with chagrin about her tryst with Scott Boyer, her treacherous heart, betraying her like that. Was it like that for Case?

So, what was left? Nothing, she answered herself. Her pride?? Laine nodded. She could carry herself with pride. Her marriage was over.

The impossible thought settled quietly in her head, seeming to finally fit into the puzzle in her head, a confusion crafted by endless tears and this numbness.

Had he tried to fight for this marriage? Her gloomy thoughts were interrupted by her mobile ringing in the kitchen. What now, she thought. She paused, listening to Judith talking to someone on her phone. No, not Case. Judith sounded too polite.

She heard her mother-in-law's footsteps approaching.

"It's for you. Jason Ballard on the line." Judith looked uncomfortable, as if she were interrupting Laine from pressing matters. Laine rolled her eyes. Jason. What could be so important he couldn't wait.

"Thanks," she said, trying for a smile and failing. She took the phone reluctantly.

"Lainie?"

She winced. It was too intimate, Lainie.

"Jason," she said, unintentionally terse.

"Laine, I have some really good news for you!" He sounded excited.

Laine grimaced. Great. She could do with some good news.

"What is it, Jason?" she said, trying hard not to sound short, rude. She stood up, restless, holding the phone to her ear, strolling along the patio. The sun was sinking fast and the sky and soon it would be a glorious tapestry of color. A sunset like that deserved good news, she thought.

"Well, it looks as if we have a sponsor for you!" He sounded ecstatic. "Word has got out there. They will put in all the money you need to do the new season's circuit, in exchange for the usual branding rights etc. Wonderful deal."

Laine was speechless.

Sponsorship meant she was free to take Donatés all the way. Without the worry of the costs, cutting shows to save money. And if she won, well, that would be the cherry on the top. Usually, the purse money would have gone towards the costs of competing in the A -Grade circuit, but that was never guaranteed. Best of all, it could mean a life where she would be so busy there would be no time to think about failed marriages, and broken hearts and bastard cheating husbands.

It crossed her mind that every last thing, everything, was pointing her towards the door marked. 'Marriage Over.' "Laine, are you there?" Jason asked, impatient.

"Yes, I'm here," she replied. "Sorry. I'm speechless. That sounds terrific!" She tried to sound as excited as she knew he wanted her to be. And of course, it was a big deal. He was right to feel elated. Full sponsorship. That was potentially worth more than half a million dollars. She might be away quite a bit. What about the girls? There were the girls to think of!

"Jason," she said, peeved with herself for sounding so lame, feeble, "I have to think about this. I have my family," her voice trailed off. Ballard read the tabloids; he would have seen everything. Who was she kidding...

To her surprise, he proved quite understanding.

"Laine, look," he said gently, "I know this is scary. But you can do it! You have the horse and you have the talent! Things will work out."

Oh please, no kindness, Laine thought, I can't do kindness today. Kindness will undo me!

"Take your time. Think about it. They are keen, and they've done their homework, seem to know all about you and Donatés, and they will put up the money, in exchange for a twelve-month sole rights option, and right of first refusal for the next twelve months.

He added, sounding pleased with himself; "I had to write a review, you know, background, abilities, that sort of thing. Didn't say anything to you, in case it came to nothing. But I got word now, just this minute! They're hot to trot. All systems go, if that's what you want?"

"Wow." It was indeed 'wow.' Overwhelming, in fact. Maybe too fast. She could feel herself beginning to panic at the enormous change this would mean.

She heard him pause, and she knew he was being cautious, choosing his words, anxious not to offend her. Here it comes;

"Thing is, Laine, this is a rotten time for you, and well, perhaps this is just what you need? Take yourself out —of all that —crap?"

Laine was silent. He was right. This was wonderful news. It was her Get-Out-Of-Jail card. Case and her, they used to dream about her being good enough, one day owning the right horse, getting a sponsorship, trying for Nationals, the Olympics.

Dreams were free, and they used to dream big, her and Case.

Case would have been over the moon, thrilled. The thought laid her low.

"You're right, of course." Laine suddenly felt tired. She forced herself to sound upbeat, Jason deserved that. "Give me some time to think about it, I'll come see you in the morning, we can chat then," she promised. A thought occurred to her. "Who are the sponsors?"

"The Tudhope Hospitality Group. They're up for it!"

Laine felt her spirits lift instantly! How fabulous! Case would have—

Damn Case! He had walked away from all of this. It was her decision now, her life.

They chatted for a short while longer, about arbitrary things, and after a suitably polite farewell, she hung up. The children were fighting about crayons again, and she could hear Judith patiently reasoning with Shana, urging the child to share her pink crayon.

What fabulous news this was. It was insane to feel so ...deflated. Case, that other Case, he would have been so very, very proud!

Laine sighed. She made a fervent promise to her new, independent self. Never, ever again would she shed a tear over Case McAllister!

She sat down on the swing.

This was really good news. Great news.

Angrily, she brushed away the tears streaming down her cheek.

THE NEWEST TINPOT

Roxie listened carefully. Phillipa sounded pleased with herself.

"Pottie has arranged everything, so around about now, the little wife should have had news of her good fortune." Phillipa took a long drag on her cigarette, "The win-win is, if the lady is as good as is being vaunted, then loads of excellent PR in store for them! If she's not, well then, it's your dime! —And a sizable dime that could prove to be, sweets!"

Roxie was listening intently. Worth every cent, if it sealed the deal...

Phillipa was enjoying both her cigarette and her story, and she was in no rush.

Roxie bit her lip, fretting. "So! It's over to the blonde herself! Will the wife go for it, do you think?"

"All in the lap of the Gods now, sweetie, that sort of thing," She replied blithely. "By the way, darling, did I mention I think this is a really crappy idea?" Phillipa added, as an afterthought.

Roxie's capacity for guilt, never optimal, had long been smothered when it came to anything to do with Case. There was no going back for her, ever.

"And she'll never find out I'm behind it?" Roxie pressed her.

At the other end of the line, Phillipa stubbed out her cigarette.

"Darling, you now have a stake in Tudhope, a teensy, tiny stake, it's true, but enough to insist upon the 'random' sponsorship of a relatively unknown equestrian. You're giving them the 'champion of unknown talent, a sort of 'housewife make good' angle. They love it! No one will suspect a thing. The entire thing is as removed from you as ever you could ever wish for. Offshore, and all that. You and tinpot dictators, sweetie, now have something in common!"

Roxie allowed herself to exhale. Dummy companies, shares, it all meant not a thing to her. For the umpteenth time, she was grateful for her decision, made a long time ago, to separate her money from Charles' beady eye. He would have scuppered this, for sure!

"I owe you, and I will never forget this," Roxie said fervently.

He was never meant to be with Laine. It was one of life's mistakes. Roxie tossed her head.

It was a small price to pay.

THE TOMORROW THIEF

THE PRECIPICE

Cases found his gut was in a knot when he approached the house, but that was becoming a familiar sensation. All the way there, he had tried to rehearse what he would say, but finally, he gave up. Something would guide him, show him the way forward... if there was a way forward. He felt Laine was already lost to him.

And there was Roxie, always there to distract him, stop him from thinking.

The children rushed to greet him, squealing and shrieking, full of noisy chatter about their new dollies. Case admired them, obligingly checking Shana's for a sore stomach. Her dolly's name was Bella, and she had eaten too much at the party, Shana announced reproachfully to Case. They looked cute and grubby, steadfastly refusing to leave his side. not to be tempted by dinner, their appetites sated on sweets, cake and ice cream.

Laine wasn't there to greet him, and he hid his disappointment. He played with the children, taking care to stay in the 'neutral zones', the living room and kitchen, feeling awkward, a guest in his own home. Judith explained Laine was upstairs, showering. She had arrived home a bit late, she explained. She seemed jumpy, and Case guessed his mother was as nervous as he was.

Which made him feel even more edgy.

What right had he, to expect anything positive to come out of this? He deserved nothing.

Sensing his apprehension, Judith made a conscious effort to try and relax him. Mother and son slowly found a way to 'chat', skirting any topic that would reveal any unwanted truths.

The children brought welcome distraction, begging him to do the honors–it was time to be bathed. He allowed them to drag him off, feigning protest, an old game. Judith was glad to see him lead his children off. It was a familiar scene, and it gladdened her heart to see it. She was relieved she had made her peace with her son.-Life was too short to squabble. She made her way to the annex, anxious Laine and Case should have their privacy.

Case was soon absorbed in conversation with the children, his sleeves rolled up to the elbow as he bathed each one in turn, first regaled by Shana, then Liesel about the events of today, both vying for his attention, with lots of news about the party next door.

He felt himself relaxing, enjoying the cheery chatter in the steamy bathroom. He laughed and joked with his daughters, relishing the distraction of their childish play, loving his small, soapy daughters with every inch of his being.

"A familiar scene..." Laine stood in the doorway, smiling. She looked relaxed, and the idea she was relaxed, that notion gave him a twinge of despondency. She looked quite gorgeous, and he felt some surprise.

How had he forgotten that?

"Hello," he said, self-conscious and awkward. "They haven't stopped talking for a minute!" He ruffled their heads affectionately, his hands wet and they yelled in protest, giggling.

"Are they finished?" she asked, looking around. The bathroom looked a mess.

"Just about. Pass me a towel. I'll take Shana." It was a familiar routine. They each lifted a dripping child out of the bath and carried the giggling bundles to their respective bedrooms. Case realized he was starved of his daughters' company, and he was soaking them in, like a gift he had misplaced. Laine left him to play with them for a long while past their bedtime, and it was with reluctance he bade them a last goodnight, and went downstairs to join his wife.

She was waiting for him in the living room. She flicked off the TV as he entered. "Have you eaten?" she asked and nodded when he said he had. Which wasn't true, but he had no appetite.

"Have you?" he asked, equally polite.

She shrugged. "I'm not hungry, thank you." The conversation was lapsing into the polite parrying of ex-lovers and Laine could feel the familiar walls closing around her.

Case too, could feel the barriers going up and he tried frantically to find something to say that might put her at ease. They both felt awkward, each unsettled by the nearness of the other, each aware that any wrong or careless word could push them into the abyss, and neither wanted that.

Case resorted to that essential anesthetic for marital discord, alcohol. He offered her a drink.

She nodded, unusually tongue-tied, mentally rifling through topics that would prove to be safe, whatever the hell safe was.

He poured her a martini, and as an afterthought, sneakily made it a double. He figured he would need all the help he could get.

Laine sipped her drink and winced. "Alcohol, the great anesthetizer," she said with a small smile. She doubted it could work any magic tonight. They sat down, she sitting forward on the couch, her back upright, he in the easy chair opposite, each searching for a place to begin, anxious to fill the alien silence.

Case felt as if someone had pushed a secret PAUSE button, and they were both suspended, waiting to resume their lives. What he wanted to ask her was 'Do you miss me?' But, instead, he said, "How are you managing?"

She ignored that and instead, answered his unspoken question. "I miss you," she said simply. There, she had said it. It was out. Popped right out of her mouth! She looked at him, unfaltering, and repeated, "I miss you more than I ever dreamed it was possible to miss someone." She looked at the glass in her hand and set it down, as if her words demanded every inch of her attention. "You've hurt me more than I ever thought it was possible to be hurt." She sounded resigned. "The worst part is, now, now mostly I feel numb. Dead inside, and I'm terrified this is how I am going to feel for the rest of my life."

"I'm sorry." It sounded trite, inane, but he said it again, "Laine, I'm so very sorry...." he said again.

His self-loathing sat strangely with him, unfamiliar and debilitating.

"Does she love you, Case, as much as I did?" she asked him. There, that was out, too.

'Did' was the only word Case heard. She said 'did'. Past tense. His heart sank. She was waiting for his reply. Did Roxie love him as much? What would she do if he went back to his wife? How would she feel? He remembered her face this morning as he was leaving, smiling, but her eyes panicked...

"It's different," he said at last.

As Case uttered the word, he realized, it was. It was for him, different.

The way he loved Laine and the way he loved Roxie. Different.

Roxie was frenzy, domination, fucking. Lots and lots of screwing.

Laine. Well, she was everything that mattered. She was the best of him. And now lost to him.

Laine thought about his reply. Different. Her eyes closed against him, shutting him out, to better find the numbness, rather than this pain. She tried to banish the mental images of Roxie, wrapped around her husband.

"Laine!"

She opened her eyes at the note of despair in his voice.

"You have to forgive me. You have to! We can fix this!" He was out of the chair, kneeling in front of her, grasping both of her hands in his, and instinctively, she pulled them away, and she saw him flinch at that small thing, that gesture of rejection.

What did he mean, she had to forgive him? As if she was the one destroying their marriage! His words stung and it showed.

He looked confused. "The children," he added, "Laine, we've got children!"

She drew her head back and regarded him with disbelieving eyes. Was he suggesting they reconcile because of the children? Not her, the children?

Laine felt a giant wave of despair. "No, Case," she said, "I thought once, what you and I had—" she flinched, "Well, I thought it was a love like no other. I was wrong," she said dully.

"No, you weren't wrong. I thought that too!" he exclaimed earnestly. "I still think that!" He stared at her, his thoughts in a whirl. I've loved her from that first day-she's filled my life with so much goodness and given me so much. What the fuck happened!? He searched her face, desperate for a hint of what he knew was impossible, forgiveness.

Laine regarded him, feeling almost sorry for him. The sentiment was alien, and repugnant. For the first time, it occurred to her that if their marriage ended, she would be the executioner, not him.

He sounded sincere, she thought dispassionately. But it was too late, her trust was gone. And second fiddle? No, not ever.

"Case," she asked, the tongue probing the aching tooth, "Do you love me?"

His eyes widened, incredulous that she could even ask, "Of course I love you!" He exclaimed, and she knew he meant it. He pulled her to her feet, holding her against him, his grip tight and fierce, wanting to ward off any insane, poisonous thoughts she might be having.

Laine allowed him to hold her, if only for these brief moments, wanting to feel at peace just one more time. She closed her eyes and allowed herself to think about the reality of losing this man whom she once believed she loved more than life itself. The thought brought a terror that made her catch her breath. Her resolve to be strong and mature fled, and in its place came those tears, impossible to hold back.

Case held her close, feeling and seeing the evidence of his infidelity. Desperate to stem the pain, he whispered endearments and kissed her softly, her face, her ears, the tip of her nose, until at last, her tears stopped. He sat on the sofa, pulling her onto his lap, and she lay with her head on his shoulder, spent, saying nothing, little gulping hiccups the only reminder of her anguish.

After a while, she found the courage to look at him, and what she saw in his face made her catch her breath. He looked agonized, defeated.

Laine stroked his face, so familiar. Her eyes were red and swollen from weeping. Yet she felt better. She had recognized him. Here was Case, the man she had married, not some detached, graceless stranger.

That he was undone gave her no pleasure, and that was strange. For so long, she had wished he would feel this pain she was feeling, and now, here it was, and she found she wanted to chase the anguish from his eyes.

Case felt her caressing his face, and her soft touch seemed to impart in him a new strength, a new resolve. This thing with Roxie had to end, but now was not the time to make promises. He had shown his treacherous heart, and he needed to end it with Roxie before he made any promises to Laine.

Tonight. He would end it with her tonight.

He breathed out slowly. Slowly. Perhaps the fog was lifting, finally.

LOVING EYES

Mia stood out of sight in the passage, listening to their laughter, a small smile playing on her lips. The girls splashed and played in the bathtub, unaware of her eavesdropping. She would give them another five minutes. But she wanted to see them, see their giggling and play, so after a moment, she joined them in the bathroom, her face soft, loving.

There was no hint, no maternal murmur of caution from a secret self, the kind of self where mothers lift cars off trapped infants.

Insanity heard their laughter too. Like a vigilant nanny, it was anxious to clean up this spillage, bring about a true peace, a peace that would be eternal.

They looked up, gazing happily into a trusted, loving face.

Mia felt absurdly pleased with their trust. It allowed the mist inside her head to settle, that necessary fog which would dull her senses while they died...

At last, the girls were bathed and in bed, Mia reflected the dolls had been a good idea. Usually, there were protests at bedtime, but tonight, tonight they were eager to put their `babies' to sleep. She looked in on Kira, for the second time in as many minutes.

It was the same. Kira had the doll in the crook of her arm and was singing softly, an old lullaby that Mia had sung to them. She felt panic rising in her. What if the child didn't fall asleep? She should have given them one of those tablets! There wasn't much time anymore. It was after eight. Rudolf would be home anytime now, and she would have to be done.

Seven bullets, that was all she had. And she had to remember to save at least one for herself.

But how could she do this thing, if the child was still awake? Bernadette had fallen asleep a while ago. Now, it was just Kira. Forcing herself to remain calm, Mia decided to give Kira a while longer. She would turn up the television to drown out the noise. They had been so sweet tonight, her girls, both still basking in the afterglow of the afternoon's party.

Soon they would be in heaven, out of harm's way.

She sat down on an upholstered bench at the landing window, gazing out. The long driveway leading to their house was obscured by trees, but she would easily spot his headlights when he approached. She waited quietly, willing the child to fall asleep.

The gun felt surprisingly heavy, and Mia placed it carefully on the floor.

When he finally came home, she would be ready There would be no mistake.

ONE FOR THE ROAD

"Okay, one more, then I go." Rudolf Reichmann muttered to no one in particular. He glanced at his watch, then remembered impatiently it was missing. He leaned over and tapped the man on the bar stool next to him.

"Bud, do you have the time?" Time to get home. The man ignored him. Rudolf tapped him again on the shoulder, this time with more insistence. "Hey, I asked you for the time."

The man swung around, irritated, then stopped short when he noted the size of the asshole bugging him.

He looked grudgingly at his watch.

"Nearly eight." He turned his back on Rudolf and resumed his conversation with the bartender.

But Rudolf wasn't finished. He prodded the man again, and the stranger swung around, clearly annoyed.

"Yeah?" He was slightly drunk, and he knew it; otherwise, he would give this motherfucker a go.

"Do you know that woman there?" Rudolf pointed toward a stale-looking brunette sitting in the corner booth. She was on her own, nursing a drink, checking out the few patrons.

She had noticed Rudolf when he walked in and dismissed him immediately. She was long enough in the game to recognize trouble when she saw it!

"Nah." The man stared in the woman's direction for a moment. "-But she's for sale." He turned his attention back to his companion.

Rudolf smiled, pleased. There was hope for this crummy joint yet. His business trip had been a success. This week he secured an order worth four hundred and forty thousand grand! He deserved a little reward and he had stopped at this flea-bitten bar for a drink and a bit of company, do a little celebrating!

He had figured her for a hooker, but it paid to be sure.

Feeling affable and generous, he picked up his glass and slid off his stool. Tonight was her lucky night!

Case stood up, wondering as ever, how the hell it had got to this. He had screwed up on such a monumental scale, how would he find his way back. He was reluctant to leave, but he could think of nothing else to say. During the evening, some of the sadness had left Laine's face, and he felt glad about that, but his own torment was right there, hard to hide.

Sitting opposite him, her feet tucked under her on the couch, Laine was striving to present a calm facade. They were on safe ground, talking about how everyone was excited about her participation in the state trials.

Case listened, masking his frustration at his exclusion from this new chapter in her life. It didn't seem right. But what was 'right' now, that he scarcely knew himself. Listening to her talk, he felt pride —and an alien fear that she might accomplish all of this, fulfill her dream, without him.

Laine watched him pull on his jacket, wondering if he was going straight back to Roxie Tanner.

Probably. Did it matter anymore?

Her feelings were a maelstrom. She noticed the deep furrow in his brow hadn't faded any, and his eyes were still troubled, but he was smiling again. Or trying to. What he would say if she told him about damn Scott Boyer. He would be hurt, angry, never, ever understand, which was ironic under the circumstances, but that was Case.

Laine bit her lip. She didn't fully understand it herself. She sighed and looked away. Mostly she was weary of it all, this angst, this heartache. It seemed such a long time since she had felt happy. When was that?

The night of his party, before that mongrel groped her.

That thought segued into thoughts of Mia Reichmann. Now there was real trouble.

"There is something that is troubling me a lot, and I need your help," she said slowly.

"Anything," he answered promptly.

She told him about her conversation with Mia that afternoon. "Please, Case. Call by and talk to her, although I think it might be too late. " Laine was clearly worried. "If she is leaving tonight, she won't last long, the state she's in. I worry about her girls." That's good, Laine. Talk about something else, she thought, anything but us.

Mia Reichmann. He frowned. That was an exercise in futility, but Case nodded. "Anything. Sure..." He was in no hurry to return to the Meridian, face Roxie in the morning, end this inanity. "I've got time. From what you say, it won't help much."

Case thought about seeing Rudolf Reichmann again. He didn't relish the idea, but Laine had good instincts. "If he's there, I'll make up something."

Her face cleared and she smiled at him, for a moment that old Laine smile.

"Their children are the reason I even mention it to you. I feel so desperately sorry for them." She sighed. There was so much trouble in the world, how come she never noticed before?

Laine was up, and she took his arm, looking into his eyes, "She respects you, Case, and she trusts you. Give it a try? Please? If it doesn't help, I'm going to call the child services in."

"Child services?? Do you think that's necessary?" he asked, disconcerted.

Laine shrugged. "Case, she needs help, these children need help. I learnt something at college, " she said, peeved.

He couldn't help smiling at her earnestness.

She saw him smile and laughed self-consciously. "Come on, I'll see you to the car."

Please don't leave, stay, ask me to forgive you and stay. Laine thought all those thoughts, but she said nothing.

They walked towards the car, their footsteps noisy in the gravel, each wondering; where was the lifeline that could fix this?

When they reached his car, he turned to her. "I love you, Laine," he said quickly, awkward. "I'm going to fix this." He looked away, his mouth a tight line, and climbed into his car. She stood perfectly still, watching him. Laine knew she should say something, anything, but no words would came.

Case looked away from her, his heart heavy.

Okay, Mia Reichmann. He glanced at his watch. Maybe a little late to go calling on her? Laine saw his glance and misunderstood. He had to rush back to her.

Her wall went up immediately. "Do you think you should leave it until tomorrow? Perhaps that might better suit you?" she said, rattled.

He felt her sudden change of mood. She thinks I want to get back to Roxie. Case looked at her and shook his head.

That other Laine was back. He started the car.

"I was wondering if it's not too late to call on Mia, that's all." Suddenly he killed the engine and swiftly stepped out of the car. Before she had time to think, he reached for her and kissed her.

Laine felt her treacherous heart leap, but almost immediately she pushed him away, shaking her head. "I can't do this, I'm sorry," she said, feeling quite desperate. Are you crazy Laine McAllister!

She hesitated, then impulsively pulled him back towards her and kissed him, a long, loving kiss.

Her eyes were wet when she drew back her head. "My first love...." she said softly, more to herself than to him. He tried to pull her towards him again, but she stepped back, out of his reach, gesturing, needing him to leave.

Case hesitated. He wanted to hold her and make everything right, but he had no right, anymore, to demand anything of her. There was the matter of Roxie. He had to sort out this mess with Roxie first. Then only he look his wife in the eye. He looked at Laine, holding her gaze. "I'm going to fix this, I promise, " he said, and climbed back into the car.

His car moved slowly down the driveway.

Laine watched his taillights, her emotions in turmoil. She was about to go back inside when she saw his car move over to one side of the narrow drive, as another car approached. The headlights were distinctive.

Kevin.

Laine groaned. She'd forgotten about that.

A moment later, Kevin's car stopped before her, and she was surprised to see Ashley alight from the passenger door.

"Laine!" Somehow Ashley managed to look both delighted and distressed at the same time.

"Ashley!" How wonderful to see you!" Laine's melancholy vanished in the face of the warmth and concern emanating from Ashley. And she was with Kevin. What did that mean?

The two women hugged each other, both feeling that new kinship of survivors.

"Hey, Kev." Laine kissed him on the cheek. "You brought a nice surprise! Come on in, it's cool out here." The three of them walked towards the house, Kevin lagging behind the women.

Case had looked away, driven on. God, would he ever relent?

He trailed the two women inside, shaking off his despair. They were here to cheer Laine up. Case and his crap would have to wait for another day!

Laine went into the kitchen to make coffee. Kevin and Ashley strolled after her. The two friends sat down at the kitchen table, Ashley, keeping up a light patter, waiting for Laine to finish with the coffee.

Laine was trying to listen to what she had to say, but she was distracted, her thoughts were full of Case and her marriage.

Could they come back from this? Was the impossible possible?

The door to Kira's room was ajar, to allow the light from the passage to banish monsters. She stared at the door for the longest time. She couldn't wait any longer. By the time Rudolf walked through the door, she had to be done! The sound of a gentle soft singing floated out the doorway, in stark contrast to frenzy in her mind. The random thought came to her that it was a while since she had heard Kira singing. Good. The child was happy, and it made Mia feel a little calmer.

She started for the door, the weight of the gun in her jacket a stark reminder of her task at hand. Abruptly she stopped. The television. Turn it on loud, very loud. It must disguise the noise. She went downstairs and turned on the TV, pushing the volume until the sound reverberated in the room.

Then she made her way back upstairs.

Kira was sitting up in her bed, wide awake, carefully removing the dolly's clothes. She was putting her troublesome child to bed. Immersed in her task, for a moment she didn't notice Mia in the doorway, looking up only to see why her light was suddenly diminished. The motionless figure in the doorway made her start.

"Mama. Is that you?" The shadow didn't move.

Mia was steeling herself, her eyes closed, praying for strength.

"Mama!" Her voice rose in panic.

Mia moved quickly into the room, hastening to reassure the child, and light once again found its way into the room. Mia turned and closed the door, then she sat down on the child's bed and pulled Kira to her bosom in a tight embrace. For Kira, there would be no more suffering.

"Why are you still awake? Can't you sleep?" she asked tenderly, pulling a lock of hair from the child's eyes.

"No, not really Mama." Kira answered earnestly. "I'm too excited. When are we leaving?" She turned her attention to the dolly's hair and began combing the hair with the toy brush.

"Soon, my darling, soon." Seeing the child's attention was on the doll, she drew the gun out of her pocket and pointed it at Kira's chest, holding the child's head towards her bosom with her free hand.

"But when is that, Mama?" Kira mumbled into her chest. She struggled and wriggled loose, looking at Mia expectantly, her expression changing when she saw tears rolling down her mother's cheeks.

Kira felt something hard, jabbing her in her chest and she looked down, suddenly alarmed. "Mama- ?"

Mia pulled the trigger. The small frame jerked, then she slumped forward against her mother. Mia held her as she collapsed like a deflating doll.

She laid the child back in her bed, carefully, tenderly.

"Now you are in Heaven, nothing can harm you anymore." she said softly. "The angels have called you."

She stroked the small fair head, seeing the life-light fading in the child's eyes. Her tears were falling, in spite of her resolve.

People would say this was a terrible thing she had done. Mia didn't care. She knew her child was at peace. That one thought kept everything in perspective. No tears or heartache. Just this urgency to join her child on the other side.

Mia covered the child, unwilling to see the blood. A red stain was spreading rapidly on the bedclothes and Mia felt her hands were sticky. She tried to wipe the blood from her hands with the bedclothes. Her hands wouldn't stop shaking, and she could hear Bernadette beginning to wail in the room next door. It was the disgruntled crying of a child reluctant to be wakened.

There wasn't time, someone might have heard the shot.

The gunshot was much louder than she imagined it would be.

And now, there was still her little Bernadette. With a last gentle touch on the bed cover covering her daughter, she turned to leave.

She brushed her hand across her face, wiping away her tears, the gesture leaving a garish smear on her cheeks. In her hand, the gun felt sticky, and there was a strange alien smell in the room.

Bernadette was now fully awake and crying in earnest. Mia rushed to attend to her. Bernadette already out of her bed and in the landing, her eyes screwed up against the light, stumbling sleepily towards Kira's room, her little face contorted in a wail.

Mia scooped the child up, hampered by the gun in her hand, blood staining Bernadette's pajamas.

"Did you wake up? Never mind, Mama's here," she soothed, and carried the bawling child back to her own bedroom. Bernadette hated to be woken up in the night. Mia brushed the soft curls with kisses. She stooped to put the child back in her bed, but Bernadette protested loudly, clamping her arms stubbornly around Mia's neck.

Mia sat down with her on the bed, holding the child on her lap, rocking her gently until the crying stopped and the tiny head began to droop. That strange smell was in this room too, and Mia realized with some distress it was coming from the blood on her hands.

Satisfied that the younger child was asleep, she pointed the gun at the curly head. Suddenly, a bright light through the window lit up on room. Headlights. She stood up, trembling. Rudolf. He had finally come home to face God's justice.

She rushed to the window in time to see the red glow of the taillights die as he switched the car off.

The gun dropped from her hand with a loud thump to the floor. There was no more time. Shaking, she picked up the gun and pointed it at the child's head. Bernadette was stirring, restless. There was no time. Mia fired, flinching at the loud bang. She saw the wound gush and heard a car door slamming.

In a few moments he would walk through the door. She had to shoot him as he walked through the door. He must have no time to act!

Mia rushed down the stairs, stumbling, almost falling in her haste. She stopped short in the hallway, trembling violently. She tried in vain to stop her hands from their shaking. It was impossible. She braced herself and lifted the gun with both hands, taking aim at the door. The cacophony from the television was deafening, and Mia blinked, shaking her head rapidly in an effort to clear the chaos inside her head.

Never again would he touch a child.

She could hear Kira's halting words, her child's nightmare with this monster, and slowly her tremors subsided.

She was ready.

THE MISTAKE

Outside in the Reichmann driveway, Case killed the engine of his car and saw with a measure of relief, Reichmann 's car was missing. He fought an inclination to just start the car and leave, he had enough troubles of his own. But that wouldn't be fair on the children, and Laine was counting on him.

He cursed softly and opened the car door.

He stopped in surprise, listening. The television was blaring fit to wake the dead. Well, she certainly couldn't be asleep with that racket going on. The kids were probably wide awake too. Christ.

Slowly, preparing the words inside his head, Case climbed the stairs on the porch and stood outside the front door, hesitating. She would never hear him knocking with that racket going on. The front door framed an opaque glass, but he couldn't see inside. To get anyone to hear him above this racket, he would have to smash the damn door!

Case put his hand on the handle and tried the door. It was unlocked and cautiously, he pushed it open and stepped inside.

Mia watched Rudolfs shadow loom against the glass. In the long moments waiting for him to push the door open, she thought of all the times when she had waited in fear for him to open the same door, dreading his fits of rage.

This time she had no terror. She was calm, ready.

He pushed the door open, and she closed her eyes and fired.

She heard him give a peculiar grunt as the bullet slammed into him. She pulled the trigger again. She heard him fall with a heavy thud to the floor and she allowed herself to open her eyes.

The nightmare was finally over. The Devil was dead.

She stared unseeing at the prostrate form, her chest heaving. It was strange, instead of release, she felt ...nothing. He was dead. He would never terrorize anyone anymore.

It was time to join her girls. She stopped, her mouth falling open in horror. The man lying at her feet wasn't Rudolf, it was Case McAllister!

Mia screamed, a long shrill scream that rose above the noise of the television. .

The television. The television was making her crazy! She turned and stumbled blindly into the sitting room, fumbling with the remote like a drunkard until she found the right button. The abrupt silence was eerie after the din of a moment before.

Mia stumbled back to the hallway, her heart thudding against her ribs, praying that her eyes had deceived her. They were both big men. She stared down at the inert form at her feet, then dropped to her knees so she could clearly see the face, but she already knew.

She had murdered Laine McAllister's husband!

Jesus Mother in Heaven.

Mia stared at the body on the floor, stunned. What had she done?? She had killed him, but it was an accident! Oh, God in heaven.

She tried to think coherently. What about Rudolf? What if someone else came, before him? They would try and take the gun from her, and then she could never join her children.

She couldn't allow that to happen.

She watched the pool of blood spreading slowly on the flagstone floor in macabre fascination, forcing herself to remain calm.

She would call Laine, tell her how sorry she was. It was an accident; she would explain it to Laine.

Mia made up her mind quickly. She needed to join her children. They were waiting for her. God would punish Rudolf.

She straightened up. Now that she had decided, it remained for her to do one last thing; Beg Laine's forgiveness.

Mia stumbled to the telephone and pressed Laine's number.

THE LULL

Kevin sat quiet, withdrawn, still smarting from Case's snub. The women were talking freely, each glad of the other, comrades in arms. Laine was glad Ashley was back and told her so. Her friends would help her through this.

Ashley and Kevin seemed close, she noted, but Laine refrained from prying. Ashley was coming to spend Sunday with her, and there would be time enough for soul-baring. She gave a little start when her phone began to ring.

"Get that, will you?" She called to Ashley, indicating the phone lying on the table. Ashley obliged and reached for Laine's phone, leaning back in her chair. "Hello. Laine McAllister's phone." She held up one finger, signifying one sugar in her coffee.

"-shot him but it was a mistake. It was a mistake." a woman's voice shrilled in her ear. "I think he is dead!"

Ashley sat up straight and her face blanched. What was a mistake? Shot who?? "Hello?" Ashley frowned. A mistake. Whoever it was, she sounded demented. "What was a mistake?" she asked, her gut churning. She saw Laine and Kevin looking at her curiously and she covered her hand over the phone. "It's a woman, and she sounds ...weird," she whispered. She pushed the speaker button so they could all hear.

"I shot him, but it was a mistake, I'm sorry, very sorry." The woman was no longer babbling, she was almost moaning now, her voice a dull monotone. This time, Ashley recognized the accent. She held out the phone to Kevin, frightened.

"It's Mia Reichmann–she says she shot someone, and it's a mistake," she stammered, her eyes wide with dread.

Laine was gripping the counter to steady herself, and a low moan escaping from her lips. A strangled scream broke from her lips.

Mia. It was Mia and she had shot ...Case! Kevin and Ashley were both gaping at her, stunned. Laine stopped her scream midway, and rushed to the phone and snatched it from Kevin's hand. Her breath was coming in gasps, try as she might, her voice wouldn't come, just this airless whisper. With a superhuman effort, she tried to stop her hysteria.

"Mia. Mia, it's me. What have you done?" Laine was panting, her voice a rasping croak.

"Laine?" Mia sounded confused. "Laine?"

"Mia, what have you done?" Laine's voice was rising again, and she was shouting into the phone. She was vaguely aware of Kevin holding her, giving her support. She was feeling faint, and Laine knew she would have fallen to the floor if Kevin hadn't been holding her upright.

"Laine," Mia spoke, her voice dull, flat, "I'm so sorry. I thought it was Rudolf, and now I have killed him, Laine." But the phone had dropped from Laine's hand and she stood there, trying to mouth the words that wouldn't come. Laine felt a terror that threatened to loosen her bowels.

Kevin had overheard enough. His blood ran icy cold. Jesus! Did he hear her correctly?

Ashley was looking from one to the other, her mouth dry. Then she jumped up so suddenly from the table, her chair fell over with a noisy clatter. She grabbed her husband and shook him. "Kevin. For God's sake!" Her shrill voice jolted Kevin out of his trance.

Laine was trying to get a grip. Mia had shot Case! Shot him. She struggled to keep her thoughts lucid, hysteria threatening to overcome her. Perhaps he was still alive??

That thought brought sanity. He needed her. She became aware of Kevin's face brushing against her own, too close, he was shaking her gently.

"Mia," she said, her voice hoarse, "She's shot Case. She says he's dead."

So, he had heard right! Kevin gaped at her in stupefied disbelief, and then he turned to his wife.

"Ashley!" he snapped. He began shouting instructions;

"Call 911, now, then wake Judith. Tell her to watch the children, and we'll call as soon as we can. Tell 911 all the lights will be on! I don't know what the street number is. The house on the right of the road. There are only two houses. Tell Judith to keep the lights off here. I'll help Laine to her car.

Where are your keys, Laine?" If Case was alive, he would need a bigger car than the Aston.

She pointed to the key rack, and he grabbed the BMW's keys. "Ashley, follow in my car." Half-dragging a stumbling Laine, they rushed out. Outside, the crisp air seemed to bolster Laine. She shrugged Kevin's hand off and began to run on her own.

Ashley called 911 and explained what she knew, or understood to be the circumstances next door. Then she ran and banged frantically on Judith's door, yelling for her to open up.

Judith opened almost immediately, panicked by the frantic pounding. She listened in sheer disbelief to the garbled words coming from Ashley's mouth.

Assured Judith understood, Ashley turned and rushed to Kevin's car, her heeled shoes biting into the lawn and causing her to stumble crazily. She climbed into the driver's seat, and the Aston roared into life. She could see the taillights of the BMW already going up the hill towards the Reichmann residence.

There was a cloud of dust and gravel as Kevin pulled up outside the house.

The front door was ajar.

Case was inside, dead or dying.

INSANITY LOOKS LIKE THIS

Kevin froze in the hallway, stricken at the grisly tableau that greeted him. Case lay face down, the red stain from his blood bizarre and garish on the white tiled floor. Near him, Mia sat propped up against the staircase, her legs splayed. She was clearly dead. There was a gaping wound in her temple. Near her lifeless hand was a bloodied pistol. He heard Laine sobbing behind him. He jerked his eyes away from the garish sight of Mia, and dropping to his knees beside Case, he rolled him gently over.

His eyes widened in disbelief at the mass of blood on his chest. Case's head rolled heavily to one side. He looked quite dead. Kevin heard Laine moan behind him, a strange, strangled sound. She was kneeling beside her husband, his limp hand in hers. Ashley stood in the doorway, transfixed at the sight before her.

"Call another ambulance. Now." He snapped at his wife in impotent fury. "Tell them it's a multiple shooting." Check his pulse, he thought. He fumbled for Case's wrist. He looked dead, but there was always a chance— He heard Laine's sobbing and he rounded on her. "No time for tears now! Stop his bleeding!"

Laine chocked off her sobs immediately. He was right.

Kevin tried to concentrate. He held the limp wrist, feeling for a pulse. There it was; he could feel it. Faint, but there. He turned quickly to Laine, who was already peeling off her sweater to use as a makeshift pad.

"He's still alive. That's good. Stop the bleeding. Anything will do. Lift his head."

Ashley was behind him, stammering, almost incoherent. "I'll find something..."

She snapped out of her funk and ran deeper into the house, looking for something, anything, to put on Case's wounds. In the dining room, the table carried the remnants of a child's party, and she stared at the trappings of happiness in disbelief, then yanked at the tablecloth, sending dishes flying to the floor. She hardly felt the shards of glass hitting her legs.

The tablecloth would do. She ran back to the hallway. Laine had already pulled off her sweatshirt and was pressing it against his chest. He had been shot in two places that Ashley could see, in his shoulder and in his chest. Ashley folded the cloth into a pad, and she pushed it gently against the second wound in his shoulder.

"Hold on, Laine, hold it firm, don't let up the pressure!"

Kevin was standing at the foot of the staircase, looking up the stairs.

"The children! Where are the kids? Oh God in heaven ...surely—! " He was talking to himself, sick to the pit of his stomach with his premonition.

Laine understood immediately.

"Find them. We've got this," she called, not looking up. Kevin pelted up the staircase. It couldn't be possible— But they must have heard the shots?

He found Kira first, drawn by a smell he would never forget. She was quite, quite dead. A blood-spattered doll lay on the floor near the bed. There was an alien sound, and he realized it was his own dry sobbing. The little one, where was the little one? He ran towards the other rooms, shoving the doors open with force, searching for the second child.

One door was a bathroom, two rooms were empty, and in the last room, he found Bernadette. She was bleeding from the head, curled into a fetal position. Her hand was flexing, as if she was feeling for something familiar.

The child had obviously tried to crawl out of her bed, and the little head hung drunkenly to the side. She had a head wound and Kevin heard himself crying, thanking some supreme deity for the sign of life.

He needed to stop the lifeblood oozing from her head wound.

"Good That's good if you're still bleeding, honey. Don't you worry, Uncle Kevin's here." His vision blurred, and he wiped at his eyes impatiently, leaving blood on his face. "Just bleed, kid, for Uncle Kev, don't stop, honey, please don't stop. If you're bleeding, it means your heart is pumping honey!" He lifted the tiny form from the bed. He reached for a stuffed toy and pressed it against the wound in her head. Kevin went down the stairs, holding her gently, but moving as fast as he could manage. Ashley and Laine looked up as he descended the staircase, carrying a child and what appeared to be a bloodied toy. Laine looked away, not wanting to see what she was seeing. She could see from the curly blonde mop that the child was Bernadette.

"Kira?" she asked, but she already knew. She turned her attention back to Case.

"We can save this one," Kevin said firmly. "Ash!"

Ashley leapt up, reaching out to take the child her was holding out to her. "Oh Jesus, no." She glanced towards the lifeless form of Mia with a new revulsion.

"She's still alive," Kevin said. "Ashley, hold her while I drive; we can't wait! Laine, when you can, call 911 and tell them I'm making my way to Mercy General. Tell them to be ready!"

Laine nodded. She had both her hands pushing against Case's chest. "He'll be alright, hon," he reassured her, praying it would be so. "Just keep your hands tight there, as tight as you can."

Swiftly he took his shirt off and clumsily, he made a makeshift bandage for the toddler's head wound. He gingerly placed the unconscious child in Ashley's outstretched arms, glad to see she instinctively knew to press hard on the makeshift bandage.

Ashley nodded to show she understood, feeling quite sick when she felt an unnatural indentation in the infant's head.

Kevin guided Ashley through the door, and they stumbled together towards his car. He opened the passenger door and helped Ashley lower herself into the seat, gently, taking care not to jostle the unconscious infant. She could feel the sticky warmth coming through the cloth and she increased her pressure on the wound.

Hazard lights flashing, and with his horn blaring where needed, they hurtled towards the city on Route 385. A short distance from the feeder road, they passed two ambulances heading in the opposite direction, sirens blaring. They were closely followed by two police cars, blue lights flashing. Once off the expressway, inside the city limits, Kevin hurtled through the streets at breakneck speed, slowing at red lights to check oncoming traffic, then rushing on, ignoring blaring horns. He could hear Ashley weeping quietly next to him.

Ashley held the little girl's sodden bandage firmly in place, ignoring the sharp shooting sharp pains in her arm from the constant pressure. A siren started up behind them.

In his rear-view mirror, Kevin saw a patrol car race up behind him, lights flashing, waving him down. Ignoring the siren and lights, he focused on the traffic ahead. The traffic lights were red, and Kevin increased his speed, pushing through them when he was sure it was safe. A glance in his mirror showed him there were now two patrol cars chasing him. One kept behind him, the other roared up to the passenger side, an officer leaning out to gesture at Kevin and Ashley to pull over. Ignoring him, Kevin pressed his horn hard to alert a motorbike before him. The biker moved quickly to the right.

"That bastard is gonna kill someone." The officer snarled to his partner. He kept parallel to the yellow Aston Martin, trying to peer into the low-slung car. The car's window was opening.

Kevin opened the passenger window, and hoped like hell they would figure it out!

The officer gaped. The woman was holding a small kid, her hand over the child's head, her hand red with...blood?

The woman's face was grim, she was ignoring everything except the kid. The driver of the car had blood on his face and he looked crazed. Suddenly the officer understood.

"Jesus, they've got a bleeding kid in there! They're trying for Mercy Hospital!!"

He pressed his foot to the floorboard and cut swiftly in front of the sports car, waving to Kevin to follow him. With the help of the siren, the traffic parted miraculously before them. Kevin followed the flashing blue light towards Mercy Memorial Hospital.

Another patrol car came out from a side street, pulling yet further ahead to assist in clearing the streets. Mercy Hospital loomed ahead at last, and Kevin's car screeched to a halt outside the emergency exit.

Ashley was aware of her door being opened, capable hands reaching in to take the unconscious child from her. A strong arm helped her out of the low-slung car and over her shoulder, she heard the car start up again as Kevin moved it out of the entrance to make way for the ambulances. An orderly in regulation green scrubs ran with the unconscious child in his arms into an examining room. She saw people rushing in and out of the room.

Ashley closed her eyes and began to pray.

A few minutes later, Kevin strode through the door, blinking like an owl in the harsh fluorescent light. He saw Ashley standing helplessly to the side, and he walked towards her. With a sob, she fell into his arms and for a short while they stood holding each other, trying to comprehend recent events. The patrolmen were hovering, speaking into their radios, watching all.

Kevin pushed his wife gently down onto a nearby chair, abruptly feeling quite weak at the knees himself. The two patrolmen said something to each other and walked towards him. Ashley could vaguely hear his words of gratitude and she saw him clasp each of their hands in thanks. They looked both pleased and somber at the same time.

The one left after a moment, and the other guided Kevin by the elbow to a nearby desk and chair, some distance away from Ashley. He was short and burly, with the flushed pink cheeks of a regular tippler. He began to question Kevin, trying and get some sense from him, but Kevin's replies were disjointed, and it was hard to understand him. He was clearly in shock himself.

He gathered it was the neighbor's kid, and the neighbor was dead. Kevin sat hunched in his chair, trying to answer the questions, but he was gazing fixedly at the door, looking out for the ambulance that should arrive soon, bearing Case. He scarcely heard the officer talking.

Ashley lifted her head as soon as she heard the strident blaring of an ambulance siren in the distance and sure enough, minutes later, she heard it stop outside the entrance. They watched the paramedics rush in, wheeling Case in on a gurney, Laine stumbling behind them, herself assisted by a paramedic.

There were a few gasps as a couple of the Mercy staff recognized their GSW. Case was wheeled into another room. Kevin stood up and took a shaky Laine towards the visitor's chairs. She collapsed in a heap beside Ashley.

Ashley took her hand, and the two women sat there, waiting. Laine waxen, almost paralyzed with shock, past weeping. A while later, yet another ambulance arrived, and two other gurneys were trundled in, one obviously bearing the tiny body of Kira Reichmann. A sheet covered her face. The other body, covered by a sheet, had to be that of Mia Reichmann.

Kevin watched silently, remembering Kira. He turned his head away; he felt nauseous.

When the gurneys were out of sight, he excused himself and made his way to the men's room.

Once inside, he stumbled into a latrine and proceeded to throw up, the retching wracking his body. At last, he felt the spasms subside and he stood up.

He had to cope, help Laine through this. No time for crap.

Case would expect him to be strong.

He made his way back to the two women. Ashley looked up at his arrival, searching his face, sensing where he had been and why. Laine stared unseeing in front of her. The door from the ward that held Case burst open, and a gurney bearing Case was wheeled out and pushed rapidly down a corridor.

A slender man in scrubs, with reddish hair and a chinless face strode out, looking around for the GSW's wife. His name tag said he was a Doctor Lurie.

"Mrs McAllister!" he called, "Where is Mrs McAllister?" Hearing her name, Laine and Ashley stood up, emerging from the chairs behind the huge center desk, Ashley holding Laine tightly at the elbow.

"That's me." Laine rushed towards him. The doctor looked grave and spoke with care, choosing his words. "Mrs McAllister?" He glanced at the two women; there was another tall guy coming up fast behind them.

Laine nodded. "That's me..."

"We're prepping him for surgery now, O R 14, on the second floor, south wing." His eyes flickered briefly at the others, then he focused on her, "It doesn't look good at all, but we're going to open him up, have a good look. We'll do all we can," he promised. He reached out quickly and touched her shoulder, a non-regulation show of empathy for one of their own.

"And the child? What about the child?" Ashley asked him, her face anxious.

He looked at her, confused. "Are you the mother?"

"No," she said, looking quite belligerent. "The mother's dead. "How is the child?"

He flinched, remembering the little girl. "I have to say the same. She's in OR 4 at the moment. Dr Kassel is seeing to her. Now excuse me, I need to scrub." Lurie turned on his heel and strode away.

Kevin put his arms about the women's shoulders. "Come on. Let's go upstairs and wait." He shepherded the two women towards the elevators.

Kevin stared after the retreating women, and his manner changed abruptly. He went to find the officer.

"Write this down." He said wearily, and the officer pulled a notebook from his pocket after a moment's hesitation. "My name is Kevin Daniels." Swiftly, Kevin gave him his contact details, the names of Case, the others, the officer struggling to spell 'Reichmann'.

Kevin lost patience, it was taking too long. "You will get your statement, but first, when," he paused, collected himself, "When my friend is out of the theatre, then I'll come downtown. Got it?"

He was wondering how he would break this to Roxie?

The officer stared at him a moment, taking in the blood-stained T-shirt and pants. They had a fair idea what went down, and this guy, this guy had saved that kid's life, if she pulled through! He snapped his notebook shut.

"That's in order, sir. We'll see you at the precinct."

TIGHTROPES

MAKING DEALS WITH GOD

They had been waiting for nearly four hours, and still no surgeon had walked through the door. They sat in silence, sometimes squeezing Laine's hand, sometimes just closing their eyes and praying.

They had been there for over three hours, waiting for news, when a thought struck Kevin, and he caught his breath sharply. Fuck.

The women looked up at his involuntary gasp and Kevin looked uncomfortable.

Roxie. What about Roxie? He should let her know, but—. He glanced at Laine, wondering how to handle this.

Laine understood and she shook her head, exhausted and uncaring. "Call her," she said, with an imperceptible shrug. "—We need all the prayers we can get." Ashley looked at Kevin, her eyes reproachful, but he stood up and walked away to make the call.

Roxie answered on the first ring.

It was impossible to comprehend what Kevin was saying, simply impossible. Roxie found she had to sit, so she sat down where she was, on the steps leading downstairs.

She had heard wrong! Kevin's words swirled in her head, little bits of insanity that threatened to unhinge her.

'He's been shot, and he's fighting for his life at Mercy Memorial'-

'It was the crazy neighbor, she thought it was her husband, shot three times...'

'—Shot her children.

'Laine is there...'

It all sounded insane, but there was nothing crazy in Kevin's voice when he spoke, his voice cracked and hoarse.

"Reporters were hanging around as I left, so it's probably going to be on the news."

"Can I go to him? I have to go to him!" Roxie couldn't breathe. It was almost impossible to speak. She had to be at his side.

"That's impossible! Laine is at his side, and the last thing she needs is more drama." His response was immediate, curt.

"But he's with me, I should be at his side! I have to be at his side, Kevin!' Roxie felt hysteria rising up, and she fought against it.

Drama. The love of her life might be dying, and he was telling her about drama!

Not go there! Fuck him! Roxie looked around for her purse. Where was her damn purse? Her hand was shaking so badly she thought she would drop the phone.

Kevin knew her silence meant trouble. "Think Roxie, do you think it will do him any good, if he wakes up—! When he wakes up," he corrected himself, "and he sees both you and his wife!" He softened, tried to reason with her. "It will be too much."

Roxie was beginning to sob, keening her anguish. Kevin felt himself relenting. Who knew what the fuck Case would want?' He sighed. "I will let you know when you can come in and see him, but for now, you'll have to wait! Just pray that he makes it."

He hung up.

Roxie tried to get a grip.

She knew what she knew, and her place was at Case's side! The thought that he could die—! She ran upstairs to her bathroom and dropped to her knees over the toilet.

There was nothing in her stomach, and the dry heaves left her feeling light-headed and spent. As soon as she was sure the nausea had passed, she splashed her face with water and dabbed her mouth.

She went again to find her purse, determined.

In minutes, she was in her car, heading for the hospital. The sun was coming up, but for her, if Case died, there would just be an endless, endless night. They had just found each other!

Well, she wouldn't let that happen.

And for sure, when he woke up, she would be there.

THE ARREST

Rudolf Reichmann drove up his driveway with increasing alarm. There were three patrol cars parked there, blue lights flashing, doors standing open and every light in the house was on. Two uniformed police officers were standing on the stairs that led up to his front door, and he could see more uniforms and men just inside his front door. He parked his car and climbed out, blinking owlishly in alarm. What the hell was going on?

A plainclothes detective appeared at his side from nowhere. He flashed his badge.

"Mr Rudolf Reichmann?" The man was in his early thirties and his face was a blank mask, save for the eyes. The eyes were narrowed, piercing. Rudolf peered at him and flung his arm off angrily.

"Fuck off. What's going on here? Why are you here?" A uniformed officer stepped up to either side of him, each gripped an arm tightly. For the first time, Rudolf began to feel fearful.

"Yes. I'm Rudolf Reichmann. What's going on? I haven't broken any laws." he exclaimed belligerently. "Where the hell is my wife? Where are the children?"

"Mr Reichmann," for the first time he noticed an envelope in the policeman's hand, "Mr Reichmann, you're under arrest." Rudolf felt his hands being savagely pulled back and handcuffs clicked shut over his wrists. There was a gleam of satisfaction in the other man's eye.

"Read him his rights."

"On what charge?" Rudolf spluttered, stupefied.

"Statutory rape."

"What! You're crazy! What kind of a charge is that? That woman was a hooker!" he bellowed, but he could feel the relief pouring through him. So that was what this was about. She had laid a charge, the bitch.

He should have killed her!

"It is for the rape of a minor, sir. One Kira Reichmann, now deceased."

He nodded to another man over Rudolf's shoulder.

"Take him away."

ONE OF THIER OWN

Case McAllister was wheeled into theatre OR 14 at twenty minutes to eleven. In the four-hour and twenty-eight-minute marathon that followed, he flat-lined twice, and twice the surgical team brought him back from the abyss with a minimum of fuss, smoothly following the procedures that worked, mostly.

Failure was not an option. This guy on the table was the wunderkind on Granger's surgical team. How the hell he had got himself shot, that was another story! How to get him un-shot, that was the challenge they faced

At three seventeen, they wheeled him from the theatre into ICU, and an exhausted Dr Lurie went to find the patient's wife.

* * *

Bernadette Reichmann was lucky.

In spite of all the blood, the bullet went through her right frontal lobe tip toward the forehead and well above the base of the skull, and so, the doctor explained to Ashley, she had relatively mild clinical damage. He looked too pleased with himself given the circumstances, Ashley thought, but she supposed a win is a win.

He went on to say they could see no rapidly expanding blood clot in the brain, and here his face sobered, "that can critically compress the important brain tissue resulting in immediate death at the scene. If the victim survives the initial onslaught, the issue is to maintain the blood pressure in the skull."

He looked at her, his face earnest. "You saved her life by keeping the pressure on her head wound". It was all Ashley could do to barely manage a nod; she felt quite weak at the knees. He went on to say the child was comatose but peaceful in the Children's ICU.

Ashley had been to see her twice in the past hours, and the ever-composed Ashley Daniels could not have explained to anyone, anyone at all, about this strange and unexpected sense of purpose that filled her being. She stood at the child's bedside, holding her tiny, unconscious hand, listening to the monitors' reassuring beeps, wondering what this new feeling was? Defiance? They had cheated death, her and Bernadette.

Love? Could you love a child so instantly? Whatever it was, Ashley knew that her life and Bernadette's would forevermore be as entangled as the web of pipes and tubes that now sustained her tiny body.

The staff knew she was not the mother. —Hell! The mother had shot this kid, so said the jungle drum.

The woman with the bloodied top had saved the kid's life, and as such, the ICU staff felt strongly that damn near earned her the right to be at the child's side.

When she shad been reassured Bernadette was 'just fine," Ashley left her side and went to join Laine and Kevin in their vigil.

Bernadette would pull through, thank God.

But Case, that was a whole different story.

INCOGNITO ABANDONED

Roxie generally felt she was quite incognito behind her sunglasses, but the woman at the reception counter had recognized her instantly. Awed and flustered, the woman picked up the phone and made inquiries.

She put the phone down and addressed Roxie. "He's out of surgery, they have him in ICU." She pointed a frantic Roxie in the direction of the ICU.

Roxie was rushing off before the woman had finished speaking.

In the next few minutes, Roxie's intentions hit a brick wall.

The brick wall wore a name tag that said: Nurse Flemming, Charge Nurse. She was the charge nurse of Mercy Memorial's Sector-B ICU. She sat elevated in an oversized swivel chair, a petite woman, her face pinched and alert, her eyes constantly sweeping the ICU 'dash'. The dashboard gave her visible alerts from each of the seventeen wards under her supervision. To her left and right were lower chairs, manned by lesser mortals. She held sway in her chair, lofty, like Jesus at the Last Supper, with her apostles to the left and right.

Rock stars did not impress her in the least.

Roxie discovered it wasn't a simple matter of merely asking for Case McAllister and rushing to his side, she had to wait to be attended to, and then, her identity notwithstanding, the dreadful woman refused her access.

'Dr McAllister? Are you immediate family?"

Roxie was forced to admit she was not 'immediate family.'

Nurse Flemming was thoughtful. That the superstar before her was clearly distressed, that was obvious, but what exactly she was doing here, well, that was not so obvious.

In the end, she dispatched a minion to call 'Dr McAllister's wife' to the ICU lobby. "I'll see if perhaps she can come through and talk to you?" she said to Roxie, indicating she take a seat.

An awestruck nurse scurried away to locate Mrs. McAllister.

There was nothing a despairing Roxie could do, but sit and wait and wonder what she could say to Laine McAllister.

After a few minutes, the nurse returned, looking flustered. Here was Roxie Tanner, in the flesh, demanding to see Dr McAllister, or his wife. Well, his wife's response had been quite clear! Foul, but succinct. In the end, she conveyed Lane McAllister's message as the good Lord would've wanted her to. She told Roxie that Mrs McAllister was 'indisposed.'

It was on the tip of Roxie's tongue to offend the young nurse's sensibilities for the second time in a few minutes, but —that would be drama.

Case wouldn't like that.

It would leak into the papers, and that would be a disaster. She smiled a wan smile at the nurse and whispered, "Could I have a word?"

Roxie indicated with a lift of her brow that some privacy was called for. She beckoned to the nurse to follow her toward the elevator.

Sure she was out of earshot from inquisitive bystanders, Roxie pushed her sunglasses to the top of her head, to convey, eye to eye, just how serious she was.

"It's like this," she confided, "Case left his wife, some weeks ago. Now we live together, but I don't want to cause trouble for the family with crappy publicity, so I'm wondering, can you help me?" Roxie appeared wretched, and her puffy eyes and smudged mascara underscored her despondency. She leaned forward. "Maybe whisper to me when his ex leaves, and I can come by then? That way, there'll be no friction! Do you think that's possible? Can you do that? " Roxie pleaded. "I'll give you my number!"

Nurse Roberts stared at her, goggle-eyed. The superstar was appealing to her, for help.

"Of course, I can do that," she agreed breathlessly, glancing over her shoulder to see if Nurse Flemming was watching. She wasn't.

Roxie breathed a sigh of relief. She gave the awestruck nurse a spontaneous hug.

"Thank you. You have no idea how much I appreciate this!" She fished in her purse for a pen, scribbled a number on a notepad and tore off the page. She thrust the note into the nurse's hand.

"The second she leaves, let me know!" The elevator door opened, and, with a sad little wave, Roxie was gone.

Laine could read nothing from Dr Lurie's face as he approached them. Her throat was closed and tight, making it difficult to speak. She watched him approach, her heart was thumping so loudly in her chest, would she even hear what it was what he had to say?

"It's over to him now," were his leading words to them, and then Laine definitely couldn't hear him. He was alive. She was sobbing and making too much noise. Kevin and Ash had their arms around her, but somehow it was impossible to stop.

Dr Lurie knew they were tears of relief, but that premature relief made him uneasy. McAllister was not through the woods, yet. He waited for Mrs McAllister—and her friends—to calm themselves. The guy's eyes were wet too. The brother, perhaps?

He explained as best he could what the prognosis was.

"He was shot with a .22, and that's why I can stand here and talk to you. It's a weapon that forgives. Anything bigger, and it would've been a completely different story! There were three projectiles, one in his shoulder, through the clavicle, pretty clean, as GSW's go, the other in the chest—more serious!" His face was solemn. "Both missed his heart, but he damn near drowned in his own blood!

One went through his right lung, and we spent a time fishing for fractured bone from a shattered sternum. " He allowed himself to look mildly pleased. "The second bullet took a bit of finding, but we got it! Found it tucked away, hiding between the C5 and C6 discs. Could be he's looking at some nerve damage in the future, but," he looked pensive, "we don't think so. We won't know the extent of that until he's up and about. I'll be having another look at him in a couple of hours to make sure there's no delayed development of hemothorax—'

Laine wanted to interrupt him and ask for an explanation, but he saw her confusion and quickly added, before she asked, "That is, kinda like a puncture we didn't spot?? Of course, it can develop, but we're watching closely for that!"

Laine nodded dumbly. Her legs felt rubbery, and she needed to sit down.

"If that happens, we'll whip him back into the OR," he said, "but for now, we wait and see."

Laine tried hard to grasp what he was saying. She would have to ask Case, he could explain all this to her.

And of course, that was absurd, but the foolish thought afforded her a small comfort, nonetheless. She sniffed, wiping her nose with the back of her hand, the Kleenex sodden and abandoned.

"So he's not through the worst yet?" Was that what he was trying to say?

Dr Lurie allowed his grim visage to soften. "Oh, he might well be. But might is the operative word! He's a biggish son of a gun, fit, and I figure he has a better chance than most. But in the clear?' He shook his head. "Nope, he has a way to go yet."

"Can I see him?" Laine felt desperate. She needed to be at his side.

Lurie nodded. "Sure. We have him in an induced coma, so he won't know anything for a while, maybe a long while, but sure, you can pull up a chair, and be at his side. One visitor at a time, only," he added sternly.

Laine and the others nodded.

"Kevin, call Judith and fill her in; she'll be out of her mind."

Kevin was relieved to hear Laine sounded calm.

Ashley hugged Laine. "I'm going back to find out about Bernadette, see how she is." She was relieved to hear about Case. Certainly, Laine looked calm, resolute even.

Laine squeezed her. "Go ahead. I'm going to the ICU.

HOLDING ON

She stayed at his side for six days, almost non-stop, reading, even chatting to a comatose Case, willing him to wake up, see she was right there, at his side. From time to time, she would go home for a change of clothing, see to the girls, and occasionally, wait at home with the girls, while a drawn and pale Judith McAllister visited her son.

Laine had a lot of time to think.

She remembered how last they had parted, that glimmer of hope, and here he was, in a hospital bed, lucky to be alive. Could she have done anything differently?

She thought about Mia.

There had been so many warning signs. But murdering your children? In the end, for the sake of her sanity, she gave up on that line of thought, it was self-defeating, and Laine knew she needed to focus on her own family. Case's affair was in all the tabloids, albeit he was the 'hero doctor' who 'tried to prevent the shooting', that was the spin, woven by God knows who. It was all out in the open, bringing its own challenges to her parenting skills.

She also knew Roxie was visiting Case, whenever she could, for a few stolen minutes. Without fail, apparently, according to a disapproving Nurse Flemming.

But Laine had made her pact with God. If Case walked out of here, he could go to whomever he liked, as long as he walked out of here. Their girls needed their father.

Laine knew she loved her husband more than anything in the world. Enough to give him up, if that's what had to happen. Divorcee? She could handle that moniker if she had to. But widow?

That was a pain she couldn't begin to contemplate.

The tabloids couldn't hurt her anymore. The early humiliation and confusion from those first weeks were behind her now. The heartache was still there, and she embraced it. Feeling pain was better than that dreadful,

dreadful numbness.

She watched her comatose husband in the hospital bed. Her girls needed protection from the Roxie affair. Try as she might to shield them, there was always school, even the damn TV. Maintaining a life as 'normal' as possible required every inch of her energy. Her days were divided between reassuring her girls and her bedside vigil.

She believed that the best thing that had ever happened to her was becoming Case McAllister's wife. Mrs. Laine McAllister, that was who she used to be.

Oh, there were pieces of her that were still intact, such as her girls, and when she was on Donatés and they sailed together over a jump, momentarily between heaven and earth, she was free for that split second of anything mundane and earthly.

Like unfaithful husbands.

Bits of her, waiting to be reassembled. Start again? Was it possible?

She just didn't know.

Obscurely, there was Scott Boyer, an incident she regretted with all her heart. She too, had sullied their marriage, and for what, exactly? Unreasonably, she blamed Case for the Scott 'incident.' Laine knew she was being unreasonable, but there it was–she blamed him! It was all his damn fault.

Could she ever confess to Case? Unthinkable.

And that upset her. What was it Kev called him? The prince. Well, the Prince sure as hell would not like to learn she had been dallying with the minions! Was it even unfaithful, when they were separated? Technically, probably not, she decided.

But her heart knew that to be a lie. Her heart knew she belonged to this man here, lying in the bed, with the wretched machines keeping him alive.

Laine sighed. It was all too much.

AWAKENINGS

IN THE MOVIES

In the movies, when the hero wakes up. there is always someone there, someone's joyful gasp as the patient's eyes flicker open.

It wasn't like that at all.

When Case came to, there was no one there.

Laine had left minutes before to see to the girls and Judith was on her way to take up the vigil. The ward was empty and quiet, save for the steady metronome of the cardiac monitor.

Case was used to wards such as this, they were the grist for his mill, but this was a different view altogether, lying on one's back, looking up at the ceiling with their moulded polystyrene tiles.

What the hell was he doing in a hospital ward?

He tried to remember, but it was hard to think. He was rescued from his rising panic when the door swung open, and a nurse strode in. She gave a start when she saw he was awake. He wanted to speak, but his lips were dry, and his voice cracked. She understood and gently raised a glass of water to his lips. He sipped the water gratefully, trying desperately to think. Who was she? Did he know her?

The nurse set the glass aside and beamed at him. Poor thing, she could see he was confused. They always were. A thought crossed her mind. Uh oh. He would ask her any minute now, what was going on, and really, what with the wife and Roxie Tanner, perhaps she should call Flemming to handle this?

There was no need.

Flemming herself blew into the ward, alerted by the dashboard light that forewarned her that patient McAllister was awake at last.

"Dr McAllister! Welcome back!" Case looked at her, blank, quite dumbfounded that it was he who was the recipient of this professional nurse-type cheer.

Flemming beamed at him, disregarding his obvious confusion. Now she would find out what the deal with the pop star was! The damn reporters were a pain in the ass! The wife clearly loved him, and yet, she was a strange one, too, the wife.

She had nothing at all to say, nothing at all, about the visits from that Tanner woman! Flemming had seen Tanner with McAllister, and she had absolutely no doubt her earlier suspicions were correct. Yet the wife, for whatever reason, was doing and saying nothing. Nothing at all. It was curious. Go figure. Well, it wasn't her business. At least McAllister was awake. She would call Mrs McAllister with the good news.

However, she foresaw a few problems ahead for him.

As if on cue, she heard him ask, "What happened? How come I'm here?"

Flemming told him what she knew, which, as it turned out, was quite a bit. The newspapers had filled her in. The essence of it; he was a hero-doctor, taking a bullet meant for someone else. The bits about estranged wives and pop divas, that she left out. Was Roxie Tanner his lover? Her pal over at Granger, she insisted that the last was BS. He adored his wife, apparently.

The shock in his eyes told her he was struggling to comprehend it all, and midstream she saw him close his eyes and nod off.

It was to be expected. The body's way of dealing with trauma. Still, it was a beginning. She left him to sleep. He would figure it all out for himself.

She needed to call his wife.

Doubtless, the Tanner creature would find out soon enough!

Case did figure it out.

He had help. It was there, in the tabloids, on the TV. What a hero he was. Trying to save the neighbor, he got shot.

It made him cringe. And worse, how Roxie Tanner was his lover. A young nurse, her fawning loyalties firmly in the camp of Team Tanner, brought him the tabloids for his perusal. But far from being grateful and thanking her, he rolled his eyes and flung them away in a fit of rage, and demanded she take 'that crap' out of his room!

Between the visits from his doctors, his mother, Ash, and colleagues from Granger, even Roxie, Case soon felt as if the door to his ward was a revolving door.

But the visits he longed for, the visits that cheered him, they were the ones from his wife.

When he saw her, everything seemed to settle. She was there, at his side. She was always warm and affectionate, and yet, he couldn't say she was loving.

From the near reconciliation on the night of the shooting, it was as if she had flipped a switch, and she treated him now like a dear friend, and Case was confused and hurt by her attitude.

He didn't understand it.

Laine didn't understand it herself. All she knew was; it was too much.

Losing him to Roxie, and then he very nearly died. The pain of his infidelity was gone, and all she felt now was stark terror at the thought of loving Case McAllister again.

She spoke about the children, brought video messages from them on her phone, and called them up from the hospital so he could talk to them, but everything she did was from behind an invisible barrier he simply could not break through. Any attempt he made to start a conversation about them, their future, Laine would close it down immediately.

And of course, there was Roxie, who always seemed to know when the coast was clear, and she had no barriers at all! When she swept into his ward, she did all the talking, a dynamo of energy and positivity. He lay back, listening to her talk, occasionally smiling, wondering when and how he could break this off.

After a few visits, he found himself wondering why he should! Laine didn't want him back. That much was clear to him. She obviously knew about Roxie's visits, yet she never said a word, didn't seem to care. He struggled to remember —had she not forgiven him, that night, before the shooting?

Roxie loved his imperfect and flawed self unconditionally.

Perhaps Laine forgiving him was all in his head?

It didn't seem so. On the third day after he had shrugged off the coma, he could bear it no longer. He was tired and defeated, and he wanted to go home, but to a loving, doting, Laine, like it was before!

That Laine was gone. Now there was this cool, kind —stranger!

Case lay back and closed his eyes. Roxie, he would deal with her. It was over, but breaking her heart too, flat on his back in a hospital ward, he couldn't do it.

He needed the right opportunity.

Later, when he was on his feet, when he had his strength back, he would sort everything out.

That was his heartfelt intention.

Then, he found out.

EAVESDROPPING

Laine was struggling. She knew Case was hurt by her reserve. Hell, she didn't understand it herself. That was just this fear, this abiding terror. There was simply no room left in her heart to lose him again, ever. It was as if a wall had gone up around her heart, protecting her, imprisoning her.

And, there was her guilt.

If he found out about that stupid, stupid tryst with Scott...

Laine was once again back in his ward. He was asleep and she sat in the visitor's chair, watching a beloved face, trying to understand her jumbled feelings, make sense of them. She, who had no tolerance for deceit, was enmeshed in a lie of her own.

Her phone started to ring and hastily she fumbled for the ringer, turning it off before it woke him.

She lifted it to her ear.

It was Josie.

"How's he doing?"

"Good," she said, her voice low, "he seems good. They've just done tests and he's back in the ward, but now he's asleep." She glanced at Case. He was out cold.

"Wait a minute. Let me go out of here, then we can talk..."

Laine crept outside and walked down the busy corridor. She stepped back, out of the moving throng of people by standing in a doorway to some or other staff lounge.

"Sorry, we can talk now..."

"Have you told him about Scott? Is that bitch still visiting him? How are the kids coping? And Judith? How's she...?" Josie fired the questions, not waiting for answers.

"Whoa! One question at a time–No, I haven't told him about Scott, he will not take that well at all!" Laine grimaced. "—And now does not seem quite the right time to confess his wife has also been screwing around. And yes, of course Roxie Tanner is still around, like stink on a damn monkey! She seems to know exactly when I am not here. Doubtless someone tips her off." Laine sighed, and told herself to breathe, just breathe. "The kids are fine, I think, for the moment. Thank God for Judith! He misses them." Laine felt her throat closing. Enough of that, no more tears. She rubbed her temple, wondering when, if ever, life would ever feel normal again.

"Well honey, if there's anything you want me to do, let me know. I'll drop everything!" Josie said, her voice soft.

"I will, Jos. Thanks. Bye." Laine turned to go and almost bumped into a nurse coming out of a door.

"Excuse me, Mrs McAllister." The nurse smiled politely at Laine.

It was that nurse from the ICU. The nurse pointed to the sign on the door. "You're in the way, perhaps?"

The sign said Nurses Lounge.

Laine grimaced. In the way, again.

Time to look in on Case, and leave.

* * *

Nurse Roberts walked swiftly back to the ICU, her mind reeling.

So, the doting wife wasn't so angelic after all. She had a lover, and that poor Dr McAllister knew nothing! She wondered if her new bestie, Roxie Tanner knew.

Probably not.

It would give them something to chat about when she popped in.

WILES VS STYLE

They bumped into each other, Laine and Roxie.

It was inevitable.

Roxie was on her phone when Laine stepped out of the elevator. The pop icon killed her call immediately when she saw Laine. She hesitated, then lifted her head high and stepped past Laine into the elevator, not saying a word. She had her trademark enormous sunglasses on, and Laine was unable to see her eyes, which, she thought afterwards, was a pity.

Laine turned and lowered her sunglasses, peering over the top of them to better see, from top to toe, what it was exactly that had so seduced her husband.

The singer looked every inch the star she was.

Vitton purse, Armani sunglasses, she was immaculately groomed from head to toe. Laine, by contrast, was in jeans and sneakers, her hair gathered in the usual knot above her head, a cavernous purse slung over her shoulders that held everything inside, from the children's nail-clippers to slinkies for their hair, wet-wipes to clean chocolate-y mouths, their overdue library books, Band-Aids.

The works. Even a clunky new bit she was trying out with Donatés.

Laine's purse alone told the world she was a wife and mommy!

She stared intently at the star until the elevator doors closed, feeling as if she were gazing at the cover of a glossy magazine.

Although Roxie out-pursed her, the star was clearly disconcerted at seeing her.

Laine stood for a long moment looking at the closed doors.

Case had always been the best version of herself, and letting go of that would be difficult. But there was Roxie Tanner, with all her glamour and beauty, offering another life.

Perhaps it really was time to let go.

Even this constant ache in her heart, it was a good thing, like the time she broke her arm. This pain was simply a sort of plaster cast for her heart, a reminder that she needed to take better care, much better care, of herself.

Starting now.

Laine headed for his ward.

She found Case sitting bolt-upright in his bed, clearly in a state of agitation.

He glowered at her, and Laine arched her eyebrows in surprise. What now? She tossed her purse onto his bed, and stood back, hands on hips, eying him.

"I just bumped into—" She wanted to say, 'your lover' but that was confrontational, and petty, and she was weary. "Roxie Tanner," she finished, her voice flat.

He seemed not to hear her.

"Is it true! Have you been screwing someone else?"

Taken aback, Laine wondered what to say, but as it happened, she didn't need to say anything; her face confessed for her.

How the hell—

Then she understood! It was the damn nurse. She must have overheard her talking to Josie and passed it on to the pop star!

"Case," she began, "He was—"

She was going to say, 'A mistake', and explain, but he interrupted her, embittered.

"So it's true." he said, enunciating each word deliberately. "Please don't lie to me!"

At those words, Laine lost her cool. "I wouldn't dare", she shot back, "You're the expert! I could never compete!"

He slumped back in his bed.

Laine felt utterly defeated. He had made up his mind, and any discussion was pointless. In fact, continuing this sham of a marriage was pointless. Suddenly, she felt exhausted.

"We're done, Case. I'll speak to Kevin." She spoke so softly her voice was almost a whisper. "You'll be fine. And so will we."

She picked up her purse on the foot of his bed, and slung it over her shoulder. Then Laine swung on her heel and walked away from her old life, her sham of a life.

She heard him calling after her.

"Laine..!"

But she was done.

IT NEVER HAPPENED

"Feel like a visitor?"

Case looked up at the familiar voice, and his smile was instant. "Kevin!"

A smile, Kevin noted, pleased. A good start. He stepped into the ward. All the machines were silent.

He had been there several times before, when Case was in that coma, and those damn beeping sounds had scared the bejesus out of him.

Silent machines were a good thing. It meant his pal was getting better. As to whether he was welcome, well, that smile said it all!

"How are you?" He was grinning broadly and were it not for all the bandages he could see through the gaping pajamas, he would have given Case a bear hug. As it was, the best he could do was reach out and touch his friend, ever so gently, on his shoulder.

Case's smile faded, and he suddenly looked upset. "Kev, I'm so sorry. Please, I was crazy, an idiot. Please—"

Kevin interrupted him, his grin lopsided. He held up his hands to stop Case from saying more.

"Yeah, you were crazy! But it's cool. I'm just glad you're around, so I can make you pay, big time!"

They smiled at each other in glad relief. It was over. It never happened.

Since Laine had marched out yesterday, Kevin's visit was the first time Case's spirits had lifted. He thought about his recent behavior, and he felt an abiding shame. But Kevin had clearly forgiven him, and once more, here at least, everything was as it used to be.

He saw Kevin had a newspaper tucked under his arm.

"What's that?" He asked, knowing already. More crap in the tabloids.

Kevin shrugged and held it out to him.

There it was, Roxie and him, in—Mexico?? Smiling like fucking newlyweds. How the hell did they get hold of that?

"Good picture." Kevin said dryly. "There's probably one of the two of you making out in the waves, but they'll save that for next week's edition." He thrust his hands into his pocket and studied his friend thoughtfully, chewing his bottom lip.

"You've fucked up my friend. That," and he jerked his head towards the discarded tabloid, "is a knife, and it's straight into Laine's heart." Kevin's manner changed. He looked uncomfortable, edgy. "She called me last night. She wants a divorce, Case. Of course, I said she's crazy, but she's very calm, quite adamant, and this, in these damn tabloids, well, that's not helping."

Case looked away. How did they get that? Someone must have recognized Roxie and snapped away, and now, divorce. And some guy waiting—

Case closed his eyes, trying to think. "She doesn't want me anymore, Kevin, she made that clear. She's already got someone in the wings, apparently."

Kevin crossed his arms and rolled his eyes. That! He knew about it. – Laine's rebound bonk. These things happened, but clearly, not to the prince. Kevin shook his head at the irony .

He sighed. What the fuck was up with Case?

"So, she wants a divorce?" Case was saying, his face miserable. He shrugged.

"—Am also thinking," Kevin said slowly, "Case, you just keep on fucking up!"

Case grimaced. "Tell me how you really feel, why don't you!"

"You're nuts, Case. Go back to your wife. Beg her to take you back. End it with the damn pop star!"

Case looked away. Of course Kevin was right. But Laine would never have him back. He knew Laine. Kevin didn't. In any event, she already had someone new!

Kevin sighed in exasperation. There was no reasoning with Case. Someone had messed with his princess, and that would never do! What a dumb bastard!

"You're a dumb bastard," he said aloud, feeling more than a little defeated. He shook his head. The best he could do, was to be around to pick up the pieces. And there would be pieces.

Kevin knew that for sure!

His body was recovering, but his mind , that was a whole other story.

Case had far too much time to think. He remembered when his life had been full of purpose and the way ahead was clear. Now, everything was indecision and confusion. He resented the forced time off for recuperation; he craved the distraction of his work.

He knew he had messed up, and Laine was lost to him forever.

He needed his kids. He longed for his wife, the other one, the one that used to be his, before she became this untouchable stranger.

His black thoughts were interrupted by the ringing of his phone.

Ashley.

"Hey, Case!" She sounded happy, friendly. He breathed easier. She asked after him, then her own news came out in a rush. "Well, the doctors say I can take Bernie home on Friday, so I am over the moon about that!" Case smiled at the happiness in her voice. Ashley would be great with the child. He never understood why they never had kids.

She was excited, happy. Kevin had agreed to be at her side, until they secured permanent custody of the child. Reichmann was in jail, and bail had been refused because the man was a flight risk.

"That's great, Ash. I am very happy for you," he said, and he meant it with all of his heart. "You'll be a great Mom, like—, like Laine," he finished lamely.

"Well, after this dreadful business—" There was a pause.

He rolled his eyes. A gay Kevin. Tabloids. Shootings. What the hell had happened to them!

Ashley was determined to be cheerful. "I suppose you are pleased about Laine's sponsorship?" she said. "God knows, she deserves it! Laine has put her career on hold for so long!

As the words left her, she flushed at her end of the phone and smacked her forehead with the palm of her hand. "I'm sorry, Case, I didn't mean it like that."

Case managed a laugh. "I know what you mean, and I agree." He hesitated. "You say she has a sponsorship?" he repeated.

That was good news, and yet why the sinking feeling in his stomach?

On the other side of the line, Ashley bit her lip in chagrin. Had Laine not said anything to him about the sponsorship? Were they not talking?

"She didn't tell you??" Ashley said. Oh shit.

Case brushed it off, and said all the right things, but Ashley could hear he was hurt.

She was glad to end the call, vexed with herself for letting the cat out of the bag. But why was the cat in the damn bag, in the first place! They had to talk, they had children, for God's sake. Laine had told her of his freak-out about her stupid rebound shag with some or other young buck at the stables.

Been there, done that, she chirped, when Laine had told her. But Ashley knew it was different. Laine, she was different. Laine would always be Case's girl, whether she admitted it or not.

CHEATED!

After Ashley's call, Case felt cheated, which was unfair, but there it was. Yet more testimony to how shallow he was.

Sponsorship. That meant traveling. Being away. Perhaps for weeks at a time. He felt upset. Why hadn't she told him? They used to dream about finding a sponsor! They used to dream about finding a great horse, a horse with heart and courage and talent. Now she finally had Donatés; she could sweep the board.

Yet here he was, feeling let down, and aggrieved. It was confusing. Worse, she had a lover herself. That thought had him churned up like grandma's butter, and there was nothing, nothing he could do about it.

He remembered his conversation with Kevin.

Had it really been just a few weeks ago?

What was it Kevin had said? Told him he was an 'innocent', 'a prince' was the term he used. Case sighed, glum. He was no damn prince, that was for sure. Fucking frog, more likely.

Juanita was asking him if there was anything he wanted.

Roxie was out and she had warned Juanita to take special care of him.

He looked at her, unseeing.

Yes there was something he wanted.

He wanted his old life back, but that was gone forever.

RIPTIDE

HOME IS WHERE

Case's hands were in his pockets and he stood on the deck at her house, morose, wondering what the hell he was doing here, at Roxie's house?

It was as if the damn riptide had swept him away.

A riptide called Roxie.

He should never have agreed to come here. How the hell had that happened?

Because there was no talking to Laine, was the answer. And he was to blame. After his outburst, it was all over. His wife was now a polite, cool stranger.

When the time came for him to be discharged, it seemed inevitable that he would be leaving with Roxie —Laine sure as hell wasn't having him back.

Roxie collected him in a new car, a Range Rover, and he tried to enthuse, she seemed so pleased with it. It was a hell of a lot easier to get in and out of, and he sat back gratefully in the plush comfort of the passenger seat as she drove them to her house.

"Let's get you home," she said, and the word 'home' made him flinch. In the end, he was tired and happy to just close his eyes and let her take charge. When they pulled into the driveway of the River's End home, he saw a few photographers outside the house, waiting patiently in the usually quiet street. Their flashes popped as she swung into the driveway.

"What the fuck!" Case cursed freely. Roxie was apologetic. "We've been something of a story, I'm afraid, since the ...shooting. They will get bored. Ignore it," she said. She made a mental note to get Maddie, her invaluable journo friend, to call off the dogs. But tomorrow Roxie knew it would be in print.

Case arriving home.

With her.

She drove into the garage, parking where the Beast once stood.

He was surprised to see her Bentley still there. He assumed she had sold it.

"Haven't you sold the Bentley?" he asked, taken aback.

Roxie laughed. "And then what would I do?" she asked lightly. "You need a car; I need a car. This is for you," she said, handing him the fob for the Range Rover, watching his face eagerly.

His reaction was instant. "I can't accept this. Never!" Far from looking pleased, he looked annoyed. "Not to mention I have a perfectly good Chevy at—" he stopped himself, but it was too late.

She looked crushed.

Home. He was about to say home. Where the hell was home? He berated himself for his churlishness. There was this sinking feeling in his gut. The Brea was no longer home.

He felt shitty. "I'm sorry, Roxie honey, but no way can I accept this," he said, trying to dial it back. "I'll make arrangements to collect my car, bring it here."

She perked up at that. He wanted to collect his car and bring it here. It was a start.

"Don't fret," she said, "If you want the Chevy, then the Chevy it is! My knight, my Prince Charming!" She reached out to touch his face tenderly, and inwardly, he winced. Prince?

The word taunted him.

THE DEBRIS

Judith was treading carefully.

However, it seemed to her no matter how cautiously she moved there was always an ominous scrunch underfoot, caused by the debris from her son's failing marriage. Laine was forging ahead with her plans for the big show in Seattle. She told Judith too casually she was taking up the sponsorship, and Judith knew, simply knew— Laine was going about things the wrong way!

Where there should have been eagerness, excitement, and enthusiasm, she saw only a dogged determination from her daughter-in-law.

Obstinacy, was something she, Judith, knew all too well.

She didn't like to ask what had changed Laine's attitude so dramatically. It wasn't her business.

All talk of Case coming home was off the table. Kevin was there last night, discussing 'business' with Laine, and he looked rather bleak himself, and Judith guessed it was all to do with Case. What was her son up to now? She had read some of the tabloids, well, scanned them, and she didn't believe a word of it. It sounded like the Machiavellian workings of that tramp! She had studied that photo of her son and his mistress —the word stuck in her craw —in Mexico, and she was suspicious about the timing of the photo.

If they, those trashy people at the papers, if they had the picture all along, why only publish it now?

It stank to high heaven.

Judith didn't care to debate such things with Laine. Laine had enough on her plate.

But this misguided rush to commit to this damn sponsor, well, that was just a mistake, Judith could feel it in her water! She could sit right down and flat-out cry! She shook her head, angry with herself. This was no time for tears. She had to get to her son, set him straight.

She squared her shoulders, her mouth a thin line of determination. That door for second chances was closing, and only she could see it!

FEET OF CLAY

Judith found the house easily enough, and it was exactly as she expected. Not particularly big, but the properties here were small, and usually, all house. There would be stairs in the front that would get you onto the beach. It was the perfect home–if you were a surfer, and not a surgeon!

She saw a Range Rover in the garage and wondered if the pop star was home. Her face hardened. Well, she could handle that too. She reached for the buzzer on the street gate.

"Mom!" She looked up and saw Case smiling down at her. He was on a small Juliet balcony, waving at her, clearly pleased to see her. A damn Romeo in his new castle, Judith thought sourly.

He disappeared, and moments later, he came out of the front door. His smile was broad, but his eyes had a hint of wariness. "I was surprised to get your call; I didn't think you would want to come here," he said, clearly ill at ease. "What's up?"

She held up her hands, placating. "Don't worry, no bad news! I wanted to see you, that's all," she lied. She hugged him, gently, because he still looked fragile. He looks tired, she noticed, definitely thinner.

"Oh." His face relaxed. "Well, that's good." Case didn't believe her for a minute. The real reason for her visit would be apparent in a short while, he had no doubt. Judith had no aptitude for duplicity.

"Come on up, there's a nice view of the ocean from the deck." He led the way, and she followed, noting the opulence everywhere, from the giant porcelain flowerpots to the double front door with its forged iron handles and embedded wrought iron in sand-blasted glass. They went through the house and out onto the deck.

Juanita appeared and Case introduced them.

Juanita greeted her warmly, gushing over Judith's 'wonderful' son. In the face of the housekeeper's genuine affection for her son, Judith dialed her responses down from aloof to polite.

The housekeeper rushed off to make them coffee, and Judith dutifully made small talk about the view.

Then they made 'small talk' about the children, skirting 'issues' until the housekeeper had left the coffee on the table and disappeared from the bright sunlight into the shadowed interior of the house.

Then, they made yet more small-talk about his health.

Five, four, three, two, one. He counted down mentally, stirring his coffee, taking his time, feeling like a twelve-year-old. He knew a lecture was coming; there was no escaping it.

He was right.

Abruptly, Judith tired of the game. Her next comment came from left field and left him wishing the game had gone on.

"Is she wonderful, you know, in bed?" she asked mildly, adding more sugar, her eyes not leaving his face.

Case choked. His deeply, deeply private mother, asking him about sex between him and Roxie. He stared at her wide-eyed, struck dumb.

She shrugged. "You heard me correctly." She enunciated again, slowly; "Is-she-good-in-bed?" She sat back, sipping her coffee. It was good coffee. "It can't be this?" she gestured with her head, taking in the house, the Pacific, everything. "—You're not that shallow."

Case paused, stalling. "What on earth do you want to know about that for?"

She grimaced, and shrugged, raising her eyebrows. "Curious. There must be something spectacular that's luring you away from your family, and it's not true love, so I am wondering. What is it? Best I could come up with, is sex," she said simply.

Case felt offended. How did she know it wasn't love? She didn't know Roxie. What did this cool, disdainful mother of his know about love, or passion??

Judith watched the emotions playing on her son's face, and suddenly she wished, obscurely, that she knew him better. She had raised him to be tough, upstanding, a hero amongst mere mortals, yet here he was before her, her beloved son, with his feet of clay. She sighed softly. It would never be about the money. It wasn't about love, not real love, she was quite sure. Therefore, it had to be about sex. She could see him losing his cool. Good, she thought.

"I don't have to answer that-"

"No," she agreed easily, "You don't. But given your wife is filing for a divorce—" she saw him flinch at her words, and it pained her, but she soldiered on. "Yes, Kevin was there last night, and she told me this morning she's going ahead; 'Moving on,' was the expression I believe she used." She shrugged, nonchalant. "I imagine you will get a call from Kevin soon enough!

He felt physically winded.

It should be no surprise, but his heart sank. Kevin couldn't really be taking her seriously! So, Laine didn't need him. A new career, and perhaps a lover?

Now, divorce?

It was all too much.

"It doesn't matter," he said unhappily, but his face said it mattered more than anything in the world. "This began with me, betraying her. But Laine —" he looked away.

"Laine? What exactly has Laine done?" Judith asked, sitting forward. "Now that she's all set to rebuild her life, does it offend you, hurt your feelings, perhaps?" she said, provoking him.

Case said nothing. He eyed his mother. What did she mean, now that she's set to build a new life? What the hell did that mean?

"What do you mean?" he asked, impatient. His jaw had taken on that pugnacious thrust Judith knew well.

She studied her son as she spoke. "She's signed a letter of intent, you know," she said, knowing full well he didn't know,"—Committing to a sponsor for the nationals, and when she gets through, gets that far—" Judith sounded confident her daughter-in-law would indeed get that far. "And she will get to that, I think! She's very determined."

Judith eyed him. If he was a dog, he would be growling.

She heard with a twinge of alarm his breathing had changed tempo, sounding a little ragged. She looked at him askance, pointing to his chest. "That doesn't sound good."

He dismissed her concern, thinking about Laine and the sponsorship. That was a big deal. "A little souvenir," he said impatiently.

"Ah." But it didn't quiet her consternation. He appeared quite shell-shocked, and for a second or two, she had a twinge of guilt. This was her son, after all, and here she was, goading him. She sighed. Her fool son!

"She signed for the sponsorship. When did this happen?"

"Oh, I gather she's committed," Judith said airily. Good. He understood the ramifications, that was a start, she supposed. "She has to get Kevin to check over all the paperwork, but I gather there's a handshake. You can imagine what that means—" She shrugged, leaving her opinion unsaid.

Case understood his mother's implicit warning. But she still thought he was deserving of Laine! Still hoping he could pull his marriage back from the abyss.

Judith kept quiet, studying her son. It was like watching him learn to walk, and just like before, she could do precious little to stop him from falling. He had to figure this out for himself.

However, it was as she had thought. He still loved his wife, yet what held him back? The damn singer??

"You were about to say something about Laine?" she prompted.

Case looked away, hesitating. "She's no better than me," he muttered, scowling.

"Oh." Judith felt her ire rising. He sounded petulant, like a child, and it was a side to him she wasn't familiar with. She stared at him, her expression closed, wondering what was behind the sullen face.

"And why do you say that?" She leaned forward in her chair, drawing closer to him, giving him all her attention.

Case looked at her, contemplating. This was his mother, but also Laine's number-one fan. She probably knew nothing about Laine's affair!

"What is it, Case," Judith pressed him.

Innocently, he stepped into the trap.

"She's having an affair."

Judith's eyes widened, and she stared at him for a long moment.

Then she struck him across his face with all her might. Weeks of pent-up frustration releasing itself in one loud, stinging slap!

Case didn't know what stung more, his face or his feelings! He sat, stupefied.

His mother had never, ever struck him before, not ever! The blue eyes were wide, his mouth opened in a round 'O' of incredulity.

"What the f—." He bit the words off.

"Fuck. Say it, 'fuck'." she snapped, trying to make the word sound commonplace, but failing completely. "It seems to be a word you understand well." She was calm again. Judith wondered who was the more surprised at the blow, herself or her son.

No matter. It was done.

"Lucas McAllister," she warned, using his given name, always a bad sign. "Think carefully before you speak again, because if you besmirch your wife's name, —your name, I might add, or I shall strike you again, as I probably should have done, years ago!"

Case pushed his chair back, unconsciously distancing himself from her anger, and despite herself, his small act of panic defused her, and she found herself smiling, then chuckling all the more at his ensuing indignation.

"Well, I am glad you find it amusing! But it's true," he said, rubbing his cheek." Whether you like to hear it or not, it's true," he asserted indignantly.

She shrugged, dismissing him, "No. No, it's not. I don't doubt the word 'fuck' is involved, but is Laine having an affair? Never!"

Case thought about that, his spirits lifting just a bit, eclipsing his awe at this new, foulmouthed mother.

"How can you be so sure?" he challenged her.

Her smile vanished. He could be so very obtuse at times. She sighed heavily.

"I almost wish she did have a lover, Case, because then I would know she isn't heartbroken, that she isn't feigning happiness, just because either I or the children have entered the room. I would be able to talk to her, and she would hear me and answer, not struggle to think about what it is that I am saying, and make some polite, distracted response!"

Judith continued; "I would know, Case, because I would see her hugging her girls and shrieking with laughter, and the laughter would be from her belly, as it used to, before ...This." Judith waved a dismissive hand, including the ocean, the house, his loathsome new life.

Her mouth was a tight, sad line.

"It's been ages since I heard her laughing, really laughing," Judith suddenly looked defeated. She was weary of this dance. She sighed, rubbing her temples with her hand, her eyes closed. Then she looked at him, sizing him up.

"Case, I don't know what she told you, and frankly, I don't care. If she slept with someone to restore her sense of self, well, that I understand. All too well. I did the same thing." She ignored his shocked face, weary of protecting her son's stupid, foolish sensibilities.

"One does foolish things, when one is in pain, Case."

She stood up. It was time to go.

"It doesn't heal the pain, of course. Makes it worse, in fact. But as for an affair—" Judith was contemptuous. "I would know!"

She wanted to be gone. His ignorance was overwhelming her.

"If she has a lover, Case, then that is a heartache I would never, ever wish for you. This," she gestured to his chest, the stark evidence of his brush with death, "this is not painful! Lose your life's mate to someone else— Now that is pain!"

Case stared at her, dumb.

He could think of nothing to say. He stood up. "Mom, she's moved on. That's obvious," he said miserably. "She not in love with me anymore." He took a deep breath, "I am going to have to make the best of it."

Judith brushed her hand against his reddened cheek, regretting her lapse of control. She tilted her head to one side, gazing at him, seeking a son that wasn't there.

"Case, infidelity does not kill a marriage! To kill a marriage, you need pride. Lots and lots of foolish, soul-destroying pride!"

Did he understand? It had taken her a lifetime to learn that one simple thing.

"Well, I must be off. Have to get back to the children. You are going to have to work something out, you know, on those weekends when she is away."

Case wasn't listening. He had failed her. Failed everybody.

"Of course, on your weekends, you can look after the girls." she was saying brightly, "You and—

He kept quiet. She was baiting him.

"Roxie, isn't it? Can't wait to meet her! Now, walk me to my car."

ENSNARED

When Roxie came home, he spoke briefly of his mother's visit, withholding from her the tidbit that Laine intended filing for a divorce. It would bring about a happiness he didn't want to see on her face. He wasn't ready for that.

Roxie didn't push him for more details. She saw his sallow color, and with a no-nonsense attitude, dragged him out to the pool, insisting he take in some sunshine, get some sun.

She was right, the sun felt good, and the water was invigorating.

After a while, she urged him to come inside, into the cool shadows of her bedroom. She wept a little when she rubbed his scars with tissue oil, her fingers gentle and caressing.

They hadn't made love yet, and he knew she was hungry for him, but Case held back, unsure, feeling almost as if it was inappropriate, not understanding why. It never felt wrong before, and of course, now she had her new life, so what the hell was holding him back?

"Lay back," she said, "her voice thick, "let me spoil you."

At first, he lay passive, allowing her to mount him in the way she had done many times before, but this time it was different. Images of Laine with someone else came into his head, and anger took over. He held her fast and pounded at her with a brute energy born from rage and frustration, but her eyes merely glazed in rapture. She came in a screaming, noisy ecstasy, and he allowed himself to come with her, let the demons out.

Afterwards, he lay next to her, tender, remorseful.

Trapped.

IN THE PARADE

She had a 'function', and he had reluctantly agreed to accompany her. Yet another celebrity brunch, this time for African music, and by all accounts, most of the music industry would be there, as well as a healthy spattering of "movie people".

There would be the damn photographers, he had no doubt, but Laine never read that trash, so in the end he acquiesced, feeling selfish.

He dressed himself carefully, wondering what was "cool" and what was not. In the end he didn't care, but when Roxie ran her eyes over him, she was clearly pleased with what she saw.

The blue of his shirt took some of the pallor from his skin, and the sun yesterday, and her own special medicine, she liked to think—had done him good. He looked hot, and Roxie wished there was time to strip him off and have an encore from the night before. And if the gods smiled upon her, and the wife took the bait.

"Why are you looking at me like the cat that got the cream?" he asked, amused.

"Because I have got the cream," she said smugly. "I challenge anyone to say differently."

Case grinned at her, ruffling her hair. She secretly hated that, but even that didn't annoy her. She was in top spirits. Case had promised last night to devote himself to shrugging off his blues, and that was a hopeful sign.

In the garage, she offered him the fob to the Range Rover, and he took it, hiding his reluctance from her. She was over the top. There was nothing wrong with his Chevy.

They were off to the Descanso Botanical Gardens, a beautiful setting to extract thousands of dollars from the celebrity guests. Case drove slowly. There was no rush. He was loathe to be on show, and not looking forward to a noisy gaggle of unfamiliar people.

Roxie had promised him they would stay for an hour or two, no more, and if he felt tired, she would leave immediately. More than that, he couldn't ask, and he determined to make her day fun.

When they arrived, Case groaned inwardly. It was noisy, trendy, and everyone there seemed hyper, excited and enthusiastic. except him. They were swamped immediately, and Roxie held onto his hand possessively. Everyone was friendly enough, but he was glad to be abandoned to the tender mercies of Sheila, Manning's PA.

Manning himself was charming enough, but Case sensed a whole heap of reserve there, and he wondered what her portly manager must have thought about the shooting? Hell, it was still hard for he himself to comprehend, or even think about! Clearly, from Manning's cool demeanor, Case gathered the man wasn't at all too happy about him and Roxie.

On the other hand, Sheila, Manning's secretary, well, she was happy! She was delighted to finally meet Laine's mystery man, and indeed, she thought, the newspapers had not done this hunky guy justice.

She patted the chair next to her, expansive and pleased to have him sitting next to her. She entertained him with interesting anecdotes, pointing out this one and that, and was pleased to see him smiling, slowly relaxing. Roxie broke her mingling to join them from time to time. Case sat affably to the side as lesser mortals came to pay homage to the golden girl of song.

He met the head of her record company, and yet again, he sensed that measure of reserve.

He asked Sheila if he was being sensitive and she giggled, confiding in him that "outsiders" were always regarded as loose cannons.

She explained; "You are an outsider. You are not in movies, or music, ergo, outsider! And outsiders are no-no." she declared with a knowing smile.

Case nodded. He wasn't really listening.

He was wondering if Donatés had traveled well, if it was a shared or a solo horsebox. It would be better shared. Keep him calm, it was a longish trip.

But Laine would have sorted that.

He had checked the Seattle weather for the next few days and Laine might be in for rain. Rain was something Donatés would have to get used to.

"Case!" He looked up from his reverie with a start. Roxie was calling him, beckoning.

"Off you go." Sheila waved him off, and turned to Case with a smile. "She's right. I think you are gorgeous! I can see why she keeps buying you those damn cars. I would do the same," she whispered conspiratorially, and turned her attention to an insistent young man on her left.

Case excused himself and went to join Roxie, bemused. What did the woman mean, 'Keeps buying you cars...'

Roxie introduced him to a spindly, long-haired music producer from the UK, and Case and the producer shook hands politely. Before they could exchange polite pleasantries, they were interrupted by Roxie's friend Phillipa.

Case felt sheepish. He remembered how they had met the last time.

Phillipa was, as ever, delightful, effervescent and openly admiring. Her plus-one was a polite little man twice her age, who stared at Case with open curiosity.

Case returned his gaze, wondering if it was the tabloid crap that had him gaping like that.

Phillipa cuffed her friend lightly.

"Pottie, you are being rude." She turned to Case. "He's gay. You're exactly his type," she said to the amusement of 'Pottie.' Case smiled politely, but something was nagging him. He felt the beginnings of a headache.

What was it the Sheila-woman had said? She keeps buying you cars...'

"So, is it true?" A big woman with an enormous bosom joined them, obviously very well known to Roxie, he judged, given her proprietary air.

"Case, this is my agent, Trish Halliwell, Trish, Case McAllister," Roxie made the introductions proudly, pleased to show him off. Case greeted the woman with a smile, noting with professional interest the faintly blue lips, indicative of a heart condition.

"Hello, Case," her voice had the deep throaty timbre of a heavy smoker.

Trish eyed him speculatively, wondering if this man would prove to be more trouble than he already was!

This was the first time she had met the man who had cost her two hundred and thirty thousand dollars in commission! Roxie refusing to do the East Coast tour still smarted. She appraised him boldly.

"So, is it true? Are you getting married in December?" She asked, knowing full well it was crap, but pleased to see the incredulity on his face.

Roxie interrupted, smiling at Trish, but her eyes were flashing fire. "You know the tabloids print rubbish, Trish, so that is not a serious question," she said, her tone warning.

Trish shrugged. "Well, Roxie dearest, the tabloids have always loved you.

You don't have to worry. " She smiled sweetly at Case, then addressed Roxie; "I would snap him up too, sweetie, he's delicious," she said slyly.

Case wondered if all the people that worked with Roxie were as transparent, as fake as this woman, or was it just that he was an 'outsider,' as Sheila said.

'No wonder she keeps buying you cars...' That's what she had said.

Cars. Plural.

Did Roxie buy that car, especially for him, the Cadillac Deville? Impossible. But she had said 'cars'. He looked around. Sheila was about to leave, gathering up her purse, still in conversation with the eager young man. He excused himself and headed for Manning's secretary.

"Sheila," he called out to her, and she looked up in surprise.

"Case?" The doctor looked agitated. "What is it? Can I get you anything?" she asked.

"Did you buy the Range Rover?" he asked, his manner curt.

She nodded, taken aback. "I do all that sort of thing, part of my job. Don't you like it? Is the color not okay?"

"No, no." I am not worried about that." he brushed her concerns aside. "Did you buy the Deville too?" he asked.

"Oh that!" She tittered. "Did I ever! That bastard didn't want to sell, but Roxie was having none of it.—Buy it any cost, she said, and wow, did she pay!" She looked at him, curious. "Although why you wanted such a heap is beyond me!" A young man was tapping her arm, and she turned away from Case to snap at him, "I'm busy!"

The youngster looked sheepish, but he extended his hand, persistent. He was holding a memory stick and Sheila took it impatiently. His mission accomplished, he slunk away, and she explained to Case with a grimace; "They are always trying to get Roxie to do their music, so they sneak into functions like this, try their luck."

Case wasn't listening. His mind was spooling back, back to the first time he met Roxie.

She had duped him, from day one!

It was impossible to imagine, but—!

He glanced over at Roxie. She was still talking to the producer, gesticulating, passionate.

He left Sheila abruptly, leaving the woman with the nagging feeling she had messed up somewhere.

He went over to Roxie. "We need to talk," he interrupted her, his face grim.

She looked at him in some surprise, wondering why he was suddenly looking so, so ... Bleak. Was he feeling ill? She felt a stab of alarm and turned to excuse herself from the producer.

Case took her arm and led her away.

"Case? Are you alright?" she asked, feeling selfish. It was too soon, all of this.

"I'm fine," he said brusquely, "I need to ask you something. His face was set, hard. A few people nearby were eying them curiously. Case glanced at them and said brusquely, "Follow me."

He walked away from the throng of guests towards a sheltered floral arbor which offered a modicum of privacy.

Roxie stared at him askance, her brows furrowed, bewildered at this meteoric change of mood. He paused, wanting to confront her, but he was wary, and glanced around for eavesdroppers and the damn photographers!

Roxie caught his hand, her heart thumping. Had he found out? "Case, let me say goodbye -then we can chat on the way home." She turned to go back, but he caught her shoulder and spun her around.

"Case!" She was shocked at his rough manner. What was up with him?

"Tell me something, —and I want the truth!" His expression was cold, his eyes narrowed, searching her face.

She looked at him in surprise, and her recent conversation with Phillipa flashed through her head. She felt herself blushing. Phillipa had said it was impossible to trace it back to her. Aware of her burning cheeks, she thrust her chin out and challenged him.

"What? What is it you want to know?"

"The car, the Deville. When you 'sold' it to me, he said, emphasizing the sold, "Did the car even belong to you?"

Roxie looked at him, her mind blank, then relief flooded through her. He didn't know. He was stewing about the damn car. Sheila must have shot her mouth off. Still, she felt a growing alarm. Case had never looked at her like that before, so very hostile—

His eyes were fixed on her. Her expression was hard to read, and he wanted her to deny it, but she stayed silent, her eyes closed.

"Well?" he was waiting for her answer.

"I– " Oh fuck. She was busted. There was nothing for it. He could check and find out for himself through the DMV. "Yes, I bought it. For you," she said quickly. "I could see how much you liked it, so–"

"So you baited the trap!" he said slowly, looking at her in sheer disbelief. "From the very beginning, you've always had a plan..."

He shook his head, as if he was having difficulty putting it all together.

"Case, please," Roxie said, pleading. "I fell in love with you from the moment, the very moment, I saw you. I couldn't just let you walk away, could I?" Now the green eyes were glistening. "And you love me too, don't deny it!"

Case looked at her and wondered which of the two of them were the crazier? Her with her manipulations, or him, with his sheer, incredible stupidity. "Are you telling me, you met my wife, you knew I was married and nothing, nothing stopped you?

"Or you, Case," she snapped, stung. "As I recall, nothing stopped you either!

Alarmed that she had said the wrong thing, she tried to back-pedal. "Case, you fell in love with me too, darling, don't deny it!" she implored. "We were meant for each other!"

She threw her arms around his neck and tried to kiss him, but he pushed her away, his face closed and angry.

Case closed his eyes against the sight of her, filled with self-loathing. What the fuck had he done?

Roxie was trying to embrace him again. but he held her away from him, trying desperately to think. How had he got into this mess? How blind and stupid did you have to be??

She watched the emotions flitting across his face and

her arms fell to her side. She stood frozen in front of him, willing him to look at her, really see her, the woman he loved. The woman who loved him!

"Case, please," she begged, "Don't deny it? We were meant to be!" He opened his eyes and looked at her, looked past her.

He had messed up Laine's life, his children's life, his own damn life, for what? He had been a willing, lock, stock and barrel, paid-for stud.

He felt sickened.

Images of his mother and Kevin flashed through his head, all trying to warn him. The tabloids– God, even the fucking tabloids should have warned him. Laine had read that shit.

And this, this was all his fault.

"Case. Please..." Her tears were streaming now, but the sight left him cold. He looked at her, wondering how he could have been so taken in, how he had almost talked himself into believing he loved her!

"I'm going home, Roxie," he said at last.

Home? The way he had said the word; home.

"Where are you going?" she exclaimed, panicked.

He took a deep breath. Where indeed...

"I'm going home to my wife, to beg her to forgive me, see if it's not too late to fix this mess," he said, and turned to leave.

"Case!" Roxie knew she sounded desperate, but she didn't care. A few bystanders were turning to see who it was that sounded so agitated, distressed. Roxie clung to his arm, uncaring. "Please, this is a mistake! She's moved on, she has her own life now!"

Something in her voice gave him pause, and he hesitated,looked uncertain.

He frowned. She spoke as if she knew Laine would never take him back?

What else had she done?

She rushed on, encouraged, "Please darling, she's moved on, you know she has. I love you, and I'm here. Please..." She was desperately trying to stop him from walking away, out of her life.

Case knew her words were the truth. Laine had moved on, and the stark reality of that overwhelmed him.

He took a deep breath. He had to fix this; he must fix this.

"That's true," he said, speaking more to himself than to her."But I am not going to give up until she forgives me." He was speaking more to himself than to her.

He ignored her tears, hardly noticed them. The fog that had been so long in his head had cleared, at last.

Case suddenly knew every minute counted! He shook her hand off and turned and strode quickly towards the exit, oblivious to the curious stares.

Roxie watched him leave, and she sat down slowly on a stone cherub bench, knowing it was futile to chase after him.

Charles Manning was approaching, a fixed smile on his face, but she could see he was concerned. She brushed the tears from her cheek. Later.

Give him time to calm down and she could sort this out.

He would understand. With some things in life, there were no choices. Oh, it all sounded insane, but that's what love did, it made one crazy.

She put her sunglasses on, taking deep breaths to calm herself, glad of the maze of floral arbors and the privacy they offered. Case felt this way, now. He was merely confused, upset.

Charles Manning was almost upon her, and she gave him a bright smile.

Later. For now, there was the wretched paparazzi!

CRUSHED

UNDONE

Case caught a cab to the Brea, and on the way there, he wondered what he could say to Laine–maybe she had already left for Seattle? His stomach churned, and in his mind's eye, he tried to rehearse the conversation.

What would he say to the girls, to Judith?

If she didn't want him back, perhaps he could stay with Kevin, until he convinced her!

That way, he could stall the divorce, ask Kevin to screw it up, delay, and play for time. He had to win her back.

Laine was his true north. His compass had been off for a while, but she had to forgive him. She had to.

He was the one who had always shared her everything, until now. He was the only one who should be there, at her side, when she had her day in the sun. And so the thoughts ran through his head.

At last, the cab was turning into the winding two-hundred-yard driveway, and Case felt his heart thumping in his chest. He glanced briefly towards the right, to the Reichmann house standing on the prow of the hill. Case shuddered.

Jesus. He could have died, and she would never have known he loved her, only her.

The driveway was at an end, and the cabbie stopped noisily in the loose gravel.

Ollie came rushing up, barking, looking fierce and proprietary until he recognized Case. He continued barking furiously as if to let the world know his master was home. Case stepped out, happy to see him, shushing him. His car was still there, in its usual place in the garage.

Her car was gone, as was his mother's. There was no one home.

The cabbie sat behind the wheel, waiting. He noted the locked doors, and the lack of people.

"Your family's out, dude. Did they know you were coming today?" he asked. Maybe another fare back to town?

Case looked around him; everything felt the same. His departure had rippled the marital pond, but now, the pond had settled, and there was nothing to see.

He paid the cabbie, giving him a generous tip, anxious to have the man gone.

The cabbie smiled broadly. Case declined his offer of a ride back into town and watched the car making its way down the driveway, appearing to move rather erratically as the driver picked the best way to avoid the ruts in the dirt road.

Inside the house, everything was the same, and the eerie quiet served to calm his troubled mind.

Everything was in its usual place.

Case walked into the study. At first glance, it looked the same, but he saw almost immediately their wedding photo was gone.

No more Laine smiling up at him, adoring him, and he, looking back at her, as pleased as punch. He set about scratching for the picture, feeling frantic. He found it, face down in the top drawer. An unbearable reminder for her?

The other photos were still there, their holiday in Colorado, in Vegas, Liesel curled sleeping next to Ollie when he was a puppy.

Case slumped down in the old chair behind his desk, wondering where exactly his family could be. Should he phone Judith? The memory of her stinging slap, her contempt, just two days ago, made him wary. She would be short, but she would tell him, he felt sure. He fished out his phone and made the call. After a few rings, she answered, laughing at something or someone on the other side.

"Hello?"

Case wondered why she was laughing. She sounded happy. They were all moving on with their lives. He heard her repeat again;

"Hello? Case?"

"Mom?" Case said, his mouth felt dry. "It's me," he cleared his throat. Had he disappeared from everyone's mind, like a blip off the radar?

The jocular tone was gone. "I can see," she said. "Is everything alright?"

"Fine, fine," he said hastily, reassuring her. "The thing is, I'm here at the house—"

"At the house?" She sounded surprised, "You mean at your house? Or—"

"At my house," he interrupted her hastily. "Thing is, Laine's not here. Where are you guys?" What kind of shit-for-brains father didn't know where his kids were, he thought, ashamed.

Judith was quiet, thinking fast. Did this mean what she thought it meant? Perhaps he had just come to collect more clothes, or his car?

"What are you doing there?" she asked, sounding harsher than she meant to.

Case flinched.

"Well, I came to see Laine," he said slowly, "see if I can make things right. I've left Roxie." Oh." There was a long silence.

"That's good, very good," she said at last.

Case waited. "So? Where is she?" he asked again, feeling anxious.

Again, a long silence.

Case wondered if Laine was with someone new.

Judith spoke at last, slowly, as if considering her words carefully "Case, we're in San Diego with Melissa for the weekend, giving the cousins a chance to get reacquainted. I'll be bringing them back on Wednesday. And Laine," she sounded unsure, "Well, Laine is off for the weekend. She's in Seattle." Case felt the tension building in him, and he took a deep breath. The show.

"On her own?"

"Oh, they're all with her, the stables crew. Two horses went up, apparently. Donatés left on Tuesday, in Ballard's trailer, and she flew there on Wednesday. It's a qualifier..." she added, by way of explanation.

He slumped back. That was a big deal, the Seattle Hunter Championship. He knew all the shows; they had gone to see the top riders in the Seattle show the year before last.

She was with the crew. Who exactly was the crew? Obviously, Ballard would be with her.

"Case?"

With a jolt, he realized his mom was still on the line.

"Case?"

"Yes, sorry..."

"Do you want to say hello to the girls," she asked.

"Sure," he said, distracted.

For the next few minutes, he spoke to each of his daughters in turn, happy to hear their little voices brimming with excitement. When the inevitable question came, when was Daddy coming home, Case answered with a conviction he didn't feel; "Soon honey, soon. Real soon."

He put the phone down, wondering what to do next. Should he call her, tell her he was on his way?

No way would she pick up, he told himself, but the truth was, he didn't want her to forbid it, reject him. Better to just 'surprise' her.

He looked at the photo he had just fished out of the drawer, both of them, so deliriously happy. He remembered the pallor of her cheeks, that terrible night, as if he was draining her of her very life force. He closed his eyes tight, trying in vain to banish the image in his head. He could hear the sound of her sobbing as he left her, walked away. He saw her face at the hospital, him yelling, her, closed and cool, indifferent.

Her love gone.

She was lost to him.

Case felt his eyes were scratchy, prickling with alien, unfamiliar tears, tears that had been too long in coming. He put his elbows on the old antique desk that desk, held his face in his hands, and wept.

Afterwards, he couldn't remember. How long had he cried? A few minutes? An hour? But through the tears and the cacophony of recriminations in his head, Case heard his mother talking, her words clear and ringing, heard the surprise in her voice.

'It's pride that kills the marriage, son, just foolish pride.' The words slowly drowned out the others, became louder, cleared the fog.

Pride. He had none of that, just shame. And there was no time for that either. He had to make this right!

Case reached for the computer keyboard and tapped it until the screen lit up.

There was a flight to Seattle that left in two hours. It would be tight. Maybe forty-five minutes to get to the airport, fifty minutes flying time, maybe an hour to the Showgrounds. He could be at her side in around four, maybe five hours. If he missed it, well, he'd get the next one.

His despair was receding, and in its place rose a tiny, fragile sense of purpose, battered and timid, but it was there.

He had to go to her, look her in the eye...Make this right.

A few moments later, he was on his way to the airport, and it was only when he was seated on the plane, it occurred to him;

He hadn't packed any clothes.

STUMBLING

From the Seattle-Tacoma airport, Case caught a cab to the State Showgrounds, wondering belatedly if he should have bought flowers at the airport. As if flowers could repair three months of insanity.

Would she even speak to him? Well, he would find her, and if she was there with this Boyer character, well, he would do the mature thing. He would pound the crap out of him, he thought, knowing he was being ridiculous. But when he thought about it, he knew he just might do that anyhow.

Crazy. The thought that she could be there with some asshole, well it made him crazy. Case knew he was irrational and hypocritical, but the reality was Laine was born to be his wife. He knew that a long, long time ago, just as surely as he had always known he was meant for her.

All the way there, he rehearsed; 'Hello Laine', 'maybe just 'Hi,' perhaps even "Need some company?"

Then, in his mind's eye, they would talk it out, and he would convince her to forgive him, he would beg her, and she would see, have to see, that he was sorry, he was so very, very sorry. When he thought of her resigned face when he was in the hospital, that iciness that kept him at arm's length, out of reach. But then, when she kissed him, the night of the shooting.

All the words in his head sounded so foolish and trite, so infinitesimally small, compared to the enormous pain he had caused her. He was diminished, ashamed. He searched for happy memories to bolster him, remind him he was once her everything, dammit.

Nothing, that was the sorry truth.

But still, he had to try. He would make it all up to her if she would just listen.

At last, he was finally at the Seattle Showgrounds. Seattle was expecting him and knew the state of his heart, so it welcomed him with dark clouds and gentle rain.

Not that rain deterred the crowds. They were out in force, milling through the halls and stands, relaxed and happy, excited. The city's Showgrounds, deserted for most of the year, had that heady energy that comes when people from all over the country gather to show off the best of the best. From marrows to pot-bellied pigs, or helicopters, they could see the best of the best. It is one of the biggest county fairs in the USA. For those riders with Olympic ambitions, placing here, at this show, was a significant step towards realizing Olympic glory.

The Seattle State Fair hosted one of the richest showjumping competitions of the season, with more than two hundred hopefuls competing for the blue ribbons and the ultimate prize of two hundred thousand dollars. Recently, Rolex had introduced a one-and-a-half million-dollar purse for the CP International, but Laine knew the competitors here all wanted one thing–the ribbon.

Case was rushing towards the arena, his heart thumping. Perhaps she had already finished, maybe left the show grounds? They had been here, together, three years ago to check out the competition. In his panic, he struggled to remember exactly where the arena was, and wasted precious moments asking for directions.

Behind the stall which boasted the finest, biggest, marrows in America, he found the entrance to the arenas. Specifically, Arena C, the showjumping ring. He went past the stalls, thinking how Laine loved all this, that smell of horses, sawdust, dubbin and leather.

Where was she?

BRING BUTTERFLIES

If ever butterflies were acceptable, today would be the day. Nerves were good.

But the butterflies stayed away, and Laine missed them. The girl with the butterflies in her stomach was the old Laine.

The new Laine stood in the stall, dressed and ready, focused on the task ahead. She was pretending to be wholly preoccupied with Donatés. Other riders came up to admire her horse, maybe hit a little on the blonde from LA.

She didn't know it, and it would have dismayed her had she guessed it, but most had her pegged as a snob, stuck-up and aloof, the rider with the stunning bay that had that weird name, Donatés.

The favorite to win the blue ribbon was a rider from Atlanta, with a horse everyone knew and admired, the awe-inspiring Bojangles.

Bojangles was owned by Mike Keller, and his horse was one of three he had here for the show. Keller was also last year's Georgia state champion, and Bojangles was a three-time Horse of the Year State Champion.

Donatés, on the other hand, was an outsider, a newcomer. Already the word was out and already the horse and his rider had a rep.

Laine felt sure her horse would prove to be as good as they thought. The question was, would she be as good? There would be around two thousand or more people out there, watching, people who had traveled thousands of miles to see this jump-off.

She figured she was on in about forty-five minutes. She knew a handful of the riders, some from way back, but Laine had little doubt this time it was different. Big competitions brought out big guns. This was a different league altogether.

Each of the horses in Hall-J5 had cost the owners a pretty penny and were worth a small fortune, including her Donatés. The difference was; most of them had a string of horses to further their ambitions, but, she only had her boy.

She reached up and put her arms around the horse, her lips brushing the side of his face. Donatés seemed to understand her tension, and he gave her a gentle, don't-sweat-it nuzzle.

"Don't you worry about the wet, Mommy's big boy! Let's just show them!" she whispered in his ear. The rain made her edgy. It was just a drizzle, but Donatés was relatively unproven in the wet. For him, it was a relatively unfamiliar condition.

"So, this is Donatés?" She turned to see Mike Keller. In the flesh, he was a lot smaller than she had imagined. She recognized him from the showjumping magazines, TV.

Keller was giving her, not the horse, the once over. "I'm told you have a magnificent animal there. Look forward to seeing what he can do. Is he for sale?" he asked amiably.

Laine smiled and patted Donatés on the neck. "Nope, he's not for sale. He," she thought about it, "he was a present, so sentimental," she finished, feeling foolish.

Keller smiled at that. "I know what you mean. I held on to my first hunter through thick and thin," he said, laughing. "And hell, there sure was some thin. Still have him, in fact.

Laine smiled back at him. That was nice. She felt herself thawing a little, warming to him. Everyone was friendly and helpful, but if she didn't get her act together, she would blow it. She needed to get ready.

"Look..."

"Mike. Mike Keller," he extended his hand, and she shook his hand politely. "Hello Mike, nice meeting you. But I have to get myself together, so —"

He held up his hands, took a step back. "Sure, I understand." Well, I'll be seeing you, probably after?" He turned to go, hesitating, wondering if she was here on her own. Unlikely. Still, he made a mental note to ask Ballard what the deal was.

Laine was relieved to see him go. She took her phone out and flicked through the text messages. Like a tongue playing with a sore tooth, she looked again at the message from Judith, sent to her the day she left for Seattle.

He's getting on with his life, you get on with yours. Girls will be fine. Go get that ribbon!

Laine flung the phone back inside her tog bag.

That's exactly what she would do. To hell with lying, cheating, bastard husbands.

Rage was good.

It kept the ache at bay.

THE FALL

In the VIP box, Mike Keller's mother settled her ample self in the too-narrow chairs reserved for Gold members and waited for her son to trot into the ring. She lamented loudly the damn rain was a 'real bitch' for the riders, and worse, it made her arthritis play up. The fact was, she hated this damn Seattle and its eternal goddamn rain. Still, it was holding up for a while, and that would do her son good. Her husband, Robert Keller was as bony as Alice Keller was broad, and he dressed as if they were still in damn Atlanta, she complained. He settled down alongside his wife and they got ready for the competitors to strut their stuff, both complacent that on paper at least, their son looked a likely winner.

Alice Keller was a doting mother, she never missed the big ones, and she liked to think that her presence out here in the stands was important for her boy. He knew his Mama was there, watching. She had a good view, but she fished out her binoculars anyhow–it helped to home in on the details. Alice had a well-deserved reputation for picking winners. The siren squawked and the first contestant came into the ring, a girl from LA, on a newcomer horse, an animal unknown to her, a fine-looking bay called Donatés. Donna-tay, was how you said it, apparently, according to Ballard.

The horse and girl came from his outfit. And if he said they were good, they were good!

Robert Keller reached for his program, wanting to read a bit more about this new pair. There wasn't too much.

That horse looked good, and the woman, well, she looked mighty fine, comfortable and relaxed. Alice studied horse and rider closely through her binoculars. The blonde looked like she was here to win this, she thought. There was a line to her mouth that Alice recognized, a set determination that she had seen in many winners over the years.

She watched the rider set quietly to the jumps. They pulled a clear round, eighty seconds. Impressive.

They were through on time.

The Kellers glanced at each other, a small smile playing on Alice's mouth.

"Well, I do think we might have some competition here. This is the gal that Ballard was on about, and she's on the right horse, for sure. Donatés. I remember the name." She looked down into the tunnel as Laine trotted past on Donatés. The rider's chest was heaving, and she looked pleased, determined.

Then it was their son's turn. The rain was holding off for him, but any minute now it could start again. Mike Keller did well, pulling the best time yet. They sat back, pleased. "I reckon he's gonna get this one, Allie," her husband ventured a cautious opinion. His wife sniffed, saying nothing. Not if the blonde had anything to do with it.

They watched the other contestants, waiting patiently for the final round.

At last, it was time.

Mike would be taking on the blonde again, and three others. The Kellers agreed; Ballard's blonde was the danger.

In the pre-round paddock with its lofty canvas roof, Donatés was proving to be quite skittish, and Laine was wheeling him around again and again, telling herself it was her. She was spooking him; he was picking up on her energy.

The butterflies had finally found a home in her stomach.

It was the third and final round coming up. She was in the running, and she could see Ballard waiting at the chute, chatting to some of the officials, leaning across the rail, waiting to give her an encouraging smile and thumbs-up as she came out.

Out of the corner of her eye, she saw Ballard glancing in her direction, his attention caught by Donatés' whinnying complaints.

It was the buzz spooking the horse. The horses always seemed to know when it was crunch time. Maybe it was that familiar big-show energy that crackled in the air. He saw Laine had her hands full, calming the prancing Donatés.

Laine could hear the crowd clapping and whistling, and the gate swung open, and the girl from Sacramento came trotting back inside the paddock, looking breathless but pleased.

Ballard cocked his ear, listening for the points-call on the loudspeakers. Four points. Two faults.

He winked at Laine, indicating the score with four fingers and then signed with finger and thumb; she was A-OK.

Laine gave him a small nod. She felt her stomach tighten.

So, it was between her and the Atlanta guy. She wheeled Donatés around and trotted towards the gate. Still no rain, thank goodness. She knew by now the course would be thoroughly churned up, and Donatés was not really used to wet conditions. But now is as good a time as any to learn, she thought, steeling herself.

She trotted out into the ring and for one crazy split second, she thought she saw Case's face in the crowd. Absolutely his double. She looked again, but the face was gone. Laine gave her head a slight shake–she needed to focus–no time for craziness! She turned Donatés to face the first obstacle.

The horse took the first six fences comfortably, and in the stands, the Kellers watched the pair tackle the jumps with effortless grace.

They frowned and exchanged looks. Their son had a fight on his hands. Alice Keller had never been on a horse in her life, but after all these years, she liked to think she had a good eye, and clearly, here was a champ in the making.

She wondered if the horse was for sale.

"I reckon Mike's gonna get licked today." Robert Keller said gloomily.

"I'm thinking you might be right," Alice murmured, jamming binoculars into the folds of her plump face. Pretty gal. She was light too, she observed, athletic, had a few pounds on their Mike, which always helped.

She watched the bay circle round to face the brick wall, and almost like a psychic, Alice sensed trouble coming. She could see it in the way the horse suddenly flattened his ears. His rider looked distracted, seeming not to notice.

Laine was looking not at the wall, but at something in the stands.

Donatés was in his gallop, approaching the wall, and too late, Laine realized she had him too short. He sailed up and she heard his hoof clip the wall. She felt his rhythm break, her balance was out and she knew instantly they were in trouble. She tried desperately to shift her weight, praying he wasn't going down.

But there was nothing for it; they were going down.

The crowd gasped in collective horror as rider and horse tumbled. They saw the rider tucking her body into an ungainly roll and disappear behind -

or under - 900 pounds of horse.

Behind the spectator barrier, Case watched in horror as Donatés and Laine went down, her helmet flying one way, and her legs folding, disappearing behind the horse's flank. Had Donatés crushed her?

The horse was back up in an instant, spooked, his forelimbs punching the air in fright before he cantered away towards the chute. A handler was running out to catch him.

Laine lay motionless, unmoving on the ground.

Laine heard all the sounds.

Sounds that lasted a lifetime inside her head, mere milliseconds to the crowd.

She heard Donatés give a frightened snort, then he was on his feet and cantering away.

She heard the sporadic spectator-clapping to show their relief the horse was unharmed. Laine lay motionless, on her back, winded and shocked, looking up at the gray sky, feeling a gentle rain on her face. Mortified, she closed her eyes.

What a rookie mistake. Distracted by an illusion. She thought it was Case, that hair—! And now, despite all her preparation, the Gods had decreed that she make a screw-up in front of this illustrious Seattle crowd.

On her back and dazed, Laine just kept her eyes shut fast and prayed the showjumping fairies would whisk her away from this stupid, idiot fall!

WHAT IT TAKES

In the stands, the crowd held their breath, willing the rider to stand up. The stewards were barreling towards her still form on the ground.

Alice Keller's attention was caught by a new hubbub below, and she tipped her binoculars a fraction down, and to the left.

A man was leaping over the barriers. A marshal moved to stop him, but the guy thrust out his hand and in an instant, the marshal was sitting in the mud, flat on his backside. The man was pelting towards the fallen rider, now he was leaning over her.

Alice Keller frowned. Her heart began racing. The guy was looking like he was damn near gonna cry!? Why?

Jesus, had the rider been crushed? She found herself sending up a prayer and peered anxiously through her binoculars. What was going on? The man was holding up his hand as the course stewards ran towards him, and they stopped in their tracks. He was a biggish guy, and she could see from his grim visage he wouldn't hesitate to flatten them too. She began to nod, in dawning comprehension This had to be the rider's guy. And she must be hurt! Why wasn't she trying to get up?

Case was bending over Laine. Her eyes were closed, and he put two fingers to her neck, feeling for her pulse. It was there, strong, and he allowed himself to breathe.

"Laine? Lainie? Can you hear me?" he said softly, his left hand held up in warning, cautioning the stewards to stand back. "I'm a doctor," he said, brusquely, "And her husband, so back off, okay."

He turned to her, shaking her gently. "Laine, he urged, "Lainie, come on, hon, wake up."

'Lainie' didn't want to wake up. She had come a cropper in front of everyone, and all because she wasn't paying attention, all because someone who looked like Case had caught her eye, and now, bam, here she was, on her backside, in the mud. She kept her eyes shut tight, knowing she was dreaming. Case was here, at her side, calling her, telling her to wake up.

She opened her eyes.

Case was here. His face inches from hers, his eyes panicked, his face tense and scared, but it was him.

Definitely him.

"Case?" Laine said, incredulous. Was she concussed?

He was trying to smile, but he looked as scared as ever she had seen him. His eyes were also wet. Was he crying? Had she hurt herself??

Gingerly, Laine lifted herself onto one elbow, trying to comprehend that Case was right here, at her side.

In the stands, the crowd saw her move and there were spontaneous whistles and claps, a collective ripple of relief swept through them that the rider appeared unharmed. Laine was vaguely aware of two stewards standing nearby, their faces anxious.

"Let me help you up, honey, I am so sorry. Laine, I am so, so sorry." There, he was saying it again, over and over, choking, hugging her to him as if he would never let go. Laine tried pushing him away, but gently, and finally, he got it; she wanted to stand up.

He helped her to her feet, and she stood unsteadily for a moment, testing. Her limbs seemed to be fine.

It was just her mind that had gone.

Case was here, at her side.

Laine looked at him. He was staring at her as if she had just been born, for God's sake, and he was saying the same thing, over and over again "I am so sorry, I am so very sorry. "

Laine knew, every part of her knew, he wasn't talking about her spill.

The stewards overheard him too, and they glanced at each other. Hell, it was just a fall, these things happen!

She heard what he was saying, and he was here, he was back, and she knew she was starting to cry, but she didn't care. Her arms were around his neck, and she was kissing him, and he was kissing her, her face, her hair, frantically, as if he couldn't get enough of her.

For a moment the crowd fell silent, enchanted at the spectacle.

Then they broke into whoops and cheers.

Case's cheeks were wet, and he didn't know if it was her tears or his, but he had his wife back!

From the exhibitor's tunnel, Ballard watched, a small smile playing on his lips. The girl from Sacramento was standing quietly next to him, her foot on the rail, observing, her lips curled in a sneer.

"Well, she's not gonna be any trouble," she said, looking smug.

Ballard turned to her, distracted, wondering what the hell she was on about. "Sorry?"

"No BMT."

He looked at her, his face blank.

" You know, Big Match Temperament, " she explained. "Hell, if they gonna cry like that, over one dumb spill," she said, smirking. "Say no more!"

Ballard stared at her, dumbfounded.

Then he threw back his head and began to laugh.

Hope you enjoyed this - look out for the next one, and please leave a review when you can. Want to comment? Leave your thoughts at https://jenniferward.uk

Your review means the world to me

REVIEW ON AMAZON HERE -

https://www.amazon.co.uk/dp/
B0D2ZDTQVT

Or follow me on
Https://jenniferward.uk

SCAN ME

FACEBOOK AUTHOR PAGE

Printed in Great Britain
by Amazon

50046148R00293